About the Author

The author went straight from school into the army, aged sixteen, in 1983 and left in 1996 as staff sergeant in the Royal Logistics Corps. On demob, he initially settled into a logistics managerial position but then realised that he enjoyed life more behind a steering wheel rather than chained to an office chair. In 2000, he upgraded his Class 2 Licence to Class 1 and has mostly been employed in the 'tramper' role ever since. Spending most of his time alone gives him plenty of time for the writing spark to germinate and grow.

Kitten on a String

To Catherine.
Thank you for helping me in my hour of need

PT Jay

P. T. Jay

Kitten on a String

Vanguard Press

VANGUARD PAPERBACK

© Copyright 2024
P. T. Jay

The right of P. T. Jay to be identified as author of
this work has been asserted by them in accordance with the
Copyright, Designs and Patents Act 1988.

All Rights Reserved

No reproduction, copy or transmission of this publication
may be made without written permission.
No paragraph of this publication may be reproduced,
copied or transmitted save with the written permission of the publisher,
or in accordance with the provisions
of the Copyright Act 1956 (as amended).

Any person who commits any unauthorised act in relation to
this publication may be liable to criminal
prosecution and civil claims for damages.

A CIP catalogue record for this title is
available from the British Library.

ISBN 978 1 80016 917 3

This is a work of fiction. Names, characters, businesses, places, events and incidents are either the product of the author's imagination or used in a fictitious manner. Any resemblance to actual persons, living or dead, or actual events is purely coincidental.

Vanguard Press is an imprint of
Pegasus Elliot Mackenzie Publishers Ltd.
www.pegasuspublishers.com

First Published in 2024

Vanguard Press
Sheraton House Castle Park
Cambridge England

Printed & Bound in Great Britain

All my books are dedicated to the people who gave me that "look" when I told them I wanted to be a writer. Yeah, THAT look. All prospective writers know what look I mean.

Acknowledgements

I would like to thank all the tyres that blew out on me and all the parts that failed on me. Waiting and repair time was extra writing time.

I felt suddenly lonely, lonelier than I thought I'd ever been. Suddenly I yearned for the touch of a loving man right now; somebody who would treasure me and protect me and respect me and look into my eyes like he was looking into hers. Somebody who would… go away and work until he'd "made it big", or whatever it was Jane had said he'd done, and then come back and claim the hand of the fair maiden. Isn't that what all women want, somebody to care for them, to cherish them, to look after them?

Chapter One

Run, I told myself, you shouldn't be here, but something made me stay. To this day I don't know what it was, why I stayed. All I do know is, had I run I would have saved myself a mountain of pain and, in addition, a whole world of joy and love. And you can't have one without the other, can you?

As he received his welcome home kiss from his wife and I stood there like a spare cog watching the door slowly close behind me, the small triangle of outside light getting smaller and smaller as the heavy door closed, seemingly of its own accord. That was what my brain was shouting at me, you see. *Run, run now, you shouldn't be here!* Part of me agreed with the voice shouting in my head, but the small part of me that was left overruled it and I didn't know why. Perhaps I was intrigued and wanted the answer myself.

Because I should have left, in fact should never had allowed myself to have gotten this far, but I was far too trusting of people. I was trusting my instincts, I told myself, but what if my instincts were wrong? How many other people who had trusted their instincts were now dead in ditches or worse? But I should have run. Anybody in their right mind would have run. To this day I still don't know why I didn't.

As the door finally closed with a soft but final click I knew that I had missed my chance, but I still admonished myself. My mentally giving myself a severe telling off was only interrupted when I saw their kiss change into a hug and her eyes open wide when she rested her smiling face on his shoulder and saw me.

'Jack, who's this?' she asked with surprise, as her hand reached out for the main light switch, missing it the first few times. Her voice sounded surprised, nothing more; no hint of danger, threat or anger at her husband bringing a younger woman – any woman – to their home. The thought that perhaps it happened all the time entered my head for a moment but I discounted it, like I'd discounted the command to run.

I was so stupid sometimes, so trusting. So far in my life nothing bad had ever happened to me. I had never ever been threatened in any way, not even by some bullying bitch at school. Some of the girls at work had mentioned unwelcome attention from men, verbal and physical, but the most I ever had to contend with was the wandering hands of the boss's son, *'Call me Ron' fucking Carswell,* and that wasn't an assault like some of the other girls had described. Part of me wondered if I would have a nasty shock one day.

This had started off as a regular pickup, though there was nothing regular going on so far. He'd serenaded me, cringingly so in anticipation, but he had a good voice in hindsight. The crowd had appreciated it, too, knowing no doubt what was to follow. The bottle of champagne that turned up in an ice bucket at the table, the approach as he was congratulated for his singing ability, the knowing nods and smiles from people he passed on the way to her table. Then the odd thing happened. He made his apologies, told me to enjoy the champagne on him, said that this had all been a mistake, knocked back the brandy that had arrived with the champagne, and left.

But yet I was still here in his home – in *their* home – standing by the door dressed in my imitation snakeskin raincoat and carrying a bottle of champagne in one hand and a half eaten taco in the other. My bag was supported over my shoulder.

After her question I looked on, seemingly frozen to the spot, as her eyes first widened, then went back to normal as she looked full into his face before looking back to me. By this time her eyes were widening again as she looked at me, as if the penny had dropped somehow and she suddenly knew, or at least thought she knew, all the answers. Then she looked at him once more, his back still to me, and her eyes started to reflect… well, amusement unless I was mistaken.

'Sorry, where are my manners. Jack, get her coat, would you sweetheart?'

Her name was Jane, I knew. I knew because I'd rifled his phone when he was in the restroom after he'd purposely left it for me to ring somebody with if I had wanted. But I am jumping ahead. What was I even doing with him in the lounge of the nearest hotel, eating tacos, drinking brandy with mixer and warming ourselves by the welcoming warm log fire?

I'd ran after him you see, after he had "bottled it". That was what the Neanderthal football supporters had said, anyway. 'Hey look, the old fella has bottled it. Get in there, Stuey, now's your chance.'

No chance. The last thing I needed was the sweaty attentions of some knuckle-dragging, football loving caveman. I'd take my chances with the "old fella".

Not that he was old, mind you, though he was obviously older than them, and me. He was also well dressed compared to them, and more bulky, though it didn't seem to be soft and flabby. His upper body was kind of like an upside down triangle, the widest bit being his shoulders at the top. He must go to the gym, I'd thought fleetingly, or maybe he was a wrestler in his former life or something. I was contradicting myself, having initially thought of him as a banker or something similar.

He had confidence, too, loads of it. I guess that being moneyed does that to you. He certainly looked that way, anyway, though looks can be deceiving. Perhaps he was just a very good stalker or axe murderer who knew that looking the part of a dapper, well-to-do gent, helped him snare his victims? Victim? Me? This victim was running after the hunter, though I still didn't know why. I told myself it was to escape the sweaty clutches of "Stuey".

As the pub door closed behind me and I struggled into my raincoat, struggling around my bag and the bottle of champagne I'd grabbed as I left, I looked around to find him. He was only a dozen or so seconds in front of me, he couldn't be far…

'Oh, is that for me?' she smiled in amusement.

For some reason I was lost for words and nervous as we were introduced and I had held out my taco-filled hand to her.

'Thank you,' she smiled, amused.

But I realised my error right at the last second and snatched my hand back, replacing it with the one holding the bottle of champagne as "Jack" tried unsuccessfully to remove my coat.

'Ooh, champagne! I'll get glasses. Bring her through here, Jack,' she said with a look at him as he finally won the battle with my coat. What their look communicated I didn't know.

Why was I so nervous around her? OK, there was the incongruity of the situation but that wasn't all of it, I admitted to myself. I'd flicked through his phone back at the hotel and gone straight to the photographs. There were scores of photos of him and her and I'd wondered why he was out trawling for hamburger when he had this beautiful piece of steak at home? But men do that, don't they, some sort of macho *just proving to myself that I can still pull* mentality, never mind how beautiful the woman at home was, and Jane was certainly beautiful and breathtakingly so, even to another woman like myself.

I remembered how I'd initially christened her *Lowercase Jane* – because that was how she was entered in the contacts list on his phone, all in lower case letters, but after seeing the photographs of her with him I changed my mind instantly. Lowercase Jane was certainly no lowercase Jane. Low... Jane was beautiful, and it isn't easy for us women to admit that about another female, us being all jealous, spitting cats on the subject.

And he wasn't "Jack" either, at least not initially. In my mind I'd christened him "Tom" after my grandmother's permanently on the prowl tomcat, and this Tom was on the prowl even though I'd seen the pale skin on his ring finger where he must have removed his ring while contemplating picking me up. Didn't he know that that was the oldest trick in the book and that even I was aware of it? But then he'd brought me home to meet his wife... 'Do you want to finish this at home?' What sort of book was he operating from?

As I'd started to panic, thinking I'd lost him, I heard a rich, confident voice amongst the other sounds of traffic and people trying to get by in the post-rainstorm urban river as water ran everywhere to eventually find a route to the drains. Some of it settled in puddles wherever there was a dent in the ground or a lack of drainage, and the puddles grew until hissed and splashed away by car tyres or treading feet.

Where could he have gone? Surely it had been only a few seconds? The street was starting to fill, now, as the rain had stopped and the Friday night revellers were starting to thicken.

I heard a voice. 'No harm done.'

Was that him? Certainly the voice was a cut above the rest. I looked to my right where some half-dressed woman, teenager actually, screamed as she tried to avoid putting her high heels into the puddles amongst the cobblestones. What with that and negotiating herself out of a taxi it seemed she had almost knocked into him.

It was him.

'Hello? Excuse me?' I called again.

Was he intentionally ignoring me? I started after him but this time I nearly became a victim of the cobble/high heel combination myself, though mine were hardly high, just semi-high sensible work shoes.

'Hello?' I called again, but the hiss of a passing car, its tyres slicing through the rain sodden road, swallowed up the volume of my words as he crossed the road after it had passed him.

One more step decided me. The heels would have to go, wet feet or not. 'Excuse me?' I shouted, this time louder.

I was crossing the road behind him and finally gaining on him when I heard the beep. Shame I hadn't heard the car it belonged to. I reacted too late and, even surefooted without the heels, would not have been able to move out of the way quick enough had it not swerved as the driver sounded his horn a second time.

I felt my ankle start to give and turned to save it.

'Whoa, there,' I heard as strong hands steadied me.

I heard 'Dumb broad!' I guessed from the car driver.

As I gratefully transferred my weight to the offered hands I felt their owner's body twist and tense as he turned towards the sound of the shouted insult.

'Idiot,' I heard from beside me as the car continued on its way. 'You OK?'

'Yes, I'm fine,' I said as I tried to untangle my feet. Thankfully my helper hadn't let me fall completely to the ground. I was wet enough.

'Idiot should drive slower on these cobbles when it's wet.'

'Yes,' I said, though I believed the fault was more mine than his.

'I bet that if he'd been alone in his car this wouldn't have happened. He was probably trying to impress some girl or his mates. Some people are just itching for an excuse to use their horns so they can seem big in front of their equally brain dead mates. Common courtesy gives out the window.'

Must admit that I hadn't thought about it that way, this was almost deep. Maybe I wasn't so in the wrong after all?

'Hey, you've no shoes on!'

I almost lost it then. My heart was pumping after my near miss and my feet were wet and cold. My stockings were sure to be ruined and they were my best pair. I always made it a point to wear best on Fridays. Thought if I looked fresh and new whilst others looked like they were in week-old clothes (like some of them were) it would give me that extra edge in the workplace.

Passers-by were looking at me in *that* way and some were giggling, not caring if they were heard or not. Nobody cared these days, nobody had any damn compassion, and this stupid man insisted on telling me the obvious, that I had no shoes on because I was chasing him in the rain because... because...

'Well done, though. You saved the clicquot, you saved the shoes and you saved the ankle. Not sure I could have done all that.'

'Well obviously you've never chased men across cobbled roads in the rain carrying champagne bottles and a handbag before,' I retorted, half mollified by his compliment.

I heard him sniff. 'Got to admit, you've got me there. Next time I bump into the old CO I'll suggest it gets added to the end of the assault course. If you can do all that then a minefield will be a breeze!'

I laughed as he guided me towards a soaking bench and laid his own raincoat down to soak up the moisture.

A squaddie, then? No, a soldier, an officer? Singing *that* song? Do officers and gentlemen listen to songs like that these days? Standards must be falling. And like I know what army officers are like, I didn't go through that *ooh my boyfriend's a squaddie* routine like some of the other girls I knew. I was already with Richard and happy for life.

Or so I'd thought.

'Look,' he said as I emptied the water from my shoes and squelched them back on to my soaking feet. 'I can see this is mainly my fault, and I apologise, but I honestly wouldn't have minded if you'd kept the champagne. And I apologise also if you were offended by the—'

'I wasn't running after you to return the champagne,' I interrupted without thinking. Immediately I regretted it. Made me feel like whatever happened I was keeping the damn bottle, like some slapper debutante impressed by some cheap Tesco sparkling wine.

His face turned to one of confusion. 'Then why, then?'

I wracked my brain for answers. 'The song,' was all I could come out with.

'Thirty Seconds to Mars? You're a fan? Good call, sir,' he said as he congratulated himself.

'No,' I answered, bursting his balloon no doubt. 'Never heard of them. There, they're on!' My soaking shoes were finally on.

'OK, now I'm confused.'

Join the club.

A silence formed, broken by him. 'Look, have you eaten?'

I admitted that I hadn't since lunch. I was shocked to realise that that was over six hours ago and my stomach rumbled as if by order.

'Come on,' he said. 'The Station Hotel's clientele is a touch above that rabble across the road and I know the food is acceptable and hot. Least I can do after I've wrecked your lingerie?'

I stopped. My what? Stockings, he meant stockings! Of course, he meant stockings! I inwardly laughed at his choice of words. Can you wreck stockings? Ruin, run, certainly, but wreck? The way men talk!

We accepted a small table which he'd secured near the glass fronted fireplace. I slipped off my shoes and gratefully inched closer as I started to thaw. Our raincoats were on the stand near the door and the champagne had been confiscated to be returned on our departure. No hassle. He'd immediately offered the solution to the staff as we'd entered. Bars were sticky about such things, I knew, and he seemed to know it too. He certainly had a knack for foreseeing possible problems and defusing them. I guessed it was the training that I presumed he'd had.

Then the thought hit me that I was presuming quite a lot. I didn't know anything about him. I presumed by what he'd said earlier that he was, or had been, a member of the armed forces, but that meant nothing, I thought he was a banker earlier. I snuck a glance down to his left hand again as he was finishing communicating our order to the waitress and, sure enough, there was the obvious pale, thin space on his finger left by a recently worn ring. Had he slipped it off this evening as I'd suspected earlier? Was it now sitting in the side pocket of his waistcoat or secretly wrapped up in a handkerchief for safety? Didn't blokes know it was the oldest trick in the book and that modern women were wise to it?

I felt myself start to grow angry until I reminded myself that he'd tried to back out of this, made a mistake. We wouldn't be here now if I hadn't stupidly run after him like a groupie chasing some rock star, but the revelation of the ring did set limits on the meeting. There'd be food and a drink perhaps, and they'd talk, no doubt, but the tired cliché of the removed ring would end it there. The last thing I needed was to be some other woman, I wanted more respect than that. Sure, he was good looking and that was probably why some... hooray Henry type horsey woman heir to Daddy's country pile had him branded as hers. And he would stick with her for the sake of the kids and with half an eye on the old codger's will, no doubt.

'You were saying about the song?'

'Excuse me?' Must admit he'd caught me out, caught up in my imaginings like I was.

'Thirty Seconds to Mars. The reason you chased me?'

'Oh!' I answered, remembering my lie. 'Yes, it was just so unexpected.'

Our drinks arrived. Two similar looking beverages to that which he'd knocked back in the pub.

'Forgive me, I thought brandy to help chase away the cold?'

What could I say, it was a better choice than my earlier gin and tonic. Or was this the obvious try and get the woman drunk routine? A fleeting thought of date rape entered my mind but I closed it down. Was I a fool to feel that I trusted this stranger? I admitted to myself that the drinks looked very warming and appealing, though, as the cut glass reflected the contents in the amber rays of the fire.

He saw me look at a small green bottle that arrived with the glasses.

'Tonic in case you can't drink it straight,' he explained as he tipped the waitress a note. It wasn't a fiver, I noticed, even though he had not flourished it in a show off kind of way. No wonder the waitress smiled. We would get good service tonight, that's for sure. Yeah, he'd thought ahead, as usual. Then my mind registered the "can't" in his last statement. Was it a challenge? 'Is there somebody you need to ring?'

Again, he'd caught me unawares. 'Uh, um,' I stumbled.

'Why don't you use my phone,' he said. 'Then if they need you and yours is dead they can always get you. I charged mine on the train.'

Of course you did, my mind told me as he placed his phone beside my drink and rose to his feet. I bet your phone never runs out of charge. Wouldn't surprise me if you booked charging points when you booked your flight and rail tickets.

'Excuse me,' he said, polite as always, as he left.

I eyed his phone, a smart new one – not like my beat up old brick – as he searched for signage and disappeared to, I presumed, the wash room.

I thought quickly. What was this? It was certainly original. Was he trying to make me trust him, was it a trick? What sort of trick? What advantage could he possibly gain by giving me his phone? Would I give anybody my phone and walk away? They could do all sorts of things.

Like an electric charge compelled me my hand reached forward and I thumbed the last dialled button: *jane* in soft lowercase letters. A time next to it showed today's date and the time.

Yeah, he was a squaddie, it was set on twenty-four-hour clock. I knew that at least.

The time he'd called showed 18.34. Whilst they were in the pub, before he'd started his pickup routine? The call duration, at least I thought it was that... *00.00.28*. Twenty-eight seconds? I imagined what he – I realised I didn't know his name – could say to "jane" in twenty-eight seconds? How long did it take to say, "Hi honey. Damn train's delayed by this awful weather. Thought I'd catch a meal at the club and pick up some floozy afterward. Kiss the children for me. Stiff upper lip and all that, old girl. Can't be helped. Top ho!"

I almost laughed at the put on stuffy voice I'd put on in my head, but the thoughts the words themselves conveyed made me uneasy.

But he backed out once and he's purposely left me his phone.

Hell! How long has he been gone?

Like it was a burning coal I quickly slammed the phone down where he'd left it and looked around. I couldn't see him, but that didn't mean he wasn't spying on me right now. Guiltily I looked around again, hoping that nobody else had seen me doing what I was so obviously doing. How long had he been gone? How long had it taken me to guess how long it had taken *him* to call lowercase jane and tell his lies? Not too long, surely?

Again my hand snaked out and I nearly knocked the phone onto the floor in my haste. A lone man reading his menu in the opposite corner looked my way, his attention drawn by sound or movement or both. I assumed a calm demeanour to combat my racing heart and smiled sweetly as he looked my way. He returned my smile before returning to his menu as I mentally told myself off.

Haven't you got yourself in enough trouble by smiling at strange men today?

Waiting a few seconds, I slowly brought up the phone and stabbed the menu button and the camera button. Then I found what I wanted. Media, then photos. I took a deep breath, looked up and stabbed the photo button. So this was lowercase j—

Lowercase jane was clearly no lower case jane. She was... joking aside, I knew us women to be jealous cats, but lowe... Jane was beautiful. She was obviously older than me, I thought, but so what. If I was honest there must be loads of women out there who were not only older than me but were much, much better looking too. Why was this "Tom" prowling the tiles when he had this cat at home? And were there kittens?

I thumbed another button and a whole suite of mini photographs appeared. I knew this was what the geeks called the thumbnail view. A quick glance showed picture after picture of JANE. Wait, the next one had two people in it. I expanded it and it was *Tom* and JANE, dressed in white. They dressed in white a lot. Or perhaps this was a specific photo shoot?

They looked relaxed and very, very happy and so relaxed in their own company that I was instantly jealous. Had Richard and I ever looked like that, so at ease with ourselves and the world? If we had, would he still be here or still be in India with Elephant Girl?

Tom and JANE were sitting on a light coloured floor strewn with pale cushions. He was resting his back against them and she was resting against him with her left hand absent-mindedly, or perhaps it was posed that way, raised and caressing his cheek. His hands were placed around her waist, though not clasped like she was property and he was scared of losing her.

One word popped unbidden into my head: *ENCHANTING*. I was almost breathless.

I knew I screamed when the phone rang and even though the damn thing was airborne I briefly saw the word "jane" flash on the screen along with one of the other pictures as a photo tag. My brain automatically worked out the possible trajectory of the falling phone and the predicted point of impact was the mini hearth on which sat the fire. Not the soft carpet, not the table or the even softer chair, but the hard tile hearth. I recalled a memory from my youth, my grandmother referring to *firestones*. Were these things, the almost mythically hard firestones?

I had visions of the phone – the phone entrusted to me by the philandering, but *who-had-tried-to-backout-til-you-ran-after-him* Tom – crashing to pieces on the ever so hard bricks. Instinctively I reached for the phone and thankfully nudged it from its path and it slid onto the floor, off the carpeted area and towards the hard floor near the bar. And I, on hands on knees, followed it, backside in the air like some slapper looking for a plastic earring. I got to it just in time, just as somebody's foot was going to absent-mindedly crush it.

Tom's foot. I saw his foot stop mid pace. My fingers were mere inches away from snatching it up and his foot was paused millimetres away from crushing it. We looked up and down at each other and I gulped.

'It... it rang.'

He looked down at me and I felt like Mr Handley, my headmaster at infant school, who had caught me playing with the illegally released mice again. Subconsciously I could almost feel the short sharp smack to my bottom.

The years ticked by.

'A mobile phone that rings?' he said deadpan as he looked down at me. 'Amazing. What will modern technology come up with next!'

He moved his foot and deftly picked up the phone and answered it as I scuttled back to my chair as quickly as I could to remove my little schoolgirl bottom from within range of the expected vengeful and calloused hand. I grabbed for my milk and took a huge mouthful to cover my embarrassment and my throat burned. I thumped the brandy glass onto the table as I coughed and cried and reached for the green tonic bottle. Through my tears I saw Tom turn to face the sound of commotion – me – and the lone man in the corner give up in his attempt not to laugh.

The Canada Dry splashed into, and over, the glass as Tom looked on incredulously and, I am sure, highly amused. I could tell from his voice that he was trying to keep his tone level but was struggling.

'Well, I thought it could be as late as nine,' he said into the phone as he turned away from me. 'But now I think it could be earlier. If I got a taxi straight away it could be eight?'

Even I knew it must be nearly a quarter to eight now. Some pickup. Spare me fifteen minutes? Good of him. I took another swallow, the mixture only just softening the burning I felt. It took me a little while to realise that he was talking to me.

'What?' I coughed.

'Sorry, I don't know your name?' he asked with his hand over the speaker part of the phone.

My name? He's speaking to his wife, that beautiful, graceful JANE, and he wants to know my name?

'Aneese,' I spluttered.

'A-knees?'

I coughed to clear my throat. 'Aneese.'

'Aneese,' he said, finally getting it right. 'Would you like to finish this at home?'

So then I was in a taxi with a man I didn't know, on the way to meet his wife for Christ's sake! My head was spinning but that might have been the brandy, my stomach in turmoil, or the half-eaten and napkin wrapped taco I had clutched in one hand. My other hand held my bag whilst forced between my legs for safety sat the last minute retrieved bottle of champagne.

What was I doing, I asked myself? Why had I said yes? And more importantly, what the fuck was going on? Two hours ago all I wanted was a quick drink to calm me down whilst the rain stopped. I had visions of a steaming bath somewhere close in my future, with possibly a large glass of wine by the side. Then? Then I'd probably veg it for the rest of the evening in my warmest bathrobe, finish the bottle whilst I flicked the channels or read a magazine and planned what to do during my enforced work break. I'd probably wake up on the sofa in the early hours and find my bed and wake up in the morning with my hair needing an hour's attention.

But instead I'd been picked up (or had I?), got a bottle of champagne bought for me (that was certain), been soaked, ruined my best stockings, nearly got hit by a car (all definites), run after a strange man (me running after a man?), eaten half a taco (a very nice one with chicken and cheese and hot sauce), embarrassed myself chasing a phone across the hotel's bar floor (no way I'm ever going there again – don't think they'll let me in anyway!)... and...

And been sang to. And stupidly nodded my head when asked if I wanted to continue "this" at home, whatever *this* was.

I had to back out of this, I decided. I stole a look across at him and he was doing what I was, just staring out his window deep in thought. Where was all that confidence and composure now, Daddy-o? He seemed almost as petrified as I felt. Perhaps his night hadn't gone as he'd planned, either?

He must have seen me move.

'I can imagine what's going through your head right now,' he said as he looked my way.

I doubt that, I told myself.

'Well let me assure you that all you have to do is say the word and I'll call a taxi and pay your fare to wherever home is. You are safe and I want you to feel that way. Is why I gave you my phone...'

So I could see pictures of your beautiful – no stunning – wife?

'Now, whoever you called will have my phone number on their received phone log. You must know that? So now I can't dump you in a ditch or harm you...'

Excuse me?

'I know that these days everybody is an axe murdering, kidnapping psycho until proven guilty, so I just wanted to put your mind at rest.'

Yeah, about that, I thought as he paused for breath. Not working.

'Oh, and the name's Kelvin,' he said as he held out his hand.

I juggled bag and taco and we shook hands. I saw the taxi driver sneak a look in the rear-view mirror. Bet he heard some strange conversations going on in the back of his cab. This one must be a doozy!

Kelvin – I'd almost forgotten it was me who'd christened him *Tom*. Tom the philandering tomcat.

He quickly looked me up and down in the half light of the taxi cab interior as he let my hand go. He can't have seen much.

'At the very least,' he continued, 'you'll have a good story to tell your mates come Monday.'

Mates? Friends? Must admit they'd been a bit thin on the ground lately. Since Richard had left it was as if their friends didn't know what to say. They certainly said very little to me. I wondered, not for the first time, if they were in touch with him? Emails or postcards or photographs (arm in arm with *her*, no doubt, all happy faces and elephant dung and beaded hair and flies. I hoped there were lots of flies).

He lapsed into silence, I guess because I hadn't said a word.

'Here it is,' he said a few moments later. Whether to me or the taxi driver, I didn't know.

The brakes squeaked as the taxi slowed – it was some sort of law of the universe.

As I straightened myself up and dusted myself down, I realised that I was still slightly smaller than him in my heels and, for some reason, that pleased me.

'This way,' he offered and he gently took my arm and guided me forward.

My heart was racing fit to burst as he pushed his keys into the lock and pushed the door open. 'Jane?' he called as he started to undo his coat.

This is it, I told myself. Last chance to run. I'm sure he'd understand. Why would I care if he didn't?

Which brought us back to now, to the present confused conundrum.

'Shall we go through?' Jane finally suggested and the man with so many names touched the small of my back and guided me after her into a large room about three times the size of my flat. We continued right through without time to pause or to really take it all in. Then we turned a corner and I could see a large table, at least eight settings a side, with one end made up.

'I thought you might be hungry?' she said as we entered, the comment obviously aimed at her husband.

I looked down at the table which laboured with plates of cold meats, cheese, assorted breads and a large covered terrine of, I guessed, stew or soup.

'Plenty for two,' Jane commented as she swept the curtain along its runner to block out the cold night and nosey neighbours.

Or six, or eight, I thought. I wondered how she kept her figure if this was a snack? Kelvin gestured me to sit and, by the time I had, I heard a twinkling of glasses as Jane reappeared. After a moment's struggle the champagne cork flew off with a bang and landed somewhere, ignored, and I could smell the champagne as it bubbled into the glasses.

'It's not too warm,' said Jane. 'So it'll do.'

Kelvin was already into his soup and, as he tore off a piece from his roll, gestured for me to help myself. He swallowed. 'No ceremony tonight. Just help yourself.'

Gingerly, on my best, most balanced behaviour, I transferred some of the cream coloured liquid to a spare bowl. I must admit that it smelt wonderful, even better than my taco. It tasted a thousand times better and I felt myself starting to thaw out. It even settled my nervous stomach.

Jane sat at the head of the table after she had finished pouring and watched us, one each side of her, eat in silence.

I had forgotten the awkwardness of the situation and was visibly enjoying the meal and was well into my second roll. Jane sipped her champagne, peering over the glass at first me and then Kelvin with an amused look on her face, whilst Kelvin chewed slowly like an admonished schoolboy suddenly lost for words. Once, I saw their eyes meet and saw that inquisitive eyebrow of hers instantly raise, demanding attention, but he said nothing.

'Gosh, this is lovely,' I gushed at the soup, remembering the incongruity of the situation.

Gosh? Who was in my head, Enid Blyton!

'One of yours, my dear?' Kelvin asked, thankfully picking up on the theme.

She shook her head, still sighting at us over the rim of her glass. 'No, Consuella's,' she answered.

'Well, I do hope she washed her hands,' commented Kelvin, 'after what I've seen her do to those chickens.'

'Well she does like her ingredients fresh,' Jane agreed.

'And that goat?'

'You'll see it on Sunday. And are you staying for lunch, Aneese?'

I swallowed noisily. When had he told her my name? How had I missed that? Lunch? Sunday? It's only Friday? Goat for Sunday lunch?

I reached out my hand and just managed the champagne glass without knocking it over. The champagne forced the bread down my throat far enough that I thought I would be able to speak. 'Honestly,' I said, hoping that I didn't sound as terrified as I felt. 'I don't know what's going to happen in the next ten minutes!'

My stomach protested noisily, whether out of nerves or other, I do not now.

Then Jane and Kelvin looked at each other and laughed as if what I'd just said was the funniest thing they'd ever heard. I found myself laughing, too. Kelvin was laughing fit to burst and banging the table and Jane was trying unsuccessfully to keep her glass steady.

'A toast,' said Kelvin, grabbing his glass and holding it up.

We women eventually joined him.

'To the queen of the ice breakers,' he said grandiosely. 'Aneese!'

'Aneese!' Jane chorused.

'Ah, oh my,' was all I could manage.

I'd heard it was bad form to toast oneself, unlucky, perhaps, but I don't think anybody had toasted me before. I had an unfamiliar warm feeling in the pit of my stomach and it wasn't the soup. I wasn't used to being appreciated, especially not lately. Lately was… just emptiness, going through the motions of living, surviving on autopilot as I continually beat myself up over Richard's and my parting. Could I have done something differently to stop him leaving? What had I done so wrong that drove him into the arms of another woman?

'So tell me how you met?' Jane asked around her laughing, and I started to. Anything was better than my own maudlin thoughts.

The glass emptied and Kelvin poured another and the explanations continued.

'So he sang to you?' Jane asked.

'After facing down the football thugs after turning off the match they were watching.'

She turned to him. 'Are you bullying the football louts again? You're such an ogre!'

I wondered if he did it all the time.

'What song?' She had her attention on me again.

'I, um, something about Mars? Something heavy and shouty?'

She turned to face him, her eyes smiling and reflecting the bubbles from the champagne. 'Not your Stiff Little Digits t—'

'Fingers,' he interrupted. 'Stiff Little Fingers, and no, not them. You know,' he said looking at her. 'The Kill?'

I watched as her eyes narrowed and her head started to rock to the beat in her head. Yeah, she had it.

'Dun nu na, du nan a, de de finished with youuuuuu! That one? Why on earth would you sing that to anybody!'

'Well it seemed like a good idea at the time. And it got her attention, she's here.'

I admitted to myself that it had but that I still didn't know why. And I certainly was here, no denying that. But why was I here?

'You know thousands of songs,' she continued. 'You could have sang anything. So did you like it?' She'd turned to face me as she'd asked the last question, surprising me at the speed at which she switched her attentions. I had a spoonful of soup halfway to my lips.

I didn't know what to say. 'It was catchy,' was all I could say, hating myself for my lack of words. I wanted to say something profound and funny. I wanted to be toasted again.

'Well this can't stand,' said Jane, rising to her feet.

I noticed his manners as he stood as well. Didn't often see that these days. I hastened to follow, not knowing whether I should or not. My spoon sounded loud as it fell back into the bowl.

'Come on,' she said as she walked out the door. 'And bring the champagne.'

Kelvin caught up with her and ushered me through the door in front of him.

Where are we going now, I thought? What could possibly happen next?

I followed Jane through twists and turns and ups and downs. By the time we finished I had the feeling that we were more or less on the same level as the room we'd just left. We certainly hadn't gone down or up any large sets of stairs. The house was obviously far larger than it looked when I'd exited the taxi and was a bit higgledy-piggledy too. There were "half downs", as I christened them in my own mind, and half ups. Small, seemingly useless sets of stairs to negotiate.

I found myself jealously admiring Jane's figure as she walked in front of me until I realised that Kelvin was behind me and could probably see. And what was he looking at, I suddenly wondered? Like I didn't know. I looked behind me once and got a smile and a wink for my troubles.

'Right, do your stuff, maestro,' Jane ordered as we finally came to rest.

We were in another large room with a bar in one corner. There were bar-type chairs and low tables and even some more plush seats. In the opposite corner to the bar was a set of drums, a guitar – no make that two guitars – and a set of keyboards. They seemed to be connected by various electronic components, wires and thick cables.

'Why, what are you singing, my sweet?'

'Oh, I'm not singing,' she answered, liberating the half empty bottle of champagne. 'You are!'

'But I've just eaten!' he protested.

'You've sang for your supper before,' she answered to stop his whine. 'I've seen you, so stop your griping.'

With that she plonked herself down onto one of the plush seats and beckoned me sit beside her. As I did, she smiled, reached across and topped up both our glasses.

'Now,' she whispered conspiratorially, 'you get to see him sing properly!'

Kelvin had accepted his fate without any further complaint. I guessed he'd just been whining for effect. I heard an electronic hum as he flicked a switch on a large keyboard and then watched as his fingers moved effortlessly across the board as he looked up occasionally and listened for the effect his changes had made.

'Did Kelvin tell you he was a sound engineer?'

I had to admit that I knew nothing about Kelvin at all.

'Well, when I say sound engineer,' she continued, 'what I should say is sound scientist, if such a term exists. The sound engineers work for the people, who work for the people,' She used her hands to get around what she was trying to explain. 'Who work for Kelvin,' she finished.

And I'd thought he was a soldier? What else had I got wrong?

'That's his next invention,' she said proudly indicating the equipment he was fine tuning. 'Going to bring in the big bucks, he says, but for now it's just a toy.'

'Oh?' I answered. I was interested but plainly not as excited about it as she was. Or was this just pride in her husband? And if it brought in the cash then who cared? They seemed well enough off to me, though, but being one of the working class, I was also a member of the couldn't-have-too-much brigade. Yes, I dreamed and worshipped at the lottery temple myself, like so many others.

'When he left the army,' she continued (and I mentally chalked one up for Team Aneese), 'he sunk his pension into his recording studio. A couple of years later he'd made it big – some music algorithm thingy that did it better than anything else – and then he came and found me, he said.'

This piqued my interest. 'Came and found you?'

'Loved me from afar at school, he said. Knew I wouldn't look at him until he'd made something of himself, he said.'

My mouth dropped open. 'And was it true?'

She looked at me sideways. 'A girl's gotta have some secrets. Shhh, he's about to begin.'

'What's your pleasure, ladies?'

'Something nice,' Jane answered instantly. 'Something that shows off your voice; a real singer's song?'

She was really egging the recipe. Was he that good? I watched as Kelvin went thoughtful.

'Problem is,' Jane started, 'is that he probably knows every damn song under the sun. 'The Power of Love',' she called out.

Jennifer Rush? Even I knew that. My oldest friend, Sianna, used to scream to it when she was drunk. Surely he couldn't hit those notes? It was meant for a woman to sing, surely?

I heard the bass droning background change as he clicked away at his magic box of tricks. When he walked forward with a microphone, I knew he was ready. I heard a piano twinkle a few notes and Kelvin spoke into the microphone. *I'll protect you from the hooded claw...*

Oh THAT Power of Love! At first I didn't recognise the song as it was a little before my time. But then the tune became more familiar when the strings kicked in and I instantly knew I'd heard it before. A sloppy dance, some family wedding, perhaps? Had Richard and I slow danced to this one night?

Kelvin was really making a good fist of it, holding the long notes perfectly and as mournfully melodic as I recalled the song to be. Part of me wondered how much was Kelvin and how much his box of tricks. If the voice was all his then Jane's egging up of him was totally justified.

She was rocking back and fore slightly, almost tearful eyes glazed over in some half lost memory, no doubt. I realised her hand was squeezing mine and, as the memories of Richard flowed through me, I squeezed back. By the time the song ended I guess I looked and felt pretty much like she did.

'Oh, bravo,' she said as she rose into his arms and hugged and kissed him. 'You never cease to amaze me, Jack.'

There was that Jack thing again.

'So what did I tell you, eh?' Jane prompted me.

I was speechless, I had to say. Had they noticed the effect the song had had on me? A song that I didn't even know that I knew?

'How much of that was you?' I asked after clearing my throat.

'Well, all the voice,' he answered as Jane looked on. 'Set up like it is it's just an ordinary karaoke machine but if I capture the frequency of a certain instrument like, for example, the piano, I can then remove it and then somebody who wants to learn the piece can play their piano over the now missing piano sections, much like singers sing over the missing words at karaoke. And then if the screens show what notes to play in a simple form rather than just the words that karaoke screens do now then people can learn to play the song on the instrument of their choice. It's all about zermumforgonding and therstig…'

Jane had her hand over his mouth by now. 'Enough,' she warned playfully.

I saw him smile and she dropped her hand away. He certainly didn't take offence like I am sure some men would. Instead he rolled his eyes and when she released him he nuzzled her neck and she screamed.

And this was the bloke I thought was picking me up for a night of extra-marital sex?

I felt suddenly lonely, lonelier than I thought I'd ever been. Suddenly I yearned for the touch of a loving man right now; somebody who would treasure me and protect me and respect me and look into my eyes like he was looking into hers. Somebody who would… go away and work until he'd "made it big", or whatever it was Jane had said he'd done, and then come back and claim the hand of the fair maiden. Isn't that what all women want, somebody to care for them, to cherish them, to look after them?

I felt myself becoming maudlin again and realised they were staring at me. For cover I moved my glass to my lips.

'Allow me, madame,' played Kelvin as he poured the last drops of the bottle into my glass. 'Oh, we seem to have run dry,' he continued. 'I'm sure the house can provide.'

Jane and I retook our seats as Kelvin opened and closed cupboards noisily behind the bar.

'There's one in the kitchen, sweetheart,' Jane said, and Kelvin dutifully trotted away without another word.

'Thanks for sharing your champagne,' Jane said softly after he'd gone. I guessed she'd gauged my mood.

'It was yours.'

'It was bought for you,' she countered.

I smiled back wanly and shrugged. 'I re-gifted it.'

She smiled back at me and impulsively we hugged. I held on tight, begging the tears not to come. Eventually, only partially successful, we parted.

'What was his name?' she asked immediately as she raised her glass to her lips.

'Richard,' I answered right back. I instinctively knew to whom she was referring.

What? I'd just hugged a woman I'd only just met and now I'm confiding her my woes? What has come over me?

She nodded sagely as I poked the corner of my eyes with my little finger in an attempt to control the tears without upsetting my make-up. I looked for my bag, not remembering where I had put it. From somewhere she produced a tissue.

'He said we were going to be together forever,' I continued as I wiped at my eyes delicately. 'I skipped college so we could be together. Didn't want to be apart from him, you see. Mum and Dad went ape but I brought them round, showed them the kind, good, loving man that Richard was. We got jobs, found a place to live, the whole thing, you know?'

I looked at her patiently listening face. Maybe she didn't know? By the look of her she hadn't wanted for anything in her whole life.

She nodded and I took that as a sign to carry on.

'We,' I struggled to find the right words, 'were very physical at first. That's the way it is, isn't it? We learnt and discovered each other. Then we saved and struggled to get a deposit together to buy a house, put off having kids, as you do. Thought we were doing everything the right way. I went clerical and he went project manager and I thought we were getting there. Then one day he told me he wanted something else, that he'd changed. I tried to respect his decision – I loved him. Turned out his "something else" was actually *someone* else. He's in India with her now doing something with elephants.' I laughed. 'Perhaps I'll get lucky and he'll get squished?'

'I'm sure you wouldn't want that,' she smiled.

I brought my finger and thumb together between us and peered through the gap my fingers had made. 'Maybe just an ickle, ickle bit,' I answered, and she laughed.

'And he robbed you I suppose?' she asked, getting serious again.

'No,' I answered. 'To give him his due, he didn't. We split our savings right down the middle. He converted his to rupees and I converted mine to a blast in Magaluf with the girls. Mum and Dad got a little bit, as you do. Then it was back to work, and alone, and Ron Carswell's – he's the MD's son – wandering hands. He knew I was single and desperate now, I guess.'

'Desperate, my giddy aunt,' she retorted. 'You're a truly beautiful young woman. Men, my Kelvin included, would wade through infected drug needles to but breathe the same air as you.'

I shook my head. 'Kelvin is totally loyal to you,' I shot back. 'Even I can see that in only the short time I've known you. He'd fight and die for you.'

I saw her eyes glaze over and knew that I'd hit a memory nerve. In a moment she was back with me.

'I'm sure things will improve for you,' she said, tapping my hand. 'And here comes the champagne,' she said as Kelvin reappeared.

I got the impression she'd said the last bit to tell me that our intimate conversation was over because her man had returned. I appreciated the thought, should it be the case.

As Kelvin opened the bottle with a flourish and refilled our glasses, I became brave. 'My turn for a toast,' I said, and before they could object I stood and continued. 'In my whole twenty-six years on this planet nobody has ever bought me champagne before, well not real stuff anyway.' I turned to Jane and she saw where I was going and nodded her permission. 'To Kelvin!'

'To Kelvin!' Jane joined.

'Heil me,' played Kelvin. 'But you are missing something here?'

He paused for dramatic effect. 'True, I bought champagne and gave it to Aneese who kindly and selflessly gave it to Jane. But this bottle,' he pointed to the one on the small table between them, 'was bought, I believe, by Jane last week?' He looked at her. 'Correct?'

She nodded.

'So in effect we have each given each other champagne!' He paused to give his logic chance to sink in before continuing. 'So I would like to propose a toast.'

'Take it away, Daddy-o!' I interrupted, gaining an odd look from them both.

We stood as one. 'To us?' he suggested.

'TO US!' we joined.

Chapter Two

I woke up the next morning feeling very refreshed having had one of those rare nights where I'd slept perfectly. The sun was shining through the white net of the already opened curtains and I could hear the birds singing. It was like I'd slept the winter through and was coming out of hibernation.

Like all bears coming out of hibernation I had a sore head, well a slight one, and my stomach roared. I tried to remember what I'd eaten yesterday. Had I eaten at all? I took a deep breath and realised that I'd slept with my arms raised above my head like I remembered doing as a child. I'd only done that rarely since then. I smiled and kicked my feet under the sheets like it was Christmas. Life felt good.

But why? My surroundings were familiar yet vague. I sat up and realised I was wearing a thin, white, cotton nightdress. Me in a nightie? I'm strictly a PJ girl!

To my right was a small bedside cabinet containing a tray which held a glass of orange juice, a glass of water and something I couldn't quite see. Its shape was warped by me seeing it obliquely and partially through the bottom and side of the glass. I reached out my hand and touched the glass but felt only its coldness. Moving the tray solved the problem, revealing two white oblong tablets and two round pink ones.

Somebody had planned ahead last night. Who did I know who planned ahead like that?

The realisation hit me. Christ, I was in the strange man's house – in the strange man's bed! I looked under the duvet and confirmed that I wore no underwear beneath the nightdress. In panic I looked around at the bed and was relieved when, to all appearances, it looked like I had slept alone. But somebody had still undressed me?

My memories of the night before starting to return. Gin and tonic, singing stalker, good looking, chasing him, being wet and falling, eating something delicious, getting caught playing with the mice and expecting a spanking (what?). The strange man again, in a taxi, COMING HOME WITH HIM! my head screamed at me.

Oh god, no!

So what's the problem? You're single and it's been a while. Was bound to happen eventually.

Single? But he's not! Shit and double shit. He has a wife, JANE, I met her?

I was missing something. I met her. If I met her...

More memories. A beautiful blonde woman with a thin waist and hair reaching down her back all the way to her waist. Not all her hair reached that far, just some. Perfectly formed legs and tits like Egyptian pyramids. Blue eyes speckled with grey. Laughing, hugging, crying, singing. More singing.

Me singing? Clapping? Dancing? Drinking white and brown stuff?

As my mind reeled, I reached for the orange juice. It was almost perfectly chilled so it can't have been there long. I gulped it down and it started to bring me to life, my memory especially.

Up to a point.

We were drinking champagne but there was no more after the second bottle. Then Tom, I mean... Kelvin... had insisted that I had a brandy "like it was meant to be drank". Yes, I'd messed one up earlier on in the night, hadn't I?

We all drank brandy. I remember enjoying it, liking the taste, being surprised. We danced, me with him and me with her and then I watched them until we all joined in.

It was after midnight.

'I should go,' I remembered saying.

'Rubbish,' she'd answered. 'We have plenty of room. And you're just being polite, you're not putting us out at all. And aren't you enjoying yourself? Have you even enjoyed yourself since Richard?'

Yes, I'd told her about Richard, must have told *them* about Richard. I remembered her closeness. And yes I was having fun.

'But, honey,' Kelvin interrupted. 'I promised Aneese that when she said the word I would get her a cab and get her home?'

And then it was after two, I remembered seeing a clock. Laughing and silliness. Then the clock was all blurry and I had to squint to see it.

Ten to three?

The room spun. Ow! Rubbing my bum.

'That's it, Cinders. I think the ball is over.'

Being carried. Unfamiliar aroma, snuggling up close, nice and safe. Grunting upstairs. 'Be careful! Watch her head!'

Far away voices. Opening doors. Being laid gently onto a bed.

'I CAN DO IT!' Think that was me.

'I'll help you – you, out! You've done your bit!'

Getting undressed. BEING UNDRESSED!

'It's OK, it's just me and you.'

Nodding, eyes closed.

'This will fit you.' Soft and cool and nice. Smells nice like... summer?

More nodding.

Comfy.

Door clicking shut. Alone.

Head buzzing.

Lights out.

Waking and smiling.

Confusion, realisation. TERROR!

Explanations, memories, order.

Here, now, drinking juice.

Relief... of a sort. At least I hadn't been raped or sold into slavery. Why had I allowed myself to come home with a stranger? That was so typically dumb of me.

OK, so some questions were answered, but some were not. Where were my clothes for one?

Before I even finished the thought I saw a pile of clothes folded neatly on a chair on the other side of the room. I slipped out from beneath the covers and... oooh, this feels nice. Thick, soft carpet on my bare feet. I flexed my toes, enjoying the feeling and smiling. I could get used to this.

The pile of clothes were actually two: mine and another set. Both were freshly laundered. Atop mine sat my underwear from yesterday, again clean and fresh.

OK, that must have been embarrassing, being undressed down to the nuddie by another woman. I must have been well out of it.

I looked at the clothes. Mine were work clothes. The other set were much better quality by far, labels I didn't recognise. It contained everything I needed with the top layer being a cream dress with small pink and yellow flowers sewn on. I held it against me and searched for a mirror. OK, it wasn't me, but it was very nice, and my clothes were work clothes after all. My short tartan skirt, sensible, semi-high shoes, cream blouse and medium denier stockings. Oh, and my jacket must be here somewhere, and where was my coat? And my handbag?

The decision made, I started to peel off the nightdress but I stopped mid-flow. Was this room en suite? There were three doors, of which one was obviously the way out. I saw from the hinges that the one to the right of the bed opened inwards. That must be the exit. That left the other two and one of them was a double door so I discounted that. I stopped again mid-step.

Nosey cow, I told myself. I ran back to the double door and swished them open. Wow, a walk-in closet, and huge. I'd always wanted one of these. It contained everything a woman could need from hats, very few of those, shoes, clothes and all the accessories. I ran my hands along the clothes like a child, making the hangers sway and click. Then there were a suite of drawers and I opened one before closing it again quickly. Underwear. Not going to start going through her underwear drawer, that would be sick. I tried another. Oh, so he got treated to the full suspender treat, did he? Lucky him.

I'd treated Richard to the whole "ish" once. It felt awkward, not sexy at all. Wouldn't have done it at all if it wasn't for Sianna egging me on, it was even her idea. Still, Richard appreciated it and it had been an enjoyable occasion. He'd hinted at it once or twice since, but there had never been the repeat performance of the bedroom whore routine.

I grew saddened, thinking of Richard again. Maybe if I had donned the suspenders more often he'd still be here?

No, no and no again, I admonished myself. I feel so good at the moment. Richard out!

I heard a sound and jumped with a start. As I turned to face the double doors opposite to the set I'd entered through, I realised that they were slightly ajar. My heart skipped a beat as I saw a shadow pass in front of them, then there was the sound of runners as, I guessed, another set of doors was opened somewhere.

My heart was in my mouth but I still crept slowly forward until I could see into the room beyond. It was their room, obviously. Although my view was limited I could see that it was larger than mine with a huge, larger than large, four poster bed slap bang in the middle of the longest wall. The colour scheme was predominantly whites and creams again, just like mine.

In front of an open wardrobe, this time a smaller one with sliding doors, stood Kelvin, struggling to get out of a tight, pale blue polo neck sweater.

My breath caught. I shouldn't be here watching him undress! I took a step back but, curiosity being what it is, only a step. My mind shouted at me not to look and I know I shouldn't have but I just couldn't stop myself. When he'd nearly won the battle and was all elbows, tussled hair and bare chest, I heard a vibration and noticed his mobile phone moving on a flat surface where he must have placed it. He snatched it up, the sweater now off and him bare chested.

'Carla,' he answered, having looked at the caller ID before holding it to his ear.

Who was Carla, I thought. Girlfriend? Mistress?

'No, it's done, checked it myself this morning. And why are you in, it's a Saturday?'

He turned his back to me and placed the phone between his ear and his shoulder and retrieved a loose looking cream coloured shirt from off a rail. As he undid the buttons to get if off the hanger I, guiltily, took in his physique, and what I saw wasn't bad at all.

I already remembered from yesterday that he was broad shouldered but, boy, was he! Whatever exercising he did made his shoulders seem to sprout out from just below his shoulder blades. If he'd had a pair of wings affixed to his back I am sure his muscle load would have coped easily. His shoulder muscles were large, too. Mentally I compared him with other men's bodies I'd seen and realised that I could see every bone in their shoulders. Kelvin's body was more padded, certainly. Almost triangular compared to their almost flatness.

Load bearing shoulders, my brain shouted at me. I must have read the term somewhere, sometime.

And were those tattoos? I hadn't noticed them at first as he turned this way and that, thought they were a trick of the light. But his left upper arm from the armpit down seemed to have dark lines drawn on it, complete circles. Rings would be the better term, I guessed. I tried to count them but with him constantly moving I kept losing track at six or eight. And then I noticed his right arm. Two grey rings.

What was this all about? Soldiers had tattoos, I knew, but weren't they all "MUM" or some girl's name? I even recalled seeing a bulldog somewhere sporting a union jack waistcoat.

He turned to face me and for a fleeting second I froze, thinking our eyes had met. My heart beat loudly in my chest.

'Well, I'm grateful, but there's plenty of time—'

He stopped, the caller obviously interrupting him (brave soul).

'CARLA,' he raised his voice slightly to interrupt her interruption. 'Go home. The sun is shining for the first time in, it seems like months! Take a walk in the park, relax, drink some wine? Do whatever you like BUT-GO-HOME!'

Not a mistress then. An employee? I don't know why I felt relief. I put it down to the fact that I hadn't been spotted after all.

Maybe he has wandering hands in the office like Call-Me-Ron bloody Carswell, I thought? No, I couldn't see that. His employees obviously felt free to call him at any time *and* felt they could interrupt him. Sign of a good boss. I couldn't imagine me phoning Carswell for any reason, even during working hours.

'See you Monday,' he finished, and he casually threw the phone onto the bed as he slipped on the shirt and negotiated the buttons. As the door closed behind him, I noisily started breathing again, not realising that I'd stopped.

Enough close calls for one day, I decided. Time for that shower.

The last untried door was, indeed, the en suite. I showered quickly, enjoying the aroma of the unfamiliar soaps and gels, I even washed my hair. Having my mop cut had advantages. As I towelled myself in the bedroom I spied my bag by the door. It was as if it had been pushed through the open door as an afterthought. I felt relief. At least I wouldn't have to go downstairs totally raw. I didn't wear a lot of make-up but, like most girls, I felt naked without it.

As I dressed hurriedly, panties and bra, a light slip and the dress – no nylons of any sort being present apart from my work pair – I realised that the room seemed different. At first I couldn't put my finger on it then I realised that the tray had gone from the bedside cabinet, so somebody must have come in. But had the tray been there when I almost ran from the connecting walk-in closet to the shower ten minutes earlier? Or had it been retrieved when I was sneaking around in the closet itself?

I started to feel sick. If my spying had been rumbled I guess I'd find out soon enough, but damn it, I was trying to make a good impression on these two... strangers?

I headed for the door but at the last minute noticed a pair of shoes by the bed. They had much smaller heels than the ones that I'd arrived in yesterday (wonder where *they* are?), but they fitted well enough so, fully dressed at last, with only slightly damp hair, I quietly left the room.

I followed my nose around corners and soon found the stairs. As I descended, trying to look as graceful as a movie star, I heard voices coming from somewhere. As I took in the scene around me, I recognised the hall from last night, with my raincoat still hanging where Kelvin must have put it after taking it from me.

'It'll have to be handled, carefully, can't just come out with it.' I heard him say as I hovered outside the partly open door. I was becoming such a sneak!

'I'm sure you can handle it, my Jack,' she answered.

There was that "Jack" thing again.

I saw the movement out of the corner of my eye but I still jumped and nearly screamed when it (she?) pushed past me and fully opened the door, carrying a tray. The "it" in question was an old, almost leather faced woman, dressed in black with dark, greying hair in a long ponytail.

As the couple turned to face us she spoke in – was that Spanish – and Jane looked my way.

'*Gracias*, Consuella,' Jane replied and even I knew what that meant. As to what the old lady had said I had no idea. I think I recognised the word, *senorita*, though.

When the door had been forced open by "Consuella" Jane had been sitting on his knee at a small table with her arms draped around his shoulders. Did these two never stop the lovey-dovey routine? But now she was walking towards me, smiling, arms open, and he had risen to his feet.

'At last you're awake.' She smiled as she kissed me on the cheek.

I froze. We were kissing friends?

She noticed my reaction. 'Oh, I am sorry,' she said, putting her hand to her mouth. 'Last night we seemed so close. I'm so sorry if I've overstepped?'

'No, no,' I said hurriedly, thinking how much I must have forgotten about last night. I had snatches, that's all. 'I'm just not used to it.'

'I really am sorry,' she continued. 'The last thing we want is for you to feel awkward around us.'

'No, I don't,' I lied. Well just a little.

There were still so many unanswered questions, though, chief amongst them being why a man would pick me up and bring me home to meet his wife?

'Did you sleep OK?' he asked, thankfully changing the subject.

'Better than I have for ages.' I could at least answer that one truthfully.

And then I sneaked around and ran my hands through your wife's underwear drawer – nice suspenders, by the way – and watched you as you changed your shirt. I smiled knowingly at the thought.

'Must have been the brandy,' Jane said, interrupting my thoughts.

'Yes, the brandy. I liked that,' I answered. 'Surprised me.'

'It came as a surprise to me, too, I must admit, when he got me onto the stuff. Can't drink it straight like he can, though. Come, sit,' she ordered politely and showed me a seat.

The table contained crumpets with jam and my stomach noisily called.

'Help yourself,' Jane continued. Kelvin already was.

'We normally have tea at this time of day but if you want coffee?'

'Tea is fine,' I answered, hungrily and hurriedly lathered butter onto a hot crumpet.

Waistline be damned today, I'll work it off tomorrow. A part of me asked why I was even bothering. Who was I bothering to keep myself thin for?

'Had you been listening at the door long?' Jane asked innocently.

Kelvin stopped his chewing and looked between us. I guessed that it was only the women who spoke Spanish, but not this woman, ie me.

So Consuella had grassed me up! I swallowed hard, remembering Jane's forthrightness from last night. Well, two can play at that game.

'About two seconds, actually. Something about "we can't just spring it upon her, Jack. It'll have to be done properly". And who is Jack?'

Jane reached out to Kelvin and touched his arm. 'My Jack of all trades.'

'And master of none,' I finished before I even knew the words were out.

'Oh, I wouldn't say that,' replied Jane instantly. A look of tenderness eased onto her smiling face as she stroked his arm, looking into his face the whole time. 'He's master of quite a few.'

Flirting? Were they flirting in front of me? Yeah, that's not going to make me feel awkward at all!

'Why am I here?' I demanded. I knew I was being rude but she'd started it.

There was silence for a while as we all looked at each other and two of us chewed. Did Jane never eat? The thought seemed to come from nowhere.

'Ultimately,' Kelvin answered, 'you're here because we like you and want you to like us. Sure, I piqued your attention and you chased me once I'd decided that I couldn't go ahead with what I'd started, but let me assure you that if we didn't like you, you wouldn't have gotten as far as the taxi home.'

I took that in. 'But Jane hadn't met me.'

This time Jane answered. 'Kelvin has great instincts and he knows I trust them. As normal, he's right. You're a beautiful, sweet, lovely young woman. A little sad, perhaps?'

OK, conflict of emotions here. This blonde goddess with the perfect body was complimenting me, but telling me I was sad? I'm not sad. Am I?

'And does Kelvin bring home young lovely women for you all the time?' I continued, unable to stop myself.

'Actually, you're the first,' he answered.

I guessed that he saw that I didn't believe him.

'No, I swear on Jane's life, you're the first. Actually, it is a great honour, believe me.'

'And you could have put the ring back on any time,' I continued. I noticed during my outburst that he was still not wearing it.

'Ring?' His brows knotted and he finally looked down to his hand. 'I've not worn a ring for years.'

I noticed that Jane was wearing one.

He chuckled, 'Oh, we're not married.'

My mouth dropped open and I saw her shake her head.

'Kelvin was married, once,' she answered. 'As I wa... am, still am.'

'But we are together, yes sir,' he continued, reaching out his hand to hers. 'In every way. She is mine and I am hers and nothing will ever change that.'

Somehow I believed him. I remembered the story she'd told me last night, about how he'd made it big and then came back for her. Obviously, she'd left out the nitty gritty. She must have been married when he rode his white charger into the little village and lifted the fair maiden onto his saddle under the noses of the evil lord and his band of cut-throats.

She smiled up at him and I realised again how close they seemed and how empty my life was in comparison.

'Please allow me to apologise for us both if we have made you feel awkward in any way,' he continued. 'It was unintentional. Now we've laid our cards, more or less, on the table. How about some quid pro quo?'

I thought about what they'd said and Jane poured the tea.

A little honesty *would* clear the air. I'd gotten the ring thing wrong, along with so much else. It was only fair, I guess. 'Shoot,' I said as I lifted the cup to my mouth. The tea was perfect, like my grandmother used to make.

'You chased me. Why?'

I formed the answer in my head as Jane sipped her tea and placed the cup in her lap.

'You intrigued me,' I finally answered. 'You went through all that effort – the football crowd, the song and all. The battle was won! And then you retreated.'

'You sound like a soldier,' he smiled.

'See, knew we'd like you,' Jane remarked.

I smiled back, feeling the ice breaking again.

'You thought it was a common or garden pickup?'

'Yes.'

'But you chased me anyway?'

I looked sideways at Jane and she noticed. 'Well you had bought me champagne – not that that's all it takes, mind you – and also…' I fidgeted. 'One of the football crowd fancied his chances after you'd legged it.'

He nodded and chuckled and she smiled.

'Well I can't fault his taste.'

'Quite,' Jane agreed.

I reddened. Shouldn't Jane be telling him off at this stage, not agreeing with him?

'Now I see your dilemma,' he continued. 'Stay for full-time and the penalty shoot-out and a possible fumble in the corner, or retreat at half-time to the assured half-time orange!'

'Well you're no mere orange,' I quipped, regretting it instantly. 'And they were tacos, anyway,' I finished, hoping that the compliment had gone unnoticed.

'And what did you think when you saw me? Knew there was me in the equation?' asked Jane.

What could I tell her? That I thought she was the most beautiful woman I'd ever seen? And that's not easy for us women to say. You know, not a model, but most of them were fake anyhow. Jane could stop traffic.

'Well that just ramped up the confusion factor even more. Some random guy picks me up and then brings me home to meet the wife? I think by then the brandy had kicked in and I hadn't eaten and—'

'But did you enjoy yourself last night?' Jane interrupted.

I paused and smiled. I remembered feeling happy, a rare state for me these days. 'Yeah, I did. Right up until I fell on my ar… rump.'

'Did you bruise?' asked Jane, seemingly not noticing my almost choice of words.

'Forgot to look, I must admit,' I answered, rubbing my right buttock.

Kelvin, who had lifted a newspaper to read something that had got his attention, was suddenly very interested. 'Perhaps I could be of service?'

This time he got the slap he so thoroughly deserved, though it was a playful one. It impacted loudly and, I thought painfully, on the bare skin of his arm, but he just shrugged it off.

'You just stick to your newspaper,' Jane admonished.

'Right you are,' he replied as he picked it up and held it upside down, shaking it nosily like he was trembling with the anticipation of seeing a young lady's buttock.

Jane looked at me, expecting me to say something but all I could see was Kelvin the comedian, and I knew from the way she was trying to ignore him that she knew what he was doing. Her arm reached out again, noisily destroying the newspaper.

'Stop that,' she chuckled. 'If anybody's looking at her bum it's me.'

He guffawed and she rolled her eyes and my mouth fell open again. I seemed to do a lot of that in front of these two.

'Well that sounded better in my head,' she said almost to herself. She cleared her throat. 'More tea, anyone?'

Whilst she topped up our cups, unbidden, I saw them share a look and a slight nod passed between them.

Kelvin was now in the chair. I'd already noticed that she left the talking to him, though I suspected that, whatever the subject, they'd already discussed it prior. He leaned forward and stirred more sugar into his tea whilst Jane looked on and I contemplated spoon or knife for the jam.

'I hope we're all friends again now?' He looked at me. 'Yes?'

I nodded because it was true. The last ten minutes had really cleared the air.

'I have to go to New York next week,' he started. 'Happens sometimes – they want to see the man behind the music, they say.'

I nodded. New York? Wow. Where was this going?

'Promised I'd take Jane on this one. Flights, hotel suite and everything are on them.'

He paused and took a sip of his tea.

'Thing is, I know how busy I am going to be and I don't want Jane, here, alone by herself in a strange city whilst I'm pumping the flesh with the clients all day.'

Realisation dawned. Surely he wasn't asking me to…

'Have you got a passport?'

I swallowed loudly and nodded, disbelieving.

'Then perhaps you'd like to come with us? Keep Jane company until I can disentangle myself? Then we could the three of us catch a show or something in the evenings?'

Oh my god! I was shocked.

'We'd be leaving Tuesday,' he continued. 'If that isn't enough notice then perhaps you could follow us out a day or two later? We were planning to fly back on the Monday morning, so we'd have the weekend to play and see the sights at least.'

I finally found my voice. 'Are you serious?'

They both nodded in unison.

I knew the mercenary in me wanted to say yes, but I hardly knew these people. But New York? This could be a once in a lifetime chance!

'Yes!'

Who said that, I asked myself?

Jane screamed and jumped up like they'd just won the lottery. Had I said yes?

Now she was hugging me tight, pulling me out of my seat to do so. She let me go to hug him and then grabbed me again.

'We're going to have so much fun!' she said this time and this time the hug was longer.

I watched Kelvin watching us, seeing the joy on his face that he'd gotten for her what she wanted. He must really love her, I thought. The hug continued and I smiled at him as she squeezed me and he smiled serenely and just nodded back.

Seemed everybody was happy and getting what they wanted. What could be wrong with that, I asked myself to assuage my mercenary guilt at accepting.

'Come on,' she continued excitedly. 'We can still catch the shops!'

Still catch the shops? Why, what time is it? I looked around as she giggled and demanded and emptied his wallet. I found a clock on the mantelpiece and my mouth opened in shock. Nearly one o clock! Hell, what time did I get up?

In what seemed like only seconds she was ready at the door and I was being hurried into my coat. She kissed him noisily three times as she opened the door.

'Lovely man,' she said to nobody in particular.

'Keep the cash for taxis,' he said.

Taxis? She must have lifted nearly eight hundred quid from his wallet, if I'm any judge.

'And use this for anything else.' He held out a Visa card to her. 'The PIN number is—'

Another kiss. 'I know what the number is, silly man. Do you think I took up with you for your broad shoulders and your cold grey eyes?'

She went to pull away but he pulled her back and he nuzzled her ear whilst he whispered something.

'OK, OK,' she answered. As she finally got away and ran for the door, he slapped her on the rump and she looked back with a smile.

I didn't know what to do with myself. I'd been ready for, oh, seconds now.

He looked at her departing form and then he looked at me. He raised his hand as if to smack me into motion and I, caught up in the moment, retreated, indicating my injured right buttock. In response he lifted his other hand and I cheekily smiled and pointed my left hip at him, egging him on. I'm sure his attempt was designed to miss which, indeed it did, but as I ran to catch up to Jane I couldn't help wondering how strangely odd and exciting it was playing and flirting with this man whilst his woman looked on and said nothing.

Chapter Three

He drove like a maniac. It wasn't true, but it was what I chose to believe because I was angry with him. At least I thought I was angry with him. I was confused. I was considering not going to New York, even though the whole point of this morning's journey was for me to collect things from my flat and put the place in order before our trip. Couldn't come back to mouldy pizza and cheesy milk in the fridge, could I?

I wanted to go, I sorely did, but I'd felt guilty enough about accepting the invitation. I knew it was the mercenary inside me, the one inside us all, who'd accepted. I was still conscious of the fact that I knew this couple hardly at all. Sure, I liked them – hadn't seen anything not to like – and if I was being honest with myself I was jealous of them in so many ways. But I was enjoying their company and the thought of going to New York was just unbelievable to me. I still didn't believe it.

And then Kelvin had spoiled the whole shopping experience and I felt angry.

Christ knows I was confused enough already. Thirty-six hours ago I didn't even know these people but since then I'd stayed two nights at their lovely house (which I still hadn't seen all of), got drunk with them, danced with them, sang with them (I vaguely recall singing something that first night), been carried, drunk, up to bed by them, BEEN UNDRESSED BY ONE OF THEM! Shared their food and accepted their hospitality, opened up to them by telling them about Richard, and Carswell's wandering hands, and all the men who just wanted one thing.

Rummaged through her underwear drawer, watched her de facto husband half undress as I watched from hiding, admired his body, admired her body!

OK, those last ones were all accidents. It's not like I set out to catch him changing his shirt and Jane and I were trying clothes on, sharing a changing room. Girlfriends do that, right? Nothing wrong with it. And I snuck a look. More than one actually, just for interest's sake. Everybody does it. Don't they?

It's not like the female form turns me on or anything, I was just confirming what I already suspected, that she had a great body. Kelvin was a lucky man if he got to worship there which, obviously, he did. If I look as good as her when I get to her age, then I certainly wouldn't complain. How old were they, anyway? Older than me, certainly, but how much more? Ten years older? Twenty years older? Possibly but probably not. It's not like we exchanged birth dates or anything.

I'd seen this dress and, boy, was it beautiful. I'd look like a movie star in it – so would Jane actually. But it was a bit pricey, almost two months' rent. It was gold and could be worn in more than one configuration. I could wear it whilst revealing my midriff or not, short or long, fully covered or off the shoulder. I'd never wanted a dress so much before, so much that I physically ached. I actually considered how I could afford it, which Peter I could rob to pay for Paul the dress. Then common sense kicked in. Perhaps one day.

I hadn't realised Jane had seen me admiring it. No doubt she saw me looking at the price tag too. I knew I'd winced when I'd seen it.

One day, I told myself. One day.

Then she'd suggested we went for a drink to get into the shopping frame of mind. There was a champagne bar she knew near Harrods. Why not, I thought. I could certainly do with cheering up all of a sudden. We got our drinks and then she excused herself for ten minutes. I thought she was powdering her nose. Then she came back and sat down opposite me, all smiles. Her normal self.

'Before we left the house Kelvin said to give you this,' she said, and she held an envelope out to me.

I remembered Kelvin pulling her back and whispering to her as we'd tried to leave. I thought he was just whispering sweet nothings in her ear or warning her not to spend too much. Like a naive fool I took the envelope before I even realised what it was. When I held it in my hand, I knew instantly what it was, though. The flap popped open and I saw the wad and my eyes bulged open as I saw it.

'Jane, I...' I spluttered. 'What the hell? What's this? I can't accept this!'

'Kelvin says I'm to accept no argument. Say's if you have a problem you can take it up with him when we get back.'

And I did, well I tried to. My argument was weak. He waved off my protests saying things like, 'Couldn't have Jane shopping and not you', or, 'You're kindly giving up your free time to look after Jane when I'm otherwise engaged'.

'As if a trip to New York, bed and board gratis, wasn't enough?' I pointed out.

His reply was that it was more than bed and board. 'All expenses paid. And clothes are an expense. Just ask my accountant!'

The shopping trip was ruined because all I could think about was how angry I was. But was I angry at him or angry at myself or life itself? I wanted nice things – who didn't – but it was always, "one day". Now I had the chance to get this absolutely killer dress which I ached just to try on, just once. I had the money (the envelope contained two thousand pounds) and all I could think about was my pride.

There was nothing wrong with Kelvin's reasoning and there was nothing wrong with my counter-argument. I knew that it all came down to my working class pride.

I was so angry I drank a lot of champagne, buying it with *his* money. That'll show him, I thought. We almost didn't start shopping again. In the end we got another hour of shopping done before even the late closing shops started closing. I spent the last ten minutes of store opening time standing by a certain dress with my fist in my mouth telling myself how much I hated Kelvin and all men. Think they can paw us; think they can buy us, own us!

When we got back to the house, I was light four hundred quid and had very little to show for it. Champagne wasn't cheap by the glass, I'd found, but I must admit I did enjoy treating Jane, albeit on his money. It was nice to be the one paying for a change. Even through my tipsiness, as soon as I thought that thought I realised how much it blew my arguments out of the water. In the end it all came down to one thing: my pride.

Kelvin had done a thoughtful and, I hope, selfless thing. I said "I hope" because deep down inside me I kept thinking that he would want something for all his kindness, one day. That was what men were like, wasn't it? Sure they'd pay for dinner and hold the door for you, but they sure as hell expected the bill to be settled later.

What I hadn't thought of before now was that Jane hadn't objected. Not once. I noticed a pattern forming. This wasn't the first time he'd done something that normal women (me) would have objected to their man doing. What was the story there? It wasn't like he was running his hands down my back or touching me up when he thought she couldn't see. Everything he did he did with, it seemed, her full approval. Was she the weak woman who accepted anything he did then cried about it later when she was alone? Somehow, I couldn't see that. I'd never seen a couple so... together as these two.

'Something on your mind, Aneese?'

I was so deep in my own thoughts that I stopped noticing his driving. It wasn't dangerous, but it was fast. He didn't rev hard and race off at the lights like some boy racer, but he certainly drove like he enjoyed it. When the lights changed, he was always first away but not because he was racing, it was because he was always ready whereas everybody else didn't seem to be. And he used the road fully too, shaking his head when all the other traffic would queue in one lane and leave the other free. I was beginning to agree with his mutterings. Why did they do that? Did I do that?

I didn't own a car, though I could drive. To Richard and I, the expense of owning a car when we were saving for a house deposit was pointless. On the rare occasions we needed a car we hired one.

I didn't answer his question. I was still confused on the subject.

'It's the money thing, isn't it?' he asked, looking my way briefly before returning his full attention to the road.

I really didn't know where to start or, if I did, what I would say. I really liked this couple and, as they'd already stated, they liked me and wanted me to like them, but there was something missing. Sure we'd had our little honesty session yesterday and it had cleared the air, but now I was feeling more awkward than I was before. Was it just the money thing or was my subconscious picking up on something that I wasn't seeing? Nobody could be as generous as these two were being without wanting something back. People just weren't that generous in real life. Then again, what did I know, I'd never met a couple like this before.

And then there was the dream. I'd had a very odd dream last night.

In the dream we were flying to New York, I just knew we were, dreams are like that. Nothing wrong there you might think, but Kelvin was the plane! Sprouting out of his shoulder muscles, yes *those* shoulder muscles, the ones I'd admired only yesterday as he'd changed his shirt, were large, white wings, like he was a Hollywood angel or something. Wings, flapping slowly like a great white bird, and he held me and Jane, one in each arm. I must have been asleep in my dream because I'd woken up and Kelvin had smiled down at me and asked me if I'd wanted a drink. I nodded back and smiled, all content and safe feeling, and a glass just appeared in my hand. I was expecting vodka with lemonade and that's what it was. It was if he had read my mind. I looked to one side and Jane was there asleep with a contented smile on her face. She just radiated the happiness, contentment and safety that I felt in Kelvin's arms as we soared across the Atlantic in the night sky. There was no cold or the feeling of rushing air. I looked below us and saw the dark sea thousands of feet below and a hint of a thin white line on the horizon. The coast of America?

'Be another half hour yet,' he'd said softly and I'd rolled over, taken a deep contented breath and fallen instantly to sleep, knowing in my dream that I was well cared for and safe.

So this morning I was determined to be angry with him about the money thing (even though I was unsure whether he was at fault or not) but at the same time I still felt the emotional after effects of my dream. How did dreams do that? In the past I'd had dreams about bad things and been in a bad mood all day for no reason! I hardly noticed him pulling over and switching off the engine.

'Aneese, I apologise,' he was saying before I even knew. 'I tried to do a nice thing but I never thought it through. I've been thinking about it all night and I now realise how you must have felt when Jane gave you the money. You see, I'd forgotten what it feels like – my parents were poor proud miners – and—'

I laid my hand on his arm and it stopped him. 'It's me, not you,' I said.

'What?' he said, shocked.

I paused to find the words. 'I, too, had forgotten what something was like. It's been a long time since anybody has been nice to me and not wanted anything back in return. And to think that two days ago I thought you were picking me up for a sordid night of extra-marital sex! But now I know you have Jane and don't need that from me, yet I am still judging you as a mere man. And you're no *mere* man.

'There are lots of questions I still can't answer, though, and maybe that is why I feel awkward all the time. Like how I came to be here and why?'

'And we will answer those questions, I promise, but please, not yet. I assure you we mean you no harm. Our ultimate wish is that all three of us are very happy and we hope, in time, that that is how it will be.

'Tell you what,' he said. 'You are off work for three weeks, right? Just trust us for those three weeks, have a good time in New York and enjoy yourself. Be yourself and let us be ourselves. I promise you that before those three weeks are up, we will answer all your questions. You will see. Please trust us. Trust me?'

I thought about what he'd said. Basically, he'd acknowledged that they wanted something of me, but did I trust them? Trust him? Last night's dream said it all, really. If I trusted him to fly across the Atlantic with me and Jane safe in his arms surely there was only one thing to say.

'I trust you,' I simply said.

He smiled. 'Good. Now prove it by giving me a hug, and before you start to feel awkward again.' He wagged his finger at me, having hit the nail instantly on the head. 'I ain't Cardwell, or whatever his name is. I ain't a groper. And you've seen the steak I have at home so you know I don't need no burger.' He stopped and looked embarrassed for a moment. 'May I point out, however, that you are far from being a burger. You're a good bit of steak yourself!'

'Why thank you,' I said as we hugged. 'I think!'

'One other thing,' he said as we drew apart and he started the engine. 'Jane and I will probably be generous over the next couple of weeks. We're not trying to buy you. Please just accept it.'

I promised I'd try.

Later, as we headed back from my, now pokey feeling flat, I noticed we were not taking the direct route.

'Where are we going?' I asked.

'Scenic route,' was all he said with a slightly wicked smile.

Lay-by drills!

I couldn't help it. The thought just popped in there, unbidden. I blamed my friend, Sianna. It was her who told me about them when she was dating that guy with the Ferrari. It was akin to the classic breaking down or running out of petrol on a quiet stretch of road or in a lay-by. Nothing to do while you waited for rescue. Nothing but get into the back seat and...

I held my tongue, remembering that I'd promised to trust. I realised we were leaving the city behind us and he eventually pulled into a lay-by and I fleetingly feared the worst. I couldn't help it, trust didn't come easy to me. I knew it was because I'd felt so betrayed by Richard and all the other men I'd dated to fill the Richard-sized hole in my heart, but knowing the reason didn't make the feeling go away.

'Scoot across,' he said, opening the door and getting out and walking around to the passenger side.

When he opened my door I was still sitting there, looking lopsidedly up at him. 'Why?'

He smiled down at me. 'Well you drive, don't you?'

'Yeah, but I can't drive this.'

'Why not?'

I paused, looking for excuses. 'Well insurance for a start.'

'Covered.'

'And... and I've never driven—'

'A car's a car,' he interrupted, correctly guessing my next objection.

'But it's old.'

'Sure is. Can't stand those new ones, they're rubbish, no character. This is a two point eight litre...' He stopped and clicked his fingers as if recalling a memory. 'Sorry, you're a girl. This is a white car. I also have a blue one, a red one and a silver one. All oldies from the eighties and nineties. I have all the cars I fancied as a young lad. Oh, and my motorbike of course.'

'You have a motorbike?' I asked, surprised.

'Yep.'

'What type?'

He smiled. 'Black one!'

I laughed. 'Of course, silly me!'

'Now scoot,' he said, almost forcing me across by starting to get in.

I hope I didn't show too much as my short skirt rode up as I manoeuvred over the gearstick. I saw him clock my legs.

Yeah, you ain't a groper but you got eyes, I told myself. Then I reminded myself how much of his body I had seen, and secretly, too. I reckoned I was still very much in credit on that deal.

I followed his instructions and, in no time, I was enjoying myself. This car was really powerful.

'So what type of car did you say this was?'

'White one,' he answered deadpan.

I played a frown onto my face. 'Really,' I growled.

He smiled. I liked his playful smile.

'Last of the Cosworths,' he answered. 'Boy racer's wet dream!'

A Cosworth? Wow! Even me, a mere girl, had heard of them. Seemed to recall one of Richard's friends waxing lyrical. Boy racer's wet dream, indeed.

'Also got me a Sierra four by four, an ST200 and an ST220.'

'Oh?' I said knowingly, but falsely. He was right. Red one, blue one and silver one. I was driving the white one, which I immediately christened "Whitey". The numbers and letters meant nothing to me.

I continued driving and he instructed me, urging me to go faster.

I shook my head. I was going as fast as I wanted to go.

'Then pull over,' he instructed.

I pulled a face. I didn't want to stop.

'Now,' he said, playing threateningly, and I complied.

'Engine off,' he ordered.

'Yes, Dad,' I said, only half playing this time. I didn't want to stop driving.

'Dad? Ouch! Much preferred "Daddy-o"!'

'"Daddy-o"?' Then I remembered that I'd called him that the other night, though where it came from I couldn't say.

When the engine had died he got out and started walking around the car and I heard noises. Then I saw the roof start to go back.

I smiled. I stupidly hadn't realised it was a convertible.

When the roof was securely down he got back into the passenger seat. 'Drive,' he ordered.

I was shocked but recovered quickly. I'd thought he was going to take over and show me how it was done. I smiled so wide it hurt. 'You got it, Daddy-o!'

It was windy and not too warm but I didn't care. It might have been sunny and warm under glass but it was still only mid-March. But the exhilaration! I went up through the gears, expecting him to instruct but he just left me to it. I'd remembered what he'd told me earlier and got a good line going into the bends and then powered out of them as the road started to straighten. I whooped with joy as I felt the car respond. I was beginning to understand why he drove like he did.

My skirt rode up slightly every time I used the clutch and I saw him look but I didn't care. The next time he looked I caught him and he knew I did but he just raised his eyebrows twice and smiled.

He reached across to my side of the vehicle and tapped the dashboard and I looked down to where he'd indicated. The speedometer was showing one hundred miles per hour. Thirty more than I'd been willing to do just a few minutes before. Just because he'd put the top down?

My mouth fell open and I started to panic. I was better off not knowing how fast I'd been going. I started to doubt myself. He must have known it was coming as he grabbed the wheel when I started to lose it.

'Dip the clutch,' he said but I froze and couldn't react.

'DIP THE CLUTCH!' he shouted this time.

Visions of all the car chase crashes I'd seen on television flashed into my head. I started to scream. I felt his hand on my left knee. Not a groper, eh? part of me said. Oh well, at least I would die having recently felt a man's touch. That was something, at least.

My brain registered his left hand fighting with the steering wheel as his right pressed down on my knee. I heard the engine scream, thinking it was the last thing I'd ever hear. Any second now, like in the films, I expected the car to flip over and leave the road. There'd be a crevasse, obviously, and the car would turn end over end and there would be an explosion. What I didn't realise in my panic was that the noise came from my right foot which was firmly on the accelerator pedal but that his hand pushing on my knee had disengaged the clutch, putting the car into neutral. Then I realised we were slowing and, as the last bend straightened, I realised he was expertly steering us towards a rough lay-by

'I need you to brake,' he said loudly, but not shouting.

I just looked at him.

'Brake, Aneese,' he said, but I was still frozen.

I felt pain on my left thigh. His hand had moved higher, the pain caused by the extra strength he had to use to keep my foot on the clutch as his hand walked higher and higher up my thigh. Any higher and he would be... Then I gasped as his fingers touched where he shouldn't, but it certainly brought me back to life.

'BRAKE!' he said once more and this time I did as I was told. Within moments we were stopping quickly, only skidding a little at the end as he removed his hand and the engine died.

'I'm sorry,' he said straight away. 'Had to get your attention.'

I was panting, not realising at first what he meant. I looked down at my thigh and saw that it was red in places. It hurt like my rump had when I fell. Was I going to get another bruise? Finally, I regained my power of speech.

'Oh, I'm sure you enjoyed it, too!' I accused, but I was more terrified and relieved than mad. My heart was still racing and my breathing was heavy.

'Well, I had no hands left. What was I meant to do, use my tongue for the brake?'

'Well it was hanging out far enough!' I answered quickly.

Then our eyes met and we both burst into hysterical laughter.

'Hanging out far enough,' he spluttered. 'That's fantastic!'

Finally we both took a deep breath and the laughing stopped. I looked across and saw him wiping tears from his eyes.

'You going to tell Jane?' I finally asked.

'What, that you have great legs? Of course,' he answered. 'No secrets between us.'

'No, you know. Where your hand was.'

'Of course,' he said again. 'Why wouldn't I?'

I was terrified and disappointed at the same time. And confused.

We swapped places and he drove home. Neither of us spoke the whole way back.

Before our goat meat Sunday lunch Jane asked me how my thigh was.

So he'd told her, I thought. Well, he'd said he would. I'd been quiet since we'd been back, wondering what would be said. Even though there was nothing in it he was still her man. If my man had touched another woman there for any reason, I knew I would have been livid. Like a guilty child I lifted my skirt to show her.

'Well, that is pretty high up your thigh. Bet he enjoyed that!'

What?

'Still, he told me it was necessary. Does it hurt?'

I must have looked like a goldfish, just standing there opening and closing my mouth.

'Well, does it?'

I recovered. 'Yes, a little.'

'Well, I can't think of anything to help. If it were an eye we could stick a cold steak on it, but not there.'

How could she be so matter-of-fact? 'Aren't you bothered where he touched me? I've been in terror all afternoon over what you'd think!'

'Sweet Aneese,' she said as she reached out and touched my arm. 'Kelvin told me what happened and I trust him. Are you OK, though?'

I struggled to find words. 'Apart from the terror I've felt ever since, I'm fine.'

'You don't feel that he acted inappropriately towards you, I hope?'

'No, he didn't.' I smiled tentatively. 'As you said, being a man he probably enjoyed it!'

'Probably,' she smiled. 'But you're both safe and that what counts. For the record I told him off for risking you both like that. Sometimes he sails too close to the wind. Did you enjoy the drive?'

I was caught out by her change of tack. 'Actually, yes, it was fantastic. The way he got me to open her up like that…'

I stopped, remembering that she disapproved, but she just smiled. Strange, I thought. I could never gauge her reactions.

'Good. Glad you enjoyed it,' she said, putting her arm through mine and steering me back towards the lounge. 'And I'm glad you and Kelvin have made up about the money thing. So we're all friends again.'

Yes, we were all friends again and I'd promised to trust and not think bad things. I was still as confused as ever, but I remembered what I promised Kelvin today. I was determined to put my doubts behind me and enjoy whatever there was to enjoy.

'Oh, and he says you have great legs and I agree. I have seen more of them than he.'

My mouth dropped open again. What was it with these two and all the compliments, always calling me beautiful and sweet? OK, it was nice to be complimented but this was getting close to OD. And when are these two going to stop just coming out with things like *oh you have nice legs?* Just as I am feeling comfortable, they say things like that and I turn to confused jelly again.

'You have good legs, too,' I blurted out before I knew it.

I didn't know what was worse, her complimenting mine or me complimenting hers. What was going on in this house! I was grateful she said nothing in reply. All she did was look at me and smile as she led me to the dinner table.

Goat lunch was superb. It was a normal Sunday lunch but just with goat as the meat. I tentatively picked at mine at first until I realised how nice it was.

Consuella came in midway through the meal, jabbering away in Spanish as if talking to herself. She picked up used crockery and walked out.

Jane turned to him and smiled. 'Seems you're a devil. I think she loved that goat!'

'Well I'm loving it now and there's enough for days, yet. Love or not, she had no qualms about killing it!'

I swallowed loudly, thinking about what he'd said. I wasn't used to food that had been running around just a little while before.

'Can I see the rest of the house after lunch?' I asked to change the subject.

'Of course,' Jane answered. 'I'd forgotten that you hadn't. Guess it's been a busy couple of days.'

Thirty-six hours, give or take. Is that all it's been? Hell, it seemed like so much had happened since I'd been sitting quietly drinking my unwanted, ordered in anger, gin and tonic.

So immediately after we'd finished, we trooped around the house carrying glasses of white wine as Consuella cleaned up after us. It was so cool having a servant to do all the tidying up.

I was shown upstairs first. Six bedrooms of various sizes, all finished in whites and creams. Four of the six had en suite bathrooms, leaving the remaining two to share the one on the landing. Then we took in the ground floor, most of which I'd seen before, but seeing it whilst sober finally implanted a map of it into my brain. Then we went down to the basement.

'I don't go down here much,' Jane admitted as we walked down the stairs. 'It's all his domain,' she said as she flicked her head and smiled over her shoulder in Kelvin's direction. 'Guess he has maidens chained to the wall or something.'

'Jane,' he admonished. 'You know very well I keep them in the lock-up down the street,' he quipped back playfully. He leaned forward to catch my eye as I was the piggy in the middle of our troop. 'It's the noise, you see. The neighbours were starting to complain.'

I smiled and nodded, realising they were playing with me again. They certainly had a healthy sense of humour, these two, that was if you can count joking about kidnapping and chaining young women to walls as humour. Was that to be my fate, part of me wondered?

Well, you do, don't you? You think the thoughts even though you know it isn't going to happen. And this pair had certainly had their chance long before now, anyway, on the first night when I was drunk as the very drunkest of alcoholic skunks.

My subconscious reminded me that nobody on the planet barring these two knew where I was. Should I contact my parents and let them know, let them know I was leaving the country at least? The answer came to me so quickly that it surprised me. No, it would be a betrayal of trust. I smiled as I realised that, despite the oddness of the situation, I did actually trust them. It was a nice, warm feeling that I was unfamiliar with. How long had it been since I trusted anybody?

'Here we are,' Jane said as we reached the bottom of the stairs.

They certainly went a long way down.

'You should get a lift,' I commented.

'To the left is Kelvin's gym.'

'His what?' I asked, surprised, then I remembered. Guess he didn't get that body from opening champagne bottles.

'His gym,' she answered, as she opened the door and reached for the light switch.

As the lights flickered on, I took in the room. It was fairly spacious with a set of expensive gym equipment that regular gyms would envy set up every few yards. There was certainly nothing cramped about it. Tread mill, cross trainer, cycling machine, rowing machine, other equipment that I didn't recognise, sets of professional looking weights, though nothing small for women to use, I noted. There were mirrors on the walls behind most of the equipment and I wondered if he was vain or just going for the same look that the fee paying gyms had, they all had mirrors everywhere. Or was it to reflect the light and make it brighter? We must be far underground – twenty feet – and there were no windows. The largest thing in the room was a suite of three large flat television screens set up so that, I presumed, one could be seen from wherever he was doing his stuff. The last thing I noticed was a small music system and speakers placed strategically around the room. It certainly looked like no expense had been spared.

I nodded approvingly. I, on the rare occasions I visited a gym, did the old iPod in the ear routine. This room must be his own personal iPod but with none of the damn wires always getting in the way.

'I use the gym only sparingly,' Jane said as I nodded.

'Because she's beautiful as she is,' Kelvin got in before she talked again.

'This is definitely set up for the caveman, here, though.'

She smiled at Kelvin again and he smiled back.

I realised that he hardly said a thing since we'd descended the long flight of stairs and once or twice I'd seen him observing me in the mirrors. What was he looking for?

'My home studio is across the corridor,' he finally said. 'Sometimes I just need to unwind and think things through so I pop in here, disengage the mind and just get a sweat up.'

'Studio?' I enquired.

'Oh, he must have music wherever he goes, as they say,' Jane quipped.

'Well, it is my profession,' he answered in his defence. 'I often work from home. Come on.'

Oh, the life of the idle – or not so idle in this case – rich!

I followed Kelvin out and Jane brought up the rear, flicking off the gym lights as she did. As the door closed he put his hand on the door handle across the hall but I stopped him.

'What's in there?' I asked.

I'd seen another door at the end of the hall.

'The garage.'

'The cars? Can I see?' I asked excitedly.

He smiled. 'Chicks always love the car.'

That was a quote from a film, wasn't it?

Jane was in first and as the lights flickered to life I saw the four cars he'd mentioned including the white Cosworth he'd egged me on in only a few hours earlier. I skipped towards it and ran my hands lovingly along the edges. For some reason I was beaming like an idiot.

'This one's my favourite, I think,' I gushed.

'You've never even been in the others,' Kelvin pointed out, but I ignored him.

I opened the door and sat in the driver's seat and placed my hand on the steering wheel. Memories began rushing back and I felt the adrenaline rush and my heart started to pump again. Then I felt his hand on my thigh and knew it felt nice even under the circumstances. More than nice, more than good. Then I realised they were looking at me with amused looks on their faces and so I stopped, feeling guilty. Thank God they didn't read minds.

I extricated myself sheepishly from the car and cleared my throat in embarrassment as the door softly clicked shut behind me. Then I saw the motorbike in the corner, a black one, just like he'd said, and my heart quickened again.

'Oh my god, what is that?' I again gushed excitedly as I trotted towards it and smoothed its dark lines.

It was polished to a high degree and the light reflected from the blackness and silver of the exposed metal.

'Can I sit on it?' I asked like a kid with his first bike.

They smiled their amused smile again but I didn't care. Kelvin graciously granted his permission with his hand and then laughed as I tried and failed to get on. The short skirt wasn't helping.

'Try again. I promise not to look,' he laughed as he placed his hand over his eyes, leaving a gap for his eyes.

'Well, that'll be a first,' I immediately shot back. *Oh shit. Jane is right there!*

She hooted a laugh.

What?

Even by pulling up the skirt beyond the levels of decency I still couldn't do it. They laughed at me and I playfully frowned back at them.

'Come here,' he said, and before I knew it he'd lifted me up and was holding me suspended above the bike, waiting for me to open my legs so that he could lower me onto it.

OK, this feels odd.

He gently lowered me onto it and, of course the skirt rose up and exposed my upper thighs again, and possibly a little of my underwear.

Ah, what the hell, they'd both seen plenty of my legs lately. Old news! But why did I have to change into this little thing when back at the flat? Who was I trying to impress or was I trying to compete with Jane?

No contest. I could never match her, younger model or not!

He raised the bike to the upright and I had to stand on my toes to touch the ground. He took his hands away and I panicked until I found the mid-point balance. It was surprisingly light as long as you kept it straight, I found. Go too far and then it needed brute strength to lift it back; strength I didn't have.

I leaned forward, took the handlebars and imagined myself speeding down the road, dressed like Catwoman, passing all the cars with a roar and a slight twitch of my wrist as I purred past them with a look of disdain thrown over my shoulder at the mere mortals behind me.

Kelvin was standing to my left and he reached across and flicked some switches after turning a key on the central handlebars.

'No, Kelvin, not inside!' I heard Jane protest, but he ignored her like I suspected she knew he would. She settled for placing her fingers in her ears.

Quickly he took both handlebars as my chin sat almost on his right shoulder; those large shoulder muscles just mere millimetres from my mouth. His scent was pleasantly strong, though not overpowering. I guessed it must be one of the expensive ones and obviously I had never smelt it before.

My right breast brushed his right elbow as he moved his hand but he didn't seem to notice. Jane was ahead of me and to my right and I wondered if she'd noticed. If she did she didn't let on but then I wondered what she would say if she did. From past experience I guessed it would be "Lucky Kelvin" or something like that.

The bike coming to life beneath me jolted me back to reality and I screamed. He looked at me and smiled and revved the engine louder and I started to smell the exhaust fumes. I saw Jane's mouth move but heard nothing, though she was still smiling. Did she ever stop? Then Kelvin removed his hand from the right handlebar and placed mine on it with his over the top. He revved again and again, letting the engine slow to almost idle before he revved again. When the engine noise subsided the third time he nodded at me and removed his hand.

'Just don't jerk it,' he shouted over the engine. 'Smooth like I showed you.' And then he moved to join Jane and slipped his arm around her waist and she reciprocated, still smiling. She'd removed her fingers from her ears by then.

I was scared. I thought that without Kelvin in charge the bike would shoot off and hit the nearest car as soon as I applied the power but the gentle throbbing between my legs was pleasant. I'd ridden a horse once or twice as a teenager and we girls had gone on about the secret pleasure that only us females could get from the experience, but this was a hundred times better. Part of me wondered how many horses were actually throbbing beneath me.

Tentatively I increased the power with my right hand and the noise level increased and I saw Kelvin nod. His unspoken approval egged me on and I made the engine roar until Jane screamed and Kelvin winced. Was I hurting his little bike? Awww, poor man. Not!

All too soon he was beside me and he thumbed a red toggle and the bike.

'No fair,' I protested. 'I wanna play. More, please?'

'If you're a good girl,' he said like a scolding father.

'I'll be good,' I promised, only half playing. 'Come on, take me out on it now. Pleeeaase?'

'You can put the lip away, it doesn't work with me.'
I frowned. Bet Jane's lip worked on him.
'Anyway, we have things to do, like get ready to fly.'
'I'm ready,' I protested. 'Tell him I'm ready, Jane!'
'Don't get me involved. You wanna ride, you charm him.'
Did she really say that?

I wanted to ride and I wanted to ride now. My decision was made, all caution gone. It was time to call their bluff.

'Daddy-o?' I purred, putting on my most silky voice as he clicked switches and turned off the key. I rested my chin on his shoulder and he stopped and turned his head a little to face me. I breathed hopefully sweet smelling air into his face. 'Aneese wants to ride and she's been ever so good,' I panted as I fluttered my eyelids and smiled sweetly.

'Huh,' he snorted and started to move away, but I reached out and grabbed his arm.

I stuck my chest out and raised my head slightly, revealing my neck. I slid back on the seat and my skirt rode up a bit more, revealing more of my panties.

I saw kelvin raise an eyebrow and I shot a glance at Jane. She seemed quite amused by the scene.

What was it with her, I asked myself for seemingly the hundredth time!

OK, I get it. It's like that game we played as children. What was it called? Oh yes, Nervous! As a child it was a way of being touched up by the boys. They would always instigate it, of course. They'd place their hand... well wherever they wanted actually, but not actually on anything they shouldn't. Then they'd ask if you were nervous. If you were it stopped but if you weren't then the hand was moved further up (or down depending on their lust that day) and on how brave the girl was feeling. I'd met Richard that way, played the game well!

Well if she didn't mind then neither did I. The memory of the bike throbbing below me as I pressed my inner thighs against what looked like the petrol tank was urging me on. I wanted more.

'Big, powerful Daddy-o, o master,' I purred again and this time I put my arms around his shoulders and gently pulled him towards me. I fixated my eyes on him, hoping his heart was beating as fast as mine. A flick of my eyes in Jane's direction again confirmed, partly to my irritation, that *she* wasn't nervous.

I leaned forward and whispered in his ear, ensuring that my tongue "accidentally" brushed his lobe just once. 'I've never been on a bike before,' I whispered and panted, using all my womanly guiles. 'I'd be afraid. I'd have to hold on *ever* so tight...'

I paused to let my intentions sink in. It had been a long time since I'd played the whore to get my way, in fact, I don't think I'd ever played the whore with Richard, barring the one suspender episode.

I moved back slightly until I could stare into his eyes and flashed my eyes, raised an eyebrow and widened by smile a little. My eyes bored into his, Jane forgotten, and his bored back. I saw him swallow and I sensed victory. Just to be sure I let go of his shoulders and leaned back on the bike, balancing the bike between my thighs as I stood on my toes. As I moved back I sensed that my underwear had not, which had been my intent. I saw him look down and lick his lips. Victory was mine. Any second now.

'Bravo,' said Jane as she clapped slowly and time returned to normal. 'Very well done, indeed, you had him in the palm of your hand. To be honest it would have worked on me, too.'

What?

I looked at her and then at him. She was smiling like she had won a great victory and he was just starting to breathe again. What was the game here?

'Sorry, Aneese,' Kelvin said. 'No insurance on the bike.'

'What? No insurance? But you can surely afford...' I looked between them again. 'You pair of... of... *bastards!*' I swore.

I struggled to get off the bike and it started to fall and he quickly reached for it instead of me, infuriating me even more. I clippitty clopped over into a corner and folded my arms as I turned my back to them.

How dare they! Making me play the whore like that. Who do they think they are! Just because they have money and...

'Sorry, Aneese,' I heard Jane say as she touched my arm.

I shrugged her arm off.

'We were only playing and—'

'You had no right!' I shouted.

There was a pause whilst I snorted like a rampant bull.

'It was rather funny, though,' ventured Kelvin.

'Funny? You think that was funny?' I turned to Jane in anger. 'And where do you get off watching your man get hot with another woman?'

Another pause.

'Oh dear,' I heard her say. 'I do think I went too far this time, Kelvin.'

Bet your sweet little arse, sister!

'Hmmm, how about an apology and a consolation prize?' Kelvin asked.

They think they can buy me! 'Fuck you both!' I snapped. Somewhere deep inside told me that they'd probably *both* enjoy that! This game was over. There was no way I was going anywhere with these two. New York would have to be... maybe next time, like the dress.

I heard a car start and turned around. Kelvin was standing by the Cosworth, holding the door open like a chauffeur.

Pedantically, I turned back to face the wall but then I heard another sound and couldn't resist turning back. A roller door that I hadn't previously seen was noisily rattling open. I bit my lip. I was mad at these two and all they could do was stand there with amused smiles on their faces and try and buy me. Fine I'll crash his car!

Yes, I actually thought that.

I turned and stamped towards the car and swivelled myself into the seat making sure that I showed nothing this time. I slammed the door and was satisfied when he winced. I smiled evilly up at him.

Jane got in beside me and I paused. So be it. She's as much to blame as him.

'Enjoy yourself, ladies,' Kelvin said as he stepped away. 'Bring her home safe for me.'

I was unsure whether he meant the car or the woman. Well tough luck, buster!

As I pulled away Kelvin said, 'And when you get back could you clean the moisture off my motorbike seat?'

I didn't believe he'd said that and my mouth dropped open. I almost didn't see the raised security pillars that were still erect in front of their garage doors. Jane and I were both thrown forward when I applied the brakes.

I glared at him. 'Well?' I said, acidly.

He walked towards my door and reached down to the key bunch and my eyes followed. There were two button fobs included.

'Black one operates the pillars, white one the roller door.'

I pressed the button and the three pillars started to drop into the ground.

He leant on the car. 'You gotta admit. It was very funny?'

'Fuck you,' I said again, but my face broke into an unwanted grin as I said it.

Jane smiled and reached over and touched my arm and I couldn't resist smiling back, then laughing. Actually, it was *very* funny!

By the time we'd returned after our drive I felt much better. She'd explained to me that she absolutely refused to let him insure the bike in the winter. It was bad enough that he rode it in the summer.

I was surprised and impressed that he would acquiesce. I couldn't imagine a man doing that for his woman. I guessed that most men just gave out the old, "Oh shut up, stupid woman. What do you know!" routine. Yes, Kelvin was certainly an enigma.

But I'd had him almost dribbling! Putty in my hands. It made me feel powerful and pleased. Life was good again.

After we returned and parked the car, Jane led me to his studio. She'd guessed he'd be in there.

'My competitor,' she said as we walked in. 'If I can't find him, I know where he will be. In the arms of his musical mistress!'

Sure enough, as we walked in he was there behind the glass, guitar in hand and earphones covering both ears. He was soundlessly playing a guitar as he sat on a stool, eyes closed and oblivious.

'Hang on a sec,' she said, and she pushed a slider upwards on the control board before us and we started to hear what he was playing.

I recognised the tune, one of the Lady Antebellum songs. Even I had a copy of this album. Three or four good songs on it, two excellent ones, and this one was one of the latter. I knew it was called '*Need You Now*', or something similar.

As we watched he opened his eyes and realised we were there, but he never stopped. He just smiled and carried on playing.

'He's recording,' said Jane.

We both swayed along to the music until it ended. I thought he played as well as the original guitarist, in fact I wondered if he was playing at all, or just pretending. And his vocals backing up the main female voice seemed spot on, too.

'You're back earlier than I expected,' he said as he exited the glass booth. He reached forward and kissed Jane on the lips and shot a smile my way.

'Starting to get cold out there,' Jane answered. 'Still only March.'

Truth be told I was freezing. I was wearing less than Jane and had only endured the cold because I was enjoying the drive. I'd even put the heater on to play on our legs, but that only had so much effect with the top down as it was.

'Thanks for bringing her back safe,' Kelvin said to me.

So he had meant the woman, not the car.

'What were you doing in there?' I asked. 'I recognised the song.'

'Oh?' he answered, raising an eyebrow. 'Think you can sing the female part.'

'I can't sing.'

'Anybody can sing,' he countered quickly. 'Just got to find the right song.'

'Thing is, all the songs seem to be the right songs for you,' Jane interrupted with a smile.

'Well, I've always wanted to sing,' I joined back. 'Just never had the voice or the confidence.'

'Don't tell me, hairbrush in front of the mirror? Who were you miming along to?'

I stopped, mouth open. He was spot on again.

'Even I used to do that,' he said with a wink.

That stopped me. I'd heard him sing and he was damn good. Somehow I couldn't imagine him miming into a hairbrush into the bathroom mirror.

'You do that, Jane?' I asked.

'When I was as young, certainly,' she answered.

I could have been wrong but I thought I saw a fleeting cloud darken her features for a second there.

'Here,' said Kelvin as he reached past me. 'Take this.'

He opened his hand and revealed a silver iPod, one of the smaller palm sized models.

'There's nearly five thousand songs on there,' he continued. 'Find some that suit you and we'll have a play.'

'Now tonight?' I asked excitedly.

'If you wish.'

'Cool. You want to share, Jane?' I asked, just to include her.

She shrugged. 'I don't sing, Aneese,' she answered flatly. 'Used to, but not any more.'

'But you sang the other night, didn't you? Sure I remember you—'

'I don't sing, Aneese,' she said, her voice slightly louder. 'Drunk or sober!'

I stopped my pushing and there was a silence between us. Did I imagine her singing that first night? Must admit I still didn't have total recall of that drunken night.

'I have things to do,' she finally said and, in a moment, she was gone.

I got the impression that Kelvin would normally have got a parting kiss at her departure. We stood awkwardly in silence for a small while.

'Did I do something wrong?' I asked.

'No, you didn't, she just doesn't sing, that's all.' He looked down to the iPod which still sat in my open hand. 'But you find a song or two and we will.'

'OK,' I answered, not believing his denial. I certainly felt like I'd done something wrong.

Deciding it was best to keep out of the way, I said I would go up to my room and listen to the music. Although it was my idea I couldn't shake the idea that I was being sent to my room like a naughty girl. I clicked the door shut and lay on the bed and let the music play on a random setting. I wasn't fully listening, I knew. My thoughts on how I'd accidentally upset Jane wouldn't go away. The music was good, though, and soon washed those thoughts away. Five thousand songs? Wow. Don't think I even knew that many!

I'm not sure how much time had passed, possibly an hour, but long enough that it would be a struggle to say just how many songs I'd listened to. Some of the songs I recognised and some I recalled just snippets of from my childhood. Some, obviously, I'd never heard before in my life.

Must admit that the range was huge. Some were punk from the seventies, real shouty sweary things, but others were middle of the road and country. Obviously, there was loads of pop music and even some from the musicals my mother used to watch with me when I was a girl. He certainly seemed to have every genre covered.

Suddenly my eyes opened with a start. Somehow I just knew that somebody was in the room.

'Sorry if I startled you,' Jane said as I pulled the earphones from my ears. 'Thought you might want a drink?'

'S... sure,' I answered, still having not recovered from my startle.

'I owe you an apology,' she said as she sat beside me on the bed. 'And an explanation.'

'No, it's OK,' I started to say, but she shook her head vigorously.

'No, I do,' she insisted. 'I was rude to you for no reason... well there is a reason, but nothing to do with you. So here.' And she handed me a brandy. 'I apologise. I'm not the perfect being I'm sure you think I am.'

'Huh, are any of us?'

She shrugged. 'Well, there's Kelvin?'

I smiled, happy that she was doing the same and that the atmosphere between us was better. 'Yeah, there's Kelvin,' I agreed.

'Now budge up,' she said and used her hips to push me more towards the centre of the bed. When she was comfortable beside me, she told me her story.

Seemed she was the best looking girl in their year at school and everybody loved her. All the boys wanted her (including a quiet, shy kid called Kelvin, apparently) and all the teachers loved her. She could get whatever she wanted with just a smile or flutter of her eyelids and, as is the norm in these cases, she was dating the best looking boy and their futures were assured.

But he went on to uni and met somebody else and then she was suddenly alone and all the secretly jealous school friends crowed at her downfall, people being what they are, but the boys kept calling. She dated them, of course, more for something to do than anything else, but there was nobody special. Then this older guy came along and before she knew it she was pregnant and, as was required those days, married soon after.

She'd given birth to a beautiful baby girl and thought she was happy but the man, Ian, was a rogue. Bit of a wide boy, wheeling and dealing but no steady job. He always left her short of money and they lived in a dingy two-room flat and the rent was always in arrears. When he wanted what he saw as his due he was friendly, of course, but afterwards he was never there. She had to virtually beg him for money to feed their daughter and he would eventually grudgingly give it.

Then the beatings started and she had nobody to turn to. Ian had long since sent her widowed mother packing for fear of violence. She suffered at his hand for years but kept it quiet out of pride. Her erstwhile school friends were laughing at her enough as it was even without her giving them more ammunition. She'd tried to leave him more than once, but he always dragged her back and then it was worse. People, including the authorities, were terrified of Ian, it seemed.

'It couldn't happen these days,' Jane assured me. 'But back then…'

He'd fill the house with his gang of mates when he felt like it and she would be required to feed them and play hostess and he would belittle her at every turn. And she'd be forced to sing and dance for them, too. She lived in terror, especially when they were drunk and playing poker. She always felt one step away from being passed around for sexual favours on those nights, she said. The threat was always there, just under the surface. It was bad enough she had to endure his forced attentions. Thankfully, she'd secretly been on the pill for years, telling him she was unable to conceive because of damage done in one of his earlier beatings.

And all the while she was struggling to bring up a child and she endured it for her daughter's sake. As soon as she could, as soon as Isobel, her daughter, went to school, Jane got a job, but her qualifications were minimal. Like most pretty girls at school she'd relied on her looks to get by. What could she do? She could wield a duster and a mop and the hours suited her so that she could get Isobel to school and pick her up afterwards. The money came in handy, though it wasn't much, but she had to hide what she brought home. Often it was stolen from her to be spent on lager and cigarettes and, eventually, drugs.

And that's when the Social Services got involved and Isobel was taken into care. But a deal was struck. Jane's mother had met a good man and they were emigrating to Australia. It was arranged that Isobel could go with them but, until Jane had sorted her life out, she was not allowed to go anywhere near her. As if she could afford the ticket, anyway.

Ian was dealing drugs by then and she was muddied by his reputation in the eyes of the powers that be. She really had no choice.

After Isobel had left there was a huge hole left in Jane's life. She needed a new goal, so she got a second job, disguised from Ian as a night school course, and opened a secret bank account. Her goal was to follow her mother and daughter to Australia, but for that she needed money. And when she eventually had enough, her dreams were cruelly dashed. Her mother had been in touch from Australia and made it clear that Isobel wanted nothing to do with her, blamed her for her far from perfect upbringing. She was happy, Jane had been told, and if you love your daughter then just let her be.

That was the last straw for Jane. The bottom fell out of her world. There was a way out but that took guts. It wasn't easy to take a life, especially if that life was your own.

Weeks passed, she said, as if in a haze. She felt like a zombie going through the motions of living. Then the impetus for ending her life appeared. She'd remembered a song from her childhood called *'Diamond Smiles'* about a good time girl who had killed herself whilst she still had her looks, so that she would be remembered the way she was without having to endure the ravages of aging. Was she the only one who thought it poignant as the song was written by Bob Geldof and performed by The Boomtown Rats, the band in which he was the singer? His estranged wife, Paula Yates, had done just what the song had dictated, some years before after losing the love of her life, Michael Hutchence.

Suddenly Jane had a new goal, she admitted. She still had her looks, so why not? It seemed a fitting end. And the money she'd worked so hard to save for her planned new life in Australia would pay for one last party. And then when the party was over... then the party would be over. Somebody else could clear up the mess.

I was in tears by this stage and so was she. We just sat on the bed, holding hands tightly and sniffing like we were attending a funeral. I couldn't believe that this woman in front of me, a woman who I was jealous of in every way, had endured this hardship. To look at her you wouldn't think she had a care in the world. You'd think, like I did, that she had lived a life of privilege all her life. She must be stronger than she looked.

'And that's when Kelvin walked into my life,' she continued. 'I was done up to the nines, just walking around town, taking a last look at the sights, when this car pulled up beside me. The driver said I reminded him of somebody he went to school with.

'He asked if I wanted a drink and it was early, but I thought what the hell? This was my last day on this earth, or close to it, so I may as well enjoy it. So he drove me to a pub and we had a drink and a meal. Told me who he was and asked if I remembered him. I did remember him a little bit. Told me he was fresh out of the army, had rented a studio and a small flat in London and was well on his way. And then I found myself opening up to him and he was a good listener. I even told him about my plans for after the party. And you know what? He never tried to stop me.'

'What?' I asked, amazed.

'No, he said he realised what I'd been through and that my life was my own. Then he told me there was another way. He told me I should go to my party and do what I liked afterwards. But at midnight he would be sitting in his car by the clock in the centre of town, just in case. Just bring yourself, he said. He'd ask nothing of me, demand nothing that I didn't willingly want to give. I even tested him on that for a couple of weeks, but he was true to his word; never laid a hand on me.

'Then he had to go away on a business trip and I realised how much I missed him. When he returned, I threw myself at him willingly and the rest, as they say, is history. Best damn move I ever made, I love him so much it hurts. And more importantly I trust him implicitly.'

I was tripping myself in tears by then. What a story. 'So what happened when you met him by the clock?' I wanted to know everything.

'Nothing. I'd decided I wanted to live, to trust one last time. I could do my *'Diamond Smiles'* routine anytime so what did I have to lose?

'True to his word, he was there sitting in his car – the blue one downstairs – reading a newspaper. He looked up as I approached. I remember I couldn't read the expression on his face, didn't know him well enough. He started the engine as I opened the door, not a word was spoken, and then with a quick look my way we pulled away and drove to London.'

'Oh, that's so romantic,' I said through my tears. Our empty glasses were just rolling about the bed as we hugged.

'And what happened to that bastard husband of yours?' I asked as I wiped at my eyes.

'Don't know. Never saw hide nor hair of him since. Half expected him to turn up here at first but now I don't. And even if he did I'm sure Kelvin would see him off with no trouble.'

'I'm sure,' I agreed.

'I hadn't seen him for a couple of days before I left, anyway. Probably in Amsterdam sorting some drug deal or something. Problem is, though, if we can't find him then I can't divorce him. But do I really want to find him, let him know where I am? And that is why Kelvin and I aren't married.' She sniffed. 'There, now you know everything.'

We hugged again, both of us kneeling on the bed.

'Poor Jane,' I said as I stroked her back. 'I am so sorry for the pain you went through.'

'Not your fault.'

'Maybe not, but then I go begging you to sing and all?'

'You weren't to know.'

'Yeah, I know, but I feel so guilty!'

We pulled away from each other, but my tears wouldn't stop. I felt the urge to kiss her and I did, full on the lips, but only a peck, something I didn't normally do to women, and then we hugged for a seemingly long time.

'Come on,' she finally said. 'Let's clean ourselves up – we probably look a state! Then we'll go and see what our Lord is up to. Well, my lord anyway. And I could sure use another drink. Or another kiss?'

My eyes opened wide. The kiss had been an impulse, nothing more. An act of empathy.

She laughed when she saw my reaction. 'I guess Kelvin will be doing the kissing, then!'

We found him in the lounge with three brandies ready and waiting, two with mixer. He looked at us for a long while as we walked in, arm in arm like old friends, and I guessed he'd noticed that we'd been crying, puffy eyes and all that, but he said nothing about it.

'Everything OK?' he asked as he held our drinks out to us.

'Everything's fine,' Jane answered. 'Just perfect.'

'Thank you, my Lord,' I said as I took my drink, earning a quizzical look from him and a snort from her.

'I just have one or two things to do downstairs and then we can relax for the evening. Seems like it's been a hell of a weekend.'

A weekend? Is that all it's been? At this rate we'd never get to New York!

As Kelvin left the room Jane turned me around to face her. 'Do you like Kelvin?'

I started to answer truthfully but hesitated. He was her man, after all.

'It's all right. You can answer me truthfully and I'd be grateful if you would.'

I threw caution to the wind. 'I think he's great!'

'Good,' she answered. 'And he likes you – we like you. A lot.'

I smiled. 'You're not so bad yourself!'

Chapter Four

Tuesday had finally come and we were up and breakfasted early. Kelvin drove us to the airport in the blue car. When I'd pouted, wanting the Cosworth, Kelvin pointed out that Jane preferred the blue, said it was more comfortable. I relented straight away (not that I had any choice in the matter). And anyway, I thought I knew why Jane really liked the blue.

Not that it mattered to me. I was like an excited little girl and Kelvin started to call me that. It didn't help matters when I playfully stuck my tongue out at him. I didn't care. I WAS GOING TO NEW YORK!

We girls giggled away in the back of the car, arm in arm like we'd known each other for years, and Kelvin drove in his normal demonic way. His driving didn't seem to bother Jane at all, even when he was doing triple figures on the motorway. It was only the cars in front that slowed him down. I wondered what state his licence was in.

We met a little snag at the airport but Kelvin being Kelvin, he sorted it in his own unique way. The problem was my ticket. Their tickets were booked by whoever he was meeting in America and had been arranged weeks ago, whilst mine had been booked by Kelvin late this last Saturday whilst Jane and I had been hitting the shops and drinking expensive champagne by the glass near Harrods. Whilst their tickets were first class, mine wasn't. Not because Kelvin was tight or anything, but because there were no first class seats left by the time Kelvin knew he needed another ticket. Obviously, he knew of the problem before he arrived but was hoping to sort it out on the day. He told me that airlines often overbooked seats by eight per cent (trust him to know that) because people often didn't turn up for flights and it was the airlines' way of ensuring that the planes didn't leave with expensive seats unfilled. Obviously, he was counting on people not turning up.

'I don't mind going in the hold,' I joked as we waited, seated near the check-in desk.

Kelvin had already approached the British Airways staff and he was awaiting a solution. They said that they would call him once they had one. Eventually they did and we three trooped back to the check-in desk, baggage still in tow.

'I'm sorry, Mr Turner,' the check-in dolly said. 'I'm afraid that all first and club class seats have been taken barring the two you asked us to reserve for you and your wife. Your friend will have to travel as her ticket indicates, in the world traveller section.'

I wasn't the only one who thought Jane was his wife, then? An easy mistake to make, I guess. And Turner? I found it amusing that I didn't know Kelvin's or Jane's surnames but here I was flying to America with them. I wondered what Jane's surname was.

'Are there more of the world traveller passengers to check in?' he asked.

The check-in girl's professional facade dropped a little and her confusion showed briefly. 'Why, yes, sir.'

'Good,' answered Kelvin. 'Carry on.'

Kelvin smiled at her and shuffled our trio to one side. The check-in girl hesitated a moment but then carried on with her job, occasionally looking our way, looking confused.

'What are you up to, Mr Turner?' Jane whispered.

'Well, there's no way Aneese is travelling alone whilst we sit elsewhere.'

'I really don't mind,' I interjected.

'And who's asking you?' Kelvin answered, but then softened the rebuke with a wink.

Just then two ladies, one older than the other, approached the desk and were asked for their tickets by the check-in staff. Before they could comply, Kelvin moved forward and intercepted them, throwing on his most charming smile.

'Excuse me, ladies,' he oozed. 'Are you travelling alone, just the two of you?'

They were silent for a moment, obviously confused as to what was happening.

'You see, I have two first class tickets here that I don't want. I would gladly swap them for your world traveller tickets?'

'I'm taking me mam for her sixtieth,' the obvious northern daughter replied. 'Taken us two years to save.'

'Then wouldn't you rather she travelled first class? Free champagne? Nice wide seats? All that extra legroom?'

'Ooo, I dunno. Would it be proper like? Don't want to be any trouble?'

'No trouble,' insisted Kelvin, turning an enquiring eyebrow to the check-in staff.

The poor girl was put back for a second but soon responded. 'I... I... well, it's most unusual... And then she looked to the girl sitting beside her who nodded slightly. 'I guess it would be OK.'

'Wonderful,' said Kelvin and with a flourish produced his two first class tickets like a magician producing flowers from a hat. 'Ladies?' he said, prompting the mother/daughter team to produce theirs.

'Kelvin, I...' I started to object.

'Give it a rest,' he smiled.

Jane snorted beside me before whispering. 'Welcome to my world. Kelvin knows best!'

The new first class passengers were checked in, still doubting their luck to the last, and then we trio presented our tickets. I angled my head to look at Jane's passport. The name read *Jane Turner*.

'I thought you said you weren't married?' I whispered as Kelvin checked us in.

'We're not,' whispered Jane back to me.

'Then how come you have the same surname?'

'Changed my name. The law says we can't get married because I can't get divorced, but things can be got around.'

I smiled and nodded. Yes, the Turners had a knack of bending the rules to get their own way, the ticket exchange as an example of that.

'Thank you, Mr Turner,' the check-in girl finished. 'That will be seats thirty-two H through to K. Have a nice flight, sir.'

It seemed an age until we boarded; my excitement made it longer and I couldn't relax. We found three seats together in the departure lounge and they sat and read whilst I sat bored and hyper beside them.

'Give it a rest will you?' said Kelvin after a while.

'What?' I answered.

'Your leg. Have you got the shivers or something?'

I hadn't realised I was doing it.

'Perhaps she needs a drink?' suggested Jane, which I was sure translated as *Jane wants a drink.*

'Have to wait until we get on board, then. First class lounge has a bar but it's not for us in cattle class.'

Cattle class? Is that what he called it? I felt guilty. A little while ago they'd had first class tickets with first class lounge and bar entitlements. And I really wouldn't have minded travelling "cattle class". It was all I'd ever known, anyway, so how would I have missed it?

'Here,' said Kelvin, breaking into my thoughts as he held out his hand to me. He opened it to reveal his iPod.

'Thanks,' I smiled.

In a moment my leg was still and I closed my eyes and made myself as comfortable as possible in the deceptively comfortable looking seats. Eventually, after at least an ice age, I noticed the boarding process starting. I started to put the iPod away but Kelvin stopped me.

'Be a little while yet,' he said. 'First class and club passengers board first.'

I frowned and Kelvin smiled at my pout.

'Cooeee, hey cooeee?' I heard as I was putting the iPod earphones back in my ears.

A few yards away the mother/daughter duo were waving frantically at us as they waited to show their boarding passes. 'Hey Mr Man?' the mother spoke loudly. 'They are giving champagne away in that there first class waiting room. Didn't know they did that. Make sure you get yours!'

'I will, Mother,' Kelvin smiled.

'See you on board, then,' she continued.

'Come on, Mam,' said the daughter, rolling her eyes at us. 'You're holding up the queue!'

Some of the other passengers were faintly amused at the scene, as were the boarding staff.

I frowned again. My mouth was positively watering at the thought of champagne. I laughed inwardly. A few days ago I would have been salivating over a bottle of fizzy water. Hadn't realised how thirsty I was until she mentioned champagne. "Mother" had also made me feel even more guilty.

'I suppose I should thank you for arranging to sit with me,' I said. 'But I feel ever so guilty.'

They both looked my way and smiled.

'There was no way we were sitting on the captain's knee whilst you were hanging onto the wheels, Aneese,' he answered.

I laughed a small laugh as a picture formed in my head of these two sitting on the pilot's and co-pilot's laps. Somehow I could see it happening.

'And I promise you we'll all travel back first class, plenty of time to arrange that. Wasn't the time for this flight. I'll make it up to you.'

He'll make it up to me? As if they hadn't given me enough already.

Just then the boarding staff beckoned us forward and we collected our carry-on luggage and trooped forward.

I know that these airline workers are meant to smile but this lot must be breaking their faces at the effort. 'It's not every day we have somebody trying to score themselves a downgrade, Mr Turner,' the senior one, a redhead, said as she checked our boarding passes. 'This way, please.'

We were the first "cattle class" to board. I realised that they'd pre-boarded us before making the actual announcement.

'I'm the senior inflight attendant on this trip.' She smiled as she seated us. 'If you need anything just ask. Oh, and there will be first class meals and drinks made available to you,' she said with a wink.

'That's really not necessary,' Kelvin started but she cut him off with an even more dazzling smile.

'Nevertheless,' she continued. 'You made that old lady's day, I think. Got the feeling they are going to drink first class dry, though, us northern lasses being what we are!'

She dropped her posh voice for the last bit and replaced it with the Geordie accent she must have been born with.

Jane reached for Kelvin's hand and squeezed it as her face showed her pride and happiness at Kelvin.

I felt proud of him, too, and empty and sad at the same time. Not for the first time I wondered why I couldn't have a man like him. Richard had been kind in the beginning, during what I later heard referred to as the honeymoon period, and later when it suited him. Funny, I didn't realise it at the time that he was only nice to me when he wanted some extra sexual favour. It all seemed so clear now. Suddenly I knew I was better off without him.

Better off without Richard? That was a revelation to me. Was I finally over him? Suddenly I could see very clearly. I *was* over him and he wasn't good enough for me, anyway, he was a wimp. Elephant Girl was welcome to him and I should thank her. I almost cringed at the memory of wanting children with him. What was I thinking!

And that wasn't all I could see in this moment of clarity. I had the window seat, and by design, their design. They knew I wanted it, somehow, my excitement perhaps? They'd deferred to me even after giving up their first class tickets and lounge. They were looking after me. To my left sat Jane in the middle of our row of three and to her left sat Kelvin in the aisle seat. He was on guard, I knew that now. He was protecting her from the bumps of passing passengers and food trolleys and they were both protecting me.

A lump formed in my throat as I looked at these two kind people beside me. I felt tears well up and hoped they wouldn't trip the dam, especially as the remaining cattle were starting to file past our seats heading for theirs.

Jane must have sensed something because she looked my way. 'You OK, Aneese?'

I reached out my left arm until it was touching both of them. 'Thanks for everything,' I said, tight lipped so as not to cry. 'Thanks for your kindness, for the window seat, for... for... for travelling with me. I feel...' I searched for the right word. 'Looked after? Special? Protected?'

Kelvin just winked theatrically back at me but Jane touched my arm and smiled back. 'As I said earlier, welcome to my world. There are bad things happening out there, bad people doing them. But to get to me they have to get past this ape.' And she playfully elbowed him in the ribs. 'And I don't rate their chances. I sleep very well at night, every night, and I wake up with a smile every morning. And I appreciate it even more because I still remember the time when I couldn't and didn't.'

I remembered her story about her life prior to Kelvin appearing. For the first time I realised the absolute terror she must have been living through. Somehow I knew that I couldn't have lived like that, I'd have taken my life rather than live another moment being downtrodden and beaten like Jane had. Whether that made me weak or strong I couldn't say, but then I remembered that there was the daughter, Isobel. I knew she'd stayed strong for her daughter, a daughter who had then refused to see her after all she had sacrificed on her behalf. Thinking those thoughts was all the help my well of tears needed.

'What the hell?' Kelvin exclaimed as Jane reached out for me and I sobbed onto her shoulder.

'Oh, don't listen to the cruel man!' admonished Jane.

In a moment, Geordie Girl was back. 'Is everything OK, sir?'

'She's just overcome,' Kelvin quipped back quickly. 'She really loves flying British Airways. She'll be inconsolable when we actually take off!'

Some of the passing cattle snorted as they passed, as cattle do. Even Geordie Girl stifled a laugh. And even though Jane was consoling me I felt her shoulders move as she tried not to laugh at his witty riposte.

And I felt like a wet fool. When I'd recovered a little, I stuck my tongue out at him and he smiled. I think he liked me playing the cheeky little girl routine. Strangely enough, I did too.

I watched out of the window as we taxied and took off. I felt the butterflies fill my stomach as the nose lifted and the aircraft seemed to leap into the sky. I started looking for the champagne.

'How long is the flight?' I asked.

Kelvin answered, as I knew he would. He was studying the plastic inflight safety brief like it was a contract he needed to sign. 'Seven and a half hours. And even though the UK time is 13.10 we will arrive at seventeen hundred local New York time. By the time we get to the hotel it will be twenty o'clock-ish but we will feel like it is midnight. Early bed tonight and we should be right as rain come the morning.'

You speak for yourself, I thought. I'd be too excited to sleep!

At last the drinks cart appeared after all the air safety briefs and tannoy announcements had finished. True to her word, Geordie Girl appeared with champagne and real glasses. The other cattle had to pay for their drinks and suffer with plastic ones.

'How come they get the real stuff?' I heard a passenger ask.

Geordie Girl must have been expecting the question. She answered as quickly as Kelvin's wit had. 'They paid for first class tickets, sir, but due to an administrative error were forced to downgrade to world traveller. I am instructed by the airline to offer them every comfort.' She looked both ways then lowered her voice to a conspiratorial whisper. 'It is hoped they won't sue the airline, then!'

She looked our way and winked as she turned away.

I liked her already.

When the meals appeared we got real cutlery and real food whilst our fellow cattle received plastic cutlery and probably plastic food. Must admit I felt a bit guilty again then, but the champagne soon took care of that.

'I guess I'd be crying if I'd paid a couple of grand for first class tickets and ended up in the cheap seats,' I heard a female passenger say.

Was that how much first class seats cost? What did they have up there, were the aisles paved with gold? I decided I would find out, if I could.

My chance came about four hours into the flight. Jane and Kelvin were head to head, snoozing, and I managed to get past them without disturbing them too much. On pretence of using the toilet I sought out and found Geordie Girl. She was sitting, taking the weight off her feet (not that she weighed anything, mind you) whilst she could. She got to her feet as I appeared even though I tried to wave her down.

'Excuse me, ah?' I looked at her name badge. 'Elaine?'

'Yes, madam?' she smiled.

Madam? Ouch! Now I knew how Kelvin felt when he'd been called "old" by the football crowd.

'What's first class like? Any chance I could see?'

'I'm afraid that's impossible, miss.'

'Oh,' I answered, disappointed. But at least I was a miss again.

Oh well, nothing ventured. 'Sorry to have disturbed you. Thanks for how kind you've been today,' I said as I turned to walk away.

'Wait,' she said softly, putting her arm on mine to stop me. She looked me up and down like a man would in a pub. 'Seems the impossible is happening quite a lot on this flight. What's another rule broken? Follow me!'

Amazed and confused, I followed her to the refreshment area three or so rows behind where I could still see that Jane and Kelvin were still as I'd left them. I watched as she shrugged out of her uniform jacket. 'Here, put this on. We look a similar size.'

My mouth dropped open. 'Are you sure?'

'Quick, before I change my mind. Good thing your hair is short. The skirt is wrong but, believe me, nobody will be looking at your legs. The men look at your bust as you approach and your ass as you pass, and you have both those areas covered, lucky girl!'

Smiling fit to burst I hastily put her jacket on and she adjusted it to regulation as much as she could. When we were done, she turned me around and pointed down the aisle towards a curtain which, I presumed, separated cattle class from first class.

'Other side of that curtain is club,' she said. 'Just walk through like you own the place, oozing confidence. Most are asleep or playing with their laptops so it should be fine. Keep going to the next curtain and then you are in first. Just poke your head in, quick look around, then come back.'

'Got it,' I gushed. 'And thank you.'

'Don't hang around in first or you'll get me sacked,' she said, and as I turned to leave, she pushed me gently on my way.

I positively tiptoed past my still snoozing companions. As I grabbed the curtain between cattle and club class I paused and took a deep breath, summoning the required confidence. After a third breath I finally had my heart rate under control. How difficult could this be? It's just walking.

As I swished the curtain aside and started to walk the aisle, one businessman looked up, gave me the leering once over and returned his attention back to his laptop. I took in the surroundings as I purposefully walked down the aisles, trying to generate the confidence that I didn't quite feel.

Of course, the club passengers sat in more comfortable seats than us cattle class. Some seats were like single business-like booths whilst others were the same but had two seats. They had much more legroom, too. I guessed that eight seats, or booths, took up the space that twenty cattle class seats took in my section.

But club was not my destination. Staring straight ahead and trying not to draw attention to myself, I continued on my way. My confidence grew, I could do this, I told myself. This is easy.

At the next curtain I stopped and poked my nose through. A quick count revealed only fourteen seats in the whole cabin. You could positively dance on the available floor space. Five wide, single, plush reclining seats graced each side of the cabin with two sets of two in the middle rear, nearest me. This was indeed luxury. I recognised two passengers immediately: the northern duo. The daughter was trying to get the last drop out of a champagne bottle whilst her mother slept, mouth open and oblivious beside her.

And this was what my friends and protectors had given up to sit with me, I thought. My heart soared with feelings of love and affection and I felt the now familiar lump return to my throat. I so wished I could return their kindness in some way, but what could I do? They were the ones with the house, the cars and the money. What could I possibly offer them apart from my friendship?

And your body.

Oh, don't be stupid, I instantly told myself. They were so obviously in love and in tune with each other. OK, so a romp with Kelvin was not an unpleasant thought but he wouldn't ask and even if he did I would not hurt Jane by doing that. No, I would have to find my own man, maybe some rich American in New York? Well, you never know.

I felt somebody standing next to me and withdrew my nose from the first class cabin and my mind from the gutter. Beside me stood one of Elaine's fellow attendants, looking at me with a confused look on her face.

'Ah, Elaine sent me?' I simply said.

'To do what?' she asked, eyebrow and nose sticking up.

'Um… ooze confidence?'

She paused as she took in my answer. 'Well could you ooze on your side of the curtain, please? Some of us have a job to do.'

Cow, I thought. Isn't Elaine your boss? I'm *so* telling on you!

Chastised and deflated I turned to leave. Unladylike words and thoughts crowded my head, the minimum of which was wishing ill luck, broken heels and severe period pains to the witch behind me.

'Excuse me, miss?' a voice said to my front and left.

I stopped, terrified.

'Could I have a blanket, please?'

'Uh, certainly, sir.'

I spun on my heel and looked imploringly at the witch who was now trying to hide an evil smile as she enjoyed my discomfort. She held one finger up and pointed towards the above seat storage area. Thankfully a blanket was the first thing I saw as I opened the locker and I took it and held it out to the passenger. He just looked up at me. The witch caught my attention and imitated shaking the blanket out and lowering it onto the businessman. I did as directed and seethed as he looked down my blouse as I leaned over him.

'Wouldn't care to join me under here, would you?' he chanced as I stood up. I smelt the whiff of vodka at the same time as I felt his hand squeezing my left bum cheek.

I was dumfounded for a second. What to do? The witch gaining obvious pleasure from my discomfort spurned me to action. I mean, what could they do? This guy had touched my ass, after all! I leaned down close to his ear. 'Sir, my girlfriend there behind you is looking daggers at you touching her real estate. If you don't remove your hand I can't say what the true contents of your next drink will be. She gets *so* jealous.'

His hand disappeared like a shot and he looked nervously back at the witch. The glare on her face, although aimed at me, hit him dead on target.

I stood and plastered a rigid smile on my face, realising that I'd kind of gotten revenge on the witch, also, by labelling her a lesbian. She was one for all I knew. Just five yards or so to the safety of my herd, I told myself as I retreated, and I'd never stray again.

Four yards. How slow was I walking? How come it was taking so long?

Three yards. I saw the curtain twitch. Was Elaine checking on me?

Two yards. I felt my mask start to slip. Breathe, Aneese, breathe!

One yard. A rush for the tape!

I pulled the curtain aside and rushed through. As I started to breathe once more, I noticed that Kelvin and Jane were awake and talking to Elaine. I heard my name mentioned. Then they noticed me and the exchange stopped. I got the slight satisfaction of seeing both my friends' mouths drop open at the sight of me.

'Seats are paid for, Aneese,' Kelvin said as I walked towards them. He'd recovered from his shock quickly. 'You don't have to wash the dishes or anything.'

I pointed back the way I had come. 'I just wanted to see…'

'But I just love the uniform,' he interrupted. 'Do we get to keep it?'

I turned to face a smiling Elaine. 'And that man touched me and your girl threw me out.'

Just then I saw a flash and realised that Jane was taking photographs of me. 'Is there a hat that goes with that?' she asked.

'What man?' asked Kelvin. 'Just show me and I'll break his arm!'

Was he serious? With him I could never tell.

'OK,' said Elaine. 'I think I've gotten into enough trouble for one day.'

She was right. Other passengers were starting to take notice. Some were grumpy, having been woken up, but some were amused. She held out her hand for her jacket and I reluctantly relinquished it. All in all, I had to admit that I'd enjoyed being a trolley dolly for five minutes.

'Don't worry,' said Kelvin as I pushed passed him back to my seat. 'I'll check eBay for the jacket. You never know!'

'So you going to tell us what you've been up to whilst we were asleep?' Jane enquired.

So I told them. About how it all came about from me wanting to see the first class cabin and how helpful Elaine had been, and about the witch and the touching man. They thought it was hilarious.

'I told you we would return first class.'

'Well I couldn't wait,' I almost whined.

He laughed again. 'I've heard that parents drugged their children on long haul flights, now I know why. We close our eyes for five minutes and you're banging on the cockpit door!'

'Excuse me, miss,' he said to a passing attendant. 'Have you any Rohypnol on board? Failing that how about a couple of brandies? She'll be flying the damn plane if we let her out of our sight again!'

The attendant looked my way and smiled. 'So I've heard, sir. I'll see what I can do.'

'And me!' joined Jane.

'Better make that three, then,' finished Kelvin. 'Doubles, of course.'

As our drinks arrived Elaine intercepted our server. 'Think we'd better get the drinks cart out again.'

'See what you've started now?' admonished Kelvin jokingly at me. 'Nobody in the cheap seats will be able to walk straight by the time we land. And it'll all be your fault!'

'I think it's you that needs calming down,' said Jane. 'About that Rohypnol?' She arched an enquiring eyebrow up to a smiling Elaine.

'Well, she keeps doing funny things,' he said, pointing my way.

'Yes, dear,' Jane played. 'Just drink your medicine, there's a good boy.' She topped off her nurse routine by feeding him some of his brandy and wiping his chin with a tissue.

'And no more for these three.' Elaine winked to her co-worker.

'Awww,' we chimed in unison.

We calmed down and stopped giggling eventually, after the second double had been delivered and consumed, and I started to fall into a contented sleep. Then there was a champagne glass in my hand and I realised I was thirsty. As I drank, I felt happy that I had got them laughing and joking by my impromptu air stewardess routine. I realised not for the first time how good company they were. Going back to work in three weeks' time was going to be hard, I thought, as I snuggled into my seat trying to find the most comfortable position.

Deplaning and collecting our baggage was a blur to me. I remember that Elaine got a hug from both Jane and I as we passed. I even got a smile out of the witch. A sober and alert Kelvin warned us to behave as we queued to show our passports.

'These people have no sense of humour,' he warned.

For some reason I was asleep on my feet. It was probably the Rohypnol, I told myself. Not the brandy or the champagne, then? My alcohol addled mind was a mess.

I started to tell myself off. I was in New York, was about to get into a yellow taxi cab, just like in the films, but I couldn't keep my eyes open. I sat between them in the taxi and my head started to roll sleepily back and fore. Eventually it settled on Kelvin's shoulder and I started to move it for propriety sake, but then Jane's head settled on mine and that ended that.

I wasn't fast asleep. I was aware of the stopping and starting as the taxi drove along and the almost continuous far off beeping of vehicle horns and road drills and overhead aircraft. I knew there were sights out there to see, sights I'd wanted to see for ages, but they'd still be there tomorrow. Sleep seemed so much more important to me right now.

'Time to move, ladies,' I heard Kelvin whisper after I'd heard the cab squeak to a halt.

I exited like a zombie and stood there swaying in the breeze as Kelvin paid the fare and discussed baggage with the driver. Even though we were standing, Jane settled her head on my shoulder and we stood leaning on each other like two meerkats on the savannah. It was cold, I realised. For some reason I'd expected it to be warm. I held my hand out to take some baggage.

'Forget that,' Kelvin said. 'It's covered. You two just concentrate on walking.'

A couple of paces only and we were into the hotel. Kelvin steered us to some seats near the check-in desk and I heard him state his name and say that a suite had been reserved for him by a third party.

Suite? Not a room, then. I wondered what a suite looked like? I'd only ever stayed in hotel rooms before. Jane was ever so comfy to lean on, and warm, too. And she smelt delish!

'Uppsy daisy.'

We were on our feet again and Kelvin was herding us again. We were in a lift and I leaned against the cool wall and felt the movement and vibration as it travelled. Thankfully there weren't too many stops before Kelvin guided us out again and I heard him talk to a man and then heard a, 'Thank you, sir', as a door closed. I guessed Kelvin had tipped the bellhop. I smiled sleepily. I was speaking American already.

I thought I was falling and panicked, but then I felt a bump and realised I was sitting on something comfortable. Not that it mattered. I could have slept on a mating hedgehog. I felt Jane being removed from my grasp and raised a reluctant eyelid.

'Be back for you in a jiff,' Kelvin said.

'... After myself,' I answered.

'Love you,' I heard Jane say sleepily.

'Love you, too,' I just as sleepily replied.

'Love you, Jane,' I heard Kelvin say.

Oh! Had she been speaking to him? I giggled. Sort that out in the morning. I heard a slight bang and a muffled curse and realised that Kelvin must be opening doors with his feet as he carried Jane.

What language, Mr Turner!

Then I felt myself being lifted and I tried to stand.

'... Myself,' I said.

'I know,' he answered.

Then I felt the room spinning and realised I was being carried in his arms. I snuggled into him. His clothes smelt nice; he smelt nice. I could sleep here. It was just like my dream, barring the wings. He laid me gently down and I knew it must be a bed. I smiled. He was laying me on a bed. He was *laying* me! I giggled inside again.

I heard a rustle and then he lifted me slightly and I felt the bedclothes move from beneath me before he put me gently back down. Then I felt my shoes being removed and I lay there compliantly, drunkenly and tiredly wondering what he would do next, all thoughts of Jane and propriety gone. My head was buzzing.

'Don't think you're undressing me,' I managed to slur.

Which meant: *Undress me! Please undress me!*

I felt his hand loosen something at my waist and I felt the beginnings of arousal.

Well I've told him not to undress me, so I've done my bit!

Then he was slipping my arm out of a sleeve and rolled me over and did the same with my other arm. Then I felt a tugging of material near my bum area and it felt so erotic. Seems he couldn't wait, couldn't get my knickers off quick enough! I smiled contently and parted my thighs slightly. I imagined what him inside me would feel like. Then I felt his hands on my thigh as he moved me into position.

Whatever you like, Tiger!

Then I felt a weight settle on my legs and raised my arms above my head in submission.

When I awoke I was still laying with my arms above my head. I took a slow, deep breath and moaned and stretched as I yawned. My eyes opened and I took in my surroundings.

What the...

Where was I? This wasn't their house. New York! Hell, I was in New York!

I leapt out of bed then stopped. My head was just catching up with me. Felt like my brain was loose. I recognised the signs of a slight hangover, but we hadn't drank that much... had we? Then I remembered reading somewhere that long haul flights dehydrated you. What had I drunk? Just three brandies and some champagne, that's all. OK, three *double* brandies and how much champagne and how little food?

Don't forget the Rohypnol!

The what? What was my subconscious trying to tell me? Wasn't that the date-rape drug? I looked down at myself. I was still fully dressed, barring my raincoat and shoes so Jane had taken my coat off me and left it at that, maybe because she was tipsy, too.

But wait. A picture appeared in my head. Hadn't Jane been carried to bed by Kelvin whilst I waited my turn? So who...

Memories started to return. As they did I realised that this was the second time in five days that I was having the *who undressed you and put you to bed* conversation with myself. This had to stop.

I remembered being undressed... or did I? OK, my coat had been taken off me by...

Kelvin.

Kelvin had taken my coat off me. He must have. Right here on the bed. But I remembered much more. My stomach turned over in dread. I looked down at myself. I think I would know if somebody had undressed me, had sex with me and then dressed me again and why would Kelvin do that, anyway? Dress me, I mean. My clothes were tight where they normally were – too tight actually; the result of having slept in them, I guessed.

Had I imagined the rest? What rest?

Kelvin making love – no Kelvin FUCKING you when you were drunk!

Kelvin wouldn't do that!

Kelvin *wouldn't* do that. Almost wish he would!

What?

OK, I admitted to myself and my subconscious. Kelvin was a good looking guy.

Good looking rich older man!

And yes, I admitted, I was attracted to him. If he was single I'd willingly crawl around above him, and beneath him for that matter. I'd wrap my legs around him and arch my back and squeal like a little schoolgirl as he had his way with me, or I'd howl at the moon on all fours as we made the beast with two backs, or kneel before him and accept what I was given and like it.

Whoa, down girl!

OK, I need a shower, I thought. Cold preferably. And I wasn't coming out until I'd gotten my head on straight.

I found the en suite bathroom. Second time in five days I've had to do that, too. Now all I need is a walk-in wardrobe and Kelvin changing his clothes in front of me.

Not helping!

I undressed angrily, not caring for the clothes. They were soiled anyway, having been slept in. I showered quickly, partly because a part of me realised I was in New York, and my excitement had returned. This was no time to be analysing myself, this was time for fun. I didn't even wash my hair. I remembered I washed it that first morning in their house so it could last another day yet. I'd run some talc through it and it would be fine for another day. Or even two.

But where was my talc? Where was my suitcase for that matter? Was I going to have to call Jane to get it for me? Was Jane even awake yet?

Your suitcase will be in your room. Kelvin will have planned it that way.

The thought was like a slap in the face, of course it would be. And as soon as I thought it, I knew that whatever happened last night happened in my mind only, I was tarring Kelvin with a very dark brush. I felt ashamed, but despite that my mood lifted. My mental judge and jury had cleared Kelvin of any wrongdoing, but it would be a good fantasy to play with later. That could be fun.

And I was in New York!

Having set my world to rights, I padded confidently out of the bathroom with nothing but a towel wrapped around me and there, sure enough, was my suitcase. I guessed it had been pushed through the door at some stage during the night. The thick carpet still showed the signs of its passing.

I smiled and my stomach growled. Yep, waking up with a growling stomach was getting old, too. Must eat towards the end of the evening instead of just drinking more. Might start putting myself to bed then! I told myself that breakfast would be waiting for me the other side of my door. Kelvin again.

I was rubbish at packing things. Most of my clothes were creased in some way and would at least need a hanging. Some would need pressing. I wondered if I dared use room service for that? Did such a service exist or was that just Hollywood?

It was time to open the curtains, I decided. What time was it anyway? Yeah, that thought was becoming familiar at waking, too. Was it morning or afternoon?

My generation seldom wore watches, I knew. It was all mobile phones. Mine was switched off and safely in the bottom of my suitcase. I knew that Kelvin wore a watch, a large chunky thing. I bet myself that it was already set to local time along with his phone and body clock. I told myself I would bet every penny I had. I was guaranteed to win a fortune!

I swished the curtains aside. "Oh my god" didn't do the view justice.

'Hey, you two,' I shouted as I ran out the door. 'Have you seen the view? It's…'

"Oh my god" quite fitted the view in the lounge, though. It was huge, the lounge I mean. And breakfast was indeed being served and Jane was getting sausage, lots of sausage. Her mouth was full with the stuff and from what I could see she must be starving. Kelvin was enjoying a bit of rump as he lay on a comfortable looking sofa and she knelt on the floor at a ninety degree angle to him. Vegetarians they weren't, that's for sure.

They were both dressed, him in a brown trousers, shirt and waistcoat and her in a light blouse and above the knee skirt. The jacket to complete his three piece was hanging nearby. Her skirt was way above her knees now, though, aided by his hand which was inside her underwear. And the underwear was the type I'd seen in her drawer, tastefully sexy and expensive. His zip was obviously undone and I saw a bit of white flesh there before Kelvin opened his eyes and our eyes met. My mouth was as open as Jane's, though not so employed, and as his eyes widened and he started to move I retreated back into my bedroom and, unintentionally, slammed the door.

It was true, that old wives' tale. Too much sex does make you deaf. I certainly hadn't been quiet as I'd burst in and come on, they had a bedroom for that kind of thing. And it was morning, wasn't it? That sort of thing was for night-times, or at least that was when Richard and I used to do it!

Obviously, I knew they did it, they must do. I know dogs do it, too, but that doesn't mean I wanted to watch them in the street. Hell, is this how children felt when they caught their parents at it? I felt so guilty. I felt my face get hot and guessed it must be crimson.

What do I do now, I thought?

Take another shower.

OK, I'd observe the view from here. Anything to overwrite the picture in my head.

What could I say about the view? Beautiful? Certainly. Expansive? Awe inspiring? All those terms fit. But unless you saw it you could not believe the scale of the thing.

Are you saying these double entendres on purpose?

The sun had risen only recently and there was a slight haze that the sun was trying to burn through. Where the sun touched the buildings I could see tints of silver, black and brown and, surprisingly, reds and pinks. The buildings were like mountain ranges rising from the sea. Everywhere was a huge, humungous building, not like London where there were only so many. Now I realised why Americans were so obsessed with size. And the greenery! New York was greener than I imagined. In the films it was all concrete and tarmac and police cars and rapes and murders. Hollywood rarely showed it from this angle. Talk about selling yourself short.

What floor were we on, anyway?

I heard a knock on my door. Shit, what do I do know? *Answer it?* 'Ah, come in?'

The door opened. Jane. Thank God, the lesser of two evils, at least! She walked over and stood beside me and placed her arm loosely around my waist.

Hope she's washed that hand!

She cleared her throat. 'Wonderful view?'

Is she for real? I hope to God she meant present tense and not past. Very recently past.

'Um, yes. I was just coming to point that out to you and... well...'

A very prickly silence developed.

'We were waiting for you, so that we could breakfast together.'

Oh, that's what you call it. Breakfast? Well, we certainly ain't doing that together, sister!

'But we kinda got carried away.'

I'll say!

'Hope we haven't embarrassed you. I'm actually so mortified. Please say something, Aneese?'

'I don't know what to say,' I finally burst out. 'I'm sorry I didn't knock!'

'You? It's not your fault. It's not as if you were entering our bedroom or something. You don't have to knock to enter the lounge, it was us two who were at fault, not you!'

Then why do I feel like this? 'I don't know how I'm going to face Kelvin!' The words were out before I even knew it.

Her head turned to face mine as if she'd been slapped.

'You're a female at least,' I quickly added, trying to reinforce what I had just said. 'He's—'

'A man?' she finished for me.

'Well obviously!'

'You like him, don't you?' she asked and I feared my silence spoke volumes.

'Of course, I do,' I answered eventually. 'You've both drummed it into me that you like me and want me to like you, and I do. Do you know how easy it is to like you two?'

I heard another tap on the door and as we both looked I saw a white handkerchief being waved. 'Sorry, sorry, sorry,' said Kelvin as he slowly advanced into the room. 'That was my fault. I'm a morning person and I—'

'I really don't want to know!' I blurted out.

Liar!

'I'm going to need therapy now,' I continued, only half playing.

'And does this therapy come in champagne bottles or in dress shops?'

he shot back immediately.

I was trying to be mad but I started to grin and they both saw it.

'Believe me, we are more embarrassed than you.'

'I seriously doubt that,' I grinned. Then the grin turned into a laugh and I couldn't stop myself. Thank the lord the ice was broken. Again!

'Come on,' said Jane once she had finished laughing. 'Breakfast will be getting cold.'

They both guided me through what I thought of as the lounge and into a dining area where a table sat with various trays and covered silver plates upon it. The table had space for six people but only three were made up.

'We ordered the full English, or what our American cousins think is the full English, anyway, and the American,' he said as Jane and I sat. 'So we have bacon, of a sort.' And he lifted a silver lid and revealed a steaming plate of what looked like gammon to me. 'Scrambled egg.' Another lid lifted. 'Hash browns, lamb chops, mushrooms and sausages… of a sort. Oh, and pancakes!'

'Pancakes?'

'Yeah, some people like something a little different first thing in the morning.'

Jane stifled a laugh and I ignored the inference.

'And there is cereal… of a sort, various juices, coffee. And tea—'

'Of a sort? I get it, thank you.'

'Well dig in, ladies.'

I couldn't help thinking that one of us hadn't been behaving like a lady only a short while ago. I smiled involuntarily as I greedily filled my plate.

'Something wrong?'

Damn, Kelvin never misses a trick.

'Nothing,' I lied. 'It's all just so unbelievable. I'm in a huge suite in a huge hotel in New York. I'm actually in New York eating breakfast – of a sort – on the umpteenth floor of a five-star hotel. What hotel is this, anyway?' I asked as I forked some egg onto a piece of toast and took a large, ravenous bite out of it.

'The Ritz-Carlton,' he answered as he served himself a large piece of so-called bacon. 'We are on the twenty-first floor, I believe, and this suite is setting back my clients around two and a half thousand pounds Stirling a night. Not,' he added, 'that they have accepted Stirling around here since about 1774!'

I vaguely heard his quip about accepting Stirling but by then I was already choking on my egg and toast. Two thousand pounds *plus* for a couple of, OK, extremely nice rooms? That was more than I earned in a month! More than a month, actually, nearly two! Even Jane coughed once or twice before regaining her regal pose.

Kelvin to the rescue. I should have guessed. In an instant he handed me a napkin and followed it with a glass of orange juice. Jane rubbed my back soothingly.

'Two grand?' I said when I'd recovered. 'Per night?'

'Yep. Glad I ain't paying it. De facto wife and little girl to support.'

Little girl? Was he referring to me or Jane's daughter in Australia? Wish he'd stop calling me that. *Liar, you love it!* 'Jesus, what is it you do for these people, ship drugs?'

'Kinda. Music is a drug to some. I certainly couldn't live without it.'

'And you?' I turned to face Jane, realising too late that I may have asked the wrong question, considering her past.

She took time to think as she lathered some marmalade onto her toast. 'Well, you know I enjoy watching Kelvin perform. Perhaps one day I'll get the kick out of music that I used to.'

My face showed what I felt and she saw it. 'Oh, you,' she said and reached out and squeezed my arm.

'So, Aneese,' Kelvin asked, partly to save me and change the subject I suspected. 'Has your first morning in New York been memorable?'

'I'll say,' I answered. Yes there was the view and the food and the suite and the... 'Oh you... you... bastard, I'd forgotten about that!'

'I'm sure I don't know what you mean,' he answered mock innocently.

We ate like pigs that morning, egged on by Kelvin. He told us that we should eat our fill as, knowing Jane and her shopping ways, we would need the energy. I had to admit that the food tasted awesome, even the pancakes which I tried a piece of before finishing one or two completely.

The conversation ebbed and flowed and I again realised how much I enjoyed their company. You had to really listen when Kelvin spoke, I realised, because you never knew when he was switching from serious to clown. He started to explain what his studio did but Jane yawned loudly and he got the hint. She'd obviously heard it all before, but I was interested.

'Perhaps I could visit your studio one day?' I asked as Jane poured the tea.

They shared a brief look.

'I think I would like that very much,' he answered.

'As would I,' Jane shocked me by answering.

What had just happened, what was I missing? I remembered other subtle communications such as this. 'I hope that one day I will have all the answers?' I said seriously, ensuring that my eyes locked with each of them in turn.

They did the look thing again.

'As do we.' This time it was Jane who spoke for both of them. A rare event.

'Speaking of answers,' I probed. 'Can you at least tell me about your tattoos?'

He stopped drinking in mid swallow and placed his cup on the saucer in his lap. 'Tattoos, what tattoos?'

How many tattoos you got, dummy? Hang on, did he have others that I hadn't seen? Where could they be? Certainly not on his breakfast sausage or I'd have seen! 'The ones on your arms, of course.'

'Oh, when did you see them?'

Good question, I thought as the panic started to rise. When did I see them? Had I seen them innocently at all or was I relying on my stolen moment as I watched him change his shirt? 'In the car as you were bruising my leg. Your left hand was on the steering wheel and your short shirt sleeve rode up and the wind caught it, too. Saw some sort of lines there, like barcodes. What do they mean?'

This little girl could lie her ass off when she had to! Truth was I'd surprised myself.

He looked at Jane. 'Go on, tell her. Where's the harm?' she said.

'So what are they?' I asked to move things along.

He looked at Jane and then back at me and then sighed. He'd been manoeuvred into this revelation, I knew, but it seemed he'd made up his mind.

'Young squaddies do silly things,' he said. 'In Vietnam it was collecting ears.'

It was? 'You were in Vietnam?' I asked.

'Don't be silly. How old do you think I am?'

'Well, I don't know. When was the Vietnam War?'

'Before my time,' he answered. 'And we weren't in it officially, though I've heard reports that our Special Forces guys paid the odd visit.'

I didn't push the point and eventually he continued.

'They're kill rings.'

'Kill what?'

'Kill rings. Every ring on my arm is a confirmed kill. The thicker ones are close quarter kills, knife or bayonet or just hands. The thinner ones are gun or grenade kills. Rules were they had to be witnessed by at least one other guy if there wasn't a body to be found afterwards. Battles can be messy and confusing places.'

Even through my shock I saw his eyes glaze over. Was he reliving any, OR ALL, of these kills in his mind's eye? He swallowed and lifted his cup to his lips but it was empty.

Jane was up instantly. 'I'll fix you another. Aneese?'

It took me a while to realise she was speaking to me. 'Ah, yes please.'

She filled our cups with delicious, stewed tea and then sat down expectantly.

'Thank you, my love.'

'Any time, dearest,' she whispered back.

I took my cup and held it in my lap. Kelvin had killed people? OK, I knew he was a soldier, obviously, but the killing people bit hadn't entered my head. Was I that naive? And didn't he say he was an engineer or something? And how could this man who I knew to be gentle and caring and generous just callously and cold bloodily kill someone and make a game of it, by keeping score?

'See, she hates me,' Kelvin said to Jane and I saw his features darken. Was I seeing him angry for the first time? Angry with Jane?

'No, I... I,' I stammered. 'It's the shock of it all, I guess. It's not every day you get told that somebody you know has... is...'

'A killer?'

'No.'

'Yes. That's the word you were looking for.'

'How many?'

'What?' he answered me.

'How many?'

'Eleven,' he said simply.

I watched as he undid his left cuff and started to roll up the sleeve. Eventually he had it rolled up far enough.

'These two, First Gulf War,' he said as he pointed to the first two lines. They were thin ones. What did he call them? Gun kills?

'Next one, Second Gulf.'

Another thin line. The next one he tapped was thicker.

'Afghanistan. Carving knife. Carving knife, would you believe? We were a small det and didn't rate a cook. My turn to cook breakfast. There I was slicing bacon under the awning of our dining tent when this raghead pops up and aims his AK at me. Don't know who was more surprised, him finding an unarmed soldier just standing there dressed in only his skivvies, or me finding a heavily armed raghead had invited himself to breakfast!

'But he wasn't alone. They'd snuck into the compound at dawn to do us harm. Suicide job. Next thing I knew he had a carving knife in his neck and his rifle went off as he fell. That and me shouting *STAND TO* woke the guys and just as well it did. There were loads of them.

'Shot his mate.' He moved his finger down to the next thin line. 'With his retrieved weapon, then the damn thing jammed. Very sloppy maint.' He chuckled, but it wasn't a happy one. 'So I threw it like they do in the films, then I started throwing tins of beans or tomatoes because that's all I had. Eggs actually worked better. Laugh if you want but nobody wants to be splattered with an egg!

'Then the first shot rang out, our shot I mean, the guys were finally awake. My mate, Simmo, was running towards me with a fixed bayonet, firing from the hip. He saved my life. I was running short of eggs by then, you see, and there were more and more ragheads appearing. Then he fell – RPG! He was dead when I got to him but there was no time to think. Shot two more with his weapon as they reloaded their grenade launcher. Stupid move on my part as there were closer targets.'

A picture of what Kelvin was describing formed in my head. I imagined dust and sand and screaming, and blood, mainly scenes I'd seen in the films that Richard liked to watch. I also noticed that Kelvin had stopped moving his finger down his arm as he told his story.

'By then there were little individual firefights going on all over the camp,' he continued. 'Somebody shouted to fix bayonets and they told me later that it was me. Simmo must have been ahead of the game on that one as his was already fixed. We grouped and advanced right at them. Either they were the worst shots in the world or we really had them frightened – no army in the world uses the bayonet like the British Army! Yanks would have retreated and called in an air strike or used missiles. We lost two wounded in the bayonet assault but by then we'd broken them. My last four were close quarter with the bayonet – you can smell their breath, smell their piss and shit when they let go.

'Final bill was one dead – Simmo – who'd saved my life, and four wounded, one critical. He recovered fully, eventually. Simmo was suggested for a posthumous MM and me the Military Cross. Simmo's citation was refused, though. It happens sometimes. When the dust settled, we counted twenty-two enemy KIA, eight attributed to me. We were very lucky.'

He stopped and stared at the breakfast table and I was instantly sorry I'd asked. But how was I to know that this was the answer?

Eight in one day, no one morning! How long had the attack lasted, I thought? The tale he'd described could easily have lasted only a few minutes.

I reached for his hand and took it and they both looked at me.

'I don't think you're a killer. Don't even think you're a bad person.'

'Why, thank you,' he answered, his playful demeanour starting to return. 'And Jane was right, you needed to know. And if not now, then when? You feel part of our life,' he continued. 'And every day you seem more of a special, special friend to both of us. Best that you found out early.'

I smiled as the pride in what he'd just washed over me. 'And the ones on your right arm?' I asked, instantly regretting it.

He was shocked by my question but not for long. He and Jane shared a glance before he answered.

'If I ever tell you about them then you're here to stay and we may as well the three of us get married!' he joked.

And whatever did all that mean? At least he hadn't asked how I'd gotten to see the two lonely rings on his right arm. That was something at least.

'Right, ladies. Have to love you and leave you,' he said as he stood. 'Car collecting me soon.' He reached for Jane and kissed her and stared into her eyes. 'Promise me you will use taxis at all times and stay safe. This ain't London. If anybody threatens you tell them your husband is a British soldier and will track them down and kill them.'

'Yes dear,' she sighed.

He made it sound so normal, like an everyday event.

'And what about me?' I asked.

'Well if you hurt her you go straight over my knee!'

What? 'I meant what If I get threatened or hurt?'

'Oh, I guess some sort of severe pamphlet campaign. That'll teach the buggers, all right. They won't do that again!'

I felt suddenly worthless. Kelvin the clown could hurt sometimes.

'Kelvin!' Jane admonished.

'Only joking.'

He moved towards me and pulled me very close. I felt like my bottom lip would quiver at any moment and my eyes filled with tears as I tried to look away. But his arms were around my waist completely, his wrists overlapping each other and holding me so close that our groins touched. He looked down into my eyes and I bit my lip as I stared up into his. They were grey, I remembered, but today they seemed brighter. I swallowed loudly, knowing that I was melting beside him. Almost with a mind of their own my arms went around him and met at his shoulder blades. And Jane was just inches away.

'I swear that I would never, through action or inaction, allow our little girl to be harmed or hurt by anybody,' he said, and I swallowed again and blinked repeatedly. The threatened tears of anger and sadness had multiplied and turned to tears of touching joy. 'And if anybody succeeds in doing so when I am not there I will hunt them to the ends of the earth, track them down and they will die begging for mercy in your name.' He looked at me and smiled. 'How will that do?'

I tried to talk but my mouth did nothing but just sagged open.

'I think you made your point,' said Jane as she pulled us apart and hugged me. 'And don't you ever say anything like that again,' she said. 'The first thing, I mean.'

'Yes, my lady,' he played, solemnly.

A phone rang and I jumped.

'Yeah,' he said as he answered it. 'Be right down.'

He closed on us and hugged us both as we were still hugging each other. I heard them kiss. 'Stay safe,' he said.

'Yes, sir.'

Then he looked at me and my heart skipped a beat as he moved closer to me. My lips parted expectantly but he just kissed me on the cheek and I blushed. 'You, too.'

'OK,' I squeaked.

In a moment he was gone and we both stood looking at the door for what seemed like a long time. I heard a sigh and hoped it was Jane, but I couldn't be sure.

'So what shall we do now?' I asked finally, more to cover the embarrassment I felt and to cover the sound of my loudly beating heart.

I saw a smile form on her face and grow until it seemed to fill the whole room. 'I guess we do New York!'

Chapter Five

And, boy, did we do New York. After a brief visit to reception to change our pounds into dollars we left the hotel in a yellow taxi.

'Where to?' the driver said rudely. He was an old guy with a leathery wrinkly face, white hair and a baseball cap. His nose was huge, I thought. Jane and I just looked at each other and he visibly grew agitated.

'How about you just drive around?' I suggested.

'Tourists, huh?'

'Yep.'

'Well it's your dime,' he finished as he pulled out into the traffic without indicating. There was a screech and a beep behind us and he wound down his window and made incredulous noises over his shoulder. It sounded like twenty words joined together to form one sound. It was like a whole new language to us.

'This is great!' Jane smiled beside me.

Did she have no fear? I guessed that if Kelvin drove you around long enough then maybe you didn't.

We were like children on a school trip. We talked over each other and constantly chattered and pointed out one thing after another to each other. We asked the driver what this was, and what that was and he ignored us as best he could so we ignored him. Eventually I pointed to a huge building and tapped him on the shoulder until he answered me.

'Whatyerwan?' he eventually said.

I pointed. 'Take us there. It's the Empire State Building, isn't it?'

'You got fifty on the metre, doll,' was his only answer.

'Yeah, well we got plenty of fifties... bud!' I rudely answered back.

Jane froze and the cabbie looked at me in the mirror and I stubbornly stared back.

'You know, you're all right,' he said finally, and I do believe he actually smiled.

Jane paid him off at the Empire State, saying we'd hail another as we left. The view from the top was awesome. Earlier, as Jane had headed towards the lift I'd stupidly said we could walk up. "It'll be an achievement and something to brag about." We gave up after eight floors and caught the lift with our tails firmly between our legs.

Hailing a cab was fun. I tried all the polite ways like we used in London. Raised my arm, politely, waved like you would at a bus, held out my hand. Then I put my fingers in my mouth and let loose with a tooth rattling whistle and two cabs almost crashed as they fought for our custom.

'Whereyouwan?'

'Tiffany's,' I answered. It was the first thing that came into my head.

'Surethin!'

'I'm impressed,' said Jane as she took hold of my hand and settled into the seat.

'I'm a quick learner,' I smiled back. 'In New York you just say and do what you want and don't be polite about it. It's dog eat dog!'

The cab pulled over.

'What's the damage, Mac?' I asked in my best put on American slang accent.

'Sixteen fifty.'

I dropped him a twenty of Kelvin's money. 'Keep the change,' I shouted over my shoulder. 'Buy the old lady a pretzel!'

Jane couldn't believe what I'd said and held her hand to her mouth and sniggered as the taxi pulled away. 'Aneese, you have a positive flair for languages!'

'Yeah, well come on, broad,' I continued in my best Ernest Borgnine. 'Let's go check out Tiffany's!'

After an hour at Tiffany's, we were happier but Kelvin was poorer. Jane bought seemingly whatever she wanted – must be nice being rich – and even I used some of my envelope stash to buy some lipstick. To be honest it was the Tiffany's bag I was after. Then Jane bought a lovely pair of gold heels which she'd refused to try on, insisting that they would fit. I eyed her up and down suspiciously. 'Are you sure you're a woman?'

She stopped and posed and opened her coat. 'I'm all woman, baby!' The looks we drew made it apparent the old lady serving us thought we were a pair of dykes!

'What next?' I asked as we stood outside.

'Ooh, I want to go on the tube!'

'The tube?'

'You know, the underground? Just like in the films?'

'Uh, OK,' I answered as I looked around. 'Say, fella?' I asked to a passing man. He ignored me. 'Excuse me, miss?' She ignored me, too.

'Oh, look a hotdog stand!' Jane said beside me.

'Perfect. Come on,' I answered as I pulled her along.

The hotdog stand looked like an old freezer that the ice cream man had in his van when I was a girl. It had a lid at both ends but a griddle in the middle with metal containers bolted to it. As we approached the aroma of onions and sausages assailed me and I realised that I was hungry.

'We'll take two,' I said.

'You wanna chilly dog?' the old man said.

'No a hotdog,' I answered as Jane looked on. She was obviously content for me to do all of the talking. 'One of those sausage things.' I pointed as I spoke. 'In a bread roll with some onions and ketchup, mayonnaise and mustard.'

'All a those fins?'

'Sure thing. And you, Jane?'

'I'll have the same,' she answered.

We watched him prepare our order.

'And say, buddy, how do you get to the tube from here?'

He stopped what he was doing and looked at us like we'd just stepped off a ship. A spaceship. 'Wadya say?'

'The tube? You know, the underground?'

It took him a few moments to answer. 'Ya mean the subway?'

'The subway! Of course,' Jane exclaimed. 'It's called the subway. Yes that.'

'Look round you, sister.'

We both did but seeing nothing we just looked back at him and shrugged.

He shook his head before pointing a hotdog filled hand behind us and we followed his gaze. 'Down there, two blocks then take a left at Central Park. Fifty-Seventh Street subway. Ya can't miss it. Nine bucks.'

'Central Park?' Jane said. 'Our hotel's near there!'

109

'It is?' Must admit I didn't have a clue where we were.

'Nine bucks, lady?' the man said again as he handed over the delicious smelling but messy looking hotdogs.

I handed him a twenty. 'Thanks awfully,' I answered in my best Mary Poppins. 'Do keep the change.'

'Sure thin,' passed for thank you. 'You have a nice day,' he plumbed back with a smile as we walked away.

The hotdogs were as delicious to the mouth as they were to the nose and they kept us quiet as we negotiated them without making a mess on our faces and clothes. Eventually, with noisy lip smacking as we sucked our fingers, we both finished and smiled.

'I still don't believe I am in New York eating a real, honest to goodness American hotdog,' she said.

'Or me. It's huge. How we going to see it all?'

'We'll have to come back and spend a couple of weeks just to explore. This is a flying visit.'

I nodded, realising not for the first time that she had spoken like I was included in her, *their*, future plans. Kelvin talked the same way. I saddened slightly maudlin. She might be coming back with Kelvin but this was surely it for me.

She must have noticed my melancholy. 'You OK?'

I smiled and nodded. 'Sure I am. I'm just conscious of the fact that all good things come to an end. I'm going to miss you and Kelvin when we get back.'

Her mouth dropped open. 'What do you mean?'

'We live in different worlds, you and I. You're the…' I searched for the right words, 'pampered de facto wife of a rich man – no disrespect meant.'

'And none taken.'

'And I'm just a working girl who struggles to make the rent.'

'Kelvin works,' she countered.

'Yeah I know, but I'm sure he doesn't have to. You know I used to think that one day I'd find a rich man to look after me and love me, and now I've found one he's taken. Life is so unfair.'

Suddenly realising that I'd said the wrong thing I dropped my eyes to the ground, conscious all the while that she was looking at me, speechless. I damned myself for saying the wrong thing. After a short while I felt her hands find mine and she pulled me close to her.

'There are so many things I'd like to say to you, right now, so many things I *want* to say to you, but I can't, not right this minute. But I can say this,' she continued after a while. 'If these couple of weeks are all we are going to spend together, which I doubt, then let's enjoy them, yeah?'

Eventually I sighed and nodded. She was right. I damned myself again for spoiling everything. 'Damn, I feel like I've been at the gin again,' I said in my own defence.

'What a good idea!' she exclaimed. 'Damn the tube. Hotel bar?'

'Damn the tube!' I responded, trying to feel cheerful.

She pulled me towards her and we hugged. As we separated, she kissed me on the cheek and I smiled. Then she kissed me full on the lips and lingered just a little bit too long, I thought, making my eyes open wide.

'If I have my way,' she said, seemingly not noticing my response, 'then you won't be going anywhere!'

And then she grabbed my hand and started pulling me towards where the hotdog man had indicated.

And I wondered what she meant; what it all meant.

We were still on our first drink when Kelvin found us. We'd gotten waylaid on the way back and had started shopping again, serious shopping. Jane was carrying way too much but she refused my help when I asked. 'You're not my servant,' she'd answered when I offered.

Eventually I hailed another cab and we used that as a mobile wardrobe until she finished shopping.

By the time Kelvin had found us we'd transferred all our purchases to the suite and were in the hotel bar. I'd splashed out on some nice underwear for myself. Nobody was going to see them but me, I thought, but what the hell; they'd make me feel good.

'Busy day, ladies?' he asked as he leaned in to kiss Jane.

'Wonderful day,' Jane answered. 'You're going to have to get a second job to pay for all the clothes I bought!'

'Huh,' he grunted.

'And we're going to need fur coats. It's freezing out there.'

'It's winter,' he said, simply, like it explained everything.

Because it did!

'So we can have fur coats?'

'Don't know why you're asking. Why haven't you just bought a couple?'

A couple? I'd just caught on that I was being included in this. 'Wait, you're not buying me a fur coat.'

They both looked my way.

'No!' I insisted, wagging my finger at them like two naughty children.

He went to open his mouth.

'No, no, no!' I said as I wagged the finger again. 'NO,' I said again as she went to speak. 'Brandy will keep me warm. You are not buying me a fur coat and that's final.'

'Then I won't have one, then,' said Jane petulantly as she folded her arms.

'Do what you like,' I answered. There was no way I was rolling over on this. They had been generous enough to me.

The impasse lasted a good thirty seconds before Jane sighed and gave way. 'Guess you'd better get some more brandy,' she said to Kelvin as she playfully stuck her tongue out at me.

'Nothing to stop you having a fur coat,' I said guiltily.

'If you're not, I'm not,' she continued playing.

'Well I'm not!' I insisted and this time I folded my arms.

We were still that way when Kelvin returned with the drinks. We both started to giggle and lower our defences as he served us our drinks.

'War over?' he asked.

We carried on giggling. Jane nodded at him as we reached out for each other and had a girlie cuddle.

'No fur coats?' he enquired.

We both shook our heads as we giggled and hugged.

'OK. I'll have to turn up the sun, then.'

'You do that,' I answered as I lifted my glass.

'So tell me about your day,' Jane finally said to him and he did just that. He told us how boring it had been and how much he hated pressing the flesh and we told him what we had done and that New York was too large to visit just for a couple of days.

'So my mission is to make New York smaller and make the sun hotter?' he said an hour and two double brandies later. 'No problem. I can do that.'

'Hooray!' we chorused a little too loudly, gaining some toffee nosed looks from some of the other clientele.

'Oh, and the big cheese wants to meet you both tomorrow, so it's dinner with his wife tomorrow evening.'

'Booooo,' I played and Jane joined in.

'But until then I am free.'

'Hoorayyyyyyyyy,' we both played. Screw the looking down the nose crowd.

'Don't know what you're shouting about,' Kelvin said to me. 'Nobody invited you.'

That stopped Jane and I dead until Kelvin's straight face started to crack and he stifled a snort.

'Damn you, you get me every time,' I said around my laughter.

'Well, you're such an easy target.'

'You're so mean to her,' said Jane as she, too, failed to hide her laughter. Then she turned to me. 'It's because he likes you!'

Although I tried to hide it my smile couldn't get any wider.

Dinner was a raucous affair and we certainly didn't improve international relations any. 'Bloody yanks don't know how to have a good time,' I whispered, loudly, at one point.

'Certainly don't know how to drink,' Jane joined. 'They'd never last a minute back home. Speaking of which,' she said as she turned to Kelvin, 'you still haven't taken me to Cardiff. Hangover capital of the world, I hear. Bet you get a good night out there!'

'I don't believe that we're sitting in an expensive hotel in New York and you wanna be in Cardiff!' Kelvin exclaimed. 'But speaking of hangovers I'd suggest we leave the alcohol there tonight. If my plans for shrinking New York come off then a queasy stomach might prove a bad idea for tomorrow.'

'Why, what you got planned?' I asked as I winked at a young girl who was looking our way from an adjoining table and attempting a smile. Her mother instantly frowned her into dreary submission.

'Never you mind,' Kelvin answered. 'Just do as you're told or you might regret it.'

'Yes, sir.' I turned to Jane. 'Is he always this demanding?'

'Normally only in the bedroom,' she replied, which started me giggling all over again.

But stop drinking we did and very soon we had finished dinner much, I suspect, to the relief of our fellow diners.

'Quiet night in, then,' Jane said as we waited for our lift in the lobby.

'Good, I'll finally have time to wash my hair.'

Jane turned to face me as if slapped. 'Can I wash it for you?'

I was about to turn her down but she continued.

'I used to wash Isobel's all the time. I so loved those times together.'

How could I refuse her after that? I could not imagine the pain she must feel about losing her daughter the way she did. I tried to put myself there but couldn't; I had no reference to work from. The most pain I'd ever felt was from losing Richard and if I could make that pain any easier for her by letting her wash my hair then I would gladly let her.

'Music, maestro,' Jane demanded as Kelvin let us into the suite. 'Not too loud, though.'

'Your wish, my lady, is as ever my command.'

As we kicked off shoes, he set up his laptop and iPod and we girls padded into their bedroom. He followed us in and started the music playing.

'I'll give you some privacy,' he said as the music started. 'Have some things to arrange for tomorrow.'

As Jane led us to their bathroom I heard the door click shut as he left.

Jane passed me a couple of towels and started to fill the sink with water. She seemed in a world of her own as she mixed and tested the water for temperature.

'Take your blouse off,' she told me and I hesitated before complying. By the time I'd opened the buttons she'd magic-ed a chair from somewhere and placed it with its back next to the sink. A rolled up towel was placed on the lip and she motioned me to sit. When I had she expertly tipped back the chair until my neck was resting on the towel-padded lip and placed a second towel over my chest to cover my dignity.

I appreciated the act, even though I had no qualms about her seeing me in my bra, my hesitation had just been because she'd surprised me.

As she softly massaged water into my hair I realised she was singing along softly to the music. I didn't recognise the song but she seemed to know every word. It was in a very high key and I imagined a black woman was singing it. If I heard correctly it was something about... was that "silly games" the singer was forcing the high notes with? It was hard to tell, especially with water lapping over my ears.

The words weren't what I was focused on, though. Jane never sang. I'd had this drummed into me on several occasions in the last week, mostly when I'd screwed up and mentioned music. And Jane's eyes were glazed over, like she was somewhere else. I guessed that in her mind's eye she was with Isobel at some other place and time.

And then it hit me. *This* was why I was here. All the while I'd been thinking why they wanted me around and, I must admit, thinking the worst. My mind went back to the scene as I'd agreed to come to New York with them, how happy that Kelvin had been when Jane was happy that I'd accepted. I wasn't some sexual plaything for Kelvin – he had this beautiful woman for that – I was here for her, as a substitute for her lost daughter!

My subconscious must have known, all the references to Daddy-o, little girl and so on. I was a proxy daughter for Jane. It all made sense now. Inwardly I relaxed. I had been on my guard, I realised, since I'd met them. I'd been expecting... well god knows what, but not this.

I saw Jane's eyes refocus and she smiled down at me. I was smiling, myself, without knowing it. Then she bent down and kissed me on the forehead as a mother would her child, and that confirmed it.

I felt as elated as Jane looked. I could do this. Gone were the nagging doubts and worst case scenarios of why I was here. I was also aware of how difficult I'd been on occasion, the don't-you-dare-spend-money-on-me moments. All they wanted to do was look after me and if that small act could make Jane as happy as she was now then I could play along. And I could do with the pampering.

'Your hair is very thick. Have you ever worn it long?' she asked as she softly massaged water into my hair. Some of the words sounded wrong as the agitated water ebbed and flowed into my ears like it did when I floated on my back in the swimming pool.

'When I was a little girl,' I answered, choosing the words purposely to please her. 'As soon as I was old enough, though, I had it cut short. Think it broke my father's heart. Long hair is such a chore when you lead a busy life.'

She paused in thought for a while. 'Would you consider growing it long again?'

My turn to think. 'Never thought about it. Guess I would if I had the time.'

'You should. You'd look lovely with longer hair.'

I said nothing, but imagined that Isobel had longer hair than I.

'Relax, you seem tense,' she ordered. 'The chair won't fall. I've done this before, you know.'

Her senses were spot on. The chair was suspended on its rear legs and I had, indeed, felt my position a little precarious. 'Yes, Mummy,' I played as I did as I was told.

The songs changed and Jane continued to sing softly along with the new tunes as she lathered my hair. Her ministrations were *so* relaxing me. Time disappeared and I felt myself relaxing into my roll of... Barbie doll plaything? I didn't care. I was happy and I was happy because Jane was happy and I was happy because all my darkest thoughts had amounted to nothing and I was happy in anticipation of how happy Kelvin would be when he saw how happy Jane was.

OK, enough of that. My brain was beginning to hurt at all the permutations of happy!

'OK, you're done,' she said as she pulled the chair upright.

I was disappointed. Felt as if I'd been woken from one of those perfect half-slumbers when the weather was perfectly warm and the far off drone of an aircraft or lawn mower had softly rocked me off to sleep.

'Can you do me, quickly?'

I wondered what she meant and looked enquiringly up at her as I wiped the excess water from my hair. She was undoing her blouse and indicating I vacate the chair.

'Quickly, mind. Then I'll comb some conditioner through for you.'

I did as I was told, but quickly as she'd asked. I tried to be as gentle as she had been with me. When I was done, she stripped off completely and quickly showered, emerging with a towel wrapped around her hair and with another protecting her dignity.

'You?' she asked, indicating the shower.

'Why the hell not. Get it all done in one fell swoop.'

All of a sudden, I felt so at ease with myself and her. There was nothing hidden now, I knew, I didn't have to be on my guard any more. And I must admit that I was enjoying doing the close girlie things that you did with a girlfriend. It had been a while, a long while.

In no time at all I was dressed as she was but without the turban. She'd led me to the dresser in their bedroom and sat me down and was combing conditioner through my half-dry hair. I hadn't even asked what brand of conditioner, which is odd for us women. Did I trust her that much?

A reflected movement caught my eye and I saw Kelvin standing watching us. I wondered how long he'd been there and why I hadn't heard him re-enter the suite. Must have been the music that Jane was singing and gently swaying along to. All those thoughts disappeared when I saw the look on his face. Was I mistaken or were those tears I saw welling up in his eyes?

'Ah, there you are,' said Jane, breaking the spell. 'Wine, please. Something light?'

So much for tonight's abstention.

I saw Kelvin swallow. 'My lady,' he said as he moved away.

He returned in no time at all with a glass of white wine for each of us. I guessed there must be a stash somewhere in the suite. Hidden fridge, perhaps? He sat on the bed and sipped his and I turned my head to him and smiled.

'Keep still,' Jane admonished softly, between hums, and I jerked my head back to eyes front.

After a while I heard a rustling sound to my right where Kelvin sat. Out of the corner of my eye I saw his jacket put onto the bed. Was he undressing? I almost jumped as his hand touched my naked shoulder.

'I'll take a shower,' he almost whispered as he pecked Jane on the cheek.

I saw her nod in the mirror, not breaking the stride of her humming, singing and gently swaying ritual for a second. In a few moments I heard the water hiss on and then decrease in volume as he must have closed the cubicle door. My mind wouldn't let me forget that he was standing naked where I had been naked only a short time before. The memory of him changing his shirt in front of me appeared in my mind's eye and I began to imagine him taking his trousers off too. Then to my horror I realised that he'd been wading through a pile of discarded women's clothes to get to the shower, my underwear included. I swallowed but kept my turmoil to myself.

He said nothing as he emerged a few moments later, dressed in a white hotel bathrobe, and padded over to the bed. My eyes followed his reflection as he passed through my field of view.

'There you're done,' Jane said. 'Put a towel round it and do me.'

We swapped places and Kelvin looked up and smiled at me as we did. He was sitting cross legged on the bed tapping away at his iPad. I guessed from his actions that he was checking his emails.

'Waiter?' Jane voiced, and held up her empty glass.

Kelvin looked up and responded instantly and soundlessly refilled both our glasses. I guessed he didn't want to break the mood either. It felt strange the next day but at the time it didn't bother me that I was standing in front of him wearing a knotted towel as my only defence to dignity. Whatever the spell that day was, whether the alcohol we'd previously consumed or just the moment, neither of us seemed to want it to end. I don't know what they felt because they were always a strangely relaxed pair, but I felt extremely comfortable in their company, like I trusted them with my life. It was a great feeling, a feeling of belonging. It was like our relationship had altered in some indiscernible way.

When Jane was done she padded over to the bed and I followed, with our wine glasses in tow. Whilst she settled beside Kelvin and laid her head in his lap I settled on the bottom of the bed, more to her side than his. He absent-mindedly dropped his arm down to her and started massaging her neck and she moaned in appreciation.

'Hmm, that's nice. Do my back.'

'Aneese, do her back, can you, please? I have to finish these emails.'

'I asked you, lazy,' Jane said, but she looked my way and smiled as she released her towel and lowered it to the small of her back.

And you know what? It felt the most natural thing in the world to shimmy over and kneel beside her and do her bidding. After a while Jane moved so that she could take a mouthful of her wine and I found myself licking my lips wondering if I dared stop to do the same. Then I found Kelvin was holding his glass to my lips and I smiled and gratefully accepted a long sip. His aim was spot on, even though his eyes never moved from his iPad.

Then I squealed because my towel had come undone and I had to stop massaging to hurriedly catch both ends of the towel as they separated. I couldn't be sure, but I thought I'd caught it before Kelvin got a glimpse of me. Either way he was up in a moment and disappeared, returning with another robe which he placed around my shoulders. The next time the towel moved I let it drop and just secured the robe around me.

That towel incident, little though it was, reinforced to me that I was right. Kelvin had no interest in my body, I thought. His only concern was making Jane happy or, in this case, keeping me happy so that I could keep Jane happy. At the end of the day it meant the same thing. I must admit I felt a little disappointed at the thought but I realised it was for the best. To have him I would have to hurt Jane and I knew I couldn't do that. And anyway, I liked this closeness that we had suddenly found. I wouldn't want to change it for the world.

'Awfully bumpy ride lately,' Jane said sleepily.

'Sorry, my lady,' we both, Kelvin and I, said at the same time.

We both laughed and even Jane smiled. 'That's more like it,' she said as I continued my massage of her.

I relaxed into my task, occasionally accepting sips of wine from Kelvin. Eventually I suspected from her breathing that Jane was asleep and, when I looked up, noticed that Kelvin's eyes were closed too, his head resting against the headboard and his iPad held loosely on his lap. After looking upon this serene scene and smiling to myself I decided it was time to move to my own room and own bed. I'd been yawning myself for quite a while.

But in a moment or two, I told myself. I didn't want the moment to end and I was comfortable. I'd just lay and soak in the atmosphere for a small moment, comfortable in the knowledge that I was not the hunted prey that I had thought I was. I wondered briefly what my future would be. This couple, my friends I acknowledged for the first time, had hinted at longevity. Did they want me as Jane's permanent live-in, stand-in daughter? I was surprised to tell myself that I could handle that, and all that it entailed.

I began to imagine a future for me as some kept woman, never having to work, just spend time with Jane and Kelvin. No more alarm clocks, no more dingy flat or thinking of myself as a second class citizen. And my duties? Just to have my hair washed and call Jane, Mum, and Kelvin, Dad. I could do that easily in exchange for a life of luxury.

As I closed my eyes, I sought out the bedside radio alarm clock. The glowing green figures showed the time as 20.17. I'd stay until half past, I told myself. Then I'd go.

This bed was comfy, even though I was laying above the covers near the bottom of the bed like the family dog. Is that what I was, the family pet? Don't be silly, I chided myself, you're the surrogate daughter, you know that now. Relax, it's not a bad thing to be, it could be worse, you could be the family whore!

Wouldn't that be better? Kelvin is hot and even Jane is warm, soft and desirable!

Shut up, Satan. Go to sleep. Riddle solved, I'm a daughter.

I emptied my mind and took a deep breath. I'd give it a moment and then I'd check the clock, then go back to my bed.

When I thought it was time, I checked the clock. I squinted in the half-light to clear my sleepy eyes. 10.12 was what I thought it said and I knew that that couldn't be right. My eyes focused again. See it wasn't 10.12, I was right.

It was 10.13.

What the...

I raised myself up with my arms. I was still laying where I'd been last night. It couldn't be morning, surely? I was still tired. I slowly looked around the room. I remembered Kelvin's bedside lamp being on. It was off now. There was light outside the heavy curtains, so it was definitely morning. I did the math in my head. Had we all slept for nearly fourteen hours?

I realised I could see more now, my eyes must have adjusted. Jane was laying more or less where I'd remembered her being, apart from the fact that her legs were now under the covers. And Kelvin was bare chested, barcode tattoos there for all to see, and, thankfully, under the covers, too, though he still sat in exactly the same position that I had last seen him in. Wasn't he wearing a robe last night? I looked down and realised that his robe was now around my legs. I guessed that Kelvin must have awoken at some time, graciously covered us both up, Jane with part of the bed covers and me with his robe, switched the light off and left it at that. But fourteen hours and not a move out of any of us?

I decided I would quietly slip back to my room. Or would I just get up? I guessed I could go back to sleep in an instant so that was out. Maybe I'd just stay here until they woke? No, I decided, that would be awkward. Back to my room, it was. My decision made I slid quietly off the bed and stood up.

'What time is it?' asked a sleepy Jane.

'Ten fifteen,' I whispered back, not wanting to disturb Kelvin. I needn't have bothered.

'Looks like our jet lag caught up with us,' he said without moving. Not even prying open an eyelid.

'Maybe,' said Jane, sleepy still. 'Or maybe it was the angel doing my back?'

'Huh, you're lucky. I had to feed my wine to the angel!'

'Well, I'm sure angels don't work for free,' she said as she moved to snuggle up to Kelvin. 'Where you going, Angel?' she asked as she settled.

They were calling me an angel? Despite myself I smiled. 'Back to my own bed.' *Back? That only counts if you were there to begin with!*

'What's the point?' she said and she reached behind her and threw back the covers. I could see that she still had a towel partially wrapped around her but her backside was almost bare.

I hesitated. This wasn't right, was it? I mean, last night was bad enough but it had felt OK. Actually getting into bed with them, for whatever reason, just had to be a no-no.

'Come on, my bum's cold,' Jane prompted as she reached out for me, her eyes still closed.

How do I get out of this without offending anybody, I thought? But then I remembered I was the de facto daughter. Daughters get into bed with their mother and father, don't they? I certainly had when I was young. *How young are you meant to be? How old is Isobel, anyway!*

I took a quick look at Kelvin. He hadn't moved a muscle. If he was awake and rubbing his hands in glee or drooling then there was no way. And I would be next to Jane, anyway…

She's naked!

And I'm wearing a robe so that's OK.

Surprising myself, I moved towards the bed and slid under the covers beside Jane. As I put the covers over me, she grabbed by right hand with hers and placed it around her waist and held it there, almost forcing me to spoon up close to her. She moaned slightly as she exhaled and settled.

This is as far as I go, I told myself. If they try and get me in the middle then I'm outta here!

But nothing happened. After a few moments of terror I started to settle, chastising myself for the black brush I was painting these two lovely, but strange, people with. *AGAIN!* I decided there and then that I had to stop judging them by other people's standards, they just weren't like anybody else I'd ever met. And, I told myself, I felt totally safe and protected in their company. I vaguely remembered something that Jane had said… my god was it only three or four days ago?

My eyes closed and the lawn mower was back again. I was at a picnic and was drowsy after eating. I was laying drowsy in the warm summer sun and content. And then somebody was talking.

'What did you say?' said Jane.

'I just wondered,' asked a still sleepy sounding Kelvin, 'how long that conditioner stuff is to stay on your hair?'

There was a pause as, I guessed, Jane's sleepy mind processed the question. 'Oh, just a couple of hours.' A pause. 'Bugger! Get up, Aneese!'

'Wha?' I half asked. 'Wass wrong?'

By now she was pushing me out of the bed. 'The conditioner! Christ, I hope I haven't wrecked your hair!'

Well that woke me up.

She pushed past me and grabbed my hand as Kelvin smiled at the view of her departing backside. I used my spare arm to check that at least I was covered everywhere that mattered.

'What time is it?' she shouted from the bathroom to Kelvin.

'Eleven thirty, give or take.'

We were all fully awake now.

'Well we're going to need that room so five minutes and you're out!'

'What, not even a kiss? Remember I'm a morning person?'

If I'd remembered he was a morning person then I wouldn't have got into their bed!

She rolled her eyes and ran naked back into the bedroom as I untangled my turban and took in the mess atop my head. They kissed noisily and I heard a slap and a squeal.

'Now out, that's all you're getting. And organise some food!' she shouted over her shoulder as she ran back into the bathroom.

'Slave driver!' I heard him reply. 'And a tease!'

Jane ignored him. 'Oh, I'm so sorry, Aneese. It shouldn't have been left on even half the time it has been. Hope we won't be needing hats!'

Hats? My hair was my pride and joy. OK, I sometimes didn't treat it as well as I should but if my hair looked good then I felt great. A bad hair day was akin to being on the rag; I just didn't feel like myself and had no confidence. Jane, I will positively kill you if you've wrecked my hair!

'I think it's the shower for you,' she finally decided. 'Come on.'

She pushed me towards the cubicle and, after I'd disrobed, followed me in. Her turban came off, too. If my hair looked anything like hers, I was going to be mad.

She doused and lathered my hair again and I could tell by the look on her face that she was concerned. I was concerned, too. Not only for my hair but also because I was standing naked in a shower with an equally naked woman. Her breasts moved rhythmically as she rubbed the shampoo into my hair and I subconsciously compared her body to mine. Yep, she was certainly in good shape. Then I realised with horror that she was looking at me, straight into my eyes.

'Christ, you're in good shape for a woman your age,' I said to hide my embarrassment.

'Thanks... I think,' she answered.

'No, I mean it. You're not loose or saggy anywhere. Hope I'm in as good a shape when I reach your age.'

'OK, enough of the age thing. I get it. I'm older than you.'

'No seriously. I've seen some older women with...'

'Tits down to their knees? Yeah, I know, but I'm only forty-four. That's young!'

It is, I found myself thinking? Sounded old to a mere twenty-six year old like me.

'There, I think we're winning here,' she finally said. 'And thanks for the compliment. I guess I just have good genes. I don't really work out but I try to watch what I eat. Guess all the brandy has pickled and preserved the rest.'

'Would you ever have any work done?'

She squeezed more shampoo onto my hair as she thought. 'Never thought about it. Guess I would as long as I didn't look like a freak afterward. Some women think they look great after surgery, but don't. Have you seen them in the newspapers?'

'Hmmm,' I answered. I didn't do newspapers much.

'There, I think that'll do it, thank the lord; looks like we got away with it. Wouldn't normally be a problem but this stuff is super strength stuff that my hairdresser got me. Can you do me?'

She turned her back to me and I doused and lathered her. Eventually she spoke. 'You know I'm glad I'm not a man.'

'What do you mean?'

'Well they couldn't do this, share a shower, I mean. Not without getting into social trouble, anyway.'

'But don't football and rugby players share a team bath afterwards?'

'Yeah, and they have communal showers in the army, Kelvin tells me, and in prison, if you believe the films. But we women share showers and changing rooms and it's accepted. If blokes did it, they'd get tagged as gays, you know?'

I nodded.

'What I'm unsuccessfully trying to say,' she continued over the sound of the water, 'is that I like the closeness we've developed. Feels like I've known you forever.' She turned around to face me. 'I'm really glad that I met you, that Kelvin brought you into my – our – life.'

I smiled back at her. 'Ditto,' was all I could say.

And then I was hugging a naked woman in the shower. First time for everything, I guess. I began to feel awkward that her soapy breasts, those perfectly formed forty-four-year-old, non-saggy breasts, were pressing against mine at exactly the right (or wrong) place. Her nipples met mine perfectly, we were so similarly aligned, and I felt a hardness there as hers pushed against mine (at least I hoped it was hers and not mine!).

'Guess it's time to face the music,' she said as she turned and stepped out.

As I watched her start to towel herself down through the misted glass I wondered if she'd felt what I'd felt, felt as embarrassed as I felt. It was just an accidental thing, like when I was a kid.

A memory of myself as a young girl sprung to the fore. I'd gone down the shops for mum and was waiting to be served. As I waited a dog, a black and tan mongrel, had somehow got in. It had sniffed around the floor and then before I knew it, it had its nose up my short skirt and against my knickers as it noisily sniffed my crotch. I'd hastily moved my hand to push him away. 'Down' – *oh that feels nice* – 'doggy!'

What was I? Eight? I thought nothing of it at the time (apart from embarrassment) but years later I realised it was my first sexual experience and I, obviously, kept it to myself. It was the first time that I'd realised that somebody – or something – touching you down there could feel so nice. I'd always thought of it as my sexual awakening.

It was years before I'd felt anything even remotely so lovely. Stuart Fanning at school, as I'd queued on the stairs to get into art class. I turned around and slapped him, but a few seconds too late and the toad knew it and never let me forget. He was always after a repeat performance after that, but consensual. I never gave in even though the act was the basis for many of my teenage fantasies. In the privacy of my head and bed I often let him have his repeat performance, and much more to boot. Poor Stuart, if only he'd known. Such a pity he was a spotty freak or he might have got what he wanted.

I felt a warmness, like a full bladder between my legs. God, if I was alone right now, I'd be shaming myself to noisy orgasm, I thought.

'Come on,' Jane called to me, reminding me that I wasn't alone. 'Got to dry it yet. And I can't wait to see what Kelvin has planned for us today.'

Ah, yes, I'd forgotten. Wasn't he shrinking New York today (whatever that meant)? Reluctantly I started to move.

When we got back to the bedroom Kelvin was gone, as per her orders. I reflected on how good natured he was as she ordered him around, he was quite a guy. Most men's egos wouldn't accept that, I guessed. He certainly seemed very comfortable in his own skin.

'Knock, knock,' I heard him say and Jane answered.

'Thought you might want some refreshment,' he said as he entered carrying a tray. It contained tea and coffee pots and two glasses of orange juice. 'You must be parched.'

We were. And he got a kiss for his thoughtfulness.

'Is that all I get? I'm short a good time, you know?'

'Perhaps later,' Jane played back. 'Once the children are asleep.'

Inside I was partly amused and partly cringing. So he hadn't got his jollies with the lovely Jane this morning. My fault, it seemed. The fact they were flirting and discussing it in front of me was a bit cringeworthy, but I couldn't stop thinking that I had got further with Jane than he had this morning and that was quite amusing.

'Oh hardy ha,' he said. 'Anyway, brunch is served. And I'm ready when you are,' he said as he retreated.

We were still in a combination of robes and towels but ready he was. One thing I was jealous of was most men's ability to be up and ready in five minutes flat. He was already fully dressed and seemingly ready to go, teeth cleaned and hair combed. He must have used my bathroom.

Hope he put the seat down!

He was dressed more casually today than yesterday, in just a pair of tan corduroy trousers and a cream (of course) shirt. My mind played with me taking him shopping to update his wardrobe as Jane brushed my hair. I had to admit, though, that he looked good in whatever he was wearing. As did Jane, even when only wearing a towel. I wondered if I did?

By one o'clock we were getting into a limousine having won the "hair war", as Kelvin had called it over brunch, and eaten our fill. We girls didn't have a clue where we were going or what was going to happen when we got there and Kelvin, despite some heavy interrogation, wasn't saying. He'd offered to tell all for thirty minutes alone with Jane but she refused. Then he offered just fifteen minutes and was refused there, too. I found the whole thing very amusing.

'Have we really got to go out tonight?' Jane asked as the limo pushed its way through the lunchtime traffic.

'Fraid so,' he answered. 'He is paying for this trip, you know?'

'Well you know I don't like meeting people. What if he gropes me? You know what you high powered company execs are like.' She nudged him with her elbow.

'Then I'll break his arm, deal or no deal.'

'And what about me?' I joined.

'If you wanna grope her, you just carry on,' he answered, quick as a flash as always.

'No I meant…'

'He knows what you meant,' Jane interrupted. 'Thought you'd have learned by now?' She smiled.

Damn it. He'd had me again!

Whilst they chattered on and giggled and flirted (did they never stop?) I took in the scenes around us. We were here to see New York after all. It was a fine day and the sun was bright and strong from this side of the glass. Outside it was chilly and I imagined myself warm and snug in a fur coat and damned my working class pride.

Oh, why couldn't I have said yes? Why did I have this stupid pride! Most women, I told myself, would have thrown their pride to the winds and accepted whatever these people had offered them, and then asked for more. I couldn't, and sometimes I hated myself for it. Life was so unfair.

Chapter Six

'I think we're here,' Kelvin said as the car slowed and took a turn.

'Where are we?' asked Jane.

'No idea where,' answered Kelvin. 'But I do know what.'

'What *does* he mean,' I asked Jane, but before she could answer I saw what I thought was the answer. A helicopter, actually, a whole fleet of helicopters on a small inner city helipad. Did I say small? It was small by American standards. In England it would have been huge.

'We're going on a helicopter?' I asked excitedly.

Kelvin just smiled.

'Did you know?' I asked Jane.

'I most certainly did not!' she answered. 'Are we really, Jack?'

'We are,' he said regally.

'I've never been in one!' I said excitedly.

'Nor me!' said Jane, sounding as excited as I did. 'Suppose you have, you damn squaddie!'

'Oh every day,' he played. 'Helicopter to work in the morning, helicopter back to the mess for lunch. Then if I was really bored I'd take a helicopter to the local pub. I mean, who's going to stop you for flying under the influence?'

'Really?' I asked.

'No, not really, you fool,' he laughed at my naivety. 'Sure, I've been up a couple of times but never for fun. And nobody will be shooting at me this time… well hopefully not.'

I looked askance at him. Was he joking this time or not?

The limo stopped and the door was opened by a man in a leather flying jacket. 'The Turner party?'

'That's us,' Kelvin answered.

'Welcome to Battery Park, sir. My name is Nick and I'll be your pilot for today.'

'Great,' said Kelvin as he exited and then helped Jane.

Nick the pilot beat Kelvin to the punch and he held out his hand to me as I swivelled myself out. He smiled at me and I blushed until I saw the wedding ring he wore.

'Just the formality of the safety brief and a quick ten-minute video to watch and then we'll have you in the air.'

'Excellent. You're aware I booked the whole aircraft, are you, Nick?'

'Yes, sir, and you don't want any of the normal tours either.'

'What have you done, Jack?' Jane asked. We'd both been ear-wigging the conversation as we followed along.

'What Jack has done,' Nick answered before Kelvin could answer, 'is booked the whole chopper for you lovely ladies and the normal tours aren't good enough for you either.' He winked to Kelvin as he spoke. 'So at no expense spared we have concocted a whole new ride just for you. You'll be in the air just over ninety minutes and by that time you'll have seen all there is to see.'

The video and safety brief were a blur and I doubt I remembered any of it. I was excited and just wanted to get in the air. Kelvin incurred the playful wrath of both of us by asking questions at the end and delaying our departure.

'Just sign here, Jack, and we'll be away,' said Nick as he held a clipboard to him.

'No problem. And it's Kelvin, by the way.'

Nick stopped dead. 'I apologise, my hearing must be going. Felt sure I heard the lady call you Jack back there?'

'That's what she calls him,' I pointed out. 'It's her pet name for him.'

'Aw heck,' said an embarrassed Nick.

'Could be worse,' I continued. 'Could be Cuddles or Fluffy or Big Boy?'

'Well, it wouldn't be Big Boy,' said Jane deadpan.

Kelvin gave her a look to die for and poor Nick's mouth dropped open. Eventually he coughed and he was all business once more as he tried to hide his smile.

'Just sign here and here, ah, Kelvin, and then I'll need to see the payment card matches.'

Kelvin produced his Amex Gold card and handed it to the pilot who checked it and returned it.

'How long you had that?' Jane asked as we were directed to the waiting helicopter.

'Got it special,' he answered. 'I gotta use something whilst you two are burning a hole in my other plastic.'

'I don't burn a hole in your plastic,' I objected playfully.

'No, but you could and I live in hope that you do one day.'

'Hear, hear,' agreed Jane.

This would have been one of those don't-know-what-the-hell-you're-on-about moments but now I was onto them. I knew their game, what was expected of me. I was the future surrogate daughter and mummy Jane's plaything and Kelvin was Daddy-o. Should I let them know that I knew or just wait until they come out with it and act surprised? A sudden thought of Kelvin playing horsey by bouncing me in his knee sprang into my mind. Well, that could be fun, I had to admit.

Jane and I squealed when the helicopter started to rise and our stomachs reacted. It was like going over a humpback bridge too fast in a car. We were both holding one of Kelvin's hands and I was surprised he didn't cry out in pain. Eventually we both relaxed and he played at shaking the circulation back into them.

To say the ride was fantastic would be an understatement but Kelvin had certainly done his job of shrinking New York. By the time we approached the Statue of Liberty we had all settled down, we were too excited to be afraid. When we were in transit between tourist sites, we travelled very close, or so it seemed to us, to the high-rise skyscrapers and that was frightening and oddly voyeuristic. We could see into the offices and see people getting on with their lives as we passed, godlike, outside. We waved and waved but nobody waved back to us. Helicopters flying past your window must be an everyday sight in New York.

When we recognised the Empire State, Jane and I jumped up and down like school girls and left Kelvin and Nick in no doubt that we'd already been there. Kelvin donned a pair of headphones and he and Nick started to converse animatedly about something. I was nervous about Kelvin distracting the pilot and said so to Jane.

'Maybe they should get a room?' she confided and we laughed.

'What was that?' shouted Kelvin over the din of the engine.

'Aneese thinks you two should get a room,' Jane shouted back and I pleaded my innocence and elbowed her in the ribs. 'Perhaps he's a morning person?' Jane continued.

I thought that was the funniest thing ever.

I didn't hear Kelvin's reply, I was laughing so much, but it had something to do with knees and spanking. Whether it was Jane or I that was being threatened so I never knew, but he'd threatened it before and was all talk. We were safe.

When I noticed we were on the way back to Battery Park I was sad but relieved at the same time. The novelty had finally worn off and my stomach was turning. Kelvin was right (as is normal) when he'd advised against a hangover and queasy belly. An hour and a half in the air was enough. I wanted to get my feet back on the ground.

'Would you like a picture, sir?' a pretty young girl said as we stepped out of the helicopter.

Even though the rotors had stopped by now my head was still buzzing and I wobbled when I tried to stand. I reached out for support and found Kelvin's hand ready and waiting.

'Sure,' said Kelvin. 'If she can stand up long enough.'

He meant me, of course, and I stuck my tongue out and the camera clicked.

'Hey, no fair,' I objected.

'Get a couple,' Kelvin ordered, and we moved together and posed and the girl smiled and clicked away.

'Get in here, Nick,' Kelvin ordered again and the pilot, feigning reluctance, joined the party. Kelvin pushed him in between us and winked at Jane who turned and posed kissing him on the cheek. Well two could play that game. I did the same and, in addition, brought up my leg to show some flesh. Jane, not to be out done, followed suit.

'I can't take that,' the girl objected. 'He's a married man.'

'Get a move on,' Jane said. 'How long do you think I can stand on one leg?'

Kelvin nodded to the girl and she took the hint and the camera clicked again.

'Sir, I should tell you that these pictures are twenty dollars apiece.'

'Just a couple more, then,' he countered and this time he took the camera off her and pushed her towards us.

She objected, of course, but Kelvin wasn't the type of person to object to. In no time at all she – her name badge said FREYA – was smiling amongst us and Kelvin was clicking away. Then, at Kelvin's urging, Nick took up the camera duties and joined us women and the whole process started again.

'Just one more,' insisted Kelvin and he made himself comfortable in the pilot's seat of the helicopter.

Jane rolled her eyes. 'Boys and their toys!'

'Hey I might get one of these,' Kelvin objected as Freya clicked away.

'Over my dead body,' said Jane. 'Your motorbike is dangerous enough. Stick with that.'

'That's all folks,' Nick finally said. 'Got me other customers awaiting.'

I looked at the party he'd flicked his head to. They were all older, even older than Kelvin and Jane. I was sure he wouldn't have half as much fun with them as he had with us.

He shook hands with Kelvin. 'Thank you, Nick.'

'My pleasure. Ladies.' He nodded at us.

'I think we made his day,' I whispered loudly and was rewarded with a bright toothy smile. Such a pity about that ring. He was cute!

Our driver smiled as he held the limo door for us. I think he'd been enjoying the show. 'Where to, sir?' he asked.

'The hotel, I think,' answered Kelvin.

The door hadn't clicked shut before Jane and I were all over Kelvin.

'That was wonderful, Jack,' she said as she held him and kissed him on the lips.

'Yeah, Daddy-o. Fantastic. You shrunk New York!' And I couldn't resist a quick peck on the cheek myself.

'Oh, double delight,' he shot back, amazed, I think, that I had kissed him. Well, he deserved it!

'But how are you going to follow that up?' Jane continued. 'Make the sun hotter, was it?'

'Yep.'

'Well, we're all ears. Let's hear it.'

'I'll tell when I'm good and ready,' he answered, crossing his arms.

'You'll tell us now.'

He shook his head. 'I don't think so.'

'I think you will.'

'I think I won't.'

'I know you will.'

'I know I won't. Not until I'm ready.'

'You'll tell us now and then I'll tell you what Aneese and I got up to in the shower this morning?'

He paused and his mouth dropped open and so did mine.

'OK, I'm ready,' he said immediately. 'Florida. Tomorrow we catch a flight to Florida and...'

We both squealed and hugged him.

'... and board a cruise ship bound for the Caribbean.'

We squealed again and hugged each other.

'How long for?' Jane asked.

'Just a week. Short notice. There was a cancellation.'

We squealed again and jumped up and down and I saw the driver look in his rear-view mirror. Good thing the glass separator was up or he'd be crashing already.

What happened in the shower, indeed? Nothing happened in the shower. Unless... did she get aroused when we hugged? It was an accident, a natural animal reaction. Surely she wouldn't mention that?

'We're going to need bikinis!'

'Well don't tell me you've forgotten how to shop?'

We squealed and jumped and earned another silent reprimand from the driver.

'So,' Kelvin said once all the furore had died down. 'I kept my part of the bargain. Now what about yours?'

'Don't know what you mean,' Jane answered.

'Don't play games with me,' Kelvin threatened. 'Spill it or, driver or not, you're going over my knee. The shower?'

'Oh, the shower. You tell him, Aneese.'

I looked from one to the other. What do I say? That our breasts touched when we hugged and that one of us, her I think, had nipples like walnuts?

'Oh, OK, I'll tell him,' she said in exasperation. 'Well I lathered up her hair...'

'You were both in the shower?'

'Yeah, it's difficult otherwise.'

'Naked?'

'Well what do you think!'

'And then?'

'And then I rinsed it off.'

'Yeah, and then?'

'Then she lathered mine up, didn't you, Aneese?'

I nodded in terror. Bruno, the dog's name was Bruno. Funny what you thought about in stressful situations.

'Then she rinsed me off.'

He licked his lips. 'And then?'

'And then we...' And at this point she paused and started to walk her fingers slowly up his chest. '... We got out and dried ourselves!'

I let go a breath that I didn't know I was holding.

'That's it?' he asked.

'Well yeah. What were you expecting?'

In relief I started to laugh but then tried, and failed, to hold it in. Even my hand over my mouth had no effect.

'You absolute bitch!' he said just as he grabbed her and began to force her over his knee.

When she realised she was losing the fight she squealed. 'Don't you dare, Kelvin Turner! The driver!'

'He's too big to go over my knee!' he said as he started to pull up her skirt and she screamed.

'Aneese, help!'

'I don't need Aneese's help, thank you,' he answered as he finally got her where he wanted her.

I laughed despite myself. That wasn't what Jane was asking. Kelvin's quick witted word turning strikes again!

'No!'

Slap!

He hadn't revealed her underwear or anything but Jane's skirts were short enough anyway. The slap impacted on her upper thigh and she yelled. Then he let her go and reverted quickly to a seated position.

What, all that for one slap!

'You bastard!' she said and then she slapped him.

'Jane, the driver!'

'He's too big to slap!' she said playfully, getting her own back on him.

He laughed as he fended off her blows and she began to realise that she was getting nowhere.

The poor driver was by now facing straight ahead. He wanted nothing to do with this.

'And thanks for your help!' she said to me. I was unsure whether she was playing or not.

'You didn't need her help,' Kelvin interrupted. 'You got yourself into all that trouble all by yourself!'

She tried not to laugh but her snort turned into a full laugh.

'I need a tissue,' she finally said.

There was a box I'd spotted earlier. This car had everything. I held the box out to her and she blew her nose.

I looked between them. I still wasn't sure what had gone down, there. Did they do this all the time, were the spanking warnings real? I'd been threatened with over the knee once or twice myself. Surely he wouldn't...

I think he would!

She settled beside him and started to laugh, first silently until it built up and she couldn't keep it in any longer.

'He thought we'd been doing the dirty in the shower!' She just got out around her laughter. Seems her spanking hadn't quelled her enthusiasm at all.

And as she laughed Kelvin folded his arms and looked sideways at her and smiled. Then he reached out and put his arm around her. 'I will get you back for that,' he warned.

They were still playing as we arrived back at the hotel. Was this a new side to them, I thought? Did they play spank all the time? What else about them didn't I know? The thought struck me: probably lots. I'd known them less than a week, I probably hadn't even scratched the surface.

We were still in high spirits when we entered our suite. I mean, why not? We were off to the Caribbean tomorrow.

'Aneese, I wonder if you could do me a favour?' Jane asked as we kicked off our shoes and Kelvin was in their bedroom.

'Shoot.'

'Could you sort out bikinis for us both, please? We're about the same size.'

'Um, sure,' I answered with a quizzical look on my face which she saw.

'The master here needs some attention, I think,' she said in answer to my querying look. 'Which he sorely deserves, don't you agree?'

I was slow in responding. Just wanted to be sure she was saying what I thought she was saying.

'Of course, if you'd rather, I could do the bikini thing and you could do the servicing the master thing? Just say the word.'

She's joking, right?

'Ah, no I get it. You carry on,' I answered, amazed and shocked that she could even discuss such a thing with me. And I got it. Translated it meant *here, here's fifty pence, go to the cinema!* Dished out the odd tenner myself, inflation and all that. Little sisters were such a pain when older sis had a boy around and the parents were out.

'If you get half a dozen or so different ones we could mix and match?'

'Are you sure you wouldn't rather a swimsuit?'

'What, are you insane? Swimsuits are for old ladies and fat girls.' Her eyes closed to slits and she examined me down her nose. 'Do you want to go over *my* knee?'

'No, I just meant... actually I don't know what I meant. My mission is to buy six bikinis. Got it.'

Kelvin had achieved his missions, I will achieve mine (and no doubt Jane will achieve hers.) *Hang on, over her knee? She gives as well as receives? Surely not! Does she?*

What I'd really meant was if we bought swimsuits then I wouldn't have to be in a bikini in front of Kelvin. Let's be blunt here, a bikini is underwear in all but name. For some reason being in a bikini in front of him terrified me and I didn't know why. Was I shy? I didn't think I was; I'd worn bikinis before.

'What goes on here?' enquired Kelvin as he appeared from their bedroom.

'Aneese has volunteered to get our bikinis whilst we take a rest.'

'Rest? I don't need a rest. Or a bikini. What you think I'm ninet...' For once Kelvin was slow on the uptake but he caught up real fast. He put on a yawn. 'Now you mention it, I guess I haven't recovered from the jet lag.'

'Why don't you walk her down whilst I turn back the duvet?'

I noticed he was going to object, probably to say that I was perfectly capable of operating the lift by myself or something, but instead he changed tack. He'd already been caught out once and was playing safe, I guessed. Jane obviously had a plan in mind and I wondered what she needed time to prepare. Perhaps it was just time to wash her hands and face, but who knows.

'OK, I'll be just a couple of minutes,' he finally answered.

'That'll be fine,' Jane simply said.

With that Kelvin nodded my way as I hastily slipped my shoes back on. In a moment we were out in the corridor and heading towards the lift. We said nothing as we waited for the lift and it felt uncomfortable. It was like a date with a long pause in conversation. Eventually the lift arrived and he gestured me to enter before following me and pressing the button for the lobby. The lift started to move and the silence continued even though we were alone. Was it because he knew that I knew that they were going to get some afternoon delight that he wasn't talking? And was it because I knew what they were up to that I wasn't saying anything, too? Wasn't like him to be so abashed, I thought.

'I haven't thanked you for yesterday,' he said, breaking the silence.

I was confused. Yesterday? What happened yesterday?

'I haven't seen Jane like that in... well never, actually.'

I looked at him, still unaware what he was on about.

'You know, she hasn't sung once in the four years we've been together, not once, not even a hum. And now you're here she's humming and singing while doing your hair. Thanks for that.'

Now I understood. Was that only yesterday? It seemed like a lot had happened since then. 'I did nothing.'

'You must have done something?'

'I just let her do my hair. I guess it reminded her of Isobel.'

'I guess so. Well, whatever you did, keep doing it. She really had a rough time before I turned up and I have only managed to…' He searched for the right word. '… Rehabilitate her so much. I offered to pay for real counselling, you know, but she wouldn't hear of it. She's nervous of people and she hardly ever leaves the house without me, just stays at home doing her embroidery and gardening.'

Gardening? I knew nothing about that. Nor embroidery, actually.

'And now look at her. Cos you're here she's out and she's extrovert. I can hardly believe she's the same woman. Whatever you are, Aneese Crosby. Angel? Well, you're worth your weight in gold. Speaking of which.' He pulled out his wallet as the elevator stopped to pick up more passengers. 'You'll be needing some gold to buy bikinis.'

'I have my stash,' I objected. The envelope containing dollars (once pounds) was in my bag which I'd ensured to bring with me.

'That's your money,' he countered.

'But it's enough.'

'Do as you're told,' he growled, earning a silent rebuke from a large old biddy who had entered as the door had opened. She was all pearls and silver hair and wreaked of money and snobbery.

He pressed a thick wad into my hand and what could I do but accept it.

'I'll get receipts.'

'Over my knee, you will!'

'Yes, Dad,' I answered until he gave me a look. 'Daddy-o, I meant Daddy-o!'

The silence returned as the elevator continued down, now nearly half full. I felt something touch my hand and realised with a jolt that it was his hand searching for mine. He closed his fingers around mine and, despite myself, I did the same. I felt him squeeze my hand and returned it. Then I saw movement out of the corner of my eye and turned to face him and our lips met. I guessed he'd been about to peck me on the cheek but I'd spoiled it.

Spoiled it? Did I say spoiled it?

Our lips touched I guess even before he knew it was my lips he was kissing. He pulled back slightly but, in a moment, pushed forward again. The second kiss was slightly longer AND intentional to boot. My lips puckered and I pushed back against him and my heart started to race.

'We love you,' he simply said. 'Be careful out there. If anybody threatens you then…'

'… Then you'll mount a severe pamphlet campaign. Yeah, heard that one,' I surprised myself by saying so calmly, considering my heart was revving up nicely.

He wasn't often on the back foot but I had him this time. The elevator came to rest at the third floor and the door pinged and opened.

'If anybody harms you, I'll kill them,' he continued. 'But slowly, very slowly.'

The old biddy couldn't leave quick enough.

I felt my chest tighten as I caught my breath. I pushed my lips tightly together so as not to cry. Kelvin always caught me unawares whether he was playing the fool or being serious. I could never relax around him as he changed tack so quickly, always hitting me with the unexpected. This time the lift stopped at the lobby and the two or three remaining travellers got out before us. One guy looked back at us as he departed.

'You find your way from here?'

'Yes,' I croaked. 'Yes, of course,' I said after I'd cleared my throat.

'Be careful, OK?' he said again.

'I'll be fine,' I said as the door started to close. He stopped it with his hand and ushered me through.

'I guess it won't take us more than an hour to rest,' he said as the door closed and drowned out the last word.

Rest, my arse!

Lucky him, he was getting his oats. I'd almost forgotten, what with the kiss and all. *One accidental kiss and one intentional one. Which you responded to!*

What was I, the starter before his main course? Last time I had oats there was milk and honey and a bowl and I couldn't even remember when that had been. And as for *oats* oats the last time had been when I'd allowed some guy to pick me up at a bar after I'd got back from Magaluf. I was still empty and feeling Richard's loss and looking for something to fill the void within me and that was nearly seven months ago. And before that there had been that fumble on the beach when we were both pissed out of our heads on the last night in Magaluf. Some nameless dago. And

I'd only done that because the girls cajoled me and bullied me into it as I was freshly single, post Richard. Neither acts were what I would call satisfying or even fully remembered. To be honest I could do a better job of it myself, and occasionally did, to my shame.

Note to self. When you get five minutes give yourself a good seeing to! I felt embarrassed. Had I even thought such a thing? I must be hornier than I thought.

The winter sun had started its short fall to the horizon as I stepped out onto the street.

Sidewalk.

Whatever.

There was a chill in the air and I realised that I hadn't even brought a coat. Better get this done, I told myself. Quicker it's done the quicker I am back in the warm.

Bet Kelvin is warm right now, snuggled up to the delightful Jane?

Hell, Jane! I'd forgotten about her. Should I tell her about the kiss?

Best had because you know Kelvin will!

Would he? Would he really tell her? I already knew the answer to that. Of course, he would. But what if he didn't and I blundered by telling her when he hadn't? Crap, could be fireworks. Now what do I do?

I only had half a mind on my shopping mission. I selected six as instructed and held one against me to test the size. I didn't have a clue what these American sizes meant. When I went to the cashier I realised that I still had the wad of money in my hand that Kelvin had forced upon me. I must have looked like a right idiot walking down the street clutching a fist full of dollars. The words made me laugh out loud, though. Good film.

Mission accomplished. I looked at my wrist and realised I didn't have a watch. My generation used phones, remember? Well, what the hell, I would buy myself a watch. I found a jewellery store only a few blocks away and bought a delicate, but beautiful looking thing, for two hundred bucks. It had been one of the cheapest in the display, but I liked it. There were others there I'd liked, of course, but they had more zeros on the end than I was used to dealing with. Yeah, people like me? Three figures and pence was as far as we went, and even then only occasionally.

I counted in my head. Bikinis bought *and* got a watch. Mission elapsed time: forty-four minutes. Not bad.

Now what am I going do? I considered returning to the suite but discounted it immediately. The last thing I needed right now was to hear them two exercising the bedsprings. Walking in on them that time was bad enough. I wondered how Kelvin was in bed? Was he ram stam, thank you ma'am or tender tortoise? I laughed to myself. Richard had been the hare at first and I had been too inexperienced to even notice. We'd fixed it eventually, though, as our experience grew. It even got to be satisfying up to a point.

Oh screw this, I need a drink!

It was mission elapsed time two hours and thirty-two minutes when Kelvin found me in the hotel bar.

'There you are. Was about to mount a search. You OK?'

'I'm fine,' I answered. 'No threats, no pamphlets required, nobody needs killing, which is just as well as I haven't yet seen a tattoo artist in this town.' I was just finishing my fourth double brandy. Neat! 'You know, this stuff is great. I understand now how you drink it straight.'

He smiled. 'Good girl. How many you had?'

'This is the fourth,' I answered. 'Double!'

'You eaten anything?'

I shook my head as I took another swig.

'Ouch, you'll be on your arse this evening. Bartender?'

'And I bought myself a watch with your change, see?' I held my wrist in his face and he pushed it down slightly to make his order.

'It's lovely. A double of whatever she's drinking, please.'

'And the same for me,' I ordered cheekily.

The barman waited for Kelvin to nod before moving away.

'You do remember we're going out this evening, don't you?'

'Yep, and you're going to break arms if he gropes but I can grope Jane and you won't break mine.'

He laughed quickly. 'True.'

'But they are allowed to grope me, right?'

He turned to face me as he accepted his drink and the barman placed mine in front of me.

'Not true,' he said. 'Cheers!'

'Cheers.' I raised my glass and nearly slipped my elbow off the bar.

I tossed back my old drink and lifted the new one. 'This iss a good game, you know. He brings me drinks and I…' I selected a note from the small pile in front of me. 'Give him money.'

'Yes, they call it capitalism,' he countered.

'Well it workss,' I slurred. 'Did I tell you I drink this neat like you now?'

'You did. I'm very proud of you.'

'And I'm proud of you, so proud. And I love you,' I said. And I said it and meant it and I didn't feel awkward at all. He just paused with his drink halfway to his mouth and I was disappointed. I wanted a better reaction than that.

'And we love you,' he finally answered.

'It's all "we this" and "we that" with you, isn't it? Did you tell her we kissed?'

He looked at me. 'Of course.'

'Wash she mad?'

'Of course not. She said, "Well I kiss her, why shouldn't you?"'

'But she… she showers with me too.'

He smiled. 'I live in hope.'

'Well dream on, buster. No way you're getting your hands on these pineapples,' I said as I stuck my chest out.

He laughed again. 'Such a shame, was counting on that. Fine pair of pineapples that they are and all that.'

'You're playing wiz me?'

'I am.'

'OK, you can have them, then.'

'Have what?'

'My pineapples.'

He smiled as he knocked back his drink.

'Bartender,' I said rather too loudly. 'Set 'em up!'

He shook his head as the bartender approached. 'Has she covered the bill?'

'More than adequately, sir.'

'Keep the change,' I said.

Kelvin nodded to him and slipped him another bill.

'Come on Cinderella, party's over,' he said as he got off his stool and took hold of me.

'I want to stay and play catapultism.' My head was buzzing like a badly tuned television, a bass-like drone.

'I think that's enough catapults for you,' he said, finally getting me to my feet. I didn't stay on them for long. Luckily, he had quick reactions.

'DO AS YOU'RE TOLD!' I imitated loudly as he stumbled until he'd adjusted for my weight.

He laughed softly. 'You know, that's not bad. Jane says you have a flare for imitating. Says you picked up the local dialect very quickly.'

'You better alieve it, buster!' BUUZZZZZZ. That damn television again. Somebody turn it off!

'Ah, your chariot is here,' he said and I recognised the elevator. How did we get from the bar to the elevator?

'My bag and the bikinis!' I suddenly blurted out.

'Right here in my hand. Looks like you did good.'

'Achieved my mission, see, like a good solja!'

'So you did.'

I felt the elevator start to move. I hadn't noticed the doors had closed. The buzzing noise had followed me in. It felt like my own personal soundtrack.

'So how was your oats? Horsey happy now?' I asked.

'Oats?'

'You know? Shagging?' I leaned in and whispered loudly.

The elevator doors opened and a young couple entered. We got a look from the man but I was used to that by now. Guess he'd heard what I said.

'Sssokay,' I whispered again. 'They don't call it that over here so they don't know. They call it—'

He kissed me hard and long and I pushed myself against him and held him tight. I squeezed and I pulled and I tried different holds on him. I tugged his shirt, I tugged his skin and my drunken strength turned us around until he was the one resting against the glass wall and I pressed against him hard using me right leg around his left as an anchor.

'Oh, get a room!' I heard and noticed that the elevator door had opened and the young couple were waiting impatiently.

'We have a suite,' I snarled. 'Many rooms so f—'

'Far away from home, we are,' Kelvin interrupted as he pulled me from the lift and I nearly fell to the floor.

He tried to get me to stand but my knees were like jelly. I felt him lift me.

'Thas it, tiger, jus like las time. Carry me to bed and undress me and fuck me without Jane knowing, like you did las time. Bet you never told her about that, huh?'

'What did she say?' I heard Jane ask.

'She's drunk. And we're so getting thrown out!'

And the television switched itself off and the buzzing stopped.

Chapter Seven

'You accused Kelvin of raping you!'

'What? I didn't!'

'You did. When he put you to bed that first night!' Her voice was an angry snarl that I'd never heard before, that I never thought her capable of.

'I thought he had. It was a mistake, a fantasy!'

'Some fantasy. Now he's in jail!'

'Jail? No!'

'Yes, and they take things very seriously over here. What will I do without my Jack? And what will he do without his reputation?'

'No, I'm sorry, I'm sorry, I'm sorry,' I sobbed. I reached out for solace but nobody wanted me. I grabbed the sheets and turned and buried my head into the pillow and howled my pain into the darkness.

'It's all right, Aneese. Calm down now, my little angel. Ssshhhh, there now.' The voice was lighter and more loving and I was grateful.

'Do you forgive me?' I sobbed.

'Nothing to forgive, it was just a bad dream.'

'So Kelvin's not in jail?'

'Jail? Why would he be in jail? He's at dinner with the client.'

'The client? Weren't we meant to be going?'

'He's making apologies for us. You did me a favour, there. I wasn't too keen on going.'

'Cos he'd grope you?'

'What?' She laughed. 'I doubt that he'd do that.'

'Then why didn't you want to go?' I asked, still actively crying and hurting so badly.

'I'm just not good with people, that's all. I'm getting better, mind. In time I'm sure I'll be fine.'

'So it was all a dream?'

'Yep.'

'So I didn't get lonely, get drunk and… and… shame us?'

'Oh, you got drunk all right.'

I howled and clutched onto her as buried my sticky nose into her blouse. 'Do you hate me? Please don't hate me? I'm sorry. It'll never happen again!'

'What won't?'

'Whatever Kelvin said happened.' Had he told her everything, I asked myself? What had he told her?

'What, that you kissed?'

I clung onto her, pressed my eyes tight shut and tried to suppress a howl as I nodded.

'Sure he did. On the way down in the lift. First one was an accident. And then later he kissed you on the way back up to shut you up and stop you embarrassing us even further. Do you remember that?'

I shook my head but then I nodded because I suddenly remembered.

'See, no harm done.'

'So we're not getting thrown out of the hotel?'

'I don't think so. Nobody has said anything and we're leaving tomorrow, anyway, so what can they do?'

Even in my pain I could understand the logic in that. 'My head hurts.'

'I'm not surprised. You certainly put those brandies away, I hear.'

I hadn't thought I'd spoken until she answered me.

'Here, drink this.'

I opened my eyes and saw that she held a glass of orange juice in her hand. My throat felt tight and hoarse, like I'd been eating gravel. I could taste my breath and it tasted awful. I took the glass and gulped the contents down. It felt like the cool liquid was forcing my veins open and rejuvenating my body as it brought me back to life.

'More?'

I nodded and she poured me another. This time she also held out two white pills and two large pink ones.

'I couldn't take them all.'

'DO AS YOU'RE TOLD,' she played and I actually almost laughed.

I reached out for the pills and held them in my hand. 'All of them? Won't I OD?'

She shook her head. 'No, the paracetamol acts on a different part of your body than the ibuprofen, so you can take them all and it's safe. Trust me, I've done it before and you'll get twice the benefit.'

'How do you know?'

'Kelvin told me. Squaddie trick. If he says it, it must be true, right? Squaddies eat ibuprofen like smarties.'

I looked down at the pills then back up at her.

'I find that if you take the white ones first and then the pink ones, it's better that way. The pinky ones cover the bitter taste of the others. Go on, give it a go. I promise you it will be fine. In an hour or so you'll feel right as rain and by the time the pills wear off we'll have you rehydrated and fed.'

I placed my hand to my mouth as I felt my stomach turn. The thought of food suddenly had me feeling nauseous.

'One thing at a time, I think. First the pills.'

'What time is it?'

She looked at my wrist. 'A little after eleven by your new watch. Lovely little thing.'

I'd forgotten about the watch. Eleven o'clock? Take the pills and better by midnight. Kelvin said so. Forgetting what Jane had said I threw all four pills into my mouth and tried to chase them down my throat with the orange juice. One pill went down but the others seemed to be blocking each other. I began to feel the bitter taste as the two remaining paracetamol won the taste war with the outnumbered sweet tasting pinky.

'Go on, get them down,' Jane said when I looked her way, and I forced more juice into my mouth. Finally, after separating the white pills with my tongue, they gave up their hold and slipped down my throat like they were greased. I made a face and coughed.

'Ah, that tastes awful!'

'White ones first?'

I nodded as I swallowed repeatedly. Next time I'd remember. *You mean there's going to be a next time? Don't you ever learn!* Eventually the taste subsided and I waited to start feeling better. I knew that Jane and I still had things to discuss. 'What else did Kelvin say?'

Jane pulled my head to rest on her chest and stroked my hair. 'That you said you loved him.'

So he did tell her everything. I felt terror well up inside me.

'Well I don't,' I said. 'Not love love, but I like him, like him a lot. Like I like you a lot. Please believe that I would never hurt you by going behind your back with him.'

'I know,' was all she said. 'And even if you wanted to, he wouldn't let you.'

And this time I believed her. I vaguely remembered a similar conversation during our first couple of days together where I'd told myself that I could take Kelvin if I wanted to. Now I knew I couldn't and do you know what? I felt better for it.

'Am I forgiven?' I asked. I really needed her to say yes.

'Of course you are. There's nothing to forgive. If you recall, Kelvin told you first that we loved you so all you did was use the same words that we used, so how could you be at fault?'

So he had. I remembered now. On the way down in the lift before he had his oats. Oh, I'd forgotten about that, too!

'So you and Kelvin... love me?' I asked before I'd even known I'd spoken.

She pushed us apart and looked me in the eye. 'Are you kidding? You're wonderful! We get so much pleasure just being with you and hopefully will get more yet.'

'Really?'

She smiled. 'Of course.'

'Well putting it that way, then I love you both too!'

We hugged and I started to feel better and it wasn't the effect of the pills.

She continued stroking my hair and I began to relax. 'You want to tell me about Kelvin fucking you?' she said eventually.

I pulled away from her and looked at her, terrified.

'That's the exact word you used,' she added.

'He didn't, I swear!'

'Well I know that, but do you?'

'You do?'

'Course I do. But you seem to think that he did!'

'I... I... it was a dream. He was carrying me and he smells nice and I was—'

'Calm down!' she ordered. 'I'm not accusing you of anything.'

'Truth is I'm horny as hell,' I continued. 'It's been over six months since I've—'

'Six months! I thought your boss was grabbing you every chance he got?'

'What? No, that's the boss's son and I don't get any pleasure from him getting his jollies!'

'Six months? Wow, no wonder you're horny! Six days and I'd be rubbing myself against the bed post! You know there's always…' And she wiggled her index finger at me as if calling me closer so I moved forward to hear her secret. 'No, you fool.' Then she wiggled her finger again and cast her eyes downward and I got the message. Boy, did I get the message. It was like running into a wall.

My mouth fell open. 'You do…'

'Are you kidding? I don't have to. I've got this hungry hound always lapping away at me every chance he gets. Won't say I haven't in the past, though. No shame in it. And men do it so why shouldn't we?'

'Kelvin does…'

She laughed. More of a bark, actually. 'Well not in front of me, he doesn't, so I can't say! But *six months*? Are you even human?'

'Hey, at least I try shoes on before I buy them!'

'Well it's hardly the same and anyway, it's not been six months since I bought a pair of shoes!'

She had me there I had to admit.

We broke down into raucous laughter and tears began to form in my eyes but this time they were tears of joy. As we finished laughing I saw Jane cock her head to one side. 'Daddy's home,' she said.

I felt fear welling up inside me and felt sick again. 'Does he hate me?' I asked. Jane and I might have smoothed feathers but what about Kelvin?

Before she could answer Kelvin pushed the door open. 'I hear laughing. You mean it's awake?'

'It is indeed,' Jane answered. 'And it's sorry and repentant and ashamed.' And then she turned away from him and said out of the corner of her mouth, 'Not to mention horny.'

My mouth dropped open. Did Kelvin hear? I could slap her!

'Sorry, missed that last bit?'

'You were meant to,' she fired back, with a wink at me.

If she told him later I would just die. I couldn't take him knowing that about me. 'Jane!'

'Fear not,' she said and she pulled her fingers across her lips, imitating a zip. 'My word on it.'

I relaxed. That was something at least.

'So how's our little brandy guzzler tonight?'

I lowered my head in shame. 'You must hate me?'

'Are you kidding, it was hilarious!'

'Glad you think so. Thought that couple in the lift were going to complain.'

'Well they did.'

Jane and I both looked his way.

'But the suite is in the name of Venture Holdings, property of one Calvin Augustine the third. Said couple complained to the hotel, hotel complained to Venture who passed it on to their boss. It made dinner very interesting tonight, though short. Calvin says hi, by the way.'

I put my hand to me mouth. 'Oh, I'm so sorry. What can I do to put this right?'

Kelvin sat on the bed beside us and lowered his voice. 'I think the best thing we can do is jump on a plane tomorrow and leave New York.'

'Speaking of which,' Jane said. 'Great choice on the bikinis. I love them.'

'As do I,' Kelvin joined.

'Glad I can do something right,' I sulked.

'Oh, you poor little girl,' Kelvin said and then he hugged me tight and put his chin on my head. I heard them exchange a kiss. 'So how you feeling?' he asked as he let me go.

'Better than I deserve, I think,' I answered. 'Took some pills about twenty minutes ago. Been promised I will feel better in an hour or so.'

'And you will need rehydration, don't forget?' Jane said.

'And speaking of which,' Kelvin said, and he got up, walked to the open bedroom door and leaned out, returning with three green bottles in his hands.

'Beer?' I put my hand to my mouth again as my stomach turned.

'Hydration – hair of the dog!'

Was that what hair of the dog was? I'd heard the term.

'Now get it down you.'

'I can't drink three bottles of beer. I'll be sick!'

'Just as well only one is for you, then, isn't it! Here, get it down you.'

I was just going to mention the fact that we needed a bottle opener when he put the bottle top up to his mouth and bit down. I heard a hiss of escaping gas and then he held the open bottle out to me. A small rivulet of foam threatened to spill over the rim.

'My party trick,' he said in explanation.

'Wow,' I said, impressed and not believing my own eyes. 'Got any more?'

He winked. 'None that I'm going to show you.'

I watched as he opened the other two bottles and handed one to Jane. 'Ladies, to the Caribbean?'

'The Caribbean!' we chorused and I watched as they both took a pull from their bottles.

I looked at my bottle, preparing myself for the onslaught. What the hell, I thought, what's the worst that could happen? Prepared for the worst I tipped back the bottle and swallowed. And then I damned Kelvin. How was he always right? I felt the beer seeping into my body like a cold fire, hitting the parts that the juice hadn't. I could have done without that beery smell, though, but the liquid itself did the job. After my second pull there was only a quarter of it left. I looked at the dregs, wishing there was more. Then I burped and the two of them almost choked on their beer.

'Pardon me,' I laughed.

'So how was that?' Kelvin asked when he'd finished his.

'Great,' I answered truthfully. 'Didn't somebody mention feeding me a little while ago?'

So room service was called and we shared a meal of southern fried chicken, mashed potatoes and peas. Kelvin had eaten dinner so only picked and we ate with our fingers and made one hell of a mess, especially with the potatoes.

'Yum!' I stated as I licked my fingers and Jane passed around serviettes. I looked at my new watch. Five to midnight and I felt much better.

'You're not packed are you?' Jane asked as we wiped our fingers.

'Um, no. Are you?'

'Yeah, did it when you were sleeping off your hangover.'

I stuck my tongue out at her.

'And I have a set of your dirty clothes packed in my case. From the shower?'

I nodded. 'In that case I'm packed. Haven't had time to unpack, really. 'What time we flying?'

As usual Kelvin had all the information in his head. It meant being up early as the car was picking us up at seven. We'd get breakfast on the plane.

'We first class?' I asked.

'Well we are.' The look on my face said I was wise to him. 'As are you by some accident.'

'Cool! Can't wait! Thanks, by the way.'

'For?'

'For everything.'

'Ah, well, we want something from you and it will soon be time to pay up.'

'Oh yeah, like what? My body?' I played, the coming flight and trip to warmer climes perking me up.

I knew damn well what they wanted and my body wasn't it. Barbie doll surrogate daughter for Jane to dress and undress and plait and curl and wash my hair as she saw fit. If he'd wanted my body he could have taken it long before now and I wouldn't have objected.

They shared a look at my flippancy, though.

'All in good time,' Kelvin answered and he leaned forward and kissed me on the forehead. 'Goodnight.'

'Goodnight,' I said as Jane did the same.

'That new-fangled watch of yours got an alarm?' Kelvin asked as he moved towards the door.

I shook my head.

'We'll wake you, then.'

'And hydrate,' Jane added. 'And speaking of which.' And she padded out of the room and returned with a plastic bottle of water. It was chilled.

Seems everybody knew about the hidden fridge but me. I'd make a point of finding it if we were staying any longer.

'Goodnight,' she said again and I smiled at her in reply. She turned off the light at the door and I settled down into the bed and reached for the bedside lamp switch. It was then I realised that I was still wearing most of my clothes.

That's odd, I thought, she's undressed me before? Then it hit me. Was she too scared to after what I had thought Kelvin had done? Then that hit me too. Kelvin must know what I'd said. If she knew then Kelvin knew. Shit! I thought we'd sorted all the fallout from my drunken escapade, now I'd never sleep. Kelvin would want his pound of flesh, somehow.

Which was why I was still awake an hour later. I'd stripped down to my underwear and decided not to dig around in my packed case for my pyjama bottoms. I tossed and turned and counted sheep and tried to think nice thoughts but I couldn't seem to switch off. I clicked my fingers. His iPod, that'll do it. But where was the damn thing? I knew it wasn't in my suitcase. Had I lost it? I'd be in so much trouble if I had.

Kelvin has it.

He has it. He asked for it to take it with him for his meeting and I'd forgotten. I stamped my feet like a spoilt child and reached for my water bottle. A mouthful and it was empty.

There'll be more in the secret fridge.

I opened my bedroom door as silently as possible and tiptoed out. The thick carpet underfoot made it simplicity itself and was lovely to walk on. The lights were off but the curtains were open and I stared in awe at New York by moonlight. I was so lucky, I thought. To think that if I hadn't gone for that drink after I'd gotten off the train after Carswell had pissed me off, I wouldn't have met Kelvin.

You mean got picked up by Kelvin.

Did I actually have something to thank Ron Carswell for? The irony made me smile.

Now where can that damn fridge be? I guessed somewhere near the eating area (which we hadn't even used – we'd eaten off trays and trollies.) Meant going close-ish past their bedroom door and through the lounge but I was sure that they are asleep by now. A few steps later, though, I thought I heard voices. Were they awake? I tiptoed nearer to clarify. Had I heard voices? I listened a couple of feet away from their door and, just as I was going to move away I heard them again. So they *were* awake and that's my name I've just heard. In seconds I was right up to their door. Who could resist hearing things said about themselves? Nobody human, that's for sure.

'So do I,' I heard Jane say.

'I mean, it's not definite, but I think she'll do it.'

'Great. So glad you chose her!'

I think I heard them kiss. Old news to me, as was their subject matter. I smiled, feeling quite superior that I was onto them. I wondered what deal I would get.

Mercenary bitch!

Well you know? Would they offer to pay me, would I be moving in, would I be able to give up work? Imagine me living with them in their house and he away earning the bacon and me and Jane doing whatever it was Jane did.

Embroidery and gardening.

'I can't wait,' Jane had started again. 'I mean, I'm nervous about it, obviously, but if it all comes off? Oooh, it'll be fan – fucking – tastic!'

I sniggered to myself. Hope I didn't let her down. Wonder when they were going to spring it? And, of course, I'd act all southern belle and surprised. *Oh I do declare, sir, that you have quite surprised me with your intentions.* Scarlet O'Hara called from my brain. Should I play hard to get?

I sniggered and placed my hand over my mouth, perhaps a little too late.

'Did you hear something?' Kelvin asked.

Damn, doesn't Kelvin ever switch off!

'I'd better check.'

Shit and shit. Kelvin was always quick to action. I could imagine him already out of bed and halfway to the door. Should I hide? No, there wasn't time and I'm sure he'd find me. And heading back was out of the question as my room was too far away. There was only one thing for it. Taking a deep breath I knocked on the door.

'Who is it?' I heard Kelvin ask.

Dumb ass, who did he think it was? 'It's Aneese,' I answered. 'Can

I come in?'

'Ah, one moment,' he said and I heard quick, light footsteps and then the rustle of bedding. 'Come in.'

I pushed the door. The lights were off and their curtains were closed and the only light was that coming in from the door in which I stood, coming from the window behind me. 'Sorry, I heard you were awake or I wouldn't have knocked. Was wondering if I could borrow your iPod?' I improvised. Well it was the truth. I did want it! 'I can't sleep,' I finished.

'Ah, of course. You've slept already, haven't you,' said Jane.

'Of course you can. Jane, would you?'

She nodded and got out of the bed.

'It's in my waistcoat pocket.'

Why couldn't he get it? Hang on, was he naked under there? Of course he was, he must have been halfway to the door when I knocked. Imagine if I hadn't knocked, him standing there in the nude (but catching me listening in in the process). Hmmm, maybe not so good then.

Jane wasn't wearing too much herself. It was a nightie but it was short. Surely she's a bit old for a baby doll? It was also thin and translucent in the half light. I could plainly see that she was wearing briefs but no bra beneath it. Kelvin would be feasting his eyes as normal as she searched about in the shadows for his waistcoat but instead he was looking at me. Odd.

I froze. *Oh-My-God! I'm in my underwear! The skimpy stuff I'd bought to make myself feel good. The stuff that nobody would see but me!*

'Found it!' Jane exclaimed. She walked towards me, seeing me properly for perhaps the first time since I'd knocked. I saw her eyes widen as she saw me.

I reached out my hand. 'Thank you,' I croaked and started to retreat, walking backwards and pulling the door.

'And are you hydrating?' she asked.

I stopped and reopened the door a little. Well I couldn't be rude, could I? 'Yes. Could do with another bottle, though.' Christ, didn't she know I just wanted to get out of here!

'Good girl. There's a couple more in the fridge which is in the dining room in a cabinet low down on the windowless wall.'

'Thank you.' I retreated again.

'And if you need a glass…'

I stopped retreating again. 'I don't. Thank you.'

'Goodnight, then.'

'Goodnight.'

The door was finally closed and suddenly it was very warm. I knew my face must be the colour of beetroot. I was halfway back to my room before I remembered the water. I heard them talking jovially as I finally got to my room carrying two bottles of the chilled water. The subject would be me, no doubt, me and my skimpy underwear. I swear I'm never drinking again!

This water better taste like champagne for all the trouble it's caused!

I sunk into the bed and pulled the duvet over me.

And the music better be choirs of angels!

I put my hands over my face and shook my head. 'What a day,' I said out loud to myself.

And then I started laughing, too. After the fact it was quite funny, though at the time I'd been terrified. I guess the laughing lifted my mood and that and a combination of the music put me to sleep. Before I knew it, I was being gently and softly woken by Jane.

She was speaking softly and smiling down at me as she softly stroked my arm. I wondered if this was how she used to wake Isobel? Kelvin, I suspected, would have just grabbed an ankle and dragged me to the floor.

'Hi,' she smiled as my eyes opened. 'Just after six and the limo picks us up at seven. Didn't want to wake you but it's time to start moving.'

I returned her smile, sighed and started to throw back the covers. I'd slept fine in the end and felt rested and refreshed. She was wearing a robe now and I guessed the nightie was still underneath. She didn't look like she had showered. As I stood up I stretched my arms and moaned contentedly as I yawned.

'Nice skimpies, by the way.'

'Thanks.' It didn't bother me that she was seeing me in them.

'And Kelvin thought they were great too. Sleep was delayed last night – got me some attention. Think you in your undies was the cause.'

What? I stopped mid yawn and stood there like some statue with its arms in the air. So de facto daddy screwed de facto mummy because de facto surrogate daughter minced past in her undies? OK, was this creepy?

'I'm sorry,' was all I could think of to say.

'Sorry? Are you kidding?'

'Well twice in one day and all that.'

'Huh, hardly a record.'

What? 'Do you ever say no,' I found myself asking.

'Occasionally,' she said. 'But rarely. Why deprive myself, it's hardly a chore.'

I let what she'd just said sink in. I guess Richard and I had gotten a little boring in the end. Sometimes I just let him get on with it for a quiet life. By the sound of it Jane and Kelvin hadn't reached that stage. What was it, four years that they'd said they'd been together? But more than once a day? Sure, at first, but not four years down the line. I guess everybody is different.

Kelvin has more experience than Richard.

Yeah that made sense. Both of us were virgins when we'd first gotten physical and learnt things as we went along. Not for the first time I wondered what that meant to Kelvin's prowess between the sheets. He must have had lots of practice in the forty years before he'd come back for Jane. Doesn't practice make perfect?

I realised that Jane was just standing watching me and had the funny feeling she was reading my mind.

'I'd better get moving,' I said to hide my embarrassment.

'OK, see you soon.'

As Jane left I started my morning routine and started to think what I could wear. I'd only brought four sets of clothes and had at the time thought that that was one too many. Now I was down to the last set having slept in two and the other was in Jane's case, dirty. I considered buying more clothes with the dwindling supply of dollars I had. There was no way I'd ask for more.

You never heard of washing clothes?

What with taxis and brandy and so on I guessed I was down to my last thousand dollars. What was that, about seven hundred pounds? I checked myself and laughed. Here I am worrying that I'm down to my last seven hundred quid. Normally I'd be worrying that I was down to my last twenty and it was still a week until payday.

Payday? Of course! I must have been paid my now. And would my holiday pay have gone in, I wondered? My debit card would work over here, I was sure, and I'd kept my credit card after paying it off, post Richard. That should still work. I'd have to remember my pin number but I think it's in my phone somewhere. Oh well, had to open the case to get underwear and clothes out, anyway. The clothes were a little creased but they would have to do. My phone was there where I'd left it in a pouch to one side of my case. I switched it on and left it while I headed for the shower. The old fashioned thing took ages to sort itself out.

I showered quickly and gathered my toiletries as I retreated out of my bathroom. As I was packing my case I remembered the phone and noticed I had messages. They must have come through unheard whilst I was showering: four missed calls and seven texts. I thumbed through the main menu to the text screen. The seven unread texts were in bold print in the inbox: three voicemail notifications and four normal texts. Two of these were from an unknown number whilst one was from Cheyanna, my pain in the arse little sis. I thumbed it open.

Hey, Neese. M&D were wondering if u r ever going to drop in and visit us. They foned work and they said u r on hols. Said they cant get u on mob so I texted. Missed u at Crimbo. Get in touch, yeah? ☺

I felt guilty. They were right and I hadn't visited for a while. I'd just thrown myself into work (for all the good that had done me) and hadn't even contacted them before I'd left the country. And as for Christmas I had spent most of it by myself, not wanting to engage myself in false bonhomie for the sake of the season. I told myself there had been little time, but how long does it take to text? OK, phoning would have been a bore with Mam and Dad asking stupid questions, but nonetheless.

Without even thinking I hit the reply button.

Hey, Annie, nice to hear from you. Tell M&D that I am fine. Apologise for me but I am in the USA, NY. Happened short notice. Loads to tell you when I return. Will visit I swear. Phone switching off now as it is expensive if abroad. Love to all.

I was just going to press send but changed my mind.

Off to Caribbean now. Gotta rush!

Send.

I couldn't resist that last bit, knew it was vain of me. Name dropper! I nearly switched the phone off before realising that I had it on for a reason. I found the pin number and recited it to myself a few times. Then I remembered the other messages.

Hi Aneese. Ron here

Ron Carswell was texting me? Didn't even know he had my number. He must have got it from HR, the swine! I read on.

just wondering if you are OK? The holiday thing is company policy so please don't be mad at me. If you feel like a chat then drop me a text

Not a chance, buster!

Rang your number a few times but no answer. Don't blame you for switching it off to chill. You've been working hard lately

Oh, just lately?

and it has been noticed. Left you some voice messages. Get in touch, yeah? I'm really not the bad guy you think I am! Maybe we could go out? My treat.

I barked a laugh. I'd rather drink bleach. Just then the phone buzzed and beeped as a text arrived. As I pressed the button to access it I realised that it was from the same number as the text I'd just read.

Aneese. My phone tells me you have just switched your phone on and got my messages

Phones could do that? Maybe expensive ones. I'll ask Kelvin.

It's a little after one thirty. Are you OK?

Oh crap I'd forgotten about the time difference. Hope I hadn't woken Annie by texting her this early.

look, get in touch. Your sister phoned the office so she is worried as I am. If you are kidnapped then I will mount a rescue, ha ha. You're missed.

But you're not, I told myself. Next message you'll be getting from me is my resignation letter, with luck!

I searched for the off button. Getting the old messages was bad enough but getting "live" ones from him was terrible. It felt too... intimate? Made me feel stalked. I felt my good mood starting to evaporate. I almost threw the phone back into my suitcase, not even bothering to place it safely, before I realised that there was another text to read. If it was from Ron's number I wouldn't read it, but it could be my mother or father.

Sianna? My best friend in the whole world! I thought she was still abroad? I thumbed the OPEN button.

Hi, 'Neese. Back in Blighty. Things didn't work out in Spain. I'm single again. Get in touch. We can go out and catch up? Know any nice guys?

Yeah, do I! The thought was out before I even knew it.

So Sianna was back? Cool. She was always fun and I'd have so much to tell her. And this time I wouldn't be the underdog. Whenever we caught up she always had lots to tell: her holidays, her plans for business (always abroad), her latest man. Mine had always been work and Richard and how much we'd saved for our deposit. Boring! But this time I'd have the lion's story which must surely trump whatever she'd been up to.

My thumb hovered over the REPLY button. It was early over in England I now knew and in any event I wanted to get the phone shut down before Ron texted again. My decision made I turned off the phone and buried it unceremoniously amongst my dirty clothes. I couldn't get the case closed quickly enough. With one last look around the room I quickly got dressed, grabbed the suitcase and went into the lounge where the first thing I saw was Kelvin sitting drinking coffee. He was dressed in a robe. Not like him at all.

'You're dressed!' he said as he saw me.

I stopped, confused.

'But it's my turn for the shared shower, isn't it?'

'Oh hardy har,' I replied. The days when he could get one over on me were long gone. 'Will we have time in Miami before we board? I need some more clothes.'

'Yeah, some. You'll be needing more cash, then?'

'No, I won't.'

Jane appeared from the bedroom, fully dressed and groomed. I guessed that Kelvin had given her first dabs on their shower.

'But you spent a lot of your money on taxis when you were shopping with me,' she said. She'd obviously overheard our conversation.

'So,' I said. 'Still got plenty left.'

'But that was New York money. You need Caribbean money now.'

I dropped my case and turned angrily. 'Look I don't need any more money, right? I have my credit card and I've no doubt been paid by now. I'm not totally without means, you know!'

I went to storm back into my room but I stopped myself. God I hated myself right then. 'Look I'm sorry,' I said, meaning it. 'It's not you two it's...' I could see by the look on their faces that I'd hurt them. I felt even worse. They deserved an explanation. 'I switched on my phone to get my credit card pin and work had contacted me. Not just work but Ron Carswell and he shouldn't even have my number. Just feel like my rotten life is intruding on the wonderful time I am having with you two.'

They both just stared at me for what seemed an age. It was actually about two seconds. Did I offend them that much?

I walked forward to where Kelvin was sitting and Jane was standing beside him. I don't know why but it felt natural at the time, but I lowered myself to my knees and then sat back on my haunches. 'I am your little girl and I seek forgiveness,' I said. I then lowered my eyes and waited for a response and when I didn't get one I looked up. They were quizzically looking at each other and then they noticed that I was looking at them.

'Up,' Kelvin said, gesturing with his hand like he was my sovereign lord and master. 'And forget it. Tea, coffee and pastries,' he said as he indicated the tray in front of him. 'Breakfast could be three hours away yet.' He got up from his chair and kissed Jane. 'Time for my shower.' He shook his head as he walked away. 'Weird child,' I heard him say, half under his breath.

'What was that all about?' Jane asked as she poured for the both of us.

'As I said. My life intruding into our wonderful holiday.'

'No the other bit?'

What, did she mean me begging for forgiveness? 'Um, I don't know. Never done that before. Am I forgiven? Christ I'm forever saying sorry to you two lately!'

She laughed. 'It's fine.'

'And Kelvin?'

'He said forget it so forget it. You could go wash his back for him, though. Sure that wouldn't hurt.'

Now she was at it as well. 'Ha, he's already asked. Said it was his turn to shower with me this morning.'

'Well it is, isn't it?'

'Oh, ha ha, you're getting as bad as him. And anyway,' I played along, 'we'd miss the flight,' I finished by sticking my tongue out.

I stayed where I was and grabbed at some food and made myself comfortable on the thick carpet. We ate and drank for a few silent moments until Kelvin called from the shower. 'Jane where's the shampoo?'

'Oh, I think I packed it by mistake.' She rolled her eyes and got to her feet. 'I'll get it.' Then she bent closer to me as she passed and whispered, 'We could have got the later flight?'

I stopped mid chew. Had to admit she had me there. One nil to Jane.

As I sat there chewing by myself a thought struck me. The client Kelvin had met last night? Didn't he mention that the deal, whatever it was, didn't go down? I wondered if that was my fault. Had I just cost them millions of pounds or something? I started to feel sick again. On top of that Kelvin had yet to take his pound of flesh about my imagined rape charge. I knew he would. I don't know which had me feeling worse, the thought that I may have soured his business deal by visibly and loudly getting drunk, or by shouting to all within earshot that he'd raped me whilst putting me to bed.

'Something wrong?' Jane asked as she came back into the room. She must have seen by the look on my face that something was.

I bit my lip. 'Did Kelvin's deal fall through because of me?'

'What? No!'

'Are you sure?'

'Yes. The guy wanted... I'll let Kelvin tell you when he's showered.'

I nodded. 'And has Kelvin mentioned what I accused him of in the lift?'

She looked confused.

'You know, what I imagined?'

'Oh, perhaps I'd better leave that to him, too.'

I gulped and chewed and swallowed, mechanically. My mind was elsewhere, my stomach and head in turmoil. Before I knew it I looked up and he was there in front of me, dressed but still wiping his hair with a towel.

'You on your knees again?' he asked. 'You'll make somebody a happy man one day.'

I had no idea what he meant. I was much too slow and anyway, my mind was full of other things. 'I owe you an apology, don't I?'

'What have you done now, I've only been in the shower a couple of minutes! You don't owe me an apology because you wouldn't come in and scrub my back, you know.'

'No, but I accused you of things, didn't I, and I'm sorry. Under other circumstances it could have been bad for you.'

'What is she on about?' he turned to Jane and asked.

'I accused you of... doing things whilst you were putting me to bed,' I said, lowering my eyes in shame as I said it.

'Well how do you know I didn't,' he shot back with a wink, and my mouth fell open.

'Because... well because... you wouldn't, would you?'

He barked a laugh but didn't reply, he just raised an eyebrow. 'Was I good, by the way?'

'Good?'

'You know, in bed?'

'Um...'

'Well that proves it. If I had you'd know.'

'Oh you arrogant bugger,' Jane accused, playfully. She turned to me. 'Thinks he's James Bond and the women drop their drawers and swoon for his charms whilst he performs for queen and country.'

'Well it's worked before and it worked with you, didn't it!'

I giggled despite myself and Jane placed her hands on her hips and faced him defiantly. Then she laughed.

'Eventually,' she conceded. 'More out of pity for your continuous whining!'

I snorted again.

'And I don't know what you're laughing at,' she said to me. 'Go on, ask about the client whilst I tidy up after him.'

With that she walked past him towards the bathroom and Kelvin tried to swat her behind as she walked past but she was wise to him and manoeuvred easily.

'The client?' he asked once she'd gone. 'What about him?'

I swallowed my last mouthful and looked up at him. My subconscious told me that I felt very comfortable on my knees before him. I don't know why, but I just did. I ignored the thought and pressed on. 'I just wondered if you lost the deal because of me getting drunk and the hotel complaining to him?'

'Oh, that? You really have got a persecution complex, haven't you?'

I went to open my mouth but stopped. Have I?

'For the record,' he continued as he poured himself another coffee. 'The client wanted something that I wasn't prepared to part with. OK, your behaviour did come up in conversation – broke the ice nicely, actually – but you had nothing to do with the deal failing.'

I visibly deflated with relief.

'He wanted my company,' he continued.

He wanted what? You to be with him, I thought stupidly.

'My capital C company,' he explained when he saw the confusion on my face. 'Offered top dollar, though, I must admit. Guess that in itself is a vote of confidence in that what I'm doing I'm doing right. He wouldn't have wanted SSI otherwise. He was *very* well informed; he'd certainly done his homework.'

'SSI?'

'Sound Systems Incorporated, soon to be Sound Systems International if I have my way. My company.'

'Oh!' The light came on finally. I was being very slow this morning. I blamed the alcohol.

Why not. You blame it for everything else!

'You weren't tempted at all?' I asked, more to look intelligent than anything else.

'Nope. Could have retired on what he offered, mind you, but then what would I have done?'

Ride your bike, drive your cars, go on holidays. Drink champagne all day. Ride Jane?

'No, I'm far from retirement age yet. I'm still young.'

It never ceased to amaze me how he and Jane thought they were still young when they were nearly twenty years older than me!

'Right, are you two finished,' Jane asked as she emerged from their bedroom. 'Friends again?'

'We never weren't friends,' Kelvin countered. 'Apart from in her confused and brandy addled little head.'

I stuck my tongue out at him again. Well he made me feel like a cheeky little girl all the time.

'Glad to hear it. Come on, I want to go to the Caribbean, not stay here chatting at your master's feet all day.'

My master? I guess it did look that way. The girl had a point!

Chapter Eight

I felt like a million dollars as we boarded the cruise liner. It was large but nowhere near the largest. Some of the others I'd seen on television were like tower blocks.

'I know what you're thinking,' Kelvin said to me. 'But this little ship was the best I could do at the last minute. Apologies and all that.'

'You're apologising? You're joking, right?'

'Oh, I'm sorry. I'd get on my knees but there's a queue behind us and I'm afraid I'd get trampled.'

I elbowed him in the ribs.

'Look at that,' said Jane excitedly.

We both followed her gaze and saw an aircraft carrier. 'Mission: Get me a ride on one of them,' she smiled.

'Aw come on. Like making the sun hotter wasn't good enough for you.'

She smiled and kissed him. 'You are right. I'm being greedy.'

As our queue snaked along I reflected on my day. I was in really high spirits and knew that nothing could bring me down.

We'd checked out of the hotel without a hitch, though I didn't know what kind of problem I was expecting. Nothing was said about my antics of the night before but I got the impression that everybody was looking at me. Whether they were or weren't I'm not sure, but I thought they were and I heard an innuendo and hint in every sentence. I felt I was a lone ant caught in the middle of the family dinner table. I couldn't wait to get to the car. I'd yearned for a pair of dark glasses to wear.

We checked in successfully for our flight though we were not allowed access to the first class lounge. This caused me to pout until Kelvin explained that it was only first class international travellers who got that concession. I felt short changed, so Kelvin promised he would try to arrange a champagne breakfast on the plane. He succeeded, of course, though we got some strange looks from other travellers, though some later joined in. I was beginning to learn that it was never too early in the day for champagne.

Kelvin remarked that *he* felt short changed as we disembarked. 'Was expecting a fashion show. What have you got against American Airlines uniforms?'

We collected our baggage and were out of the airport by one o clock with a couple of hours to spare before we were due to board ship. Kelvin arranged for our luggage to be stored and we got a whistle stop tour of Miami with a little bit of shopping thrown in. Towards the end I left them in an open air cafe and stole away to do some shopping of my own. When they said they would come I told them that they needed time to themselves, as a couple without me in tow. They objected but I'd made up my mind and wasn't taking no for an answer. I had a mission of my own to achieve.

I bought myself a couple of light dresses, two pairs of shorts, two short skirts and a selection of tops. Then I got more underwear and a sun hat. Realising that Jane didn't have one I bought one for her too. I needed some light footwear so Jane got a pair of them as well, so that was half my mission done. I had decided, you see, to buy them something, anything, just to repay them for their kindnesses. And what the hell, that's what credit cards were for, yeah? I'd pay it off on the never never.

But what to get for Kelvin? Buying for girls was easy, I was a girl! But blokes, especially a special, unique bloke like Kelvin was going to prove difficult.

Self tattooing kit?

He didn't smoke, so a fancy lighter or something was out of the question. A tie? We were off to warmer climes, for Christ sake. An item of clothing? Hardly, that was Jane's job if she wanted it. The last thing I wanted was him modelling boxer shorts I'd just bought him. Jewellery? OK, that had possibilities, but what? He had a watch but apart from that didn't seem the decorative type. He wore no rings so I didn't want to queer the pitch there. What do you buy the man who has everything?

A box to put it in?

OK, well he was musically inclined, that was a clue.

Harmonica?

What could I do, buy him a guitar or some other instrument? He had all of them.

Time was getting on and I was starting to panic. I'd promised them I'd only be an hour and I only had twenty minutes left and I had bags to carry and I had to remember what kerbside cafe I'd left them at and get back before they launched a search party.

'Can I help you, miss, you seem lost?'

The shop assistant was oriental but American sounding. Very pretty girl.

'I'm rubbish buying for men,' I confided.

'British?'

'Um, yes,' I said absent-mindedly. I wondered if that made a difference.

'Is he a relative, a friend or that special man in your life?' she continued.

Good question, I asked myself. Theoretically he could be all three soon. 'He is certainly the most special man I know,' I opted for.

'Then something passionate, perhaps?'

'Um...' What could I tell her? No his wife, de facto, has that covered? 'Problem is he has everything.'

'Don't all men. Cake and eat it.'

True enough. This girl was smart!

'So what's he like? Give me a clue. I've found it's often easier from the outside looking in.'

'Well, he's funny and smart and quick witted and has a dry sense of humour; he's always catching me out, wondering whether he's joking or not. He's generous, plays most if not all musical instruments and can sing like a canary.'

'Does he work out?'

'You mean in the gym? Body to die for.'

'Does he cook?'

I thought. Does he? 'I don't know. Not so far.'

'Control freak?'

'Um, he's in control. Don't know if that makes him a control freak. He makes the plans and prepares the surprises, champagne, holidays, always trying to buy things for me, throwing money at me, always saying he'll drag me into the shower.'

Where did that come from?

'Is he good looking?'

'Yeah, though older than me.'

'Rich?'

'Yeah, I think so.'

'Well I think I have just the thing, then, miss?'

'You do?'

'Yes, my card!'

How's that going to... I looked down at her face – she was slightly shorter than me – and then the laughing started and I leant against her and she joined in.

'You British are known for your sense of humour,' she said as we gained control of ourselves.

'Thank you, though you did pretty well yourself.' I looked down at her name badge. 'Crista.'

'You're welcome.'

'Aneese, my name's Aneese.'

'That's a beautiful name. I think it means sweet tasting woman.'

'It does?'

'I'm studying ancient languages at college here in Miami. I'm only a first year student, so I could be wrong.'

'And what does Crista mean?'

'That my mom and dad tried very hard to integrate when they arrived here from Vietnam.'

I laughed again. 'You are a scream,' I said. 'But it's not helping me select a gift. Hang on, what's that?'

Something behind her had caught my attention. I almost pushed her over in my haste to get to it. It was a picture of a handsome, long haired angel standing on stormy, angry looking purple and blue clouds with a full moon in the sky. And he was all muscles and tattoos and he held in one arm a heavy chain, ready as a weapon, and in the other arm he held a scared, but beautiful, long haired woman who was dressed in a torn robe, whom it was obvious he was protecting from whatever horror was off camera. And to cap it all, leaning against them both was a guitar which reflected the moonlight. The picture itself was sunken into a marble plinth, designed to look like it had been planted in the rock like some Arthurian sword in the stone. It ticked all the boxes.

'What is it?'

'What, that piece of junk? It's a CD cover in glass.'

A CD? It was too big. It was more like... Yes, my dad had some old records. It was an LP record cover hardened and sealed in hard plastic.

She lifted it and nearly dropped it. It was quite heavy.

'How much is it?' I asked, suddenly excited.

She carefully turned it around. 'It hasn't got a tag.'

'I'll give you a hundred dollars?'

She bit her lip. 'I should really check how much it costs.'

'Two hundred. I'll pay with my credit card. If it turns out to be any more just bill me for the rest.'

I could see her mulling over my proposal.

'Please, Crista, I must have it. It's him, don't you see?'

'What, your man?' She turned it around with difficulty and took a closer look. 'Did I mention my card?'

I smiled despite myself. 'Please, I must have it, and time is short. I have a boat to catch.'

'And if it costs less?'

'Then keep the change.' I could see from the look on her face that she was weakening. 'But I'll need it engraved?'

She was still considering it. Come on, damn it!

'Bill?' she shouted. A voice answered her from somewhere in the back of the shop. 'Can you do a quick engraving job?'

I sighed in relief.

'Sure, but how quick depends on how many letters.'

She looked at me. 'How many letters?'

'What?' I hadn't even thought of that yet. 'Um, My Angels, No! Make it How I See You.'

"Bill" appeared. He was old and grizzled and wore a sweat stained and faded baseball cap. There were white faded letters on it, intertwined together, but the hat was so old that I couldn't see what they were. He had an unlit cigarette hanging from his mouth. 'What's your name, honey?'

'Aneese. Make it "What I See When I look At You. Aneese." Can you do that?'

'Sure, but it'll take a while.'

'How long?'

'An hour.'

'I don't have an hour.' Just then I heard a ship's horn sound.

'She has a boat to catch,' Crista offered.

Bill looked all thoughtful and the cigarette miraculously moved from one side of his mouth to the other. 'How about "How I See You. Aneese"?'

'Perfect. How long?'

The butt moved again. 'Twenty minutes?'

'Fifteen?' I'd still be five minutes late getting back but it was close enough. I'd get down on my knees and beg for forgiveness. Kelvin was a real stickler for time.

'Pay the lady,' Bill said as he retreated to the back of the store. 'I've got the album on CD if you want it, too,' he shouted over his shoulder.

'Wait, you have?'

'Sure. Jim Steinman, the one and only.'

'I'll give you fifty?' Another box ticked. Kelvin was going to be tickled pink even though he probably had the album laying around somewhere.

'Shit, you can have it for ten bucks,' he said as he carried my gift to the back of the store. 'Here Crista, can you get it from my truck out back? I got some engraving to do.'

I saw movement out of the corner of my eye and flinched. Crista caught the set of keys that Bill had thrown.

'I can't leave the store,' she said, looking at me. 'You go.'

'You go,' I countered. 'I don't know his truck. If somebody comes in I'll keep an eye on them until you return.'

She thought about it briefly but then she moved. She was back in a few minutes and thankfully nobody had come in whilst she was gone. She handed me the CD case. It was greasy and cracked slightly.

'Here let me clean that up for you,' she said.

She worked on it for a few minutes and when she gave it back it was in a much cleaner condition, though the case was cracked and chipped. Some present, I thought, though I knew he'd appreciate it.

'It still plays sweet,' shouted Bill from the back. 'Not a scratch.

Don't let looks deceive you!'

Looks were everything and so were memories. I remembered the dream I'd had before we came to New York, of Kelvin as an angel flying across the Atlantic with me and Jane safe and content in his arms. I couldn't have painted it better than this.

I gave my credit card to Crista and crossed my fingers as I entered the pin number. I'd paid for my other purchases with the cash from my stash. 'And give this to Bill after I've gone,' I said, and I pushed fifty dollars into her hand. She went to object but I shushed her. 'You have no idea what this means to me.'

She smiled as she thanked me. 'And I suppose you want it wrapped?'

I nodded. 'Quickly if you could.'

True to his word Bill finished in fifteen minutes and I hugged and kissed them both as I hastily retreated.

It took me twenty minutes to get back to the cafe carrying my shopping and trying to back track and I was later than late. As I saw them in the distance they got to their feet and started to walk away. It was only by shouting and waving frantically that I managed to get their attention. I almost tripped as I speeded up.

'Sorry, sorry, sorry,' I said. 'It'll be worth it, you'll see.'

He looked at my bags. I could tell he was miffed. 'Yeah, it'll be worth it seeing you in your new hat.'

What if I were wearing only the hat? 'Are we too late?' I asked. 'Can we still make it?'

'With luck,' he answered. 'If we get a cab straight away and traffic is kind. Remember we have to pick up our luggage yet.'

'Give me some of those bags,' said Jane.

At least she wasn't miffed. Kelvin walked a small distance away, looking for a cab.

'Timing is a squaddie thing,' she said as she rolled her eyes. 'It's his worst character trait. He can't stand anybody making him late.'

'I can still hear you, you know, I'm not deaf.'

Jane rolled her eyes again as I lowered my voice as we sorted and adjusted what we were carrying. 'Can I kiss him to apologise?'

'Huh, you've never asked permission before, why start now?'

I blushed but smiled my thanks.

'Taxi is here. Quickly now.'

'Yes, Master,' I said as I walked past him to the already opened boot. *Trunk.*

Whatever.

This driver was on the ball.

Jane squashed past Kelvin as he held the door open for us. As I followed I felt a short sharp impact on my backside and I yelped and glared at him. What was this, Daddy smacking naughty daughter or something else? He glared back, daring me, but I backed down after only half a second. As I made myself comfortable between them and Kelvin pulled the door closed I saw Jane silently laughing, her shoulders lifting up and down but her lips firmly shut. I play scowled in her direction, pouted and rubbed my injured bum cheek.

But traffic was kind and we got to our luggage quickly and Kelvin and the cab driver left the car to get it.

'What did you buy?' Jane asked.

'This and that,' I answered. 'Got us both a sun hat and pair of summer footwear.'

'Oh, you shouldn't have.'

'And then something quite special for you both. You're going to love it, I just know you are!'

'Hey, you're really wired. What's got into you?'

'You'll see. I can't wait to give it to you!'

'Well you have to smooth the master's feathers first.'

'No sweat, got it covered. Remember the motorbike?'

She paused as she recalled. 'Ah, yes.'

I turned and winked at her.

'What *has* got into you?'

'I'm just excited, that's all. Aren't you?'

'Well I've kissed Kelvin before, actually.'

I paused and looked confused. What was she on about?

'Ha, got you!' she said.

'Damn it, you and him between you, I've really gotta watch myself!'

We were still laughing and joking when I felt Kelvin sit down beside me. As the driver shut his door I winked at Jane, got up and plonked myself down on Kelvin's lap and placed my arms around his shoulders.

I placed one of my knees over the other, the effect making my skirt rise halfway up my thigh. With satisfaction I saw his eyes open wide. I'd surprised him.

'Oh great and worthy master,' I played. 'Please forgive your little girl for being late. She is very sorry but hopes that you in your infinite wisdom will understand that there was a very good reason for my tardiness, which you will see when you realise what I crawled over broken glass to buy for both of you.'

I stared into his eyes and awaited a response whilst Jane guffawed. I saw his eyes drop, guessing he was looking at my legs and imagining where they went.

'Your knees don't look like they're bleeding to me?'

I was lost for words for a little while. 'Good point,' I finally conceded.

Now for the big guns. I closed the distance between us and our lips met and as usual my heart began to race. I felt him try to pull back and when I opened my eyes he was looking at Jane sideways, our lips still touching but his firmly closed. I flicked my eyes in her direction too, just in time to see her smilingly nod her assent to him and for the first time I remembered, he kissed me back, put his arms around me and pulled me close.

There was no doubt this time. It was daylight, I was sober and this was definitely not a dream. I felt his tongue probing and my lips opened to let him in. I gasped slightly as I felt his tongue brush mine. I pushed against him even harder and used one of my hands on the back of his head to draw him even closer to me as my tongue started to get active. I felt the unfamiliar and almost forgotten pangs of arousal and yearning rise up in my stomach, or was it just below that? We broke once for air but then started again. The second time we broke I was breathing heavy and so was he. He leaned towards me to give me a final quick peck on the lips. I took a deep breath and sighed.

'You're forgiven,' he said softly.

'Bravo,' said Jane, clapping her hands quickly.

'But now you gotta kiss Jane too.'

I opened my mouth to object.

'Well you nearly made her miss the boat too?'

Fair enough, I could play dare. I slid off his knee and on to hers and caught the driver's eyes in the rear-view mirror. Whatever else we were doing this trip we were certainly giving the drivers a good time. She made a face as my weight came to rest on her. She wasn't built as solidly as Kelvin.

'Oh great and worthy mistress...'

'Just cut the crap and pucker up,' Jane laughed.

And what could I do, I was committed. It was a dare, surely, and I was very good at playing the Nervous game. I moved towards her expecting her to break away at any second. Was she expecting the same from me? But I didn't – I wouldn't – but would she? We went closer and closer and I told myself that I was not backing down. Our lips finally tentatively touched and I saw that both of us had our eyes open. Then she smiled, almost daring me to continue, and pushed her lips to press against mine. I did the same and then saw that her eyes closed and I followed suit. Then I felt her tongue experimentally touch my lips and I gasped in shock and tried to hide it. She was really going for it.

I will not lose this game, I told myself. I will not be nervous first!

Time to up the ante. Kissing her was hardly unpleasant so taking it up a notch would hardly be a chore. She had very soft lips – softer than Kelvin's – and smelt like... like a woman.

My mind screamed at me, telling me to stop, that what I was doing was wrong, but I found my body vetoing it as I responded. Somewhere in the darker recesses of my subconscious I told myself that it was smoke and mirrors, conditioning almost. Only a few moments before I'd been responding to Kelvin's kiss and now my body still thought I was kissing a man and was responding the same. It would help me win the game.

Eventually the kissing stopped and I opened my eyes and saw that Jane was opening hers too. I was breathing heavily, but slowly, and so was she by the look.

'I've never done that before,' she whispered. 'Not like that.'

'Nor I,' I said, hearing a voice that didn't sound like mine.

'But it was nice, very nice,' she continued. 'Wouldn't mind trying it again sometime?'

I wordlessly nodded and then Kelvin's clapping broke the spell and time returned to normal and I started to be aware of other sounds and other things apart from Jane and her luscious, soft lips.

'Bravo, indeed,' he said. 'Looks like your forgiveness is unanimous!'

'Ah, thank you,' I whispered as I removed myself from her lap and sat down between them. I felt each of them take one of my hands and realised they were smiling. I felt myself smiling too and I held their hands tight and they squeezed right on back. I felt Kelvin's lips on my cheek and then Jane did the same and I smiled. Neither of us said another word for the remainder of the twenty-minute journey. It ended far too quickly, our pleasant bubble burst.

But while it continued I realised I was at war with myself. I was like a broken record, the scratch causing the needle to continuously jump to the beginning of the loop. I felt close to these people, very, very close, and I was numb, almost glassy eyed. I had to remind myself to blink. I kept replaying in my mind what had happened and telling myself that it was wrong (but it made me feel like this), but it's wrong (but it made me feel like this), but it's wrong (but it made me feel this *GOOD*). My heartbeat had still not returned to normal ten minutes later.

I snuck a glance at them both. They were both quietly looking out of the taxi window. I remembered they were each holding one of my hands. I gently squeezed Jane's hand and she squeezed back without looking at me. Then I did the same to Kelvin and he looked my way, smiled and squeezed back. I returned his smile before shyly lowering my eyes. I guessed they were feeling and thinking the same as me, but what was I actually thinking? Was it just high spirits going too far and they regretted it? Was that what I was thinking?

And then we saw the boats and we girls had started to get excited and time blurred as the taxi stopped, our luggage was taken away and we'd commenced the boarding process. During this time we stayed holding each other's hands as much as possible, it just seemed natural. Kelvin was his normal composed self but, of course, this was his plan and he knew what was coming. There was so much to see, so much to take in. I don't think my eyes were still for a second. I guessed that to casual onlookers we looked like a happy family experiencing the beginnings of the cruise and being caught up in the moment. Occasionally Jane or Kelvin would reach out and hug and plant small kisses on me and, indeed, each other. I found myself doing the same.

After Jane had commented on the aircraft carrier we set foot on board our ship for the first time. Kelvin gave us both a card. 'This is our room card,' he said. 'It will get us into our rooms and if you need anything then just show it to the server and the cost will be charged to our account. Don't lose it,' he admonished.

I looked at the card. 'What could I possibly need that you two haven't already provided?' I asked. It was more of a spoken thought than anything. I mean, how much do cruises cost? It must be thousands of pounds per person, surely? That got me thinking. I hadn't even thought about the cost. Very unlike me.

In response to my question Kelvin theatrically clicked his fingers and a waiter appeared with a full tray. 'We'll take one each, please,' he said and he handed a glass of champagne to both us girls. I watched as he showed the waiter his card and the number was noted. 'Cheers!'

'Cheers! Champagne on tap. Don't think I'm going to be sober for the rest of the week!'

'Nor me,' said Jane. 'And what a week it'll be.'

Kelvin guided us towards the rails and I looked at the scene before us as I leaned and sipped my chilled champagne.

This was like something from a film, I thought. Everything was here: the band, the ticker tape, the waving and cheerios to the people below. There was a light, cooling breeze this far up (and I'd thought our ship small!) but it was still hot even after its effect. My skin was so warm I felt I could cook toast on it. Another few moments in this heat and I might faint. I felt a hand find mine and turned my head to find Jane to my left.

'This is wonderful, isn't it?' she said without looking at me.

'It's a dream,' I answered and I found a lump forming in my throat.

'You OK?' Jane asked.

I nodded as I felt tears start to form in my eyes. 'It's just that if somebody had told me I would be on a cruise ship in a week on the way to the Caribbean after visiting New York I'd have told them to see a shrink, but here I am. Is it like this all the time with you two?'

She snorted. 'Hardly. We've spent most of the last four years getting me back on my feet and his company off the ground. This is our first trip, actually.'

Four years? What kind of a mess had she been in?

'I'm glad you're here to share it with us,' she continued.

I smiled and swallowed and laid my head on her shoulder. 'I must have done something very good to deserve you two.'

'Aww, well whatever it is, keep doing it.'

I squeezed her hand. 'Speaking of which,' I said. 'Where is the master?'

'Oh, he's just making sure everything is all right. Said he'd be back in a jiff.'

He was back a few moments later carrying hats for us. They were the ones I'd bought earlier. The words *control freak* jumped into my head but I ignored them. He was just looking after us, that's all, he was controlling for our benefit, not his. Most women would call it being attentive.

'Thanks, Jack,' Jane said as she accepted the hat without a second thought. I guessed she was used to him thinking of everything for her.

'How did you know?' I asked incredulously.

'Warm day, hardly difficult. I swear I didn't look at any of your other purchases.'

I kissed him softly on the cheek. 'Never crossed my mind that you would.' I took his arm and pulled him until he stood between us at the rail. As Jane noticed us she slipped her arm through his and leant her head on his shoulders. I kept holding onto him. I was so happy I was actually tingling.

'This is wonderful,' Jane said wistfully. 'Thank you so very much for this and... everything.'

'Anything for my ladies.'

He'd included me in his answer. I smiled, though I knew he'd probably meant the singular. I imagined that Jane was thanking him for more than just the trip. Her life and the last four happy years, perhaps?

'Shall we explore?' Kelvin asked as he deftly secured three more drinks from a passing waiter. I thought it was orange juice but it tasted funny. 'Bucks fizz,' he explained. 'Champagne and orange juice. We can stay mellow and hydrate at the same time.'

'Good call, sir,' Jane said as we turned from the rail and started walking slowly along the deck.

We were as one, still holding onto each other as we trod our path. It meant that other people had to walk around us or get out of the way, but I didn't care. Most were by the rail, anyway, waving their goodbyes.

The ship may have been small compared to the larger ones I'd seen but it was large in itself. We occasionally stopped and poked our head in when something caught our attention. I saw beauty salons, barbers for the gentlemen, bars, restaurants, basic self-service eateries, more bars, a casino, shops of every kind, pools, and mini golf courses. Was there anything this ship didn't have? We didn't linger too long in any one place. Did I mention there were bars?

'This is just the recce,' Kelvin had said. 'We've plenty of time to explore fully.'

I didn't know what recce meant but I think it meant a quick look-see.

By the time we'd arrived back to where we'd started, we were on our third glass and had eaten some savoury pastries that Kelvin had acquired from somewhere. I was grateful for the food and determined that I would not drink without eating again and as for my "never drinking again" well there was always after the holiday.

'We're moving,' Jane said.

To be honest I hadn't noticed. It was only now that I saw the slight distance between the shore and our boat that I realised. I hadn't even felt the engines spooling up like I had when I'd gone on a ferry with Richard. This was smooth sailing indeed.

'We have to go to our cabins soon,' Kelvin said. 'They like us to start the lifeboat drill in our cabins so that we know the way to our muster point.'

I started to ask a question but a tannoy crackled and came to life and invited us to go and find our cabins. Kelvin, right as always.

Everybody was happy and in high spirits and it was contagious. For some, like us, this was their first time on a cruise ship and the excitement was palpable. The old sweats, the ones who had been before, were obvious as they had an air of quiet superiority about them. They seemed to know where they were going and loudly proclaimed it so.

I was amazed by the cross-section of people, not only of nationalities but the ages of the passengers. I'd always thought that cruises were for the elderly who had retired or the rich who could afford it, but there were quite a lot of family groups with children of all ages. I smiled and took it all in as a big adventure as I observed everything and tried to count the number of languages and accents I was hearing. English was, of course, the prominent language but spoken in so many different ways. And everybody was *so* polite as we edged and barged passed each other as we tried to find our rooms.

'Do you know where you're going?' I asked without thinking.

Kelvin sighed theatrically and shook his head and Jane laughed and tutted. 'Don't you ever learn?'

'Sorry, Master,' I said and kissed him on the cheek. 'I am young but I will learn.'

'Here we are,' he said eventually. 'Deck eight room eight-four-five-five.' He put his card in the slot built into the door handle and pushed against the door. He stepped back and gestured for us ladies to enter. 'Perhaps I should carry you both over the threshold?'

Jane snorted and I gave him an odd look. Was this the honeymoon suite? What was he on about?

But it was a suite, and a large one. It wasn't a patch on our hotel in New York, of course, but I could see it was luxuriously adorned. I ran to the large curtains and swept them back on their runners. We even had our own balcony. Jane busied herself opening doors and generally being nosey and I tingled with excitement even more.

'This is great, Jack. Well done.'

He smiled at how pleased we were. 'Well, I opted for this suite because it was the only one left with a balcony available at short notice. A cancellation. Somebody's loss, our gain.'

'It's fantastic. Everything is!' I said excitedly and I hugged them both. 'I'm so spoilt by you two. Thank you isn't enough. How can I ever repay you?'

They shared a look. 'And you are so worth it,' Kelvin said. 'But you don't have to repay us in any way. Believe me, you just being here is enough.'

'There's only one bed,' I said without thinking. It was meant to be a private thought.

'No, this is a suite, so there will be at least one other room somewhere, and even if there wasn't then there'll be fold out beds or whatever, just like a caravan. We're in a ship. Space is limited.'

'OK.' Guess I'll be changing into my jimjams in the bathroom, though, if there was only the one room. There was a bathroom, wasn't there?

The tannoy crackled again and we were invited to muster. It was a formality and therefore boring and what's more there was no champagne on offer. What kind of way to run a ship is that! The whole thing lasted about twenty minutes and then we were released back to our cabins. Kelvin left us briefly and caught up to us as we turned the corner into our corridor. He had an ice bucket, champagne and three glasses. Jane and I cheered.

'Oh, look our baggage has arrived,' said Jane as we approached our door.

'Oh, great, wait til I show you!' I'd forgotten about my present for them until I'd seen the suitcases and shopping bags.

As Kelvin struggled with the ice bucket and slipped his card into the door's lock, I rummaged through my bags and found what I was looking for.

'Can't it wait until the cases are in and the champagne is poured?' he asked.

'No,' I answered. 'Well actually, yes. Champagne would be good.'

Kelvin filled the glasses and then brought the luggage in from the hall. I offered to help but Jane just stood aside and sipped from her glass. It was obvious that she was used to being looked after by Kelvin and that I wasn't, but I got the hint when he play growled at me and wouldn't let me lift a thing.

'To us,' Kelvin said as he lifted his glass to his lips.

'To us,' we chorused.

'And to a lovely cruise,' I added. 'Now wait til you see what I got for you.'

I put down my almost empty glass and saw Kelvin top us all up. As I carefully manoeuvred their present out of the bag there was a knock on the door and Kelvin took delivery of two more bottles of champagne.

'Trying to get us drunk so early?' Jane asked.

'For the journey,' Kelvin answered. 'And anyway I have a nice buzz at the moment and I don't want to lose it. I feel relaxed and comfortable and ready for the cruise. Do you know how long it's been since I've been on holiday with two lovely ladies?'

'I hope you've never been on holiday with two lovely ladies,' Jane replied, deadpan.

'Good point, well presented,' he countered.

I knew what he meant about the buzz because I felt the same. I'd felt the buzz start to fade during the muster formality but it was back now. OK, we'd drank a couple of glasses of champagne each but we'd eaten something too. It wasn't as if it was the stronger brandy we'd been knocking back. Do it properly and you could drink champagne all day.

'For you both,' I said as I struggled to hold the heavy package out to them.

Jane accepted it and as I took my hand away she almost dropped it. 'What on earth?'

Kelvin was there in a moment, of course, and held it and tested its weight. 'An artillery shell. Thank you, Aneese, I've always wanted one of them.'

'It's not an...' Damn it, he almost had me again. 'Go on open it.'

Kelvin held it in place and Jane tentatively unwrapped it, the thick paper crackling loudly as she pried it open.

'It's just to say thank you for all you two have done for me in the last week. I don't deserve any of this and I can't remember being so happy. I still don't believe this is happening!'

Finally their present was exposed and Jane looked at it, frowned quizzically and looked up at Kelvin with a raised eyebrow.

'I got it engraved,' I said excitedly, then watched as Kelvin turned it so that they could both see.

'How I see you,' they both read together. 'That's how you see us?' Jane then asked.

I smiled and nodded. Then I started to panic. What if they didn't like it, had I insulted them in some way? Then Jane turned to face me and I saw that her eyes were filled with tears and she was biting her lip.

'It's perfect,' she simply said and then she reached out for me and we hugged as relief flowed through me. I saw Kelvin nodding as he smiled.

'Thank you, Aneese,' was all he said as he reached for me, but I could tell that he loved it, too. He hugged me so tight that my breath caught. Was he trying to break my spine?

When he released me I saw Jane wiping at her eyes with the end of a finger. She cleared her throat as she did it and I realised I'd done good.

'That is no doubt the best present anybody has ever bought us,' she said as she sniffed.

I looked at Kelvin who just nodded, tight lipped. Kelvin speechless? Worth every penny!

He cleared his throat as well. 'We, too, have gifts.'

'No I haven't finished,' I said as I rummaged in the bag again and brought out the CD. 'This is the actual CD that the picture is based on. See?'

I handed the scratched and broken CD case to him and he turned it over and started to read. '*Bad For Good* by Jim Steinman? Never heard of it.'

You haven't? YES!

'Heard of Jim Steinman, of course, who hasn't?'

It was a hypothetical question but Jane and I both raised our hands.

'He wrote *Bat Out of Hell*, amongst other things, the whole album. He also wrote that Bonnie Tyler classic, 'Total Eclipse of the Heart'.'

Well I'd heard of that, who hadn't? Jane nodded, too.

'But I didn't know he'd done this.' He turned it over and read with interest. '1979? Where was I in 1979, how come I missed this? I knew they fell out after *Bat Out of Hell* was released. Were these songs meant to be for the next Meatloaf album but he used them himself?'

Jane and I just looked at each other. It was obvious to me that Kelvin was thinking aloud. 'Well done,' she stage whispered. 'You beat the music man.'

'She certainly did,' he admitted. 'Does it play?'

'Sweet, I'm told.'

'Cool, looking forward to that,' he said as he looked around the room. I guessed he was looking for somewhere to play it.

'Later, Kelvin, eh?' Jane said. 'You mentioned we had gifts?'

'So I did,' he said and then he grabbed us both for a group hug. 'That was very thoughtful,' he said to me. 'We're touched.'

It was my turn to fill up with tears. 'Well you're always thinking about me, both of you.'

'You don't know the half of it,' answered Jane cryptically. 'And now we have gifts for you.'

We broke apart and I wiped my eyes. 'You don't need to buy me anything, you two. Haven't you done enough?'

Kelvin handed me my champagne glass as Jane opened one of the suitcases. When she stood she had a medium sized box in her hands.

'First there's this.'

First? I put down my half empty glass and accepted the box. Was it a shoe box, I asked myself? Sure enough it contained a pair of shoes: golden shoes. I remembered her buying them. 'They were for me? I was there when you bought them. Didn't realise they were for me!'

'And this,' she said as she held out another, smaller package.

It wasn't wrapped, either, unless you count the thin crepe-like paper it was wrapped in. I saw straight away that it was a small clutch bag, what the Americans called a purse.

'Thank you,' I said as I moved forward to hug her. I couldn't remember how much the shoes had cost but I knew they weren't cheap. I seemed to recall that it was triple figures. She didn't let me hug her for long and, as she gently pushed me away, she accepted a large box which Kelvin had magic-ed from somewhere.

'And there's this,' she said as she took the large, flat, white box and handed it to me. It wasn't heavy at all, I noticed, if her handling of it was anything to go by.

'What the hell, what have you done?' I asked as I accepted the box and laid it on the table. I put the shoes and purse to one side and tentatively started to flip the lid off. 'If there's a fur coat in here, I'll be mad,' I said, but I knew I wouldn't be.

'So will I,' smiled Jane.

I saw them smile at each other in anticipation and Kelvin moved forward and slipped his arm around her waist. Neither of them took their eyes off me the whole time.

The lid came off and I saw the same sort of packaging that the purse had been wrapped in. I moved the paper aside and spied something gold, gold fabric. A memory popped into my brain from seemingly a long time ago. It was like when somebody held the door open for you. You'd thank them but you wouldn't even recognise them a few minutes later if asked.

But this was more familiar than that.

I moved more of the protective layer away and then it revealed itself. A dress, a golden dress that I'd had to use all my reserves of strength to force myself *not* to buy less than a week before as Jane and I had shopped prior to our departure for New York. *The* dress. I knew Jane had clocked me looking at it, she'd even taken a look herself. I guessed at the time that she had liked it too but just hadn't bought it out of respect for me.

But how? The shop had been closing and was going to be closed for a week for some sort of refurbishment, not opening for another week. And we'd flown on Tuesday. How did they get this?

This time I totally filled up with tears. 'How did you?' I stopped as I put my hand to my mouth in an attempt to hold in my tears. I failed. 'Damn you both,' I said as the tears began to fall and Jane reached for me and folded me into her arms. I sobbed with abandon onto her shoulder and felt Kelvin come near.

'Don't cry. Have we done something wrong?' he asked softly.

Men, they didn't know a thing!

'Fuck you,' I managed to say, but then I reached out and hugged him, crying on his shoulder, too.

'Go try it on,' Jane said softly. 'We want to see you in it.'

I nodded and cried and sniffed and pulled myself away from him as Jane pointed behind me to the bed. I went to move away but she held me back. 'Don't forget these,' she said as she handed me the shoes and the purse.

I was still sobbing as I placed the box on the bed. I quickly undid my dress and went to shimmy out of it. 'Don't look,' I said over my shoulder.

'You're shy all of a sudden?' Kelvin said. 'You weren't shy last night coming into our room in just your bra and knickers.'

I'd forgotten about that, was that only yesterday? I blushed slightly. 'No it's just that I don't want you to see it until it's on me,' I half lied.

'Quite right,' said Jane. 'Come on, you, turn around,'

I waited until they had and then reached out for the dress box, but I stopped myself. I searched for and found a box of tissues on one of the bedside cabinets and started to clean myself up. There was no way I was getting tears and snot on my new dress.

My dress, my *new* dress. When had I even treated myself to any new clothes? OK, there was before I'd been to Magaluf but I'd bought rags for one time use, certainly nothing like this. In fact I'd never owned anything like this in my whole life. I smiled and sniffed. Play your cards right, girl, and this could be the first of many, the more mercenary part of me said.

Any why not, I thought as I changed? Why the fucking hell not? I deserve it, don't I? All I have to do is be the preened and prim and proper surrogate daughter and be company for Mummy Bear. OK, riding the pony on Daddy-o's knee might be a problem, all things considered, but I'd grit my teeth and bear it.

Grit your teeth, my arse!

OK, so kissing Kelvin was fun. Come to mention kissing Jane was bearable, too, albeit a bit weird.

I needed a break, no, I *deserved* a break after what I had been through lately. Richard leaving me, all our plans going by the board, the heartache, the loneliness, the "Yes, Mr Carswell", through gritted teeth, the drinking wine alone at night and then wondering how come it was Sunday evening already and I had work in the morning? No, life had finally dealt me a winning hand I wasn't going to let it go.

'What's taking you?' I heard Kelvin say from behind me.

I heard a slap. 'Ignore him. Take as long as you like.'

Quickly, and with a growing sense of excitement, I finished cleaning myself up, stripped quickly down to my undies (stopping briefly to check that their eyes were averted first) and stepped into the dress. I looked for a mirror and found one aback a dressing table and smoothed the silky soft material over my stomach as I took in the view. Hell, I'd fancy myself in this.

How should I wear it? Was I demure or was I the raunch today? Better play safe and go with demure, the screen goddess look. I wore it full length which meant I didn't have to tuck the rest of the material away into the belt. The integral shoulder straps I wore loose over my shoulders rather than high up on my collar bone.

It fitted, of course, as did the shoes. I wondered if Kelvin had chosen me purely because I resembled Jane so much in size? I mean, did he know Jane so well that he could judge my size just by looking? Richard didn't even know what size shoes I wore, never mind bra or dress size or anything else.

Eventually I was ready and I gathered myself at the foot of the bed. I took a deep breath and then smiled even though I was trying my best to play it cool. I gulped. Why was I feeling so nervous? I cleared my throat and walked a few steps towards them. On cue they turned around.

'Oh my,' I heard Jane say.

'Oh my indeed,' Kelvin echoed. 'What have we created?'

'Stop it,' I blushed and gushed.

Jane walked towards me and looked me up and down from various angles whilst Kelvin stayed where he was and wolf whistled. 'Give us a twirl, then,' he coaxed and I found myself complying. I felt like I was on the Paris catwalk and my confidence started to soar as I walked and twirled and generally put on a show.

'Not tight anywhere?' Jane asked.

'No, not a bit.'

'And the shoulders?'

'Not restrictive at all, but if I breathe in, I have the feeling it may fall down.'

'No, your boobs will take care of that, and is it heavy?'

'No, it's like wearing air, honestly. Do you want to try it?'

'No, it's yours and your alone.'

'We can share. I wouldn't mind, honest.'

She shook her head.

Whilst we were talking shop Kelvin was just looking on admiring the view. I tried to compose myself when I saw him pointing his phone at me but it was no use. When it flashed my smile was so wide it hurt and I felt tears of happiness well up again.

'Thank you so much,' I managed to say before I felt the urge to jam my lips together in an attempt not to go all gooey again.

'It was her idea,' Kelvin said, indicating Jane.

'Well you approved and organised it all and paid the bill. It was a joint effort.'

I was lost for words. Eventually I found my tongue. 'I'm touched and flattered,' was all I could manage. Kelvin handed me another full glass of champagne. 'You trying to get me drunk?' I joked.

'Yep, so we can have our wicked way with you. Bet you look fantastic out of that dress?'

I saw Jane catch his eye and thought she was going to tell him off – well there's a first time for everything. She playfully slapped him often enough, I guessed that passed for a telling off, though it never seemed to stop him. I felt so wonderful that I didn't care, and I could always push back.

'Well, you two keep on buying the dresses and the champagne and you can do what the hell you like!'

'You hear that, Jane?' Kelvin answered without missing a beat. 'What do you say? You up for some fun?'

I saw her mouth open but she caught herself. 'Sure, why not.'

Oh I get it, I told myself. We've played the dare game before only this morning. 'Bring it on,' I said as I put down my champagne glass. Or was it the champagne that said it? What the hell. I really *was* so happy I didn't care. Or at least I thought I wouldn't.

They both approached me, Kelvin from the front and Jane from one side. I folded my arms in defiance but Kelvin grabbed my wrists softly and forced my arms down to my side as I looked defiantly back at him. He brought his lips close to mine but I cocked my head at the last minute and moved my lips away, raising an eyebrow playfully as I did. I felt Jane close by.

An idea came to me. I raised my nose and looked down at him like he was somebody I'd never deign to speak to, like he was the footman and I was the queen. Then I removed my wrists from his grasp and turned to face Jane. I'll show him, who needs him! He could do with bringing down a peg or two. Jane saw my intention and she played along. I leaned towards her and we kissed just like this morning. Kelvin wasn't going to get a bean from me.

Or so I thought.

I would have gasped if Jane hadn't been kissing me, playing the game. I felt Kelvin's arms around my waist and his hands snake up until they cupped my breasts. I started to object but then he started to nuzzle my neck and my knees went weak as I melted and leaned back against him. My eyes opened wide in shock when Jane really started to kiss me with no holds barred. Despite myself I moaned in appreciation of this double... attack? Was I being attacked?

'No!' I cried out as I pulled away from her and wriggled away from him.

They withdrew immediately.

'Aneese, I've never done this before,' she said softly and anxiously.

'We've never done this before,' he joined. 'This is consensual, Aneese. Just say the word and it stops.'

What's consensual? They don't mean... all the way?

He slowly returned his lips to my neck and I let him, knowing that Jane would probably re-engage too. When she did, I found my tongue starting to explore her mouth as I had with Kelvin only this morning. Her lips were soft, softer than any man, and I found myself gently sucking on them. Realising my compliance she moved closer and kissed me more forcefully.

This was going all the way. Did I want it to go all the way? Hell, I knew I was horny as hell for no other reason than that it had been a long while since I'd had any attention. Or was that not it? Was I attracted to them both? Kelvin was a no brainer, obviously, and there was the shower thing with Jane and the kissing. Did they mistake my playfulness for something else?

But, oh god, this feels good!

I gasped and came up for air when Kelvin moved his hands up my waist and cupped my breasts again. It had been a long time since anybody had been near me, barring the office groper, and this felt wonderful. I hadn't realised how much I'd missed a man's touch.

Man's touch? Did I say *man's* touch? I realised that Jane had stopped kissing me and felt a slight pulling of material as she softly pried the straps from off my shoulders. I felt the dress start to give and gravity start to affect it. All the while Kelvin was doing wonderful things with his mouth, teeth and tongue on my shoulder and right earlobe. He found the zip with one hand and slowly lowered it down the small of my back as Jane resumed kissing me. Then, as I stepped out of the dress he found and undid my bra clasp. I momentarily panicked but then I felt the familiar relief from constriction that accompanied undoing a bra. It was like I'd been wearing a badly fitting bra all day and was finally free of its prison. On this occasion, however, there were so many other feelings to consider, a barrage of unfamiliar thoughts, emotions and senses.

Part of my brain was asking me if I wanted this whilst another part of me was shouting at me to stop. I told myself that I could stop any time I liked. Hadn't they already backed off when I'd objected? What was the harm in trying something once? How would you know you liked it or not unless you did?

I was leaning against Kelvin and I knew that the pressure to my lower back was not his knee or even his wallet. Through half closed eyes I saw that Jane was just looking at my exposed breasts now, her kissing stopped. I knew then that she (they?) had spoken the truth. Jane had certainly never done this to a woman before, I guessed. I reached for her hand and placed it, beneath mine, onto my skin and when she experimentally touched my nipple my back arched, I let out a loud moan and my legs felt the urge to open immediately.

I heard her gasp and I half opened my eyes and smiled at the expression on her face. If she felt anything like I felt then I knew what she was going through. Lucky, lucky girl. All the while Kelvin was nuzzling and biting my neck and I writhed and squirmed as I reacted to their dual attentions. Part of me wondered if her brain was going through the same cascade of emotions as mine. This was wrong, wasn't it, she was a woman, like me, and you weren't meant to do this to another woman? And then there was the additional thought that there was a man doing things to me too.

Confusion. None of this felt remotely wrong to me, in fact, for once it felt profoundly, totally right.

Doing things *to* me? I suddenly realised that I was being much too passive here. Like an electric shock to the brain I realised that I wanted to do things to them, both of them. The realisation was both exciting and frightening at the same time.

We were three consenting adults so what could be wrong? There was nothing wrong with three people mutually giving each other pleasure and I hadn't had any brandy so I couldn't be drunk. As I said the words to myself I realised that that was exactly what a drunk would say anyway and a part of me knew that I was making arguments to justify what I was doing. Twenty-six years of adhering to society's taboos couldn't be undone in an instant.

'My dress,' I sighed and Jane got the message. As she raised my feet to remove the material from around my feet I quickly turned towards Kelvin and kissed him long and hard. Then I turned back towards Jane and reached towards her and started to undo the buttons of her dress as he started to kiss my shoulders. Her mouth briefly dropped open in shock and I guessed that she thought that I wouldn't want to do things back to her. A few moments earlier and she would have been right. I saw her shock disappear and she smiled at me and then at Kelvin who, no doubt, smiled back.

I was expecting Kelvin to attack my breasts but it seemed he was content with watching his wife – I have to stop thinking of her as that, they're not married – being undressed by another woman.

'The bed' I said. 'Not here.'

Was I really saying this? *Take me to bed!* Did I mean that if we were doing this it was being done properly in a bed and not on some settee or over a table?

'She's right,' said Jane.

There was a brief pause before Kelvin spoke. 'OK.'

I looked at Jane and she looked at me. I guess neither of us wanted to answer first. We were the ones breaking most taboos, after all.

'Or this could be a chance to back out,' Kelvin continued, even though I could feel in the small of my back that he wanted to continue. 'Wouldn't want it to go on if it meant any of us hating each other.'

I bit my lip. 'I couldn't hate either of you.'

'I don't want to back out.'

Jane and I had both spoken at the same time and we smiled at the realisation.

'Nor I,' Kelvin said, cementing it.

We were soon near the bed where my discarded clothes were the first thing I saw. Jane moved them to a chair that I hadn't even seen when I was changing only a few moments before. Whilst she was doing that I sat down on the bed and Kelvin stood off to one side and I appreciated the fact that he must have been waiting for Jane to return before we continued. I knew that this was another chance to back out. My bra was in my hand and my briefs, thankfully the good stuff I'd bought, were still on. Jane returned to the bed and her bra was still on but she'd unbuttoned her dress top and was reaching for the zip.

A strange thought hit me. I found myself wanting to see her bra off, wanted to touch her like she had me. Wanted to see her lips part and hear her moan like I knew I had. Of course I wanted to see and touch Kelvin too, but I had been with a man before. Somehow the forbidden idea of being with a woman excited me. And, I told myself, it's not as if I'm a lesbian or anything. There is a man here too.

Bisexual.

The word echoed through my head. So fucking what? If it felt good and everybody was consensual and nobody got hurt then what was the problem? I realised that Jane was back and that nobody was moving. 'Nobody must know,' I said without thinking and I looked between them and realised that this confident pair and the super-confident man were suddenly human like me. Was this doubt I saw?

They nodded in unison.

I stood up and approached them and took a hand from each of them. 'I want this,' I simply said. 'Want you both.'

'And this was my idea,' said Jane. 'So if it all goes wrong don't go blaming Kelvin. We were making love and I just happened to say that it would be nice if we could find a third person who we could connect with like we do.' She smiled before continuing. 'We're just so compatible in the bedroom, you see.

'But I didn't expect Kelvin to start searching for somebody. I nearly died of shock when he brought you home!'

I smiled as I remembered her eyes opening wide as she first saw me in the shadows as she had been kissing Kelvin. 'I remember.'

'And you are the only one I have brought home, I assure you,' Kelvin interjected. 'Nobody else just seemed to fit the bill. You seemed perfect in every way, fantastically beautiful, but maybe not knowing it. Do you know what a goddess you are?'

I was dumbfounded. What did this perfect couple see in me? I was just an ordinary girl. I was starting to fill up with tears and feel a super warm glow.

'You seemed above everybody else, aloof and superior. We wouldn't want somebody whose every word grated on us, or who the limit of their knowledge was who won *Big Brother* last year.'

I was close to tears. This wonderful looking, perfect couple were telling *me* how good *I* was?

I swallowed. 'I hope I don't disappoint you.'

'Don't think that's possible,' Jane said, and then she closed with me and then we were kissing and I think I made the first move.

I felt Jane press closer to me and I went to move my hand to touch her breasts but I still had my bra held in my hand. Instantly I dropped it to the floor. My last defences gone?

Jane undid her own bra as she felt me fumble and I gasped as our breasts touched. Then Kelvin sat down beside us on the bed. I'd almost forgotten about him. How could I forget about Kelvin!

I felt a kiss and knew from the soft lips that it was Jane. The fingers gently squeezing my right nipple were hers, too, and then so too were the lips and teeth on my left. I gasped and my legs started to open as if she'd hit a switch. I felt a hand snake up to my waist and touch my underwear, just *there*. I knew it must be him. I wasn't used to the emotional overload of this dual attack. At this rate I'd be coming in seconds.

Oh, this was heaven. All thoughts of me not being so passive disappeared. I just wanted this pair to do things to me, do whatever *they* wanted to me. I knew I would not object to anything. When his finger slipped inside me I groaned loudly, almost panting. I hadn't realised how wet I was. I recalled a comment about his motorcycle seat and almost laughed. It must really need cleaning.

I felt my underwear being removed, deliciously slowly with each new revealed patch of skin being softly kissed. He stopped at my knees. I was surprised that I didn't care that these two virtual strangers were seeing me naked. Not just naked but NAKED, defenceless and open for all to see. I felt a touch between my legs and gasped audibly even though Jane was kissing me once more. When I felt his tongue enter me I gasped even louder, almost screaming. I started to pant like I'd just run a marathon and when my senses returned I realised that I was suddenly not being touched in any way.

What the hell? I was mad, I wanted attention. They can't stop now! I unscrewed my eyes and raised my head and saw them starting to kiss. He was sticking his tongue out, daring her to taste him, to taste me on him. I cleared my throat, loudly and they both looked at me and smiled.

'God, she's insatiable,' Kelvin said and then he moved towards me, swiftly undressing as he did.

I saw his manhood spring free of his pants – not boxers – and I licked my lips.

He saw me and a crooked smile appeared on his face. 'As you wish.'

Had I wished? Licking my lips had been involuntary. Richard used to cajole me to go oral on him, ply me with wine. What was happening to me? I actually wanted this man in my mouth! He positioned himself beside me and I turned my head and opened my mouth to accept.

Involuntary again, I asked myself? Felt voluntary to me.

As he entered me my tongue sought him out and I realised I liked the taste of him. First time for everything, I guessed. Then his tip was past my lips and I almost gagged as my eyes opened wide and seemed to plead with him. He withdrew a fraction and I started to work my mouth along his length. A quick glimpse in Jane's direction showed me she was fully naked too and I felt my eyes drawn to her pelvic mound – I couldn't help it! The hair there was slightly darker than that on her head.

She saw me and smiled and I noticed that her eyes almost glowed in intense animalistic glee. Guess she was enjoying seeing her man being sucked off by another woman. Was she enjoying it as much as me? I must admit that I'd only done it with Richard for a quiet life, certainly got no pleasure out of it. But this time I wanted it and I found my hand helping me as Kelvin closed his eyes and moaned above me.

And then it was the end of the world, or so it seemed to me. I hadn't realised that Jane had knelt before me but when she tentatively kissed me *there* and then explored me with her tongue I just exploded loudly and shamelessly. My body wasn't my own, it seemed, and I felt like I could hardly breathe. For a quick moment there I thought I was having a heart attack. Pain was so close to pleasure, they say, but this pain was... oh so very nice!

I heard Kelvin grunt above me and saw his eyes open and mouth open wide. Surely he wasn't going to... He told me later that the sight and sound of me in orgasm was just too much for him.

He tried to pull away, like the gentleman he is, but almost didn't make it. I felt a hotness strike my cheek and then a moment later my breasts and when I realised what it was it started me off all over again.

I'd been coming down from the orgasmic plateau but now I was back up there again. My first of the almost mythical double yolkers!

So they do exist, my subconscious mind cried out victoriously. The magazines were right!

I was screaming and panting and feared that some passing passenger would hear us. I heard a thud and when I opened my eyes I realised that Kelvin had fallen to the carpeted floor. Jane had stopped her ministrations and was sitting on her haunches, mouth open, observing me, her face and eyes seemingly fully alive. I shook my head at her and tried to talk but nothing came out. I was thinking poor her, here's me and Kelvin and she had nothing. I was trying to say that I would put that right in a moment, just give me time to recover. It had been my first orgasm for... well I couldn't say how long, and because of that it burned intensely.

Then she moved and kneeled beside me and held me and stroked my cheek.

'Oh, you lucky, wonderful girl,' she said. 'That was so hot, you are really something else!'

I managed a smile as my breathing started to return to normal. 'K... Kelvin,' I managed.

'Oh don't you worry,' she said, shooting a quick look his way. 'He's fine.' Then she squealed and kissed me and squealed again. 'Everything we hoped for!' she said excitedly as she bounced up and down on the bed.

I saw movement to my left and saw that Kelvin was shakily on his feet again. I weakly smiled up at him and he smiled back. My eyes were drawn to his penis and I saw a strand of silver thread like material, almost like a filament of spider web, hanging from his tip and moving as if affected by a slight breeze.

I did that! My subconscious told me, but I knew it to be wrong.

Kelvin and I had been merrily engaged in what we were doing but it was Jane who had started the chain reaction by unexpectedly using her tongue between my legs. In but an instant I was gone and poor Jane had nothing to show for it. No almost painful pleasure like we had. I – no we – would have to put that right, and soon.

My breathing finally returned to normal after what seemed like an age, an age in which Jane continually stroked and touched me and Kelvin started to kiss me.

'No,' I said.

They both stopped instantly, thinking that I didn't want to go any further.

'Jane,' I finished.

I got up off the bed and guided Jane to where I'd been lying and the relief on their face was obvious, though I inwardly appreciated the fact that they had stopped when they'd thought I didn't want to play any more.

I softly started to explore Jane with my hands and eyes as she lay before me and it was like I was seeing the female form for the first time. I hadn't realised before how beautiful we women were, the contours of smooth skin, the hard softness, the velvety pungent aroma. I felt like I was her master, all powerful. Is this what men felt when a woman finally surrenders and opens herself totally up to them?

I realised that Kelvin was watching me and I gasped and smiled all at once. Jane moaned as I touched her and Kelvin lay down beside her and found her left nipple with his mouth. She gasped and her back arched a little.

Oh yeah, I know that feeling, sister!

I couldn't bring myself to do what Jane had done to me so I just slipped my finger tentatively into her. I was exploring, watching her face the whole time. This was so new to me.

I felt a hand on my shoulder and turned to find Kelvin's lips seeking mine. We kissed for only a short time and then he pulled me down to lay on the bed. We were each one side of Jane and she turned her head towards me and we kissed as Kelvin took over the finger duties as he continued to nuzzle her left nipple. My mouth found her right one and I knew from experience that she wouldn't be able to stand this attention for long. She'd have to be frigid to resist this. She took longer than me to react but when it happened I was awestruck and wide eyed. I'd never seen this before. Oh, the power it gave me!

When she finished moaning and shuddering and stopped biting her lip, she was panting. 'Oh god, oh my god,' she said as she fought for air. 'Better than fantastic. Worth waiting for!'

'Ain't she something?' Kelvin said, meaning me.

I blushed and smiled. 'Takes two to tango.'

'Or even three,' Jane added. She licked her lips as her breathing seemed to return to normal. She flicked her eyes to Kelvin. 'Do it,' she almost whispered.

He smiled and nodded.

I was confused until I saw her reach down and softly grab his manhood. Then she looked at me and the old light in my head went on.

'I want to watch,' she said, as if to reinforce her order.

'Hey, don't I get a say in this?'

Kelvin was quick to reply as normal. 'Sure you do, bottom or top!'

I was laughing before I knew it but I didn't get the choice I was promised. Instead I was pushed down onto my back and he straddled me and entered me in one swift movement and I almost screamed. OK, having a tongue or a finger inside you was an invasion but nothing compared to an erect man and it had been a long, long while since anybody had had the pleasure. I was sure I'd almost healed up through lack of use.

And a pleasure it was, too. After thrusting deeply in and almost all the way out a few times he stopped.

Surely that's not it, I thought, even Richard could do better than that! Were all my fantasies just that, wishful thinking, an Aneese directed version of what I wanted to be? I opened my eyes just as he started touching me, running his hands down me, appreciating my curves like I was a beloved sports car. I smiled up at him appreciating me and he smiled down at me, open mouthed, almost like he couldn't believe he finally had me where he wanted me.

'You're beautiful,' Jane whispered into my ear and Kelvin nodded and how could I help but smile.

She reached up her left hand and caressed his shoulder. Then she slowly brought it down his back and he sighed in appreciation. When she reached his buttock she took a firmer grip and pushed him into me. It was obvious what she wanted and I wanted it too.

So he hadn't finished!

He started, slowly at first, and I held onto him, staring into his eyes as he did the same to me. Jane was so close I could smell her but she was content just to watch, her eyes wide and her mouth slightly open.

Kelvin's rhythm increased and I closed my eyes as I started to feel the now familiar build up to orgasm. I opened my eyes again and he was still watching me.

'No, stop watching me,' I gasped but he smiled a small smile. I knew it meant that he had no intention of stopping. This time he was relishing the power.

I bit my lip and screwed my eyes tight shut and then I was orgasming again. He rammed into me one last time and held it there and my legs closed around his back and I held onto him tightly as I bucked and shuddered in pleasure, secretly ashamed of my panting. When I finished and finally opened my eyes and started to regulate my breathing he was still looking down at me, himself panting slightly. When he moved inside me I realised he was still erect.

'You didn't…'

'Takes longer the second time round,' he explained for me. Then he lowered his head and kissed me once, tenderly.

'Again, then!' Jane demanded.

I'd forgotten Jane was there. I mean, come on, I normally didn't sell tickets and perform to a crowd!

'Again?' I almost shrieked. Surely not? I was spent. She must have really enjoyed the spectacle, the horny miss!

Kelvin winked at me and slowly withdrew. 'Again sounds good,' he said. Then he lay down beside me and pulled Jane towards him. 'Come on, ride the pony,' he demanded.

She looked disappointed for the briefest time but it was only fleeting, and she sure didn't take no persuading to do his bidding. She straddled him and hovered above him until she felt she was in the correct position. Then she slowly lowered herself down onto him and exhaled slightly as he was forced into her.

This time I got to watch. Part of me screamed that this was wrong but I couldn't drag my eyes away. They'd both watched. When in Rome…

Kelvin was quite content to let her do all the work, it seemed. He seemed hypnotised by the swaying of her breasts and I must admit I could see the appeal myself. He had each of his hands on her backside and as Jane increased her riding speed, he surprised me by swiftly and loudly smacking her bum cheek with his right hand. She closed her eyes as she rode faster and then he slapped her twice more. Seemed the pony was getting the whip and liking it.

'Yes,' she responded, urgently, but to what I had no idea.

She was galloping now and her breasts were no longer in rhythm, I noticed. Kelvin reached up with his left hand and found a nipple and pressed his palm against it. I guessed the friction of her movement did the work for him, the lazy bugger. In no time at all she was loudly orgasming until her eyes opened and she noticed me. Then she bit her lip and tried to lower her volume but the attempt didn't last long. In no time at all she was coming with abandon and then Kelvin shuddered and groaned and dug his fingers into her bum cheeks as he gripped her hard.

This was fantastic. I never thought I would see sex like this. Doing it was good enough but actually witnessing the act was… ecstasy itself, but a guilty ecstasy.

'Come here, you,' Kelvin said as Jane dismounted and lay beside him. I was shocked to realise he was holding his hand out to me.

I did as I was told and settled down beside them. It felt great to be here beside him, resting my head on his chest and with his arm reassuringly around me. I saw Jane open one eye and smile briefly before reaching a hand over to me. I grasped hers and sighed and closed my eyes contentedly. I guessed we could all do with a rest. Just for a little while.

And a little while was what it was. Then somebody moved and that was all it took. The heavenly hell started all over.

Chapter Nine

It was the morning after the night before and I needed to feel the cold wind upon my face, not that the breeze was cold, mind you. It was fresh and warm even at this early hour. I knew that they knew that I'd sneaked out early. Part of me guessed that they also understood why; the cold light of day had put a new slant on the events of the previous afternoon and evening. Suddenly, what had seemed normal and acceptable last night had turned into turmoil and doubt and... anger? I had to sort my head out.

It must have been the alcohol, I told myself, but I hadn't had much.
How many glasses of champagne?

I wouldn't have had a threesome under normal circumstances. Never had before, never even thought about it. Couldn't say it was even on my wish list. OK, the subject had come up during conversation occasionally. Somebody would always bring it up at a party or whilst at the pub and no doubt most of the crowd who'd said they had were probably liars. Richard had mentioned it once in passing but I had given him such a severe look that he never dared again. Christ, what would he say now? And I also didn't know if I was actually angry and if I even was, was I angry with them or myself, or should I say them *and* myself because I'd already decided that I wasn't too impressed with what I had done.

I felt nauseous but I didn't know if that was hunger or regret. We hadn't eaten after we'd returned to our cabin after the muster yesterday, just drank champagne and... *fucked* – there was no other word for it – repeatedly. Something to eat would help a great deal.

It was easy to find an eatery, just follow your nose at this time of the morning. I settled for a toasted teacake and a cup of tea. I thought the tea would be easier on my stomach than coffee. I found a table and banged my tray down on it. I was angry because I had to use the room card to pay for my snack and I didn't want to use anything given to me by them. I chastised myself, telling myself not to be stupid. My head was really screwed up.

Then my self interrogation began. Where to start? Why hadn't I backed out? I know they would have backed off if I had asked. OK, things would have probably been awkward but that's not the point. I guess that's one nil to them, then? They would have stopped if I'd asked but I didn't. There were at least two opportunities to back out and I never took them, in fact I told them that I didn't want to back out. Two nil to them. I felt my anger with them dissipating.

It must have been the alcohol. One way to test that, I told myself. Give it a try sober? I didn't believe I was even considering it.

Why not, you obviously enjoyed it!

Is that why I felt ashamed, because I'd enjoyed it? I'd broken a taboo, possibly two or more, and enjoyed it immensely. I won't deny that to myself, I really enjoyed it. Is that why I was angry? What does it say about me that I enjoyed having sex with two people at the same time, and who was I, anyway? Where has the old Aneese Crosby gone?

You mean the doormat that Richard and "Call Me Ron" thinks they can use and drop, that Aneese?

Well isn't that what them two did to me? Used me?

Well they haven't dropped you or groped you?

Groped me? Groping me would be a walk in the park compared to what we had done yesterday! Hell I was arguing with myself. First sign of madness!

Parts of the night were more salient than others, fresher in my memory. Jane fondling me and me liking it, Kelvin inside my mouth, Kelvin inside me… down there and me holding onto him and seeing nothing but his eyes as he looked down at me and made me orgasm. And I'd even double yolked the first time! Shit I was such a whore. Just buy me a pretty dress and I'm yours.

And an envelope with two grand in it, and an all expenses paid trip to New York and a Caribbean cruise?

OK, so I was an expensive whore. Makes no difference.

Yes it does!

And here's foolish me thinking that all I had to do to earn my life of ease was be the surrogate daughter.

'Well I know that look, girl?'

'What?' I didn't even know that anybody was near me.

I focused and saw a young man all dressed in black with studded leather bracelets and the like. A goth?

'Tomas,' he said as he thrust out his hand.

I sighed. Sometimes not being ugly was a curse, men just couldn't leave it alone. Seven thirty in the morning and sex was already rearing its ugly head. As if I needed that right now.

'I'm really not in the mood,' I said as politely as I could. Even then, I was surprised at how forthright I'd been. Christ, it wasn't even eight o'clock in the morning yet!

'This isn't a pickup,' he laughed. 'Sweetie, I play for the other team, doesn't it show?' he said as he took the seat opposite from me.

I wasn't really listening. What was he on about? I searched my brain, trying to remember what he'd said only a few seconds ago and what it was he meant.

'I was saying I know that look,' he continued after I hadn't answered for a while.

'What look?'

'That one,' he said, pointing at me. 'That "Oh my god what have I done and what the hell do I do now" look. And before you deny it let me save time by telling you that your teacakes are cold and hard and your tea is, at best, lukewarm.'

What? What is he talking about? I've only just got this tea, it'll be scalding.

'Go on, try it,' he persisted. 'Prove me wrong.'

I found myself moving my cup to my lips to take a small, hesitant, hot sip. It was cold. I opened my eyes wide in surprise and he took this as a sign to continue.

'Saw you come aboard yesterday. You're with the blonde and the guy with the shoulders. *So* not your parents, but he's hot by the way. Hope he gets that chest out by the pool! So which was it, him? Or was it her?'

There was no way I was sharing my shame with a stranger. I sat poker faced.

'Don't tell me it was both?'

I must have reacted somehow because he knew. So much for the poker face.

'Both? JEE-SUUUS, no wonder your tea is cold! And don't tell me... you enjoyed it but now you feel guilty, yeah? But last night it felt the most natural thing in the world? Yeah, I remember that. And now look at me,' he indicated himself with his right hand. 'Happy as Larry. Best move I ever made.'

I still hadn't told him a thing. If this was a mind reading exam, he'd have passed with a 2:2.

'You see, everything costs in this world. By the looks of them they are well enough off and you're the middle class working girl, right?'

I opened my mouth to speak.

'Don't answer, don't need too. Well listen, girl, they chose you cos you're special, don't forget that. Not everybody can do what we do and unless they're ogres and beat you or something, then what's the problem? You must at least like them or you wouldn't be here and they must more than like you.

'What did you have before? Work and a lonely social life because you're different from the rest, yeah? Well that's not why they chose you. They chose you cos they know, or at least suspect, that you are perfect for what they want and, what's more, they want to *share* something with you. They ain't taking anything from you, they're *giving* something to you, something unique, something special.' He paused and sniffed whilst I took all that he'd said in. 'And the rewards could be substantial.'

'I don't want anything from them; I don't want payment.' As soon as I opened my mouth I regretted it. I knew I was admitting that his presumptions were right.

'Ah, she can talk! No you're right, neither do I. I don't want fifty quid left on the dresser every morning but I live in a nice house and I drive a killer car and I want for nothing, and you know what?'

I shook my head.

'I'd do it all for nothing and do you know why?'

Again my head shook.

'Because I love him. I didn't always love him, in fact I ran away once but found out I missed him too much so I came crawling back. Don't make the same mistake I made.'

'Now do you like them? Do you like just one of them?'

I nodded dumbly.

'Do you love just one of them?'

I nodded.

'Say it.'

'What?'

'Say it, say you love them.'

I thought for a moment. 'I do love them both, I think.'

'So it's yourself you're mad at, then?'

I nodded.

'Because you think you've broken the rules?'

I nodded again.

'Well whose rules, who do you think creates those rules? The Normals, that's who. The normal people who hate themselves for not having the balls to take off and soar like we do, it's their defence for their cowardice. Why should people like us abide by their cowardly rules? Isn't it enough that the Normals are sad? Why should we join them?

'Listen you can back out at any time. Until then, why not give it a try? You might find you like it. And believe it or not, liking it is more than just enjoying it.'

'Your order is ready, sir,' the server said as she held out a package to him. She was all smiles and bouncy with energy like all the crew.

'Thanks. Gotta go,' he said as he accepted his package and revealed his room card. 'Johnny does like his sausage hot in the mornings. No pun intended, sweetie.'

Wow, this was so right. Was this guy a sage or what? 'Wait,' I said, interrupting the payment process. 'Charge his order to my room.' I pulled out my room card.

'Thanks, but you don't have to,' Tomas said.

'I insist,' I answered, making sure that the girl complied. 'It's the least I can do.'

He smiled, and not a bad smile at that. 'Thanks, swe…'

'Aneese,' I interrupted, holding out my hand which he shook.

'Aneese,' he echoed. 'Thanks for the sausage.'

'Thanks for the advice,' I said as I rose and hugged him. 'I hope that this is allowed,' I smiled, coyly.

'As long as nobody sees,' he replied with a wink, and then with a last smile he was gone.

What has just happened, I asked myself? I looked around, wondering if the event I just witnessed had actually taken place. Did I dream this? Whatever it was I felt much better.

'Would you like a refill, miss?'

I looked down at the suddenly unappealing snack. 'No. Throw it overboard,' I said as I stood to leave.

And suddenly my stomach felt fine and so did I.

By the time I'd walked back to the cabin, though, I'd made a decision but I also had some questions. I heard them stop talking as I opened the door and as I stepped in I noticed that they were still in bed and looking my way. He was sitting up with the pillows behind him and she was leaning on his chest with his arm placed protectively around her shoulders. Their eyes followed me as I walked in.

I pulled a chair to the bottom of the bed and sat in it like I was going to interrogate them. Chair with the back facing them and me astride it like... *like I had been astride of Kelvin at least once during last night's play!* I could see by the look on their faces that I had their complete attention. I made them wait. I was going to enjoy this.

'I have questions,' I said simply.

When it was obvious I wasn't continuing, Kelvin said, 'We imagined you would.'

I paused, using the time to form the questions in my head. 'This was always the plan, like you said last night?'

They both nodded but said nothing. So much for my surrogate daughter theory.

'But it's not just sex,' Kelvin finally said. 'If that's all we wanted I'm sure we could have just picked up the phone for that.'

Jane nodded.

I guessed they could. Money talked.

'We want a... permanent live in equal to... augment and better our relationship. This isn't a master/slave thing; you are not a plaything or a servant, but a friend.'

I nodded, glad to hear that at least. One of my questions answered. But there was one question still remaining and it was a biggy. 'Why last night? Did you purposely wait until I was trapped on this boat and couldn't get away?'

Kelvin looked offended. 'Of course not, it could just as well have happened in New York. We were hinting enough.'

They were?

'Believe me,' he continued, 'if you want off this boat and back to England then I'll arrange it and you'll be off today, and with no hard feelings, either.'

Oh yeah, how was he going to do that?

'And don't think I couldn't, either!'

My doubt must have shown on my face. He was right. This was the guy who shrank New York and made the sun hotter. I had no doubt that he could arrange my departure never mind what rules and authorities were against it and what they put in his way.

'No hard feelings,' Jane echoed. 'But there will be apologies from us. That and painful regrets. You're a lot to lose.'

Kelvin nodded in agreement.

There they go again, telling me I'm something I'm not.

They can see that you're special Tomas echoed back at me.

To be honest I'd already made my decision before I'd entered the room. The questions were just reinforcement. I sat in thought for a little while, though, and they stared silently right on back at me.

'Then budge up,' I said finally and I quickly unbuttoned my dress – I was wearing nothing underneath in my haste to get out this morning; I couldn't even *find* my underwear. In a moment I was standing on the bed wearing nothing but my flat shoes. I put on a show for the three footsteps that it took me to get to them, making sure that I swayed like I was on a catwalk. My dress fluttered to the floor and I kicked my shoes after it as I made a space between them with my feet. One went where I'd intended but the other rebounded loudly off the wall before bouncing off the bed and onto the floor. And I started to tingle with excitement, the fact reinforcing to me that I had made the right decision, helped by a stranger dressed in black. Didn't mean I wasn't nervous, however, because I was, and then some.

The look on their faces was to die for. Initial shock, I knew, but Kelvin recovered more quickly than Jane. Before I turned around to lower myself between them, I knew that his mouth was mere inches away from my sex and I felt a sudden catch in my throat as I saw him lick his lips. He hadn't done *that* fully to me yet and I found that I suddenly wanted him to. Then his gaze switched to my rump as I turned around and so did Jane's.

'The view is awfully nice in this cabin,' joked Kelvin as I snuggled down.

'Quite,' answered Jane.

I cleared my throat for the second time in twenty-four hours (or was it twelve?) demanding attention. 'I'm waiting, you know. What's keeping you?'

Turned out nothing was.

I felt two arms around my waist and then one of them dropped lower and I didn't know or care whose. I was being kissed by one of them and both of my nipples were being attacked by finger and lips. And I felt happy, as well as instantly aroused. I was enjoying it, I was sober and I thanked myself and a stranger dressed in black for preventing me spoiling it all. I felt myself smile and then I heard a gasp and realised it was me. And then I was lost.

It took us three days to leave the cabin, three days which I realised later were a form of honeymoon. I don't need to describe what we did – you can guess – but at the end of it we were one and I was totally happy. I couldn't ever remember being so happy. We were sweaty and breathy but we didn't care. We were like three people getting reinfected by a recurring cold virus. Two of us would do something and that would arouse the third who had been up to that point exhausted. So as those two were finishing the third would start something and so the delicious tag match would continue. At times I'd feel sated and think that I couldn't do it any more. I was sore in certain places, my nipples especially. Is this what breast feeding mothers felt like? But like a drug I... we... kept going back for more, time after time.

I'd like to say that I gave as good as I got but, truth be known, I *was* their plaything most of the time, never mind what they'd previously said. And you know what? I didn't care. They were both very careful with me and treated me like a china doll, a favourite china doll at that. Not once was I forced into anything I didn't want to do. At times I was guided, wordlessly into what they wanted but it was never unpleasant.

On the morning of the third day Kelvin lifted me out of bed and laid me in the bath that Jane had already prepared. There, I was pampered and washed like I was an Egyptian Princess. When I was clean they joined me and it was a tight fit – it was only a normal sized bath. I remarked that there was not the space for a sunken bath on a ship. Kelvin and Jane shared a look and asked if I'd been spying in their personal en suite back at the house. Seemed they had a large one at home and I couldn't wait to use it. I wondered how come I hadn't seen it already?

Of course we couldn't continually screw each other silly for three days straight, we did other things, too. We joked and did silly things that seemed perfectly normal at the time. We massaged and caressed each other – Kelvin had rough hands which were great for massage. We even spent hours just talking, believe it or not.

More often than not, Jane would have her embroidery in her hands when we weren't being physical. I don't know where she kept it but it would always magically appear and she would start working away as she talked and joked with us. Kelvin and I would play at holding a glass to her lips so that she wouldn't have to stop. We kept our own clock; we slept, day and night, and we loved, day and night. The real world clock outside our cabin door meant nothing to us. Occasionally Kelvin would ring for room service and we'd receive food and drink at the door. A new trolley would arrive and the old one would leave. We fed and watered each other mouth to mouth like an orgy at some Roman villa.

We had the Do Not Disturb sign on the door but it still took our own personal stewardess a day or two to realise what Do Not Disturb actually meant. We didn't want clean towels, we didn't want the bed made or the curtains opened or the flowers replaced. We just wanted privacy. On the second morning she received a growl from Kelvin after she had knocked, received no answer, and then tried to enter using her pass key. Something along the lines of "What the fuck part of Do Not Disturb don't you understand!" sent her packing and she didn't reappear until we tracked her down and requested her services a few days later. Poor young lady looked terrified every time she visited after that.

We listened to music quite a bit, Kelvin and I, whilst Jane did her embroidery on the bed. I realised it was the perfect hobby to bring with you. A needle set and some coloured thread and some blanks of cloth took up no space at all. She was working on a new piece and didn't want us to see until it was finished so every time she started we two would leave her do it. She never complained at the noise we made, jumping around naked and playing air guitars and table bongos and singing, shouting and laughing.

Oh, and having sex. Sooner or later, normally sooner, we would be at it again. Sometimes she would leave us to it, she seemed to enjoy being the voyeur, but mostly she joined us or put her hobby away and ordered us back into bed.

Music-wise, we would share his iPod and have an earplug each. Then, eventually, Kelvin damned himself for his stupidity and plugged it into his laptop and we listened via there. Jane didn't seem to mind the noise and occasionally hummed along to something. We had to pretend not to hear her because once she realised she was doing it she stopped. I'd recalled what they had told me about her previous life and how happy Kelvin had been when she had been humming and singing when doing my hair. He'd also told me that she'd only started to do that in the last week or two and put it down to my presence. Whether it was true or not I didn't know but it made me pleased that Kelvin attributed it to me.

'Sing this,' he'd order and I would try if I knew it. Then he'd frown. 'No that's not you, try this.' His fingers would fly over the keyboard and something else would start. I'd sing again, not feeling self-conscious at all (a mixture of alcohol, familiarity, trust and the sense of ease I felt when with them). If I didn't know the song he was referring to he would show me the lyrics and demonstrate the key to sing it in, himself. I realised his voice had quite a range compared to mine. I really wanted to sing for them but he made it all seem so easy whereas to me it was like gargling sand.

'I can't do it,' I said petulantly at one stage. I stopped short of stamping my feet... just.

'Yes you can,' he said, using his fingers on the keyboard once more. 'You just don't know it, like you didn't know you're a good fuck!'

My mouth dropped open and my eyes bulged.

Jane almost choked on her tongue before reaching out, stifling a laugh, and tapped his arm. 'Tut tut, Jack, diplomacy!'

I put my hands on my hips in mock disgust but secretly I was proud at his referral. I was soon smiling, despite myself. My hard taskmaster then handed me a glass of champagne which I drank quickly.

'Now try this,' he ordered and I complied.

Yeah, he could wrap me around his little finger, as the saying goes. He sure knew what buttons to push to get me to do his will. Sexually and on the music front.

'Now we're getting somewhere,' he finally said. 'That's more you.'

I was overjoyed. 'Who am I?' I asked excitedly.

'Well that was a Debbie Harry song you were singing.'

'Debbie who?' I asked, but I know I'd heard the name somewhere.

He rolled his eyes. 'Save us from musical heathens!'

'Hey, I'm no heathen, I know lots of good music.'

'Like?'

'Like… like… like Take That!'

He snorted.

'What's wrong with Take That?'

'I said music.'

'Nothing wrong with Take That.'

'No, not if you're half deaf or infantile.'

'Oh, like Debbie Harry isn't.'

'How would you know, you've no idea who she is!'

It came to me. 'Wasn't she from the seventies?'

'1978,' he corrected. 'Singer with the band Blondie and 1978 was their first British hit. By the time they'd split they were the biggest band in the world.'

'So?'

So back and fore we would argue good naturedly whilst Jane would embroider and laugh at our antics. But in the end I would always do as I was told and in the end I was ordered to learn half a dozen songs that I was to perform for him and Jane when we got home. A couple were duets and I was so looking forward to performing them with him. He promised to video me if I was good enough, so that I could see myself and show my family. That really appealed to me. Kelvin would tutor me in the shower. We even did some singing, too!

We could have stayed in the cabin for a month and we still wouldn't have run out of music. He'd put on a song and say, 'You could sing this', or, 'We could sing this', or, 'Listen to the guitar on this'. Listen to the drums, the timing, the way the music speeds up or slows down, that this section was a tricky bit, that this song was recorded live but you wouldn't know it until the crowd applauded at the end. If you listen carefully you can hear a cough in the background or a scraping chair or somebody calling out somebody's name or laughing. Listen here and you will see the singer failed to reach the correct note or strained so much to get there it sounded wrong.

Most of the time I heard nothing out of the ordinary and my face betrayed it if my voice didn't.

'I can't hear a thing,' I'd say, exasperated.

'Well it's there. Listen again.'

I'd listen again. 'No, still can't hear it. Are you having me on?'

'He has a good ear,' Jane would comment without looking up from her therapy. 'I've heard the coughing one. Cliff Richard clearing his throat after the recording has started.'

'See, I told you!' he'd exclaim. Then he'd punish me pleasantly for doubting him.

I say pleasantly because he – they – never hurt me, not once. It got so I trusted them implicitly. If they'd told me that they were going to soak me in water and plug my nipples into the electricity for a more satisfying orgasm I would have willingly done as I was told. There was even a bit of over the knee playing, but I will come to that later. If I was nervous at anything Jane would instruct me and tell me to relax, that I'd enjoy it. I told her to prove it once or twice and was surprised when she did. Found out that I enjoyed a bit of the voyeur bit myself. After the demonstration she would tell me how and why and what she'd enjoyed about it. Well, what could I do after that but allow it to be done to myself? I thought I didn't enjoy certain things at first but later I would find myself wanting more. Then I would reflect and not believe what I had just done.

What was happening to me?

Once Jane played at restraining me whilst Kelvin did as he pleased. Then he would pin me down and I would wiggle and squirm and Jane would say I was her prison bitch and it was my duty to do anything she demanded OR ELSE! I found it oddly stimulating to pull against my captors but not be able to get free. We also would have played at dress up and role playing but, they said, we didn't have the time (or the wardrobe). We'd wait until home for that.

And Kelvin said that he wouldn't spank me for real until I asked him to. Like that's going to happen!

It all started the first time I transgressed and I was pulled across the both of them as they both sat up in bed. Jane had her needlework in her hands and was following what we two were up to with her eyes as her hands automatically did her bidding.

'No! Jane, tell him!' I implored as he held me over both their laps. I was more over his than hers with my knees over Jane and my head over the side of the bed. I felt the blood start to rush to my head.

I was naked, of course – we all were – but they had a thin sheet over their lower halves. I was meant to be getting another bottle of champagne but I'd cheekily given them the finger and started to drink from the bottle, and played at keeping it all for myself.

Kelvin struck like a snake and whilst I was busy chugging away, and before I knew it, he had my wrist and was pulling me back towards the bed. He'd deftly taken the champagne bottle from me and I felt dribbles escape my mouth and nose as he positioned me where he wanted me.

'Don't you dare!' I said at first, though a part of me was hoping, daring him to continue. That masochistic part of us we all have, deep down inside us, that we refused to acknowledge. Then I'd asked Jane to intervene and managed to look back and just see her smile as she ignored me.

'Jane!' I screamed, but part of me was playing. I wanted it to sound real, though.

'Jane it is,' Kelvin said. 'First honours, my sweet?'

I saw Jane look, almost a comic double take. 'Oh, that is so beautiful. Such a lovely view,' she said as she took in the delight of my ready rump. I tried to picture what she could see but it didn't take much effort. I knew she could see everything from the whiteness of my flesh to the darkness of what Kelvin referred to as my chocolate coloured star fish: my bum hole itself.

I felt her lay her hand on my upper thigh and run it slowly and softly up until she came to rest on my right bum cheek. Surprisingly I felt a warmness of anticipation in the bottom of my stomach. Her little slaps were more a caress then an attack, though. I watched as she seemed to almost shiver in appreciation. Then she moved her hand away as if she didn't trust herself to leave it there any longer. She sighed a deep breath as she did.

Then he put his hand where hers had just been and I tensed myself in preparation for what I knew was coming. I stayed tensed as long as I could but he didn't do it. I relaxed and slowly looked back at him and found him looking at me with his crooked smile. Then he lifted his hand slowly and I tensed again but as I eventually opened one eye I realised he was teasing me.

Just do it part of me screamed at him. *Get it over and done with!*

Then he moved his hands and I fell to the floor, first catching myself with my hands like I was doing a handstand and then rolling sideways on to my knees. I was dumbfounded and I think it showed. I hadn't been expecting mercy.

Awwww!

I stayed on my knees and stared in disbelief for a while.

'I won't do that for real until you ask me,' he eventually said.

'Like that's going to happen!' I spat back, but I was only playing angry. *Now let's not be too hasty.* But my heart was racing and my breathing was fast and wild. I felt really alive. And really cheated!

I realised that there was so much I didn't know. To innocent little me sex was the two or three positions that Richard and I had tried, though more often than not the missionary. When I was tiddly and he nagged enough there had been a bit of oral, me receiving more than giving. I realised that I'd been pretty selfish in the bedroom department with poor Richard. Or was it that my subconscious knew that he wasn't the one for me, that I wasn't totally comfortable with him? Or was it the fact that we were both young and relatively inexperienced?

Of course I'd read the women's magazines, all those letters and articles which were probably lies, and, to be honest, I just didn't get it. I thought it was make believe to sell the product and make us all feel inadequate. Boy, how wrong had I been? I was beginning to think that if I'd read who'd submitted the letters it would have been "Satisfied of Kent" or "Daddy-o of Bromley"!

On day three we emerged, more from my nagging than anything else. I had a killer dress I wanted to wear and in any case we were on a floating palace and we hadn't even seen most of it. I had seen rather a lot of the cabin ceiling, though, probably all of it. The bit over the bed, the bit over the table and the soft and hard seating. I was also intimately familiar with every scratch on the table and with how nice the thick carpet smelt and felt. And not only underfoot.

We were happy. I was so happy I was numb and I never wanted it to end.

It's funny how time is, isn't it? How does something bad last forever and something good fly by in an instant? The last three days had flown so fast but at the same time I felt like I'd known Kelvin and Jane forever. I couldn't imagine any other place I wanted to be and I certainly couldn't imagine being without them. No, sir, this was the place for me and I knew it. This was home, my home.

It wasn't until the second morning of our "love-in" that I realised that I was owed an explanation. We'd just made love for a couple of hours (reinfecting each other with horniness!) and were settling down in the afterglow. I was caressing Kelvin's chest, just running my fingers softly through his chest hair, when I noticed the tattoo rings on his right arm, the two lonely grey ones that he hadn't explained to me yet.

I sat up like I'd been electric shocked. 'Hey, didn't you say you'd tell me about them once you'd had your way with me?'

'What? What's happening?' said Jane as she sat up. She'd been laying spoon-like with Kelvin wrapped around her and me wrapped about him. I think I woke her.

'Kelvin's tattoos,' I explained. 'It's explanation time. You promised.'

'What I actually said was that if I tell you then...'

'Something about me staying forever and marriage,' I recalled. 'Well surely this qualifies? I'm one of you, now. You said.' I watched as he pondered. 'You promised and it isn't fair for Jane to know and not me. Equals, you said.' I got the impression I was winning so I said nothing further.

'Actually, Jane doesn't know,' she said, addressing herself in the first person. 'We've never discussed it.'

'Though she's probably guessed,' he continued. 'She's not stupid, you know.'

I remained silent. I knew I was winning and that he was just delaying the inevitable.

'Why do you want to know?' he finally asked me.

'I just do,' I answered. 'I see them every day and I want to know. I know so little about you both, still.'

He pursed his lips and looked enquiringly at Jane.

'I guess this is the time,' she answered his silent question.

'Sure you won't hate me?' he asked.

She shook her head and then he looked at me.

'As if,' I answered. 'I love you to bits. We both do!'

He sat up and untangled himself from us and we all made ourselves comfortable. Then his mouth opened but he stopped and closed it again. He was silent for a while and I didn't push him. If he'd changed his mind and decided not to spill then I wouldn't have pushed him. He seemed to be a little lost for words and I felt guilty for my insistence.

'With these,' he said as he pointed to his left armful of tattoo rings, 'there was a form of honour. OK, they were terrorists, but soldiers nonetheless. I was armed, they were armed, they were fighting for what they believed in and I was doing my job.'

He trailed off, seemingly lost in thought, and I thought that was all we were going to get.

'But with these it was different.' He used his left hand to point at his right shoulder. 'I couldn't bring myself to put these on my left arm with the combat deaths because it would have somehow demeaned the whole process, dishonoured the dead, so to speak. And I couldn't make them black like the others for the same reason, so they were done in grey. Shouldn't have put them up at all, in hindsight, but that's macho vanity for you.'

I looked at Jane and then at him. His eyes seemed glazed over again, like they were when he was telling me about Iraq and Afghanistan.

'This guy.' And he indicated the topmost grey ring. 'Tried to kill me so I killed him partly out of revenge and partly because he was trying again to kill me. Self-defence, you could say.'

My mouth dropped open. I knew it must have been something similar to what he had on his left arm but I wasn't expecting this. In hindsight I mocked my stupidity. What else could it have been?

I saw his finger drop to touch the second ring and he rubbed it before continuing. 'But this one was pure murder in a way. He wasn't trying to kill me, though he did order others to do it for him. My blood was cold when I did it so I can't claim self-defence. I found him, he was hiding, his cronies were gone. I had help, you see. Fired up a flare and the cavalry rode over the hill to help me.'

He trailed off and I gave him time to carry on. Or perhaps he was finished.

'Like all bullies he begged for his life when the time came but it didn't help. It had to happen because there was no other way. Too much had happened to let him go and he was a potential threat to my future with Jane.'

'With Jane?' I asked.

'Yes,' he answered simply. 'You see this ring is...' He tailed off and swallowed.

'My husband,' Jane finished for him. 'Ian.'

He turned to face her. 'See, I knew you knew.'

'Well you only had the left armful when we... you know? For the first time? And then after you had me safe, I noticed the right arm. Once I knew what the left ones were I guessed the rest.'

'And you don't mind?'

'He was a bastard!' Jane said with real vehemence. 'He deserved it, the things he forced me to do lost me Isobel!'

My mouth dropped open in disbelief.

'And you're not angry that we couldn't get married because you couldn't get divorced because I put your ex in the ground and they can't serve him papers in hell?'

'Well it's a disappointment, but I accept you did the right thing for the right reasons. Ian wasn't somebody who would let us ride off into the sunset unmolested, you had to do it. To be honest it helped my sanity greatly knowing – or at least suspecting – that he couldn't come back and hurt me.'

'I would never have let him.'

'I know,' she said. She smiled and touched his arm.

I had been listening, agape, up to now. This was so... WOW! I knew and accepted that Kelvin was a soldier and killed people *in the line of duty* but this was different. This was, as Kelvin said, murder to some extent. He'd taken the law into his own hands. How did I feel about that? I'd been a totally law abiding person all my life, as had Richard, my family and everybody that I knew.

'So do you hate me?' Kelvin turned and asked me.

I didn't know what to say. I was still shocked and astounded.

'See she hates me.'

'No I don't,' I protested. 'It's just that I...'

'You never knew what it was like,' Jane said. 'Ian wouldn't have let us go. He would have found us and sent men after us. It was a pride thing, what he called his respect. He was a yob, a gangster if you like. The law couldn't touch him, were afraid of him. No, Kelvin did the right thing. Took me a long time to realise it, that I was condoning taking a life, but then it dawned on me. Ian and his yobby drug dealing friends did much worse every day. Kelvin stopped them and saved me in the process, probably saved others, too, if you think about it.

'Kelvin didn't want to take them on. He came home to the village he grew up in once he'd left the army, looking for me. He had saddle bags with money over his shoulder, a cowboy hat and cowboy boots.'

'He did?' The picture formed in my mind. This time it was my turn to talk as if he wasn't here.

'He didn't want confrontation,' she continued. 'He just wanted to use his payoff to make a life for himself. Then he had the misfortune to bump into me.'

'Hardly misfortune.'

'Shut up, I'm talking, they almost killed you!' she admonished him before facing me fully. 'Kelvin thought he was dropping into the local where his father used to drink, but what good people there were left in the village drank elsewhere. The place was unrecognisable from the place he knew as a youngster, the whole village was much larger for a start. Like most local places it was now owned by Ian. Not legally, mind, protection and drugs and threats. Kelvin should have left then but he was too stubborn, wouldn't leave me.'

'Not once I'd seen you. Couldn't leave you there.'

'So you see, don't hate him for doing what he had to do. Not everybody can make the difficult decisions and do what's right. I was a crack-whore, not by choice but–'

'That's enough!' Kelvin said threateningly. 'No you weren't!'

I knew him well enough to do as I was told. So did Jane.

A silence developed between us, which was broken by Kelvin. 'So there you have it. You have the power to send me to jail for a very long time. Jane too, actually.'

'I would never do that,' I answered. 'I love you, love you both.'

I reached out and found both their hands and squeezed them. 'And I would never do anything to hurt either of you. And anyway.' And I smiled impishly. 'I don't think they do mixed cells for three!'

They smiled at my attempt at humour.

'I'm here and I'm staying here with you two. I don't care about the past.'

Chapter Ten

'OK, let's see what this tub has to offer,' Kelvin said as he closed the door behind him. Then he slipped his arm around Jane's waist, whose arm was already around mine, and away we sauntered.

We'd discussed the world on the other side of the cabin door. Sounds odd doesn't it? But we agreed that we shouldn't be too overt about our relationship. To be honest we tried but we failed. OK, we weren't openly snogging each other on the sundeck but neither could resist the urge for a quick peck here and there or a lingering touch. I'm guessing most thought of us as father, mother and daughter but I suspect there were a few who didn't. And there were some who damn well knew what we were.

Take "the boys" for instance. They knew. But who were "the boys"?

The boys were actually the band. We came across them on the afternoon of our first day out of our cave, as we referred to our cabin. In our cabin Kelvin was the hunter gatherer and would speak in mono syllables. 'Me hunt. Bring home bacon for cave women.' Then he'd lift the phone and room service would be provided. But eventually we just had to come out of the cabin and explore things for ourselves, hunt our own food.

The band were setting up as we walked past one of the ballrooms, seemed they'd come aboard yesterday at some stop or another. News to us; we didn't even know the ship had stopped anywhere! Of course, Kelvin was drawn to the instruments like a moth to a flame.

'Don't touch the equipment,' some cockney sounding guy had said challengingly. He was all greased back hair, dark glasses and leather jacket. And he had a ponytail.

We were standing by the stage observing, just like some of the other passengers were doing. Kelvin had inched us a little closer than the rest.

'Not touching,' said Kelvin. 'Would never touch unless invited.'

'Yeah, well we ain't inviting.'

'Is it yours?' Kelvin continued in a far nicer tone than the guy deserved.

'Yeah,' he grunted as he eyed up both us girls. I guessed he wouldn't even be speaking to Kelvin if he didn't have a pretty girl on each arm.

'So what do you practice on?'

'What ya say?' the man answered, still undressing us with his eyes.

'Well you use this beat up old thing on the stage but I doubt you practice on it,' Kelvin continued. 'Got me a Fender Telecaster myself and a Gibson for when I want to really get creative. But when it's just me and my axe I either use my Broadcaster or my Gretsch.'

His head moved towards Kelvin like he'd been slapped. All of a sudden he wasn't interested in us women any more. 'What ya say?'

'Broadcaster or Gr...'

'I heard what ya said,' he interrupted. 'Thas expensive in it?'

'About a hundred grand.'

'Shit!'

Shit indeed. Kelvin had a guitar that cost more than I'd probably ever earned. I guessed by Jane's lack of reaction that she already knew.

'So what music do you play?' Kelvin continued like everybody owned an expensive guitar.

'Uh, the greats, you know. Elvis, Roy Orbison, The Stones.'

'Not a fan of The Rolling Stones.'

'Not a fan of... Are you for real?'

Kelvin nodded. 'Not a fan of the Beatles, either. Prefer my guitar music to scream at me like good sex, you know? Not that I don't mind the odd bit of grunge or heavy punk.'

Well I'd remembered his fingers making me scream like a good guitar only a few hours ago. Jane too!

'Oh yeah?' the man said.

I guessed by his tone he was disbelieving.

'Give you a demo if you like?'

The leather clad guitarist chewed on his lip. 'Be my guest,' he finally said.

Kelvin untangled himself from between us and gingerly picked up the black guitar. 'Good weight on it,' he commented as he placed the strap around his shoulders and experimentally thumbed a few strings.

From the sound I knew that the guitar was plugged into a speaker of some sort.

'Your drummer set up?' he said finally.

The man hesitated and then rolled his eyes before gesturing to the drummer who was adjusting something or other on his set. 'Hey, Topper? Join in with this guy if you like. Says he owns a hundred grand Fender Broadcaster. Think he's shooting the shit myself.'

The drummer, too, rolled his eyes but sat ready as he had been told.

I jumped when Kelvin started strumming. It was loud and fast and with heavy bass and he was straight into it with no preamble as he sang along. I vaguely recalled the song so I must have heard it at some stage. I was a Take That and West Life girl, though, so this wasn't really to my taste. Or it wouldn't have been three days ago. If Kelvin was playing it, then it was heaven to me. I watched his fingers and tried to interpret the noises he was making from his finger positions. Beside me Jane started to rhythmically rock to and fro in time with the music. I noticed that a crowd had started to gather now that Kelvin had broken the semi silence with his raucous display.

'That's Green Day,' I heard one of the older teenagers whisper loudly to the girl on his arm.

She nodded in agreement. "Basket Case'.'

My little sister was into them and used to drive me mad playing them loudly whenever I visited. What were those words? Some of them were too fast to catch and the noise of Kelvin's playing made it worse. Something about a melodramatic fool not having enough sex? So, it wasn't written by Kelvin, then!

Then the drummer, who had been silent until now, joined in and the noise became louder. Out of the corner of my eye I saw movement and noticed that other band members were picking up guitars and joining in. Kelvin was really giving a display like he was on a stage, rocking his head first this way, then that, as he shouted out the words. He began to play the guitar more expressively, almost like he was showing off. The drummer was drumming so fast that his sticks seemed to be a blur of movement.

The crowd grew bigger and I noticed more and more people running in from the deck outside to see what was going on. By the time the song was obviously winding down and Kelvin was really holding some of the singing notes – not that you could tell from the volume and pace – there were perhaps a hundred people there with more appearing all the time. Kelvin held the last note after the drummer had stopped banging away and there was silence briefly until a round of applause and cheers went up from the ad hoc audience.

'Yeah, not bad. Plays well, um…'

'Spider. Spider McGraw,' the guitarist said as he held out his hand for Kelvin to shake. All of a sudden "Spider" wanted to know Kelvin, it seemed.

'Kelvin Turner,' he returned.

'Not bad, Kel, not bad at all. So tell me about this Broadcaster?' Spider asked as he turned Kelvin towards the stage. 'Where'd you find it?'

The rest of the band joined them and sat on the stage as they talked animatedly. I inwardly laughed at the scene. They were all dressed in black and leather with bare arms and dirty vests. Some of them had ponytails and large, multicoloured intricate looking tattoos. As for Kelvin he was wearing light colours as he normally did, cream shorts and a white short sleeved shirt which was still immaculately pressed with straight, sharp creases on the sleeves. To all the world he looked like a naval officer circa 1930s, relaxing on shore, or a plantation owner. That made the boys either his crew or his slaves!

'We not getting any more?' one of the teenagers said to nobody in particular, before shrugging and moving away.

It was obvious to me that they weren't. Kelvin and "the boys" were too engrossed in shop talk to even notice us women. I could have stripped down to my bra and pants and I guessed I wouldn't even get a look in.

Well maybe.

'Come on,' said Jane. 'We've lost him for the afternoon, I think. Let's try the shops.'

'Are you sure?'

'What do you think?' she said, gesturing towards where Kelvin was the centre of attention at the stage. A waiter brought a tray and the group all took a glass. It looked like whisky to me. As Kelvin took his glass, he noticed us and went to stand but Jane waved him back down. 'We'll see you later,' she called out to him.

I saw his lips move but didn't hear what he said.

'Yes I'm sure,' Jane replied, obviously more used to his body language than I. 'We'll hit the shops.'

He nodded, smiled and kissed the air in our direction. I couldn't resist opening my hand to catch the kiss and Jane laughed at me as I closed my fist.

'Come on, you,' she said as she placed her hand in mine.

'Are you sure? Will he be OK?'

'Will he be OK?' she echoed. 'He's in hogs' heaven!'

So we hit the shops. There was so much we needed, little things mostly. 'You know you can spend what you like, don't you?' Jane asked at one stage. 'You're one of... me now.'

What did that mean, I asked myself? Was I Kelvin's de facto wife too? That sounded odd. I was one of Kelvin's wives? Must admit the thought was appealing. Mrs Aneese Turner? Yeah it had a good ring to it. I noticed Jane watching me. Did she know what I was thinking?

'This is going to take some getting used to,' I said.

'Yes, for me too. I know I wished for this – wished for you – but the reality of it is that I never once expected it. Dreams, fantasies, are frightening when they come true.'

'I know. I always wanted a rich man to sweep me off my feet but I never once thought it would happen. And now I have the bonus of you, too, and I'm not just saying that,' I finished.

'I know,' she nodded. 'You know, I can't wait to get you home to share our life.'

'What, you want the cruise to end?'

'No, silly, but even our routine humdrum existence will be better with you around. It won't all be cruises and holidays, you know.'

'It won't?' I played. 'I'll have to check the small print, but I'm sure it's mentioned somewhere!'

She laughed as she put her arm in mine and turned me around. 'Come on, I have to find a dress to match yours for the formal night. Can't have you dressed to the nines and standing next to this old hag in a rag.'

She took my hand and I allowed myself to be pulled gently along by her. I found myself squeezing her hand just so that she would smile at me. When she did, my heart turned cartwheels and I shyly returned her smile.

'I really want to kiss you right now,' I whispered as I leaned towards her so that any passer-by wouldn't hear. 'And you're nowhere near a hag.'

She squeezed my hand and smiled back at me. 'Come on, in here,' she said.

I was slightly disappointed, I expected more of a reply than that. Was she not feeling what I was feeling?

'This will do for a start,' she said as she picked a green silk dress from a rail. 'And this one.' The second one was turquoise. She headed for a changing room. 'Help me, will you?'

I followed her in and pulled the curtains behind me. It was just a normal sized changing room with a mirror, a padded bench and hooks on the wall to hang things. She turned to face me after placing the clothes hangers on a hook and before I knew it she was kissing me and my disappointment evaporated.

'There,' she said. 'Happy now?'

I smiled and nodded.

'We have an advantage, I think?' she said.

'What do you mean?'

'Well we couldn't share a changing room with Kelvin in the high street, could we?'

I made a play of thinking about it. 'I guess not.'

'Help me with this,' she said as she turned around and indicated the zip of her dress. She lifted her hair out of harm's way and I worked the zipper. I found myself kissing her neck and she moaned appreciatively. 'See, what did I tell you?' she said softly as her dress fell to the floor and she stepped out of it. 'It's going to be so much fun having you around. A friend and a lover to boot!'

She turned to face me and unclipped her bra in the process. 'Really too hot for bras, but what's a girl to do?' She reached out to the hanger for the first dress but stopped and looked at me. I knew I was licking my lips, I couldn't help it. I was hypnotised by the movement of her breasts. I felt desire welling up inside me.

'You want some?' she asked playfully.

'Yes, please,' I answered breathlessly.

'Well only a bit,' she said. 'Don't want to get us thrown out.'

I moved towards her and placed my hand fully on her left breast and brought my mouth down to her right nipple. I rubbed and sucked and I heard her stifle a moan as she grabbed my hair. I took this as her reminding me that my time was up and pulled away, but she instantly pulled my face to hers and we kissed hard and passionately.

We heard voices as somebody passed our cubicle and we pulled apart. I inspected the curtain to reassure myself that it was fully closed and when I turned to face her again she had her finger to her lips. Then she reached out and started to unbutton my dress and my mouth fell open so she shushed me again. In no time we were kissing again and my dress top was around my waist. Then I felt the material sliding down my legs as it fell to the ground. It felt like an electric shock as it touched my skin. She grabbed my head and started to kiss me again and I embraced her tightly and kissed her in return. Then I felt her hand inside my underwear and I whimpered but managed to bite it down to a hiss. I felt my wetness as her fingers entered me.

We slithered and ground against each other for what seemed like an age, my brain shouting at me to stop – we were in a public place for Christ's sake – but my body not wanting to. I felt for her underwear and started to peel them down over her buttocks. Just then I heard laughing and the clippity-clop of shoes as somebody passed by the curtain. A curtain, I told myself. There was nothing but a curtain separating us from prying eyes and ears.

Reassured that we were safe for the moment I turned to face her again. She'd used the time to remove her panties and I was disappointed and happy at the same time. I'd wanted to remove them. But I was happy because I was rewarded with her standing fully naked in front of me, panting like she had run a mile. I saw her beautiful body in the mirror behind her. I pictured her deliciously round rump raised up for all to see as she lay over my knee. I found that I was panting too, but unfortunately this wasn't the place for that.

I would have to settle for something else. I knew what I wanted and it was strange because it was one of the few things that I hadn't done to her yet. I pushed her down onto the seat and she raised her knees up and opened her legs. My tongue was there in an instant and I heard her stifle a gasp and bang the wall accidentally as she reached out for a coat hook to steady herself. I was kneeling on our clothes and I reached back and placed them over my legs as I knelt before her. Now if anybody bent down to peak under the curtain they would only see a pile of clothes. What could be more natural in a changing room than that?

So this was what a woman tasted like. It was similar to the taste of a man, but sweeter, less salty, but a little more pungent.

I was new to this but, of course, had had it done to me. I experimented with touching her, trying to translate what I had felt when it was being done to me into where to do it to her. I was guided by her reactions, or perhaps I should say her stifled reactions. I heard shoppers passing occasionally but we were too far gone. I knew that if somebody swished back the curtain then I just wouldn't care.

Then, surprising me by how quickly she did, she came, and I looked up at her and saw her lips and eyes screwed tight shut as she tried her best to stay silent. A thin sheen of perspiration covered her body. I heard somebody passing again and I coughed and banged the walls to cover the noise. I reached up and swished one of the dresses on the hangers and hoped it sounded like somebody was struggling to get into or out of a dress. When I looked back up at her she was smiling weakly at me and she brought her hand down to touch my cheek as she fought to regain control over her breathing.

'Oh, that was wonderful!' she gasped. 'Once we kissed, I just couldn't help myself!'

I nodded and smiled back. 'You're right. It was only the kiss I was after but once we started? Wow!' I leaned forward and kissed her.

'What have you done to us?' she panted as we moved apart.

'Me? What have you two done to me, you mean. I'm just an innocent working girl!'

'My arse, you are!'

We both laughed at that.

'Come on, I guess we'd better try these on,' I suggested. 'Somebody is bound to get suspicious in a minute.'

She sniggered. 'I hope I haven't stained anything?'

I wondered what she meant but then the penny dropped and I

sniggered too. I put my hand to my mouth. 'How embarrassing would that be!'

Eventually we mutually chose the turquoise one. It looked wonderful on her and made her look as voluptuous as she actually was. Kelvin would trip over his tongue. I'd probably choke on mine.

As the assistant charged our purchases to our cabin we tried to keep control of ourselves. The thought of what we'd just done within hearing distance of just about any passer-by refused to leave my head. Although the shop girl wore her uniform smile at all times she must have been thinking behind her facade that these two were a right strange pair of birds!

As we left the store we just burst out laughing as if we had been holding our breath for ages. We earned ourselves more odd looks from other passengers as we held on to the wall and each other to support ourselves, but what the hell. If they knew what we'd done they would be doing more than giving us strange looks.

'Come on, let's find Daddy-o.'

'Hey, that's my pet name for him,' I objected playfully. 'Use your own.'

'Right you are, Angel,' she replied, and I glowed at her use of my pet name.

We found him where we'd left him. He was sitting on the stage with a guitar on his knee and his scurvy crew were still rapt with attention at what he was saying. Around them were a lot of empty glasses and beer bottles.

He saw us enter the room and immediately stood. 'There's my ladies,' he said, smiling as he did so. 'Don't forget,' he said to Spider, 'you have my card so any time any of you are passing give me a call and we can jam. If you're lucky I might let you touch my pride and joy.'

'Speaking of which,' he said as we neared,. 'Here are more of them. Say hello to the boys, ladies. This is Spider, Leo, Decker, Topper and Mitch.'

'Hi boys,' we chorused. Suddenly they weren't interested in guitars any more.

'Pleasure to meet you, girls,' Spider said. 'Your old man's a mint, missus, a real mint.'

'Hey, less of the old,' I shot back.

'I meant it to mean your dad, little un.'

'Well he ain't me dad,' I answered, twisting my voice to sound like I thought a cockney would.

'But I...' Spider wore a confused look.

'But he is my daddy,' I finished and I grabbed Kelvin and roughly kissed him on the lips.

Spider and the boys shot a look at Jane, their question obvious.

'Oh he's my daddy too, in case you were wondering,' she said and as I pulled away from Kelvin she took over and Kelvin's hand strayed down to squeeze her rump as she kissed him.

Kelvin was smacking his lips like he was trying to identify something that had somehow appeared on his lips. After he and Jane finished he was still doing it. Then his eyes opened wide. 'Have you two been back to the cabin?'

I looked at Jane and she looked at me and realisation dawned. 'Um, no.'

'No? Well how do you account for... where were you?'

'Shopping,' Jane said innocently, winking at me. 'Had to try things on, you know.'

'In the changing room. Bye boys,' I said as I put my arm through Kelvin's free arm and led him away. 'Nice to meet you.'

'Yeah, a pleasure,' finished Jane as she flashed them a smile. 'Don't forget what the master said. If you're passing...' She let the sentence hang as we put on a wiggle show as we left the room.

'Uh, you smell like cabbage and sweat,' said Jane when we were out of earshot.

'And stale whisky,' I said.

'And you taste like f—'

'Ah,' said Jane, holding up a finger. 'That's enough. Explain yourself?'

'You explain yourselves,' he shot back.

'Well it's pretty obvious, isn't it? We got carried away.'

'Yes, and it was wonderful,' I babbled excitedly. 'I only wanted a kiss and didn't think Mummy Bear knew, but then she was kissing me in the changing room and was undressed and people were outside and there was only a curtain and—'

-'OK, calm down, Angel. He gets it, I think.'

'You pair of bitches! You couldn't wait?' he asked playfully. 'Thought you were sore?' he said to me.

'Well my tongue wasn't,' I quipped and Jane snorted.

'So now you explain?' she said to him, poking him playfully in the chest.

'What's to explain. Me and the boys were jamming and drinking and then they went out for a fag so I joined them.'

'You smoked?' I asked incredulously. I hated the smell of a smoker and Kelvin smoking would be such a turn off.

'What? Course not.'

'So where did the cabbage smell come from?' I asked.

Jane was saying nothing, just frowning. I suspected she already knew.

'Let's just say that I don't think it was tobacco they were smoking,' he explained.

'So what were...' I'd led such a sheltered life. Drugs had never reared its ugly head anywhere near me. 'You don't mean we—'

'Sshhhh!' said Kelvin. 'You'll get us... and them, thrown off or arrested or something. What was I to do, run away like some scared kid in the playground? *Grass*,' he emphasised the word, 'them up?'

I was dumfounded.

'Either way, it's the shower for you,' Jane said. 'And then you'll get to see my new dress.'

'Nice, shower sounds good,' he leered, squeezing us both tighter as we walked along.

'Not a chance, cowboy,' Jane countered. 'Not while you smell like that!'

So we returned to the cabin and Jane readied her fashion show whilst Kelvin showered. I went with him, just to make sure he scrubbed the smell totally off him, of course. We were both squeaky clean when we finally emerged and Jane play snored on the sofa.

'I thought you were sore?' she asked with an amused raised eyebrow.

Yeah, I was getting that a lot today.

We dressed up for our first night out of our cave, though not in our best. Jane and I both wore cool summer dresses and Kelvin wore long plantation trousers and a fully sleeved casual shirt. He'd rolled the cuffs up slightly, as was his way.

We ate in one of the top restaurants on board. Kelvin explained that we had to take what we could get as meal allocations were planned to the nth degree when the cruise was booked, and that we were late booking and lucky that there was a cancellation. So we were actually eating in the restaurant that whoever had cancelled our cabin had selected but it was very good and the service and food were excellent. Kelvin and Jane ordered lobster and I, because I'd never tried it before, did too. We all had scallops as a starter and I was surprised how good they tasted. There were five courses including the desert, cheeseboard and liqueurs. Kelvin ordered a different wine which each course and Jane told him to stop showing off.

'It's our coming out party,' he'd said in his defence.

This was all new to me and I revelled in it. Normally if I was taken to a restaurant I'd get three courses of overpriced stodge and have to gratefully pay for it in the bedroom later. I laughed to myself as I thought that this time I'd paid in advance, and probably for the next month, too!

A piano softly tinkled in one corner as we ate and afterwards a man came out and crooned along as the tables were cleared. He was very Frank Sinatra and appreciated by most but not our table, though we gave him the applause and respect he deserved.

'I bet you play the piano too, don't you?' I shouted over the final applause as the performer bowed and smiled his exit.

'A little,' he answered. 'But nowhere near well.'

'Is there anything you don't play?'

He smiled. 'Hard to get.'

Jane snorted. 'Yeah, you're such an easy lay!'

Kelvin ordered us champagne in the interval. Whilst we drank and chatted and generally soaked up the atmosphere there was activity in the piano corner as things were set up. I wondered what was happening and observed with interest. In time I realised that a small four of five piece ensemble was being prepared.

'Are we staying here all evening?' I asked.

'We'll stay for a little while, if that's OK. Promised Spider and the boys we'd pop our heads in later if you're willing. Then there are themed pubs or nightclubs or whatever takes your fancy.'

'Wow, this ship has everything!' I exclaimed.

'Sure has,' Jane agreed.

'I wanna go nightclubbing.'

Kelvin and Jane both winced. 'If you insist.'

'I do.'

When the music started couples decamped to the dance floor and I watched enthralled. There was none of the normal women dancing with women thing that I was used to seeing in the nightclubs I occasionally visited. It was mixed partners or nothing, fathers or brothers or boyfriends with mothers or sisters or girlfriends.

'Would you care to dance?' I heard Kelvin say and I saw he was speaking to me. I couldn't dance like this, I thought, and I went to answer him but Jane beat me to it.

'I'd love to,' she answered, and as she rose and accepted Kelvin's arm, he and I shared a look.

Don't tell me, Jane doesn't normally dance either? Well at least it took the pressure off me.

I followed them with my eyes for as long as I could but they were soon lost in the crowd. Occasionally I'd catch a glance of them and they'd wave and I'd wave back and smile. I must admit that they looked a lovely couple and I was close to tears as I watched them enjoy each other's company. I did feel a little awkward sitting alone by myself, though.

The music ended and I saw them returning to our table through the applauding crowd. I noticed that they were both smiling and their eyes sparkled. I felt a momentary stab of envy and wondered if Kelvin would want me once Jane became... fully functional... which she surely must do eventually. I pushed the thought to the back of my head but it wouldn't go away.

'And what about you?' Kelvin asked as he returned Jane to her seat.

I shook my head. 'I can't dance like that,' I said.

'You think I can?' he countered. 'I just move around the floor and try and make it look good.'

I was tempted. 'No, I don't want to leave Jane here by herself,' I finally said.

'You mean like we just rudely did with you?' Jane asked. 'Sorry about that.'

'No, it was fine. I enjoyed watching you.'

'On your feet, soldier!' Kelvin ordered. 'We'll just shimmy around right here, close to Jane.'

'No, I…'

'Go on,' said Jane. 'I'll be fine. And fair is fair.'

Reluctantly I did as I was told and Kelvin took me and held me firm with his right hand in my left and his left in the small of my back. He hummed and played at slowly turning me around and I looked at Jane and smiled. As I did there was a flash and I realised she had a mobile phone in her hand and was taking photographs with it. I'd forgotten she even owned a phone but then I remembered the picture she'd taken of me when I was wearing Elaine's air stewardess uniform on the flight to New York. That time seemed years in the past now.

It felt great being in Kelvin's arms and as he shuffled me around my confidence grew. So much so that I was disappointed when the dance finished.

'You looked like you enjoyed that,' Jane whispered as we sat back down.

I smiled. 'It was fantastic. Kelvin shimmies well!'

'What are you two plotting?' Kelvin asked.

'Nothing,' Jane said. 'Just about your shimmying. You do it quite well.'

'It's easy. You just look like you know what you're doing and Bob's your uncle.'

'Good old Bob,' she answered.

We sat through a couple of boisterous pieces and drank champagne. I was beginning to feel hot and started to fan myself.

'There'll be a cooling breeze on deck, no doubt,' Kelvin said. 'Shall we?'

He pulled our chairs back and we linked arms and left the music behind us. Kelvin snatched the half empty champagne bottle and made sure we kept our glasses.

'Are we allowed to do that?' Jane asked, I guess meaning carrying bottles and glasses around.

'I guess we'll find out, though it is ours and paid for,' he replied.

He was right (as always), the breeze on deck was just what we needed. We walked along in silence for a while as fellow passengers thronged around us in various degrees of rapture. It was all still so unreal to me. I kept thinking that this was a dream and that reality would soon intrude. I would wake and it would be time for work and drudgery and no doubt I'd downed a bottle or two of wine the night before and hadn't prepared any clothes for work.

I felt somebody squeeze my arm.

'You OK?' Jane asked.

I tried to speak but my voice caught. 'I'm just so happy,' I said. 'Happier than I thought I'd ever be.'

'Yes, us too,' Kelvin said.

We continued in silence and squeezed each other's hands. I felt tears coming and started to blink them away. 'I love you two so much,' I said before I even knew I was talking. 'I don't need cruises and holidays and such like, I'll be happy in a tent or on a deserted island wearing nothing but palm fronds.'

'So would I be,' said Kelvin the letch and Jane slapped him on the arm.

'Stop it, Kelvin. You're spoiling the moment.'

'You're right. I apologise. Please forgive me.'

We walked along in silence a little while longer.

'Can we just go home,' I said. 'Back to the cabin, I mean? I don't want to go clubbing.'

'Anything you want, Angel,' Jane answered.

We started to turn around but messed it up as we turned different ways. Before we knew it we were in a messy huddle and laughing at our stupidity. I found myself hugging Jane and as we pulled apart we kissed and we didn't care who saw. Then Kelvin and I kissed and then I watched as they did. A wolf whistle sounded from somewhere and there was the sound of passing laughter but we didn't care. We walked almost trance-like to our cabin and speechlessly kicked our shoes off as Kelvin locked the door after replacing the Do Not Disturb sign. Jane headed for the bathroom.

'Can we go straight to bed?' I asked as Kelvin squeezed the last drops of champagne into our glasses.

Jane stopped and opened her mouth as if she was going to object, but then she simply nodded and unwrapped her dress from around her. Kelvin opened the porthole for air and in no time at all we were the three of us on the bed, naked and wrapped up in each other with me in the middle.

I waited for some sort of advance or touch, though I was happy just to lay where I was, happy and content and safe. My eyes closed and then it was dawn and neither of us had moved an inch since last night. I smiled. I felt happy and refreshed and rested.

I felt movement down by my belly button and watched as Kelvin, or part of him, anyway, awoke. One part of him always woke first and I watched in awe as it seemed to unravel and swell like one of those noisy whistles with a paper-like long balloon that you filled when you blew it. Before that it looked like a walnut whip! It seemed to have a life of its own. It seemed to knock on my stomach as if requesting entry and I smiled, knowing that I wouldn't refuse.

'Oh, it's awake, is it?' Jane said sleepily beside me as she rested her chin on my shoulder.

I nodded.

'If we keep quiet then maybe he won't notice,' she stage whispered.

'Fat chance,' said Kelvin without evening opening his eyes. He reached out and grabbed and the first hand he found was mine. He wrapped my hand around the target and I got the intent. Yes it was going to be another good day.

We finally got out of our cave just after lunch and headed for the pool. We'd all had a bit of a workout by then and could do with a couple of hours laying in the sun. I was exhausted. But happy. Deliriously, unstoppably happy. It had been ages since I had been in a bikini and I felt self-conscious at first, but after just ten minutes of being surrounded by similarly dressed women I felt at home. Jane looked lush, like she belonged in a bikini and I told her so.

'You're kidding?' she answered. 'Have you seen yourself?'

I smiled at the compliment.

'Well I apologise,' Kelvin said as we entered the pool area. We were the three of us arm in arm with him in the middle. He was wearing swimming shorts and a loose shirt and sandals, no socks. 'I have the better deal. I get you two beautiful specimens and all you get is me.'

'True,' said Jane with a wink at me. 'But you can redeem yourself by making sure we get a good spot and some cool drinks as required.'

It was no sooner said than done. Kelvin had to negotiate with two teenage boys who had taken the middle two of a block of five sun loungers. They moved to one side, leaving three in a row for us, but moved away completely a few moments later. Kelvin then found two small tables and placed them between the chairs and disappeared to get drinks.

We settled down when the drinks arrived. It was mainly fruit juices, Kelvin told us, but with enough alcohol to keep us relaxed. He promised to up the alcohol content as the afternoon wore on. We had nothing special to do that evening as we were slumming it as far as the night's eatery was concerned. We were allocated to one of the more cafeteria type venues and it would probably go un-noticed if we turned up tiddly and loud. In fact, we would more than likely fit in better.

Even through the occasional sound of splashing and screaming teenagers I soon settled down with Kelvin's iPod in my ear. I was still officially learning the songs that I'd been ordered to learn but I was also searching for a song that I could sing to them or that Kelvin and I could duet, that I had picked myself. I had no qualms about Kelvin not knowing it. If it were on his iPod, chances were he did. Jane read when she wasn't just soaking up the sun and Kelvin actioned emails on his tablet. At one stage he excused himself and said he had to make a phone call but he returned with fresh drinks, his call made.

'Everything OK, Jack?' Jane asked as she accepted her drink.

'Yeah,' he nodded. 'Just a little thing that needed the boss's guidance. Do them good to have to operate sans the boss for a change.'

As they continued their exchange I saw movement to my front and across the pool from me. Somebody was saluting us (me?) with their drink. I let my sunglasses slip down a little in an attempt to see more clearly. I didn't recognise whoever it was at first but then he sat up and I saw that it was Spider. He was wearing cheap trainers, a black T-shirt with something or other written on it and a tatty pair of cut-off jeans. I stuck my nose in the air and ignored him but as I settled down I saw something else and this person I did recognise, and he was in trouble.

It was Tomas, the goth from the cafe on our first morning aboard and he was sitting on a sun lounger next to another guy. There were four youths standing beside them and there seemed to be a confrontation of sorts going on. I saw one of the youths look around surreptitiously before kicking the sun lounger that Tomas was on. I saw Tomas get up and face off the youth, almost nose to nose, and the three others move closer, almost surrounding him. His friend joined him but they were still outnumbered two to one. I guessed that nobody else had seen the exchange.

'Kelvin, tell me you love me and will do anything for me,' I said, quick as a flash.

Kelvin and Jane both stopped talking as one and then faced me.

'Tell me!' I demanded.

After a few moments of incomprehension he did as I'd demanded.

'Then go over there and stop that fight before it starts. That boy is my friend.'

He turned his head to see the direction I'd pointed in. 'Which boy?'

I pointed again. 'That one. Four lads squaring up to those two. The taller one is my friend.'

He looked at me. 'How do you know him?'

This was no time for jealousy. 'Later, Kelvin, please!'

'OK, OK,' he said as he raised his hands in submission. 'There's meant to be plenty of security on these cruises but I guess they are never around when you need them.'

Jane and I watched as Kelvin negotiated his way between sun loungers and around the pool. He was in no hurry, it seemed to me, and I nearly got up to hurry across myself but Jane stopped me.

'Relax, he has it covered,' she said, laying her arm across my legs to stop me getting up. 'Running across there would ramp up the situation, I'm guessing. Arriving slow and cool could diffuse it. Relax, I've seen him at work before. He'll try diplomacy before he goes to war, believe me.'

I looked at her enquiringly but she wasn't forthcoming. By the time I looked back Kelvin was standing in what I perceived to be a nonthreatening stance, slouched and with his hands in the pockets of his shorts. He was standing facing the four youths, to all intents and purposes amiably passing the time of day. We girls both watched, almost holding our breath, as we waited for something to happen but there seemed to be an impasse. At one stage Kelvin pointed our way and the whole seven of them looked our way. Tomas even smiled and waved upon recognising me. They exchanged words for a few moments more and then the situation seemed to heat up and I saw the leader of the youths point past Kelvin towards Tomas and then try and lunge at him after I'd seen Tomas's lips move. I guessed he had said something about Tomas and hadn't liked the reply, hence the lunge.

Then Kelvin's friendly stance was gone and he pushed the youth back, who almost stumbled before regaining his balance. Occupied sun loungers were almost knocked over and a mild scream arose from the scene. The four surged forward, taking off their shirts as they did. One of them, the leader, had two dark rings on his left arm. Kelvin quickly took off his shirt and flung it aside and the situation cooled as quickly as it started. The one with two arm rings nervously eyed up the foreboding figure of Kelvin before him. I guessed the other guy had clocked Kelvin's tattoos and knew he'd been trumped.

The uneasy standoff continued for a few moments more until cruise security men arrived and Jane and I let out a huge breath. Questions were asked briefly until the security men got the gist of the rights and wrongs of the situation and then the four agitators were herded away. The head security man, or so he seemed to us, watching the silent display from the other side of the pool, then turned and shook Kelvin's hand and I saw Tomas mouth a "Thank You" in my direction. The remaining trio, Kelvin, Tomas and, if my memory was right, Johnny, headed in our direction.

'Thank you, Daddy-o,' I said as I jumped up and hugged and kissed a beaming Kelvin.

'Not a problem,' he said in reply. 'Nobody died.'

'Just as well,' I quipped back. 'Don't think this tub has a tattoo parlour!'

'Thought it was going to get hairy for a second, there,' Jane added. She turned to the other two. 'I think some introductions and explanations are due?'

'Right,' I said, taking my queue. 'This is Tomas and...' I raised an enquiring eyebrow. 'Johnny?'

'Spot on,' Tomas said and he and Johnny shook hands all round. 'Oh shoot,' Tomas suddenly said as he looked behind him. 'Seems we lost our place after all.'

We all followed his gaze where a young couple were starting to make themselves comfortable, ignoring the fact that there were belongings left on the loungers.

'Excuse me?' Kelvin growled across the pool. It wasn't a shout but it carried to the ears of the lounger scroungers, as well as everybody else, just like a leopard's low growl would travel for miles in the jungle or African savannah. It seemed like Kelvin had won the battle and was unwilling to relinquish the battlefield in his absence.

When the couple looked our way Kelvin gave them the universally friendly *fuck off* sign, by holding up his hand, palm facing him, and shooing them away like he was saying "move along". The couple looked at each other and shared a few words but it wasn't until a lady next door leaned over and whispered something to them that they hurriedly packed up their belongings and departed. Kelvin had acquired a rep, it seemed.

'So how did you all meet?' Kelvin asked as if the whole scaring off the lounger scroungers thing hadn't happened.

I told him and drinks were ordered and we as a group swapped stories and introductions. Of course, I didn't delve too deeply into Tomas helping me get my head screwed on straight, but I suspect I didn't have to anyway. Neither Kelvin nor Jane are dumb.

As the two boys started to return to their own, recently fought for, sun loungers I hugged Tomas and whispered in his ear. 'You'll do anything to see Kelvin with his shirt off, won't you?'

'Ah, you remembered,' he smiled back with a wink.

'Thanks, Daddy-o,' I said again after they had gone. 'And now your reward.' I held out a bottle of suntan lotion to him and he smiled as he got the message. I turned over and undid my bikini top and made myself comfortable.

'Oh, and me too,' Jane said, and followed suit.

Kelvin carried out his task, lingered over the areas close to my breasts and buttocks. I felt mildly horny by the time he'd finished.

'Pity there are all these people around,' I whispered as Kelvin rubbed lotion into Jane's back.

'Quite,' she winked back.

'We could always slip away and return later?' the ever hungry hound said, hopefully.

'What, and have to fight for these loungers all over again? No, let's stay and enjoy the sun,' Jane finished.

'But you have won yourself a good time later,' I said. Then I slipped into my innocent little girl routine. 'And I'll do *anything* you say,' I finished, all breathily and heavy breathing.

'OK, then,' he smiled. 'It's a date.'

We all settled down and relaxed and, as us girls sunbathed, Kelvin tapped away at his laptop. I didn't know he'd brought the damn thing with him to the pool. It seemed he never totally switched off.

'That key tapping is awfully loud, you know?' said Jane lazily a few moments later.

'Sorry, sweetheart,' he said.

'You are meant to be on holiday?'

'I know, but I have to prepare a statement for the good Bahadaar.'

'The what?' I asked.

'The head security guy. He's an ex-army Gurkha. Bahadaar means "warrior" and is the most respectful thing I could call him.'

'Ah, no wonder you got him eating out of your hand so quickly,' Jane said.

And I felt rotten. 'Oh, I'm so sorry,' I said as I raised myself up to look at him. I held my hand across my bikini top lest it slip away. 'This is all my fault and now you have to work and do a statement.'

'No sweat,' he said as he continued clicking away. 'I have a reward to look forward to and, in any event, I'll be done in a few moments.'

He continued to tap away and I smiled crookedly up at him and had a naughty thought. 'Would you mind if I went topless?'

'Yes!' they both chorused instantly.

'If you want to go topless and get an all over tan then I will find some secluded spot,' he continued. 'Not having you display your wares for all and sundry to see!'

To be honest it was the answer I was looking for and I smiled as it made me feel wanted, protected and special.

'And anyway,' he continued. 'You get your pineapples out here and my lips will be on them in an instant and then we'll be in trouble.'

'Mine too,' added Jane.

Must admit it was very hard to relax after that. I kept imagining my nipples being sucked and caressed and I couldn't settle. Was beginning to regret that I'd even brought up the subject. I was still fidgeting when Kelvin left to hand his memory stick to the security guy. In the end Jane suggested that I get us some more drinks and it made sense. A good strong cocktail might settle me down. I made my order at the bar, brandy Alexanders, purely because they had brandy in them, and hoped they would be nice. I felt a shadow block out my sun.

'How you doing, little un?'

Where had I heard that before? Oh Christ. 'Mr Spider,' I said as friendlily as I could. I turned around just in time to see his eyes averting from my bikini-clad body. 'Can I get you a drink?'

'Sure, whisky,' he said, and I nodded at the barman. 'A double,' he added.

I nodded as I OK'd his order and we stood looking at each other silently for a while.

'And it's Spider, OK?'

'Mr Spider will be fine,' I said. In truth I was only being nice to the leering git because Kelvin knew him. I was on edge, though, expecting a hit or inappropriate... something or other. He didn't take long to disappoint me.

'You know, if you ever tire of your...' He searched for the right word. 'Life, you could always jump ship and sail with me?'

'And why would I want to do that? I have everything I'll ever need right where I am.'

'Well you never know,' he persisted as his drink arrived and he took a long pull at it. From the smell he'd had a few already. Being a brandy girl, the smell of whisky was off putting.

I decided to attack. 'Did you see Kelvin's tattoos during the recent fracas?' I asked.

He nodded as he tossed off the rest of his drink.

'Well each of those tattoos is a spider that he had to pull the legs off for straying onto his… ah, web?'

He gulped. 'Really?'

I nodded. I know I wasn't being totally truthful but it was close enough. We stared into each other's eyes silently for a while. I hoped the message was getting through to his whisky sodden brain.

'What I mean is,' he continued. 'You're quite a girl and I was wondering if you and I could—'

Seemed he couldn't take a friendly hint.

'I can imagine what you have in mind for you and I. And haven't you got a Mrs Spider at home back at your web?' I asked sweetly.

His silence said it all.

'Don't touch the equipment!' I heard a familiar voice say behind me. I turned to see Kelvin leaning on the bar and leaned back into him. I felt his arm snake around my bare midriff and pull me closer to him. I tingled as his hand touched my bare skin just above my bikini line. How Spider hadn't seen him approach I don't know.

I watched as a look of terror fleetingly covered Spider's face but, credit where credit is due, he recovered quickly. 'Ah, I wouldn't unless invited.'

'As if that's going to happen,' Kelvin returned instantly.

Spider smiled, remembering the gist of their recent introduction. 'Would it help if I said I had an expensive one at home and that you could use it if you were ever passing?'

Kelvin threw back his head and laughed. I smiled too. Mr Spider went up a notch or two in my estimations.

'No, it wouldn't,' Kelvin finally said when he'd finished laughing.

'Can't fault a guy for trying, right?' Spider smiled, partially, I suspected, with relief.

'Yes… and no,' Kelvin answered truthfully.

Just then my order arrived on a tray. The clever barman had added a third drink to my order and I smiled my thanks at him. Kelvin saw my smile and slipped the guy a twenty-dollar bill. I didn't even know he was carrying any cash.

The barman mumbled something and waved it away but Kelvin insisted. After looking left and right he smiled and made the note disappear.

'Well, thanks for the chat,' Kelvin said as he picked up the tray. 'We'll try and pop in for the show tonight. We had an early night last night. Jet lag caught up with us, I think.'

'Yeah, I'm sure,' he said, switching back into leering mode.

'Don't spoil it,' I admonished with my finger. 'Spider!'

His mouth dropped open at the use of his preferred name. It was as if I'd said yes to his intention. I don't think I could have paid him a higher honour.

'See you later,' Kelvin said as he guided me and the tray away from a speechless Spider. I giggled. 'He's harmless,' Kelvin said.

'No he's not,' I answered. 'But I told him you'd pull his legs and arms off if he laid a hand on me.'

'And so I would.'

'I know.'

I couldn't help myself. I stopped and turned and in no time at all I was kissing Kelvin passionately with tongues and sexual intent as he hugged me as best he could with a tray of drinks in his hands. Nobody whistled this time, though I'm sure that all eyes were on us. I could have sworn that the noise level dropped considerably.

'And that's why I love you,' I whispered when we'd finished.

Jane was smiling when we approached and I was sure she'd seen.

'Quite a show,' she said.

'Plenty more where that came from,' he said and then leaned over her, supporting himself on the floor with one arm, and they kissed as I smiled down at them. The surrounding conversation level dropped again. When they finished Jane looked up at me and raised an eyebrow.

'Don't think we should,' I answered, guessing her question.

'I think you're right,' she answered. 'But wait til I get you back to that cabin!'

Chapter Eleven

The afternoon was a joy. We laughed and drank and frolicked in the pool, though Jane never liked putting her head under the water. Kelvin had to watch over her only once as she breaststroked a length of the pool. After that everybody got the hint. No splashing Jane when she dropped into the pool to cool off or the alpha male would get you!

Or at least that's the way I saw it. Either way, it worked just fine.

As for Kelvin and I, we spent a great deal of time in the pool, just swimming and splashing around. We broke some of the rules, I'm sure, like when he'd launch me up out of the water and into a dive. We'd always ensure there was nobody else around when we did it, though. It wasn't as if we were taking over the pool like Kelvin was the local tough or anything. I knew that Kelvin didn't, wouldn't, work that way and I loved him the more for it.

We also broke the "No Petting" rule… ish. I remembered being in a pool as a young girl and seeing the "No Petting" sign and wondering what it meant. I made the mistake of asking my best friend, Sianna, and being the butt of the joke for a long time afterwards. There wasn't actually a sign on this pool that I could see, but I knew it was almost universally accepted as the norm. We didn't grope each other or anything like that but we kissed quite a lot. Nobody complained, so no harm done.

Eventually, things around the pool settled into a kind of normality, a normality policed and sheriffed by a watching, but silent, Kelvin. If anybody got too boisterous or the teenagers started bomb diving into the pool, then one look from Kelvin stopped it instantly. The adults present started to appreciate the safe haven status of the pool and soon there wasn't a spare lounger to be had. Word somehow got around that this was the well behaved pool and everybody who wanted to be noisy or lark around went elsewhere.

This was King Cat's watering hole in His jungle and here you played by His rules or you didn't play at all. I even noticed the Bahadaar drop by, nod approvingly, and with a flick of his head send his security men elsewhere, somewhere where their presence might be needed more.

And all this had been done without Kelvin intentionally saying or doing a thing (barring seeing off the rowdies who were threatening Tomas and Johnny). We found out later that somebody had heard the yob with the arm rings tell his mate what the arm rings meant and that word had travelled. After that nobody wanted to mess with Kelvin.

They didn't know Kelvin. To me he was the most gentle, loving man I'd ever known. He rarely raised his voice to Jane and never raised his hand. He never had to, but that didn't stop some, I knew. I could see, however, how others would find him scary and most of it was down to confidence (and that superb body of his). Problem for the bad guys was that he had the ability to look after himself which was the foundation of his confidence. He explained to me once that he put it down to having been to dark places and coming out the other side, nothing "phased him" any more. He'd seen the worst that man could do to another man (he hinted that some of it had been done to him) but he was still around to tell the tale. I'd tried to dig deeper but he wouldn't tell.

The next round of drinks were brought over by the barman and they were free. Whether they were on the house or charged to other guests' rooms we didn't know at first, but they kept coming. All we were told when Kelvin enquired was that they had been paid for. Occasionally we caught the eye of our patron when the drinks were served and we saluted them with our glasses. One time it was a smiling Spider and I thanked him with a full megawatt smile that I was sure would have him fantasising for a year.

We hadn't been back in the cabin five minutes before Kelvin dragged me into the bathroom. Jane left us to it as she wanted to take a nap and then take time to get ready for the night's festivities. I jokingly pleaded with her to stay but I knew she wouldn't.

'You promised the hero the good time,' she said to me as she left us to it.

'But what about the kiss you promised me back at the pool?'

She about faced and pulled me close to her and we kissed deeply and sensually as she caressed my skin and slowly moved her hands all over my body. When she was done I was ready for whatever Kelvin could throw at me, but Jane just yawned.

'Oh thanks,' I said in mock anger.

'Sorry, the sun just does that to me. No reflection on your good self, I promise.' She yawned again, using her hand to stifle it as she closed the door of the bathroom behind her. 'Try and keep it quiet if you don't mind,' was her parting shot.

As the door clicked shut behind her I looked at Kelvin, smiled and started to move towards him but he stopped me and my mouth fell open in confusion.

'Lay down,' he ordered.

My confusion must have shown on my face.

'So much for anything I asked,' he said with a shrug.

I jumped to comply, remembering my promise. I noticed that he had piled towels on the floor and I guessed that they were meant as my destination. I made myself as comfortable as I could, as comfortable as a girl wearing a bikini laying on a pile of towels in a ship's bathroom could be. My heart started to beat faster, partly in anticipation and partly out of a kind of fear of the unknown. I knew that Kelvin wouldn't hurt me but I was unaware of what was to come. It was plain old trepidation.

Slowly he knelt at my feet and I followed him with my eyes. He seemed to just be looking at me, savouring me with his eyes. Just like his hands had done earlier when he was applying my sun lotion, his eyes lingered over certain parts of me longer than others.

For some reason I swallowed nervously and my heart rate increased.

'What—'

'No talking.'

I went to answer, "Yes, sir", but stopped myself. No talking meant no talking. I felt my heart beating in my chest.

He reached forward and placed his right forefinger on my stomach just above my bikini bottoms and slowly dragged it down and over my bikini until it rested on my right upper thigh. Then he spread all his fingers and dragged his hand down some more before stopping again. I tried to look into his eyes and gauge his intention but he was totally engrossed in what he was doing. He started to move again and I felt that his hand was now moving the other way, back up my thigh. But this time his fingers invaded under my bikini bottoms and I gasped as I felt him touch my pubic mound. He applied pressure and rubbed slowly and I felt the friction between his skin and my pubic hair as it occasionally pulled against his rough hands. My breath caught and my legs opened a fraction as if he'd hit a switch. At this he slowly removed his hand and I opened my eyes. I hadn't even realised they were closed. Was he teasing me?

'Turn over,' he ordered softly and I hurried to comply. He undid my bikini top. At last. Something I was at least expecting, I told myself.

He let the straps fall as I had when I'd been sun bathing. Then he massaged my neck and shoulders slowly but with firm pressure. He was positively pulling my skin until it could reach no further and then it would slowly return back to its original place but with the friction of his hands pulling on it still. It was like being massaged with smooth grain sand paper but, strangely, it was most satisfying. I wondered how he knew such things.

All too soon I realised that he'd stopped and I raised my head to try and meet his gaze. I saw that he'd taken off his shorts and was now naked and was settling into a sitting position against the wall. As he did, he pulled me towards him and I ended up leaning against him and snug between his open legs with my back resting on his chest. My bikini top had stayed on the towels and I felt his hands immediately cup my breasts and my nipples start to harden as he tempted them with his forefingers and thumbs. I threw my head back and started breathing raggedly and he bit hard down on my shoulder which just made me gasp even more. He continued by nuzzling my ear and neck and intermittently biting when the need took him. I never knew when he was going to and it was like an electric shock going off in my head.

I felt my arousal building and I almost turned to face him so that I could kiss him and lay my hands on him but I realised just in time that I was doing his bidding and he hadn't yet given me permission. Instead I let out a loud, satisfied groan and visibly opened my legs further. He got the hint and slipped his right hand into the front of my bikini bottoms and I secretly smiled at my victory. Then he had fingers inside me whilst he still nuzzled and bit and teased my nipples. I felt the need rising within me and I didn't fight it. My climb had already started and soon my cascade and my orgasm would follow.

Too late.

I squirmed around as he played with me, moving contra to him so that his fingers went deeper into me. He took the hint and started to frig me with abandon as I writhed and squirmed and moaned in pleasure. Suddenly I went rigid and pushed my body against him as I bit my top lip. It wasn't long before I was erupting in noisy rapture as the waves of pleasure vibrated through me. He moved his left hand from my breast and covered my mouth with it and, strangely, this only heightened my pleasure.

Was he doing this so that I wouldn't disturb Jane or did he know the effect it would have? And if he did know then *how* did he know?

He continued to flick his fingers back and fore inside me as he stifled my orgasm and I felt myself start to shake uncontrollably like I had no control over my own body. After what felt like an eternity, I finally went limp like a rag doll as my orgasm ended. How it hadn't turned into a double or even triple yolker I don't know. It had certainly seemed like the longest orgasm I had ever had.

He removed his hand from my mouth and let me go limp. I found the strength to turn my head and our eyes met. He wore a small victorious smile, damn him. He knew exactly what he was doing. I was the proverbial putty in his hands, his to do with as he felt fit. And I was grateful, I was his completely. If he could see through my eyes into my soul he would see that at that precise moment in time I would gladly flail off my own skin and roll in a vat of salt if he but uttered a hint. I managed a weak smile and his widened slightly.

I remembered that somebody had recently called him a control freak. Well if that meant he had control over my orgasms then so be it. He could be a control freak any time he wanted.

I felt him remove his fingers from inside me and some of the sticky dampness come with them, but I didn't care. Then he put his hands around my waist and I felt him relax and I joined him, my breathing slowly returning to normal. He was comfortable to rest against, even with his promise of something more digging into my back. Part of me suspected I could be laying on a beach full of sharp rocks and pebbles and I'd still have felt blissfully at ease.

So that was a reward for him? Felt more like a birthday treat for me!

'Oh boy,' I finally said.

'NO TALKING,' he growled.

You mean we aren't finished? I was.

Wasn't I?

He pushed me gently forward and I ended up face down on the towels again. I felt him tugging at my bikini bottoms and raised myself slightly so as the ease the way for their removal but he slapped my rump.

'No!'

Hell, I was only trying to help him, I told myself. Did I really deserve that?

'Hands and knees,' he ordered once I was fully naked and I complied instantly.

I felt his skin brush mine as I heard him position himself behind me. I relaxed slightly. So it was going to be the good old doggie style, was it? Well I'd done that before so nothing to worry about there. And I remembered that so far he had done all the giving and was due a little taking. As Jane would say, fair was fair.

I smiled to myself. So I was finished, was I? Funny how I wasn't all of a sudden.

I patiently waited for him to enter me but he was taking his own sweet time about it. Dare I turn around and enquire? Ah, that's what he wants me to do and then it will be punishment for noncompliance. Snowball's chance in hell, honey. Wise to you, yes, sir!

Eventually I felt some pressure on my rear and I almost jumped. He was off target slightly, not like Kelvin at all. I wiggled back and fore a little bit to help him but he seemed to miss the honey pot completely just as he was almost knocking on the door. I felt him try again but still he got it wrong. He ended up almost ready to knock on the back door. What was wrong with hi…

Realisation hit me. Surely he wasn't intending to…

Well you did say ANYTHING HE WANTED!

I quickly turned my head and our eyes met. He was looking at me, daring me to speak. I shook my head slowly, my eyes silently imploring. I watched as he slowly raised his right hand above my bottom, the threat obvious. My mouth opened, almost letting out a word, but I stopped myself in time but shook my head more. He stayed the same, watching me with his hand ready to drop. He wore a crooked smile on his face and his eyes shone bright.

I was caught between a rock and a hard place, a very hard place actually. He wouldn't actually do it without my permission, would he? I'd never speak to him again!

Is that why you're moving away?

No, he wouldn't. I trust him. He'd never hurt me.

He motioned me with his hands to avert my gaze and look straight ahead but I couldn't. My eyes were drawn to his manhood which I could just about see behind me. I could see that it was ready for anything. Surely it wouldn't fit in *there*!

This time he motioned me sternly to turn my head back around and I found myself complying. I tensed up all my muscles, positively holding as tight as I could to the towels until my knuckles were white. I screwed my eyes tight shut and clamped my jaw closed and waited for whatever I was going to receive, though it didn't take much guessing.

I don't have to do this. I can stop this. He'd never hurt me. I'll move away. He won't do it, he'd never against my will. But as long as I'm complying, I'm willing. No, I trust him, he'd never hurt me. HE'D NEVER HURT ME!

I let out a scream when I felt his attack at the back and I moved forward as far as I could but without moving my hands or legs. Slowly I naturally sprang back into position acknowledging that it hadn't been half bad so far, in fact far from it. It was fear of the unknown, the waiting, that had done me in. Before I was back at my starting point I felt the same pressure again but I was ready for it. I realised as I again gasped that he must have moved forward a tiny amount. Again I moved forward on my natural spring and I started to look behind me, against the rules or not, to see what he was doing. Before my head had completed the turn, though, he attacked me again, harder this time, and my arms gave way and my nose buried itself into the towels as he continued.

I felt an electricity bolt of pleasure run through me and I cried out. Then when I thought it couldn't get any better it suddenly would and I would moan loudly again, all thought of not disturbing Jane gone.

Then I realised that it was his tongue he was using on me. The semi-softness of his tongue against the softness and sensitivity of the little private, least used part of my body. He did it again and I gasped again but when he removed his tongue I was already aching for the next intrusion. I tried to anticipate the next attacks but misjudged the first couple. On the fourth attempt I judged it perfectly and moved back just as he was moving forward and it was like a perfect moment in time. I gasped even louder and tried to stifle it down but soon I had to give in and move forward. This time my legs gave way too and I was suddenly laying flat on the towels.

Then the main attack of pleasure started. With my natural spring gone I had nowhere to go and his tongue went in and it stayed in as he tried to push deeper and deeper into me. I squirmed and I thrashed about and I bit my lip and screwed my eyes tight but I would have died if he'd actually stopped.

Hell, this was heaven. PLEASE NEVER STOP!

The words rushed through my head and I knew I meant them. I felt his hands on my bum cheeks and he forced them apart and pushed his tongue harder still. I felt like I was going to split in two but I didn't want him to stop. My breathing caught, surely I'm not going to…

He must have noticed because he stopped and I felt the sweet rise start to fall.

'No!' I pleaded, but I needn't have worried.

In no time at all his penis was inside me, in the front door, and I was galloping on it as much as I could with his weight laying atop me, getting every inch of pleasure out of it I could. My breath started to become ragged and noisy and I panted at every breath and my breathing got faster and faster until I could hear myself and was secretly ashamed at my wantonness. I went silent for the last two or three seconds but I knew it was the calm before the storm. Then the storm broke and it was a force ten hurricane. I bit down on the towels but probably I was still waking everybody on the ship. Then Kelvin grunted and I swear I felt his explosion inside me like high pressure water being squirted into a cup. He grunted again and thrust forward one last time and held it as long as he could, his hands pulling on my shoulders in an attempt to get further into me. Then he collapsed on top of me, the both of us panting and spent.

I felt his breath by my left ear, loud and ragged like mine. After it had slowed a little he softly pulled out of me.

No no no!

I heard him flop down beside me like a big wet fish and I turned to face him and he gathered me in his arms. We said nothing, just lay, nose to nose, breathing each other's air and smiling inanely like a pair of idiots. He reached back and removed a sweat sodden lock of hair from my forehead. I smiled back, my breathing still not back to normal.

'I'll not,' he started to say but found he didn't have the breath. 'I'll not do the other thing until you beg me,' he finally got out.

'I'm begging, I'm begging!' I answered.

He smiled and it turned into a laugh. 'Well your timing is awful!' he said. 'Just give me a minute to recover.'

The minute passed and then it was sweet oblivion. We were still asleep when Jane popped her head around the door a few hours later.

'Oh, you're alive?' she said. 'Always a bonus, I find. Don't move,' I thought I heard her say as she left the room. When she came back she had her camera phone in her hands and was snapping away. 'You look like a pair of friendly dogs sleeping all wrapped up like that.'

Kelvin woke up. 'Well we were dogs at one stage.'

I snorted. How did he do that? He was straight from slumber to sharp in nothing flat and it was funny too.

'What time is it?'

'Little after seven. Thought I'd better wake you if we're going to eat for eight. Have you showered?'

Kelvin yawned as he helped me up. 'Didn't get that far. Hope we didn't disturb you?'

'Well you didn't really. Thought you were killing her at one stage, though,' she said, pointing to me.

'And you came in and saved me?' I returned cheekily. 'Must have missed that bit.'

'Oh, sounded like you were beyond saving. Come on, you, shower!'

She grabbed my hand and pulled me into the shower. We women always showered first as we needed the time to get ready whilst Kelvin would be ready in five minutes flat. Part of me hoped that she wouldn't get amorous in the shower but only part of me. I was spent. I laughed at myself. Where had I heard that before!

As it turned out we didn't get into anything heavy in the shower but we did enjoy washing and soaping each other. We kissed often and Jane told me how wonderful I was and I returned the compliment. I was such a lucky girl, I told myself for the hundredth time. Two people love me and I love them. How could my life change so much in just two weeks?

When we left the bathroom we were met by a still naked Kelvin carrying two glasses of chilled bucks fizz. 'It'll bring us back to life,' he said as we accepted the drinks.

I hadn't realised how thirsty I was and gulped mine straight down.

'Another?' he asked.

I nodded. 'Yes, please.'

'What *have* you been doing to her!' Jane exclaimed.

'What hasn't he been doing to me, you mean.'

'Prey, tell.'

'Oh I will. Later. I'm looking forward to it.'

'Me, too. Now shower, you,' she said the last bit to Kelvin, slapping his bare rump as she did so. 'I'm starving!'

Somehow Kelvin changed our food booking and we ended up eating in the most luxurious restaurant on board that night, so we were semi-dressed up. Tomorrow was the penultimate night, I knew, and the formal dress up night. Tonight was semi-smart, second best togs and all that.

The food was exquisite and we purposely ordered different dishes but shared what we had between us. To the outsider it must have looked like a dangerous, confusing melee of food laden forks, but none of us were even remotely injured.

I was aware of the staring attention we were getting from some of the other tables but I didn't give a hoot. I was enjoying myself, I was deliriously happy and, in any event, if anybody wanted to complain they would have to go through Kelvin first and somehow I didn't think that anybody would. And nobody did. At least not on that occasion.

I'm sure that some of them thought we were unkempt and uncouth heathens but I would rather be that, and happy, than posh and stern and po-faced and sad like them. You can't please all of the people all of the time, I'd heard somewhere. Well we weren't even trying. We were pleasing ourselves.

I had no doubt that some were happy when we finished and left the place, Kelvin in the middle with his arms around us both. I noticed scowls from some but that wasn't all. I could have been wrong but I was sure that some of the men were jealous of Kelvin, who wouldn't be with him having two lovely blonde ladies (even if I do say so myself) on his arms. I also saw wild-eyed desire from some of the women present. One of them I recognised from the pool earlier as she had always been looking our way and trying to meet Kelvin's gaze and smile at him. Her husband, partner, whatever, looked like he was terrified of her and wouldn't have dared object if she'd stripped naked in front of us and wiggled her finger Kelvin's way. Either way I knew she wouldn't get anywhere with Kelvin and the thought gave me a warm glow.

I'd never felt so proud being on the arm of any other man. There was total trust. I knew he wouldn't hurt me, would look after and protect me, would never stray, would never even let his eyes wander. He would provide for my, our, every need. Isn't that what every girl wants in a man? And a MAN was what he was, too, not some metro-sexual wimp who couldn't change a fuse and needed his female partner's permission to breathe and who used conditioning creams and make-up. Hell, we had to force him to use suntan lotion on himself!

I felt my pride turn into desire and then I noticed that Jane was watching me. She looked as happy as I felt.

'Do you feel it, too?' she asked.

'Oh yes,' I almost panted. 'Back to the cabin?'

Kelvin barked a laugh. 'We promised Spider we'd attend,' he said. 'And this is the last chance before the ball tomorrow.'

'Fuck Spider,' I whispered a little too loudly. At least one head turned at my coarseness.

'I'm sure he'd be happy if you did,' said Jane before turning to Kelvin. 'You do know that he wants to bounce our little angel up and down on his web, don't you?'

'I'm sure lots of men here, do, and to you, too,' he answered, squeezing us both tighter.

'Well he can forget it. Closest he'll get to that is webbed fingers,' I answered, proud at my quick wittedness.

Kelvin laughed.

'I don't get it,' said Jane, which made me laugh some more.

I was amazed. Even Richard and I played *The Man from Atlantis* occasionally. Jane never had? Surely not!

'I shall explain when the time is right, my dear,' Kelvin answered.

No, I was amazed. They never had but I had. I smiled to myself. Maybe little old me could teach my masters a little something after all!

So we went to the band, even though Jane and I tried a mega pout at Kelvin.

'Half an hour?' he pleaded with outstretched hands. 'Then I promise we'll go back to the cave and darn, or whatever it is we do to pass the evenings.'

I mouthed the F word to Jane and she nodded and smiled back at me.

'OK, twenty minutes, and that's my final offer!'

So we went to hear the band and, to be honest, they were very good. Spider started to show off, I think in an attempt to impress me, but I purposely ignored him. When I thought twenty minutes had gone I looked at Jane and winked and she joined me as I surreptitiously started stroking Kelvin's thigh. We left within minutes after that and were at the cabin in short order. We were pulling at each other's clothes before the door was even closed.

Seemed we all had intentions that night, each of us fighting to actively do things to one or both of the others. It turned into another battle, all swords and charges and attacks. I had to surrender first (well it's hard to fight two against one) but a sweeter surrender I could not imagine. In this war being conquered was the best you could hope for, and I was being conquered a lot. In fact I could have changed my name to France. Do I have to say that other countries are available?

Then it was dawn and I was awake, having woken earlier than I'd thought I would. I was getting used to waking up feeling calm and loved. Before I met Kelvin and Jane I used to wake up feeling either agitated or depressed with either work or a lonely weekend to look forward to. That all seemed like a long way away now, a lifetime ago.

In the half-light I could see the faces of both Kelvin and Jane without even having to move, they were that close to me. But I didn't feel squashed or uncomfortable or anything, just loved and secure and looked after and special and excited. I felt like kicking my feet under the light sheet we used to cover us on the warm nights, just like I had when I was a young girl and excited about Christmas or a school trip or something.

I just knew that I wouldn't sleep any more that morning so I lay still and fantasised about how my life would be from now on and it didn't need too much in the way of imagination. There'd be friendship, love and fantastic sex, my every need catered for. I'd buy a car – Kelvin wouldn't mind, would he – or perhaps I'd just drive one of his? I'd make sure that I'd drive where everybody that I used to know in my old life could see me and I'd be Lady Muck and a lady of leisure and they'd be downtrodden and on the way to work and have to worry about paying bills. All I'd have to worry about is which part of the ceiling I'd be studying that night, or afternoon or morning – like I gave a damn!

And we'd have more holidays, no doubt. I wondered where we'd go?

I felt a slight stab of guilt. Was I wrong to be thinking this way, was I being mercenary? No, I'd more or less been told that my future life would be that way, or pretty close to it, anyhow. Kelvin would be at work and I would be at home with Jane. That in itself would be nice. I began to feel aroused at the thought of being alone and unescorted with Jane all day, what would we do all day? Yeah, like I needed telling. Then Kelvin would come home and Jane and I would fight to bring him his pipe and slippers and then the evenings would be even nicer. And we'd have cooked dinner for him and...

What?

Well, that was a shock. I actually found myself wanting to cook for him, for them. With Richard, with both of us working, it had been a chore. Whoever got home first got the duty and I'm sure he delayed coming home sometimes so that he could shirk. OK, I'd considered it once or twice but never actually done it. Well, OK, just once, but it made me feel so guilty that I rushed home to ensure that I was home first for the rest of the week.

A sudden thought struck me. Can Jane even cook? They had that Consuella creature to do all that. I wondered if Kelvin could cook but somehow I erred towards the positive. Yeah, it wouldn't surprise me at all if he could cook, being the Jack that he was.

'Good morning, my angel,' whispered Jane as she moved to kiss me on the lips.

I smiled back. 'Good morning, Mummy Bear.' She'd never once commented on the name I'd adorned her with. I guessed she must like it.

'I was watching you,' she continued. 'You seemed to be elsewhere if your face was any judge.'

Guilty as charged. 'I was thinking about our future,' I whispered honestly. I saw no point in lying about it.

'And was it good?'

'Heaven. I still don't believe I'm here with you two, loving two people and being loved back, and one of them's a girl! And the sex? I've orgasmed every time!' I started to giggle but stifled it with my hand. I didn't want to wake Kelvin. *Liar!*

'Sometimes more than once, you greedy girl!'

'I know. Was it like that with just the two of you?'

'More often than not, ninety-nine per cent of the time. I'm sure there were off days but they were few and far between.'

'Wow. With Richard it had been the other way around. How come we always seem to do it?'

'I believe they say that arousal is fifty per cent in the body and fifty per cent in the mind. It helps if you at least fancy the person you're doing it with.'

'Oh, I do. Both of you!'

She smiled. 'And, of course, Kelvin is very attentive, he knows his way around a woman's body, that's for sure, and he knows some tricks. And he isn't selfish, either. Some blokes all they want to do is get pleasure. Kelvin likes to dish it out and have you noticed how he always makes sure we're satisfied before he finishes?'

I nodded. 'Quite a guy, isn't he?'

'I'm sure he's loving us talking about him like this, the rogue.'

I looked below his flat stomach. 'No, he's asleep,' I whispered. 'Walnut whip there for all the world to see.'

'Walnut whip? What do you mean?'

Then she got it and used her hand to stifle a snort. 'Walnut whip! That's hilarious, that's just what it is!'

'And just before he wakes it unravels like one of those noisy whistles you have at children's parties.'

I watched as her face turned from confused to humour as she got what I meant. This time she put her whole hand over her mouth to stop disturbing Kelvin but I was surprised that he wasn't awake yet, considering the noise we were making and the movement of the bed as we stifled our giggles.

'I don't think I'll ever be able to blow one of those things again,' she said around her hand.

I turned around to face her and we lay there nose to nose like two little girls plotting and sharing secrets on a sleepover. She smelt of clean laundry, soap and perfume.

'So tell me,' she said after kissing me. 'You OK with the whole girl on girl thing?'

I thought for a suitable answer. 'Better than I'd thought I'd be. Not, I might add, that I'd ever thought about it. Everything I do with you – between the three of us, actually – feels natural. No second thoughts, no regrets. Couldn't do the girl bit with anybody but you, though.'

'Nor me,' she answered. 'But I can't complain because I did start this.'

'Must admit that doing the bloke bit with anybody but Kelvin feels pretty alien at the moment.'

'Very glad to hear it. Keep it that way.'

'And I think your bum is fantastic,' I said as I lowered my eyes in shame. 'I could look at it all day. And your breasts? Wow! How come I never noticed how beautiful the female form is before? All that time wasted!'

'Probably just as well, considering,' she answered. 'But it's fun catching up on lost time.'

We grew silent, just looking into each other's eyes and smiling.

'You know,' I said finally. 'Some mornings I'd like to wake up with just you and me. Is it wrong of me to think that?'

She shook her head. 'It'll happen, too, Kelvin does business trips.'

'But I wouldn't want to be without Kelvin either,' I said, suddenly feeling guilty at not including him.

'Don't worry, I know what you mean. And I'm sure there will be times when you want there to be just you and Kelvin and I will probably want just Kelvin and me on occasion. Let's not worry about it. But when that time comes I want you to tell me. It's not like I ever go anywhere, don't think I've left Kelvin alone in the house since we've been together!'

'Not even once?'

'No, nowhere else to go, nobody to visit. Wouldn't want to, anyway.

He's been my rock and my crutch these last four years. I'd be lost without him.'

My good mood lessened slightly at the thought of the hell that she'd hinted she'd been through before Kelvin came back into her life. 'You know, I'm so sorry about the bad things that happened to you. Makes me angry just thinking about it and I know next to nothing about those times.'

'Why, thank you, but that's in the past and I have you two now and I'm happy.'

'You know, if anybody tried to hurt you, I wouldn't let them. I'd kick and scratch and bite and…'

'Call Kelvin?'

'Yeah, but if he wasn't around then I'd…' I found myself lost for words and a lump form in my throat. The thought of somebody hurting Jane or Kelvin made me want to bare my teeth and rip throats out.

Yeah, like anything could harm Kelvin!

'I know,' she said, stroking my cheek. 'And I'd do the same for you, sweet Aneese.'

We softly kissed, playfully biting each other's lips and taking our time about it. Suddenly she put her finger to her lips and pulled me with her out of the bed. She passed me a short, thin robe and we loosely slipped them on as we padded hand in hand to the balcony door. She put her finger to her lips again and cautiously slid the door open. When we were out, she closed it behind us and I started to breathe once more.

'Good. Didn't want to wake him. Not often he gets a lay in.'

I leant on the rail and watched the lightening sky and the white, bubbly fluorescence of the ship's wake. The breeze was strong enough to upset our hair but it wasn't chilly at all. I felt her join me and her arm felt good around my waist, just like Kelvin's did.

'It's odd, isn't it?' I asked. 'Been in the cabin for a nearly a week and we haven't been out on this balcony once. It's beautiful, especially this time of the morning.'

'It is,' she agreed. 'But I have been out here once. When you and Kelvin were in the bathroom yesterday, just briefly.'

From somewhere I smelt the delicious aroma of bread baking and it reminded me of the first morning aboard as I ran to sort my head out and met Tomas. She had both her arms around me now, like a man would. If we were in a social gathering it would denote ownership, I knew. And I loved it.

'You know, I still don't believe this,' I said.

'Well believe it. Your life is going to be quite a bit different from here in.'

'It'll take some getting used to. I keep expecting to wake up and that it's all been a dream. I'll be so disappointed if I do.'

'Well don't wake up, then, stay here in the dream world with us. Tell me about the bathroom yesterday and you'll stay asleep longer.'

So I told her everything and she nodded and commented because she'd been there herself, more than once.

'So you've... you know... up the bum?' I found myself asking.

She smiled and made a kind of face before answering. This was hardly a topic for civilised society before breakfast. 'Sure.'

'And was it OK?'

'More than OK. Wouldn't want to do it all the time but once in a while is fine. More than fine, actually. And an anal orgasm is, strangely, better than the normal one. Or perhaps it's just that absence makes the *arse* seem fonder!'

I laughed out loud at her creative reply. 'But doesn't it hurt?'

'A little, but Kelvin is careful. And pain is so close to pleasure, they say. And weren't you positively begging for it by the time you'd finished yesterday?'

'Well, yeah, but that was yesterday.'

She pulled me closer and kissed my cheek. 'Relax, you haven't got to do it and nobody will force you, least of all the monster in there.'

'But he wants to. What if I say no?'

'Well you are allowed to, you know. You can say no to anything you want.'

'But won't he be upset?'

'No, but you are missing the point here.'

'I am?'

'Yes. Kelvin will not be taking anything away from you when and if you do it, he'll be giving something to you.'

Oh he'll be giving you something, all right! And wasn't that what Tomas had said?

I was confused and it must have showed because she continued. 'Yesterday in the bathroom when he was... tasting you down there? Did you enjoy it?'

'Yes,' I answered quickly, there was no denying that. 'It was unexpected and new and... I didn't want it to stop and it was such a surprise. It was almost like the first time you find out you can do something more with your fanny than just go to the toilet with it.'

'And it'll be like that when you do the other, too. Well maybe not unexpected, but you know what I mean. And tell me, do you want him to use his tongue on you again?'

Well that was a no brainer. 'God, I hope so. If he doesn't I'll complain!'

'And that is how you'll feel when you're not an anal virgin, my little angel. You'll want him to do it again and you'll be mad if he doesn't.'

My mouth dropped open. 'Honest?'

'Cross my heart.' She went through the motions. 'Trust me, trust him!'

I smiled, partly in relief. Suddenly I was looking forward to losing my bum cherry although I was still a little apprehensive.

'You could always be, shall we say, under the influence the first time?' she suggested.

'Were you?'

'Well, yes, but not intentionally so. It wasn't as if I purposely drank to numb myself, we'd just had a drink, that's all.'

'And have you done it sober?'

'Of course. What do you think I am, some sort of lush!'

'No, I didn't mean that.'

'Relax, I was only playing. We're British and as such we drink. It's in our history.'

'It is?'

'Yeah. Kelvin will tell you all about it, I'm sure. He knows about stuff like that.'

'He does?'

'Sure, he's a history buff. Military history mainly, but the two sometimes overlap.'

Another thing about Kelvin I didn't know. Perhaps we should speak more instead of fucking all the time? *Yeah, right. Like you want that!* I stayed silent and reflected on all that Jane had just said. My eyes were drawn to a seagull floating on the breeze and when I looked, I noticed that Jane was watching it too.

'Morning, my ladies,' I heard just as I heard the small rumble as the door slid on its runners. We both turned and were caught unawares when the phone flashed and I heard the artificial sound of a camera shutter.

'You both look more than ravishingly beautiful this morning. That'll be a great picture.'

'Oh, you. You surprised us.'

'That's how you get the best shots.'

We joined and kissed our good mornings.

'Didn't mind waking up alone, did you?' Jane asked.

'Not at all. I was in a half slumber and knew you'd come out here.'

'We woke early and were trying not to wake you,' I explained.

'Thanks, appreciate it. So you want to breakfast here on the balcony?'

Jane and I shared a look and deliberated. 'Yeah, that'll be great.'

'So what were you talking about, out here?'

Suddenly I was mortified. I knew Jane and Kelvin had no secrets.

'Never you mind. Girls talk,' was all Jane answered. I was so grateful I would have licked *her* arse, there and then.

Hmmmmm, I found myself thinking. Now there's a thought?

'OK, I'll get breakfast ordered if you're going to be boring.'

'You do that,' she answered deadpan, before sticking her tongue out at his retreating back.

'Thanks, Jane,' I said when he'd gone. 'Though I feel bad that you've kept it from him I'm glad you did. I know you have no secrets from him.'

She smiled. 'Well, there are three of us to consider now. Couldn't have my favourite girl squirming as I blabbed.' She paused before continuing. 'Though actually, that would have been fun to watch!'

'Oh, you wouldn't!'

She smiled. 'Well maybe I would?' she answered all coy, like a little girl.

The breakfast trolley arrived a short time later and we enjoyed the coolness of the morning breeze as we ate. This was the earliest we'd risen so far this week, though we'd yet to make the actual sitting breakfast. Time was running out for that event. The cruise was close to its end.

'So what's the plan for today?' I asked as I polished off my plate. I was ravenous this morning and eating outside in the fresh, salty breeze only seemed to enhance it.

'Whatever you like,' Kelvin said. 'I have a few calls to make but that won't take long.'

'But you're on holiday,' Jane objected.

'It won't take long and you'll hardly notice anyway.'

'I was thinking of you.'

He smiled. 'Thank you, my sweet. Gotta be done, though.'

'Can we lounge by the pool,' I asked. 'Still got bikinis we haven't worn.'

'Yeah, lets,' answered Jane.

'But there's so much of the ship we haven't seen yet,' he said. 'How about a bit of exploring and then relax by the pool until it's getting ready to go out time. It'll give the sun a chance to rise so you're nice and hot by the pool?'

As usual there was a lot of sense in what he'd said and we nodded our acceptance.

'Not that you two lovelies don't look super hot as it is,' he added.

'He says the nicest things, doesn't he,' Jane said to me before turning to him. 'And I'll want to get to the hair salon later today, too.' Jane added.

'As will half the ship.'

'Well in that case phone and book me now, dammit.'

'You have such a way with words, my lady,' he played as he rose to carry out her request, no, demand.

'And Aneese, too!'

'No, I'll be fine. My mop is easy,' I shouted so that Kelvin would hear. 'I'll just wash it and it'll be fine.'

'Are you sure?' she asked.

'Yeah. I'll just wash it and blow-dry it and it'll be perfect.'

'Can I do it for you?'

'Well only if we set an alarm for the conditioner this time.'

The two of us sat quietly for a small while as we listened to Kelvin negotiating Jane's hair appointment over the phone. He was right (as usual) and most of the appointments had been taken. It took him a good ten minutes of good natured bribery, charm, coercion and wit before he was successful.

'Yeah, done,' he said. 'But it is the very last appointment of the day. Seventeen hundred, ask for Gail.'

'That's five p.m. to us normal people,' she said to me before turning back to him. 'And what did you have to promise her?'

'Said she'd recognise you because you'd be carrying a bottle of champagne and a large box of chocolates. Got the impression that Gail was of the tugboat persuasion. Guessed she'd appreciate the chocs.'

'Tugboat persuasion? What on earth is that?' I asked.

'You know,' he motioned with his hands as if drawing a football in the air. 'Big girl?'

'Tugboat?' I again asked.

He sighed as if he was explaining to a child for the umpteenth time. 'You women come in two types: tugboats and liners. You two are obvious liners. Fine, racy lines, pleasing on the eye, turn heads wherever you go, people want you to visit their port and want to get inside you when you do.'

'Kelvin!'

'Then there are tugboats,' he continued, unperturbed. 'Bit more power and bulk, less speed. Everybody knows that tugboats are necessary but nobody wants to sail in one. There are three or four tugboats to every liner but nobody sees them even though there are some in every port.'

My mouth dropped open. 'That's cruel.'

'Life is,' he continued. 'Haven't you ever noticed that when unattached women go out on the town they go in pairs? One is a tugboat and one a liner. It's a... what do they call it on *Star Trek*... symbiotic relationship?'

'Say what?' I said it but the confusion was on Jane's face, too.

'They both get something out of it. The liner looks even better with the tugboat in tow and the tugboat gets to visit places and see things that tugboats don't normally get to see. Everybody wins. And, of course, when the liner sets sail, or pulls,' he said with a wink. 'The tugboat returns to port and waits for the liner to return so she can nudge it back into its berth. Couldn't be simpler than that.'

I opened my mouth to object but something stopped me. I *had* seen women like that out on the town. I just hadn't looked at them through the critical and analytical eyes of a bloke, and an almost surreal, witty and intelligent bloke at that. Wow, this was almost deep.

I looked at Jane. 'You know he does have a point.'

'I guess,' she answered. Her mind seemed elsewhere.

There was silence for a short while as if neither of us knew what to say. Jane ended it. 'Why don't you shower first this morning, Aneese?'

I looked her way and her eyes were boring into mine like she was trying to tell me something.

'Kelvin and I need to discuss... champagne and chocolates for tugboat Gail.'

OK, that might have meant something but it meant nothing to me. What does getting alcohol and chocolates really mean?

'Alone,' she leant forward and whispered, winking as she did so.

Got you, bit of one on one. The penny finally dropped. I got up to leave. 'Yeah, good idea. Need to wash my hair,' I lied. I'd wash it later after I'd been in the pool.

I want some one on one! But then I remembered that I had had some yesterday. I was being way too greedy.

I hurried to the bathroom feeling like I'd been sent to my room. I felt envious, I didn't want to be excluded. Then I remembered what Jane and I had discussed only a half hour or so before and I smiled. I could have one on ones too, with both of them, and had quite recently. That thought kept me smiling all the way through my shower and even as I dried and marched back out into the cabin with a towel wrapped around me.

Then I stopped. In my reverie I'd forgotten why I was showering alone in the first place. I mean, like I showered alone any more!

Jane was spreadeagled on the bed with her knees slightly raised. Her hands held Kelvin's lower back as he lay atop her in the traditional missionary position and slowly moved into her. When he was in as far as he could go he slowly, very slowly, pulled out and so the process continued. My mouth dropped open and I saw that Jane's was, too. I could hear her breath catching as Kelvin gently moved another small amount into her. It was like they were savouring every movement but in slow motion.

A slow screw! God this was erotic!

I continued to watch, transfixed, as he lowered his head and slowly pecked her lips. I saw her lips stick slightly to his as he pulled away, as if they were temporarily stuck together, before slowly coming apart and unsticking themselves. Then Kelvin moved his left hand and slowly caressed her right breast whilst bringing his mouth down to her left. She moaned in appreciation and I saw her mouth open wider and a ragged gasp escape. Her eyes opened wide for a moment and I thought she was going to orgasm right this second and I knew that I would stay and watch, guilty feeling or not. Instead, she swallowed, seemingly regaining control of herself, and Kelvin continued with his slug-like pace. Then he moved his left hand down to her right buttock and squeezed so hard that I thought he would bruise her. I heard a ragged breath-come-moan again, longer this time, and Kelvin upped the speed, but only slightly. After a few moments of this, with her getting more audible at every, still slow, thrust he backed off on the speed again. She objected, audibly breathing, 'No' but he ignored her.

The bastard is teasing her, I realised. *Say when, my dear!* It wasn't only her he was teasing. I already felt like I needed another shower.

Then her right hand grabbed as far across the small of his muscular back as she could reach and her left arm curled around his neck and she pulled him down on to her as she started to buck and writhe in her pleasure. I saw her eyes close and she started to bite down on her bottom lip. I heard her grunt, stifle it, then grunt even louder as she lost control. Kelvin went to ramming speed and I realised that he was playing catch up but he didn't have to for long. In no time at all they were as close as any two people could be but they were holding on to each other so tightly that they could have been just one bucking, writhing, groaning animal.

I want some!

I continued watching and saw his bum cheeks tense and dimple as he emptied himself into her. She moaned loudly, like she was signalling in Morse, and then the two of them came to a halt and I could hear nothing but their heavy breathing and feel nothing but desire and my heart beating loud in my chest.

Just then Jane looked my way and smiled. 'Oh, you were watching, you bitch!'

'That was so hot!' I couldn't help myself from saying. 'Now I know why you like watching all the time.'

'I most certainly do not,' she exclaimed weakly.

'Yes you do, you're always watching us. You're quite the voyeur!'

She made a face. 'Well maybe sometimes.'

I made a face back.

'OK, maybe more than sometimes,' she conceded gracefully.

'So when do I get to watch?' asked Kelvin. His voice was muffled because his mouth was still buried in Jane's shoulder.

I looked at Jane and felt my arousal. 'Right now, I guess.'

I threw off my towel as I advanced on the bed and Kelvin moved off, and out of, Jane. I saw a satisfied smile appear on his face as he made himself comfortable on a chair.

But Jane protested. 'No way, I'm spent!'

Yeah, like I hadn't heard that before. She saw by my face that I was having none of it.

'And I'm all… gooey.'

I played at smacking my lips. 'Hmmmm, even better. Man taste and woman taste all at once.'

Kelvin laughed at my cheekiness.

As I approached her she tried to get up but I grabbed her wrists and held them above her head and forced her back down.

'I said no,' she said, but I saw by the smile on her face that she was playing.

Either she let me overpower her or I was stronger than her and in no time at all I was laying on her and kissing her hard. She played at moving her lips away from mine once or twice but as my tongue brushed hers she stopped resisting and kissed me back forcefully and I felt her arms around me, pressing me closer to her. I hadn't even realised she'd broken free. Maybe I wasn't as strong as I thought.

In our play fight my sex brushed against hers and I felt a tingle of excitement. I made it happen again, purposely this time, and was rewarded with her eyes opening as if electricity had suddenly shocked her. I felt the same but I was expecting it after the first accident.

I am making this happen, I told myself. I have the power!

I ground my groin into hers and felt a rush of pleasure. This was just like we'd discussed earlier, finding a new use for a piece of your anatomy. We were beginners at this – there were no instruction books – and we were learning and feeling our way. This was the one aspect of our three-way relationship that Kelvin couldn't coach us on. It was trial and error and even the error was worth dying for.

I positively forced my hips as hard as I could up to hers. This is how men do it, yeah, I asked and told myself? I'd just seen Kelvin doing it (albeit slower). Is this what a man feels? Normally us women lay back and hope the man does the right thing, this time I was pushing here or rubbing there and feeling my excitement climb. In the back of my mind I vaguely remembered our conversation about Kelvin making sure that we were satisfied before he took his own pleasure. I didn't know how he did it, I just wanted to take, take, take. ME, ME, ME!

I was close, so close, and part of me wanted Jane to be close too, but another part of me didn't care. If she came, she came, but if she didn't then tough!

Oh, how very selfish of me!

I felt something touch my skin and realised it was Kelvin. I'd honestly forgotten he was there. I felt another touch and my rhythm was spoiled and I became momentarily angry. Then I felt him start to enter me from behind and his pressure on me translated into more pressure between Jane and I. He took over the thrusting duties – he was so much more practiced at it then me – and every time he thrust in it forced me against Jane and we all got the benefit of his greater experience at this. Part of me wanted to say that he was only meant to be watching, but I pushed that thought aside. If he stopped now I would hate him forever.

Somehow I found the time to look down at Jane and to my horror she seemed almost in pain. She was panting small breaths like she was hyperventilating and her eyes were open unnaturally wide. She wasn't blinking. I was concerned for her but at the same time I didn't care enough to want this to stop. I was getting the pleasure of Kelvin inside me *and* the additional stimulus of the grating and grinding against Jane. There was shame in there somewhere, shame that I didn't care about Jane's apparent hurting but it was over-ridden by everything else. The urge to gain as much pleasure for myself was strong and overpowering and everything else came a distant second.

And talking of coming second, it was Jane. I was first by a hair's breadth and it seemed an age until Kelvin did but it was actually only a few moments. For those few moments I was just a useless spare part, I thought. I'd served my purpose and now I was worn out, but Kelvin was still trying to get some use out of me. When he grunted and thrust even deeper into me I knew he'd succeeded.

There was a cacophony of sounds and voices and I honestly didn't know whose was whose. I felt Kelvin's weight fall onto me and mine in turn push down onto Jane. I relaxed and tried to get control of my breathing but something was disturbing me. I opened my eyes and realised that Jane was trying to talk to me but somehow seemed unable. Then I realised that she couldn't breathe and my shame at her prior lack of well-being sprang me to action.

'Get off me!' I shouted to Kelvin as I tried to wiggle myself free.

'What?'

'Get off, Jane can't breathe!'

He only needed to be told once. In no time at all he had not only got off me but was lifting me off her as well. When she was free she took a huge noisy breath and sat up as she dragged air into her lungs.

'Jane, I'm sorry,' Kelvin said urgently.

'We're sorry,' I added.

Jane held her hand up to us once as if to stop our apologies and then continued to regain control over her breathing. Then she shook her head. 'It was fine,' she managed to say before taking in another breath. 'Until you both collapsed on me at the end.'

'We're sorry,' we chorused.

She waved our apologies away. 'Don't worry.'

We both watched her as she finally started taking normal breaths. 'Before that, I gotta say it was fucking fantastic!' she exclaimed, and relief washed over me. I thought I'd hurt her, played too hard.

'You're OK?' I heard Kelvin ask, concerned.

'Am now,' she answered. She held out her hands towards us both and gestured with her fingers the traditional *come on* sign. 'Come here you two lovely people,' she said and we both went to her like relieved children, relieved because we'd been expecting a scolding. 'If you don't do that to me again then I swear I will never speak to you again. Ever!'

We laughed.

'What, right now?' asked Kelvin.

'No, not right now,' she answered.

'Just as well because I'm s...' I was going to say spent but changed my mind. That word seemed to be a red flag to a bull these days. I'd have to find a different word.

Chapter Twelve

So it was after a light lunch that we finally got to the pool; the boat tour was cancelled. As we negotiated around the pool area this time I was aware that we were getting some serious attention from behind the sunglasses and upside down books. I just knew we were. About time, I thought. If it's one thing a girl hates more than being ogled, it's not being ogled. Yeah, you men can't please us.

Kelvin can!

But then I noticed that it wasn't only the men looking at two gorgeous fillies in bikinis. Some women were looking, too. Why on earth? Were they all lesbians and fancied a bit of girl on girl? Surely not. And surely they didn't know what Jane and I got up to when we were alone? In my mind I presumed that, if they guessed anything, they just thought that Kelvin had two women in his stables. I mean, he'd been seen kissing both of us in public so it was no secret on board ship, I guessed.

Kelvin found three loungers in almost prime position – they could have been purposefully left for us – and we settled our bags and belongings among them. I felt positively under the microscope and said as much to Jane as Kelvin went to organise refreshments.

'Yeah, I feel it, too,' she whispered.

We sat back and tried to relax but it was like I could sense something with a magical sixth sense. It was like I knew that something was going to happen but couldn't for the life of me imagine how I knew, and so I disbelieved it. Strangely, I didn't disbelieve it enough to fully relax. My head might have been still but behind my sunglasses my eyes were everywhere.

Then I had it. I noticed that, suddenly, there were more women at the bar than there normally were. Could it be coincidence? No.

'They're after our man!' I whispered frantically to Jane.

'Just got there myself,' she answered. 'I was just going to say the same.'

'What do we do? This happened before?'

'Well, no, but I guess that this situation is unique. We've always been a couple up to now, but now there are three of us. And Kelvin's alpha male performance the other day must have set the bitches on heat!'

'What do we do?' I asked urgently, staring at the trespassers through slit-like eyes. *Keep off my turf! I'll bite!*

'Um, nothing for the moment,' she finally answered. 'Let's just... Kelvin would call it "observe and report".'

'Got it, but I don't like it.'

If Daddy-o even looked at one of those trollops, I would hate him forever!

I watched him turn away from the bar carrying a tray with three glasses and a pitcher of orange liquid. He almost bumped into one of the bitches – she'd arranged it that way, I saw. I saw him smile and mouth something to her and she smiled and mouthed something back.

OK, that's allowed – just being polite – but if you look back at her you're dead meat!

He didn't look back at her. I felt relief well up inside me. But that relief turned to anger when she looked back at him and I saw her chest heave.

'Did you see that bitch!' I hissed to Jane beside me.

'Relax, will you. Kelvin didn't spare her a second glance, and hardly a first. He knows which side his bread is buttered on.'

But she didn't stop watching him either.

Then he had to walk around two more bikini clad women and that was it for me.

'That's it!'

'Aneese, what are you going to do? You'll cause a scene!' I heard her hiss as I stomped towards Kelvin.

By the time I reached him he was past them, having sidestepped them cleanly. I stomped past him, barely giving him a glance. I didn't know what I was going to do or say when I caught up to them but by god I was going to do something.

'Whoa, easy there. Point made, I think,' he said quietly and softly. He'd grabbed me with his free arm and had me trapped against his body as he effortlessly half pulled, half carried me along as my feet comically tried to propel me the other way.

'Did you see those... those...' I spluttered as I pointed past him at the retreating wiggling arses. 'Mutton dressed as pig!' I finally got out.

'Yep,' he simply said. 'Just like I see every bloke ogling you and Jane all day and every day. What do you want me to do, kill them all?'

'But they were—'

'Yes, they were. And I think you taught them a lesson, my little protector, you!'

I was mad as hell and ready to eat nails but his compliment deflated me a little. And when he followed it up with a wet and noisy kiss on the cheek my face cracked into a wide smile and my storm of a mood evaporated instantly. I felt proud and six feet tall as he allowed me to travel under my own steam again, patting me on the behind as he shepherded me back to my pen.

'Have to watch this one,' he said to Jane with a wink. 'Got us a wild cat here.'

'Indeed we have,' Jane answered as I play scowled in the direction of the enemy and plonked my recently patted derriere down onto my sun lounger. 'And I'm so proud of her.'

How could I scowl after that? 'Well they were—'

'Yes they were,' Jane interrupted, just like Kelvin had a few moments before.

'And they deserved a—'

'They certainly did, my fierce little angel-cat, and you would have, too.'

'Damn right. Not having the competition get their hands on my, I mean our, man!'

'Competition?' Kelvin joined. 'What competition?' he asked as he removed his shirt and dropped it casually on the floor beside him. Was he dumb? Just now he said he'd seen. 'I don't see any competition,' he continued.

I turned to face him incredulously. I found his eyes boring into mine but he wore a slight smile.

'You're not listening, are you? I said I didn't see any competition.'

I just stared back at him, confused.

'Because there is no competition,' he explained. 'I have the cream of the crop and nothing else will do for me. You get me?'

My face softened and I smiled again and nodded.

'Good,' he continued. 'Now be a good girl and Kelvin will give you a slow screw,' he said as he handed Jane her cocktail.

What? I looked from right to left. Did I hear right? 'You mean just like Jane got?'

'Just like Jane got,' he repeated with a nod.

'When?' I asked.

'Right now if you want. Right here.'

'Right now?'

'Yeah, going to dare me?'

Was I going to dare him? Calling Kelvin's bluff was a potentially dangerous game. I had to clarify this. 'You're going to give me a slow screw right now in front of all these people?' I asked slowly.

'Yep. And then we could have sex on the beach afterwards.'

'Ooh, count me in,' joined Jane.

Beach, what beach? There was a beach?

I looked at Jane and caught her trying not to giggle as she sipped her drink. What was I missing here?

'Must admit this slow screw tastes wonderful, Jack,' she eventually said.

My mouth dropped open as the penny dropped.

'Your slow screw, miss,' Kelvin said as he handed me my glass.

'Oh, damn you,' I answered. 'I'm going to war for you and you're taking the piss!' *And I wanted a real slow screw like Jane got this morning!*

I was mildly upset, actually. I think they both realised after a few moments.

'I apologise, Aneese,' Kelvin was the first to say, followed quickly by Jane. 'I don't know what else to do because I'm flattered and a bit lost for words. The last person who had my back had a gun and all. I'm just not used to it.'

They both watched me, waiting for a reaction, but I too was lost for words.

'So I seek forgiveness. My humour always sails a bit close to the wind and sometimes I cross the line. I am sorry if I've offended you.'

He finished it by opening his arms and before I even knew it we were both sitting astride his lounger and hugging. I smiled victoriously to Jane over his shoulder and she smiled back as she squeezed my arm.

'I love you,' he said softly, and my head turned to gush. 'And I would never intentionally do anything to hurt you.'

Dammit, how did he have this effect on me? I knew that if he wasn't holding me I would be a jelly-like shape on the floor before him. I saw that Jane's eyes had moistened up and looked how mine felt. She was biting her lip, too.

'I love you too,' I managed to get out around my control. I swallowed and mouthed "you too" silently to Jane. My brain might have been mush but I hadn't forgotten we were in the public eye. Damn society's conventions!

'So am I forgiven?' he finally said.

I nodded quickly, still afraid of what would happen if I opened my mouth.

'And shall I oil you up for the sun?'

I nodded again.

And then he deftly undid my bikini top with just two fingers of his left hand as he held me tight with his right. I gasped at the unexpectedness of it all. I knew that it was only the pressure of me against him that was preventing my top coming off completely. He swapped hands and held out his right hand and accepted the suntan lotion from Jane and, as he took it, he lay back and I was forced to follow suit or reveal my breasts to the world. Then he squirted some lotion onto my back as I lay atop him in a public space and started to rub it softly in. He looked into my wide eyes and smiled his superior smile. I knew he was daring me to back down but I wouldn't. We were certainly putting on a show. Even Jane was agape.

When he'd oiled up all the places he could reach he slithered from beneath me and touched up everywhere else. When he'd finished I was thoroughly oiled up in every way and wished we were alone. I wanted some serious one on one.

'Jane?' he enquired, holding up the sun lotion to her.

'Ah, yes,' she answered after a pause. 'But I think we'd better do it the conventional way,' she continued. 'Don't think anybody around the pool has breathed for the last five minutes.'

She turned to lay on her front and unclipped her top as she did so and Kelvin started on her. We shared a smile and I winked at her. Slow screw, a public fondling and a promise of sex on the beach later. Not to mention a truly orgasmic morning. Was I beginning to take all this a little bit for granted? Oh, what the hell, get it while you can. Nothing lasts forever.

Why not!

We settled down to sunbathe and life slowly returned to normal beside the pool. I'd even forgotten about the trespassers and slipped into a half slumber as I relaxed and had horny dreams about being taken roughly – but not too roughly – from behind by a masked assailant who I knew to be Kelvin. He had an accomplice with a lumpy jumper and long blonde hair. She threateningly held a bottle of conditioner to my head and forced me to stick my bum in the air and accept whatever I was given as she watched and licked her lips.

Yeah, my life was hell. Poor, poor me.

I was disturbed by the sound of somebody close by talking. I willed Kelvin to tell them to go away but instead he joined in. Slowly I opened one eye and recognised the head of security standing before us.

'I am so sorry to disturb you ladies,' he said in slightly accented English. 'Please accept my apologies.'

He was dressed in shorts and a Hawaiian shirt. I'd noticed that all the security men were dressed similarly, I guessed in an attempt to blend in. Unfortunately, it had the opposite effect.

'That's all right.' I searched for the word that Kelvin had used. 'Bahaader?'

I knew I'd got it right when his leathery brown face broke into a smile and he grew an inch or two in height.

'You honour me, miss,' he answered. 'Would you mind if I had a word with your... man, here?'

Jane was the last to wake and the bahaader nodded his greeting to her also. 'Come on,' said Jane to me. 'I'll teach you to breaststroke.'

She went straight from sleep to action. I wondered why she was in such a hurry. Without waiting for me to answer she grabbed my hand and led me to the pool and before I knew it, we were swimming side by side as a protective personal bubble of space formed around us. I looked Kelvin's way and saw that he had a protective eye on us as he animatedly made a point about something or other. He needn't have bothered about his overwatch, though, as it seemed that everybody had got the message about leaving us alone whilst in the pool.

'So what was all that about?' I asked Jane as we plodded along, side by side.

'All what?'

'You back there. Couldn't wait to get away from the bahaader. Don't you like him or something?' I had a sudden thought that Jane was racist in some way and didn't like non-whites.

'Oh, sorry, normal reaction for me. Do it without even knowing,' she answered as she stroked along slightly ahead of me.

I wondered what she meant. Was she racist or not?

'Throwback to the old days, I'm afraid,' she said as she concentrated on turning around at the end of the pool without bumping into me. 'When Ian had conversations with other men I realised quite early that it was better not to know and so excused myself. Became a habit. As I said, I do it without even thinking. I do hope I haven't offended him?'

There it was again and for the umpteenth time I wondered about Jane's previous life. How fucked up is she? How fucked up must she have been four years ago! And, of course, I felt guilty about making her remember things that she obviously wanted to forget. Seemed I couldn't mention anything without reminding her of her "old days". Still, she was speaking about it easily enough. That must be a good sign, surely.

We swam along in silence for a short while as I pondered. I guessed it was early days yet. No doubt I would get the whole story eventually. It also reinforced the fact that although I felt that I'd known these two forever there was so much I didn't know about them. I was so looking forward to finding out.

'Come on, let's us get the drinks this time,' she finally said and we finished our next length of the pool close to the bar and lifted ourselves out.

I was conscious of the fact that nobody seemed to be watching us as we padded to the bar, but I knew that everybody actually was. The men were ogling, no doubt, as Kelvin had rightly stated. I laughed to myself.

We all knew that we all did it. Us humans were a funny bunch.

'Sex on the beach, please,' Jane asked the barman and it surprised me. For some reason I'd been expecting her to defer the ordering to me.

He nodded and went to work. Whether he got his jollies chatting up women with that icebreaker, I don't know, but he had more sense than to try it with us. He didn't even ask for our room card which was just as well as we didn't have it.

'Oh, and if you know what the security fella, there, drinks then one of them too,' she added.

'Fiery ginger ale with ice, m... miss.'

I laughed to myself. I got the impression he very nearly called her madam.

'So what about you walking the walk as well as talking the talk?' Jane said to me as she planted her lovely, wet behind down on a bar stool.

'What?' I answered. She'd caught me unawares. I didn't have a clue what she was on about.

'Earlier. With the bitches?'

'Oh,' I said, feeling instantly ashamed. 'Don't know what came over me.'

'Well I'm proud of you,' she said, touching my arm and beaming at me. 'You're braver than I.'

I knew my face had coloured and I bit my lip and looked down at my feet. 'Actually, that could have been quite embarrassing if Kelvin hadn't intervened.'

'Yeah, cat fight,' she agreed. 'I'm sure the blokes would have loved it.'

I winced again. 'Yeah, kinda wasn't thinking straight.'

'Maybe,' she said. 'But your heart was in the right place. Good on you, girl!'

I smiled at her compliment though, truthfully, I was secretly ashamed of myself. I'd never ever done anything like that before; the green-eyed goddess of jealousy had never visited me before. What did that tell you about my life and my previous relationships? That they weren't worth fighting for, maybe? But Jane was right, I'd talked the talk earlier on today when I'd told her that I wouldn't let any harm come to her or, by default, Kelvin then I'd walked the walk to back it up. I *did* feel secretly ashamed of myself but I also felt a fierce pride.

'I'd do it for you, too,' I said.

'I know. You told me and I believe you and now I have two people looking after me, two lovely people.' She looked to see how close the barman was to us, leaned forward and lowered her voice. 'Two lovely, wonderful, *s e x y a s f u c k* people!' she finished with a smile and a wink. 'I'm such a lucky girl, I don't deserve you, either of you.'

'Ditto,' was all I could say.

A drinks tray appeared in front of us and I rushed to grab it.

'You're not my slave,' Jane said straight away. She picked up the tray and turned to head back and I trotted after her.

Again she was going out of her way to reinforce that point. I somehow knew that with anybody else but Jane I would be treated as a newcomer in a situation such as this. These two people were really perfect and well suited. I hoped I could match their perfection. Somehow I suspected that I couldn't but I was young and I would learn.

'Refreshments Mr…'

'Gurung, miss, and thank you. Fiery ginger ale?' he asked as he spied the tray. 'Why, thank you.'

He'd started to rise as we appeared before them but Jane waved him down. Such manners.

'Barman knows your order,' Jane explained. 'All I had to do was ask.'

'Well, much appreciated,' he continued. 'Some wouldn't think and it is a warm day.'

'Beautiful day,' I joined as I filled three glasses with red sex. 'So what were you boys talking about?' I enquired.

'Oh, just reminiscing about old times,' Kelvin answered.

'What, you know each other?' I stupidly asked. I knew it was a stupid question as soon as I'd asked it, but it was too late now.

'No, unfortunately not,' Mr Gurung continued. 'We trod the same dirt but at different times, walked in each other's footprints, so to speak. The British Army is a relatively small group if you think about it.'

'But the best,' said Kelvin raising his glass.

'Indeed,' Gurung answered, and he touched his glass with Kelvin's. 'Your Kelvin was telling me about his work in nonlethal warfare. A very interesting field in this day and age.'

I almost choked on my drink. Kelvin and nonlethal warfare? How ironic was that. The evidence of people he'd killed was there for all to see. His tattoos had been lethal to some, that's for sure.

'My cousin works the cruise ships in the Indian Ocean,' the bahaader continued. 'They have sonic cannons on all the liners now and they are a most efficient way of deterring the Somalian pirates.'

Pirates in this day and age? I watched the news; it was amazing to me that they were even allowed to operate. Why weren't they hunted down and… and what? In the old days they hung them didn't they? Was society too soft these days? And what was a sonic cannon? A sound gun, was that it?

'True, but it's a shame we couldn't just shoot the buggers.'

'Kelvin!' Jane objected.

'Well it's true. Criminals chose to be criminals. Forget all this *I had a tough upbringing* nonsense. It's bol… rubbish.'

Well this was a side to Kelvin I'd never seen before. Although he was smiling when he said it, not standing on a soap box and lecturing like some I'd seen in central London, it was obvious to me that he believed in what he was saying.

'No, I fear for society,' he continued. 'It's gone weak, got all the wrong people in charge, all the lefty hoody hugging lawyers and social workers.'

'Hear, hear,' said Jane. 'Down with all social workers,' she said, raising her glass.

I turned to her in shock. Then I realised that social workers must have had something to do with her losing Isobel and I found myself sympathising somewhat. I also realised what a trouble-free life I'd had in comparison. Lawlessness had hardly touched my young life. I was naive enough to think that if you didn't upset anybody then they wouldn't upset you. I'd had that drummed into me by my father from an early age.

'Well I'd like to stay and chat,' the bahaadar finally said as he drained his glass. 'But I am on duty and there are things to do.' He turned to me and Jane. 'Thank you for the refreshments, ladies.'

'You're welcome,' Jane answered and I smiled as my response.

'You will be by the pool for a while?' he asked as he stood.

'Til about seventeen hundred, or there abouts,' answered Kelvin.

'Good, then I bid you a good afternoon,' he said and then he was gone.

'So what was that really about?' Jane asked after Gurung was out of earshot.

You mean it wasn't all about Kelvin reminiscing with another ex-soldier, I asked myself?

'Oh, nothing,' Kelvin answered. 'Just shooting the breeze.'

'Jack?' Jane admonished. 'I don't normally ask, as you know, but this time I am.'

He pursed his lips, deep in thought, but then he answered. 'Right you are, my love.' *I wanna be called that.* 'Well some of it was an update on the four youths who upset Aneese's friends, Tomas and Johnny. They have been given a very stern warning and have been told that they are being continually watched. One foot out of line and they are off the ship.'

'Quite right,' Jane answered and I nodded in agreement

'And they can forget about a refund, too.'

'Well I should hope so.'

'And part of it was two ex-servicemen shooting the breeze, as I said.'

Jane nodded and I flicked my head from one to the other as if I was watching tennis.

'And part of it was a friendly telling off for a public show of affection, almost bordering on pornography, that Aneese and I demonstrated earlier. Seems somebody complained.'

My mouth dropped open and I felt myself getting angry.

Kelvin held up his hands to us both and we both stopped. I could see that Jane wasn't happy either. 'I know what you're going to say,' he said. 'But we were in the wrong. This is a family ship and we were out of line.'

Kelvin was rolling over and taking a slapping. I didn't believe it.

'Yeah, but they just reported us because—'

'Yeah, I understand the psychology of the situation,' Kelvin said, interrupting me in the process. He raised his voice slightly, just like he had when he'd told the couple to vacate Tomas's and Johnny's loungers yesterday. 'The little people are jealous of us because they haven't got what we have because they haven't got the guts to reach out for it. They haven't got me and they haven't got you two and they haven't got our money, houses or cars.'

Was Kelvin doing this on purpose, I thought? Was he?

'These poor people have to live with themselves at night, poor things, and all we can do is sympathise with them for their sorry, cowardly existences. They are jealous, simple as that, and they know it, and they know they will never be able to match their actions to their thoughts like we do. Like brave Aneese did earlier.'

He was. I looked at Jane and she was biting her lip, suppressing a smile. And to think I'd thought he was rolling over and taking it. He was giving it!

'So we'll take our telling off on the chin like the grown-ups we are and leave it at that, OK?'

Neither of us answered.

'OK?' he asked again.

'Yes sir,' we both chorused with a smile.

'We were out of line, though. *I* was out of line and I accept that, not you two lovely ladies.'

This was probably the longest speech I'd ever heard him say and the effect wasn't lost on me or the listening crowd.

'But then he had the cheek to ask you to police his pool for the afternoon,' Jane offered.

'Oh, you noticed that, did you?'

I hadn't. Dumb blonde or what?

'And what does that tell you?' he asked.

I looked at Jane and she looked at me and we both shook our heads.

Kelvin leaned towards us and lowered his voice so that only we could hear. 'The telling off was just for show,' he winked theatrically.

Ah, of course, I told myself. Kelvin was right, a friendlier telling off I couldn't imagine. Why, he'd even stopped for refreshments.

The rest of the afternoon passed uneventfully and I caught up on some sleep and acquired the beginnings of a tan. Then it was back to the cabin to prepare for the big night.

Jane looked stunning and I felt wonderful. If I looked half as good as her then I'd be extremely happy. I was finally in my dress and I was getting some serious looks from men and women alike, but after the last two days I didn't know whether that was because I looked stunning or because of Kelvin.

I wondered, briefly what they thought of me, of us, of Kelvin? At the end of the day I didn't give a damn. I was happier than I had ever been and, what's more, I knew it. Nothing could change what I felt for my two lovers and I hoped that they felt the same. Tomas the sage was right; the "normals" just didn't have a clue, poor things.

I understood what Kelvin meant, now, when he'd mentioned about men ogling earlier on. They were good at it; they almost turned it into an art. Kelvin had briefed me on it as a topic of conversation whilst Jane was at the salon getting her hair done. I'd hoped that we could get physical, but I realised that I just had too much to do to get ready for the dress night. And when Jane had come back there was no way she was going to get down and dirty with me. She just wanted to preserve her hair (not that I could see much difference from when she'd left) and wash and dry mine. As a result I was horny but happy and there was always later, I told myself. In fact, we had the rest of our lives. The thought filled my whole being with happiness. I couldn't stop smiling if I wanted to and I didn't want to!

Everybody was done up to the nines and the atmosphere was electric. Everybody seemed excited and, to be honest, so was I. There were guys in kilts and tuxedos and young teenagers who were obviously being treated as adults for the first time. I watched as a Scot, kilt and all the accompanying finery, slowly danced with his teenage daughter as she beamed at all around her. I imagined that normally she wouldn't be seen dead dancing with "the old man" or be in a ball gown. I saw the look of pride on his face and wondered if my father would be proud of me right now.

OK, best not go there, I guess. He was too staid, too set in his ways. I secretly thought it took an influx of money to finally gain his approval after I didn't go to university, but stayed with Richard instead. He'd been proved right there, eventually.

Damn Richard again and double damn him. Bet he wasn't having as much fun as I was right now, though, and I bet he never felt as I felt right now. I certainly never felt this way about him.

Bringing up children must be really hard, I thought. I wondered if I'd ever have children now? It had always been on the cards when I was with Richard but what now? Do I bring the subject up, do I even want children? I damned myself for my timing in thinking such a thing, today of all days. This was meant to be the party night and I pushed the thought away and blamed it on the Scottish guy.

Everybody was so well behaved tonight, not that they normally weren't anyway. Then the thought struck me; do they possibly think of us as badly behaved? Must admit we hadn't gone out of our way to make anybody like us. I remembered we hadn't cared about other passengers' feelings and opinions when we'd been loudly drinking and swapping food between each other and I'd known that we were pissing some of them off at the time.

Screw 'em. Didn't they complain about you at the pool today?

I let that thought disappear too. What was wrong with me tonight? This could be the best night of my sorry existence of a life and here I was thinking maudlin thoughts. I wondered if there was any gin in any of the cocktails we'd consumed today?

It seemed that nobody wanted to sit down and eat this evening. Everybody seemed to be doing a lap of honour of the ship so we joined them. I wondered if our table would be occupied when we eventually got to it, but then I told myself not to worry. Kelvin would see them off if it were. We had a prime table booked in the best restaurant for this night. I must raise a glass to our mystery *cancelled* benefactor.

So we did the tour and picked up drinks along the way. There were bands playing light music and even fireworks to make us ooh and aah. We had our photographs taken by one of the ship's photographers and I overheard Kelvin say to the girl that she was to take as many of us as she could throughout the night. Oh yes, this night would be well remembered even if we were on our collective asses before the end.

'You two look stunning,' Kelvin said softly as we negotiated a path through the celebrating masses.

His voice was different, I thought. This time he was being himself and not being Kelvin the clown or anybody else, I thought. He really meant it.

'You really do,' he reinforced as he stopped and turned us both so that he could see us both. We smiled and he softly kissed us both on the cheek. The photographer caught him as he kissed Jane. She was good to her word, at least.

'You don't look so bad yourself,' I answered.

He was dressed in a white tuxedo with dark trousers. I was secretly glad he wasn't wearing white all over, he'd look like Andre Previn or something if he did.

'You know, when I make it big I want to see you both with diamond necklaces around your necks, and earrings to match. Boy, you'd shine, then.'

I smiled and filled up with tears and pride. A look at Jane showed she was doing the same.

'But aren't you a rich or something?' I couldn't help asking.

'Well, we're not going to starve anytime soon,' he answered. 'But poor Jane, here, doesn't have a diamond to her name.'

I turned to her. 'Not a one,' she sighed theatrically.

'Oh, poor you,' I said, playing along. 'Here,' I continued, 'when we get back to the cabin I'll dig the ones out of my watch and you can have them. I was assured there were some there.'

We laughed at our stupidity as we sought out our table now that we had returned to our restaurant.

'How come you have your cars but Jane has no diamonds?' I asked cheekily as he held our chairs out for us now that we were back at our table. I was trying to rag him but I didn't get the chance. Jane was straight in there in his defence.

'You obviously know nothing about cars. Add them all up together and you might make ten grand. Couldn't buy any good diamonds with that piddly amount. And anyway, he deserves his cars.'

Sorry I'm sure! 'And the bike?'

She pursed her lips. 'OK, I admit that I wouldn't miss the motorbike. I think they're dangerous.'

'So it's settled, then. I'll sell the bike and buy you both a tiny diamond each.'

What, I thought, but I haven't been for a ride yet! 'How much would you get for the bike?'

'Couple of grand, max.'

I made a face. 'Not going to get many diamonds for that. You may as well keep it.'

'Why, thank you. It is awful being as poor as we are. Good thing you mentioned you wouldn't mind living in a tent with us, the other night,' he continued. 'Could get crowded, though.'

'Oh goody,' I answered. 'Bagsy me in the middle!'

'Come on, let's go eat,' he said after they'd laughed at my quip.

'Perhaps we should just order one meal and share it,' I continued. I was warming to this poverty theme. Warming? It had been my whole life!

'Good idea,' he answered. 'Waiter, one meal but three forks, please!'

The subject got me thinking, though. Although it wouldn't matter to me whether they were millionaires or benefit scroungers, I realised that I'd taken a lot for granted. 'Are you OK, though? Financially, I mean?'

'What? Of course, we are,' he answered.

'Because I haven't got to stop work, you know?'

'What?' he asked, incredulously.

'I could stay at work. The money would come in handy if you're short?'

Kelvin started to cough and reached for a glass of anything. Jane patted his back. 'Aneese, you are priceless,' he finally got out, before starting a coughing fit again. 'Isn't she great?' he asked of Jane.

'Priceless, like you said,' she answered. 'Trust me, we're fine,' she said, turning to me and smiling. 'The very first thing Jack did with his first million was put it away. It's our... what did you call it... fall back money?'

'Yeah, that's it. If the world goes to hell in a handcart then we have that as our comfy blanket. I'll have to add to it now that we're three of us, though, add another half a million in gold just in case paper currency goes to the floor, maybe. Make sure it's enough for three of us to live on comfortably. And how did we get onto this subject anyway?'

'Was you mentioning diamonds,' I said.

'Well you'll have them, you both will.'

'I don't need diamonds,' I said. 'I have everything I need, here.'

'I'll have yours, then. More for me!'

Well I couldn't help laughing at that. Neither could he.

'And what will you get?' I asked when I'd regained control of myself.

'You two, naked, but wearing diamonds. What else could I want?'

'Seriously,' I asked. 'I wanna know.'

He went thoughtful for a little while and still hadn't answered by the time a waiter brought our menus. 'I've recently spotted a Lotus I quite like.'

A car? Of course. 'What type?' I asked.

'A yellow one,' he answered immediately.

I laughed, remembering our conversation as he'd told me about his cars that time. God, was that only a fortnight ago? Less?

'No. I'm serious. I saw this yellow Lotus and I thought, "Wow that's nice" but I have no idea what car or spec it is.'

'Really?'

'I swear,' he answered. 'I was standing looking out of my office window and there it was, growling by below me. My knees went weak and my mouth fell open.'

'Wow, must be love,' Jane said.

'Oh, I know that feeling,' I added with a smile.

'So how much do Locusts cost?'

'Lotus, dear. L O T U S,' he spelt out for Jane, laughing as he did so. I thought it was hilarious, too.

We'd all been on the sauce all day, cocktails by the pool followed by buck's fizz at the room, and it was beginning to show. I thought we would have to slow down but I wasn't going to mention it first. Some food would help; we hadn't eaten since breakfast really. And anyway, I was enjoying the buzz. I felt I was present but looking over my own shoulder. The trick, I knew now, was to stay that way. Didn't want to drink too much and get into the don't-know-what-the-hell-you're-doing stage. That way meant only disaster. Had to keep it just right; drink enough to keep the buzz but not cross the line. This could be a long night and I didn't want to miss a bit of it.

Finally we all stopped laughing and he wiped the tears from his eyes. 'Come on, let's eat.'

I don't know why but I was fancying something salty, and said so. And what Kelvin suggested wasn't on the menu, at least not until later, anyway.

'And a large bowl of chips,' Kelvin said as he finished giving our order to the waiter.

'We don't serve chips in this restaurant, sir,' he responded quietly, almost at a whisper.

'I know, but it is requested that tonight you do. I don't care who has to be bribed or killed, just get it done and put it on the bill.'

The poor guy looked like he was going to say something.

'Did I mention that the customer's always right and I'm a good tipper to boot?' Kelvin finished with a wink. 'Now chips, and lots of them.'

'I'll see what I can do, sir,' he said, before retreating.

'Are you all right,' asked Jane to Kelvin.

'Yeah, fine. But as soon as Aneese mentioned something salty I had a sudden urge for fish and chips wrapped in newspaper. My Dover sole will have to pass for cod. I'll have to rough it.'

'Poor you, having to suffer with Dover sole as a substitute. Hopefully the economy will improve and you can return to cod again,' I said.

'We can only hope,' he answered, playing along, but Jane and I couldn't keep a straight face. This was getting very silly.

'You know?' he talked over the last of our wheezing laughter. 'I have the urge to get roaring drunk tonight. Who's with me?'

Jane and I put our hands up, as one.

Just like any other night, then!

'It's unanimous, then.'

'Are you sure? I demand a re-count,' I said, banging the table noisily and incurring the silent wrath of fellow diners. 'You know,' I said loudly. 'I'm getting damn fed up of the starched shirts who don't know how to enjoy themselves and frown at us because we know how to. We're British, damn it, and as such we drink. It's part of our history!'

I knew I was parroting something Jane had said this morning but I didn't care. It sounded right.

'Hear, hear,' I heard from somewhere close.

'Ooh, did you hear that?' I asked. 'I'm a hit!'

'I did,' said Jane. 'And you are.'

'Yeah, I could get to like this.' I suddenly felt very brave, stood up with my recently arrived glass and said, 'A toast. To the British. May the rest of the world learn to drink like we do!'

'Hear, hear,' I heard from somewhere else and it was joined by the banging of tables and the twinkling of glasses. I saw some of our fellow Brits raise a glass and I smiled as I raised a glass back.

'See, I am a hit. The jungle drums have spoken.'

'Hey, you can't do that,' Kelvin said, mock offended.

'Do what?'

'Smile at innocent men like that. They have no defence, you know!'

'And what about you?' I asked, putting on the full million candles.

'Or me,' he played, going all dew eyed.

'Or me, for that matter,' Jane added finally.

'Oh, poor you,' I said as I leaned towards her playing kissy kissy.

She leaned forward and kissed me noisily on the lips. Part of me panicked because we were in public and the other part of me did a victory dance. Who's going to see, anyway, my semi-drunken mind, thought.

When we stopped I smiled victoriously at Kelvin.

'What about me?'

'You got to earn yours,' I said.

'Well that's not fair. I earn mine every day but it goes unnoticed.'

'Oh, yeah, like how?' I asked cheekily.

'The fact that you're here, the fact that you're dressed in fine clothes, the fact that you're unmolested—'

'Mores the pity,' joined Jane, but he ignored her and carried on.

'The fact that you're safe and well fed and haven't got a care in the world?'

Oh yeah, he was right. 'Sorry, think I fucked up!' I answered and Jane positively roared at my choice of language.

'Yes you did,' said Kelvin, playing at being offended.

He was playing, wasn't he? I saw Jane looking at me with a raised eyebrow and realised that I may have crossed the line there. Her look said that some form of recompense was required here.

'Handsome and brave Daddy-o,' I started. Always a good way to start. 'I am only a little girl, your little girl,' I emphasised. 'And I am young and inexperienced and on the way to roaring drunk at your request. Please forgive me for my trespasses at this time. I am young and with your guidance I will learn.'

I hoped that would do it. He seemed to wait an awfully long time before breaking his face. 'Perhaps I could offer you some guidance over my knee?' he finally said.

'Perhaps, but I haven't asked you to.' Yeah, I remembered his statement. Not until I asked him to, he'd said.

'Just checking,' he said with a smile. 'Oh good, food's here.'

Three servers arrived carrying plates and our main courses were positioned in front of us. As they departed Kelvin comically looked around and was rewarded when a fourth server positioned a large bowl of chips in the middle of the table.

He looked up and beamed at us in victory. 'Ah, smug mode,' he said as he pushed a note into the waiter's pocket. I think it was a fifty.

'Only mode you know, isn't it?' smirked Jane, and I laughed despite myself.

The chips didn't really go with my chicken in white wine sauce, but what the hell. I dug in and they tasted wonderful. Couldn't remember when I'd had chips last. Jane dug in, too, her pasta and bacon dish matching as much as mine did.

'Can I have a taste?' I asked. I'd never tried that before. She obliged and I was impressed. It tasted oily but spicy and I wished I'd ordered that. 'We didn't have starters,' I finally exclaimed. Look at me, a week of good eating and I was the connoisseur.

'Yeah we did,' answered Kelvin, shaking his glass in his wrist.

'And what about desert?'

He shook his glass again.

'Oh, good,' I answered. 'More alcohol, just what I need.'

I ate my meal and soaked up the atmosphere (as well as the champagne) and looked around me. It might have been my alcohol slanted view but all of a sudden even the starched shirts seemed to be having fun. I even saw somebody at a table close to ours point enviously at our bowl of chips as they made their order with the serving staff and I stifled a guffaw. Seemed we'd started something.

When we finished our meals we were offered desserts and ordered cheesecake, chocolate fudge cake and apple pie. Kelvin always had cheesecake, I now realised, and the chocolate fudge cake was for Jane. My tastes were simpler.

'I think we'll have to move house next to a gym when we get back,' I mused.

'Or I could work you harder?' Kelvin offered.

'But you'll be at work,' Jane said.

'Leaving just me and Jane.' I sighed. 'It's going to be hell.'

'Indeed,' Jane finished with a faraway look in her eye.

Kelvin played at sulking whilst Jane and I smiled victoriously. I was having ice cream with my apple pie but it wasn't cooling me down any. Suddenly I was all hot for some reason.

'Oh god, keep your hand on your knickers,' I suddenly said. I'd seen a familiar form standing by the door. He seemed to be searching the crowds but his eyes lit up when he saw us. Kelvin followed my gaze and turned around just as Spider arrived at his shoulder.

'Kelvin, mate, you gotta help me?'

'I'm at dinner if you haven't noticed?'

'But this is an emergency. You gotta help us or we're dead.'

'Dead?' he enquired.

'Well, financially speaking. Our lead singer, Leo – you met him – is ill. If we don't finish this week then we lose the rest of the season. Just gotta get those ticks in the boxes for this last night and we're in.'

'Ill?' Kelvin enquired. 'What's wrong with him?'

Spider stopped and I saw him lick his lips. If I was any judge of character it was a sign that he was contemplating lying. He looked left and right and lowered his voice and leant towards us. "E's had too much weed. His missus has left him, see, and 'e's been over indulging a bit. Can't blame him really.'

So he'd elected to tell the truth. Good on him.

'Don't know what you expect me to do,' Kelvin answered. 'There's no way I'm singing Elvis, The Rolling Stones and The Beatles.'

Spider licked his lips again as he considered his options. 'Well sing what you like, then. We should be able to follow you.'

Kelvin pursed his lips as he thought. 'No, I'll pass.'

'But Kel, we're desperate, mate. We just need tonight and we're in. I'll pay you?' he said in desperation.

'As if I need the money,' he shot back. 'Anyway, they'll know I'm not him. I don't smell of cabbage for a start.'

'Doesn't matter,' Spider continued. 'All we need is the tick in the box that the last night's entertainment was good and we're in. Your welcome packs in your cabins contain a questionnaire which is just tick boxes. We get over sixty per cent and we get the gig for the rest of the season.'

I saw Kelvin considering. Surely he'd jump at the offer.

'I promise I'll never try it on with Aneese again,' he begged.

Kelvin drained his glass and turned his head to look directly at Spider. 'As if you stood a chance. If you did I'd have acted.'

'Oh, Kel, please? Tell him, missus?'

'The name is Jane,' she answered imperiously and stuck her nose in the air.

'Jane, tell him. Please?' he begged. 'This is important.'

'Spider,' Kelvin finally answered. 'Lookee over there.' He indicated us two women. 'I'm sitting here with two beautiful women and the food and champagne is excellent. We've been imbibing since about noon and I am wondering whether I'll remember in the morning what I plan to get up to with these the lovely ladies later on tonight.'

I sniggered at that.

'So why, pray, would I want to get up on the stage and sing whilst playing a second rate guitar for my supper?'

I saw Spider deflate because he knew he'd lost and I felt a little sorry for him. If Jane's face was any indication then she did too. A silence formed as Spider slowly looked down to his feet.

'Because you love to play,' Jane said softly, breaking the silence. 'And possibly because I'd rather watch you perform than watch you and Aneese dance as I sit by myself, or possibly because I know that you want to but poor Spider hasn't got the words to cajole you in the way you want? I know you, Kelvin Turner. You can't turn him down for two reasons. One, you always help if you can because you're a nice person who likes to help the little people, and two... because I know that you're just aching to get up there and strut your stuff with a live band behind you!'

I watched as Kelvin bit his lip and the ignition of hope returned to Spider's eyes.

'Well, I guess it would be a good test of my software,' he mused. 'It hasn't been tested with more than one player yet.'

I watched again and Spider smiled and the spark turned to a flame.

'So you'll do it?'

'How long we got?'

'Thirty-five minutes til curtain up,' said a reinvigorated Spider.

'And how long's the set?'

'Two forty-minute sets with a fifteen-minute interlude.'

'I'll need your guitar? That double necker you were hiding and thought I hadn't seen?'

'You got it.'

'And I'll need my laptop.'

Jane rose from her seat. 'We'll get that,' she indicated my way as she did.

'And there's a leather bag of leads in the cupboard hanging on the door.'

'I know it,' said Jane as she pushed her chair back indicated me to follow.

'Oh, and my iPod, unless Aneese has worn it out.'

I stuck my tongue out at him.

'And my phone and your phone.'

'And mine?' I asked, even though I didn't have a clue why he wanted them.

'Android?'

I shrugged.

'No, then.'

We all stood.

'In the lounge where you first met us, then,' Spider said before setting off with a spring in his step.

Kelvin went to follow him but Jane stopped him. 'Thank you, Jack,' she said as she kissed him. 'I knew you wanted to, you know.'

'Did I?'

'Yes you did. And part of the reason I love you is because you help people. Now run along and make it work. We'll get your stuff.'

292

Chapter Thirteen

In five minutes we were in the lounge with the items Kelvin had requested, but he didn't notice us at first. He was standing on the stage with his back to us strumming and adjusting a double necked guitar. I guessed he was tuning it, but what did I know.

'Oh there you are, finally,' he said and Jane motioned for me not to bite. We'd been waiting a good five minutes to get noticed. I guessed that she'd seen him this intense before and I was momentarily jealous that she knew him so much more than I did. He took the items from us and then it was if we didn't exist again.

We found an unoccupied table which had no chairs around it and leaned against it. I hoped we weren't going to spend the whole evening standing this way. Our ever attentive friend was elsewhere and had other things on his mind as he sat hunched over his laptop, adjusting it and plugging various cables in everywhere.

'Hi, what's going on?' I heard beside me and I almost jumped. I'd been totally engrossed in what Kelvin was doing.

I turned. 'Tomas! Hi.'

He was dressed smartly and reminded me of a Mississippi riverboat gambler. 'Your man's in the band?' he enquired.

'Shhh, it's a secret,' I said. 'Some emergency. One of the band is sick and Kelvin is standing in.'

'Cool,' he finished. 'Can he play?'

'Can he play?' Jane interjected with obvious pride. 'You just listen!'

'Great, looking forward to it. We have chairs if you wanna come join us?' He indicated into the shadows where I could just see Johnny waving at us.

'Why not bring the chairs here?' I asked. 'Better table, right at the front?'

'They're a bit prickly about that type of thing in their ballroom,' he answered. 'Stuck up... ah, people that they are.'

'Well I don't care,' said Jane. 'I'm not standing resting my butt on a table and I'm not sitting at the back. We're here by request, you know. We had a lovely table right by the dance floor until Spiderman sent his SOS and fired up a flare.'

Tomas looked at me with confusion in his eyes. 'I think that means bring the chairs down here,' I translated.

He shrugged but walked away and did as he'd been told. Nobody said a word when they brought the two chairs for Jane and I to sit on but as they brought the other two for themselves a member of the ship's crew intervened and she wasn't taking any crap from us. I saw Jane's face cloud and she opened her mouth. Was I finally going to see Jane bite?

'Hey, they're with us,' I heard a voice shout from the stage. We all turned and saw Spider standing on the end of the stage. 'These two are our roadies,' he said as he pointed to Tomas and Johnny. 'And these two are our... uh, groupies,' he said. 'They've been working hard all week making sure that we could play every night and this is their reward, see.'

The hard faced bitch was still ready for war.

'The head of security knows all about it,' Kelvin intervened over his shoulder as he carried on sitting with his back to us tapping away at his laptop. 'Feel free to check with him. Kelvin Turner's the name. Now run along, we're busy and time is short.'

We all froze whilst the uniformed Rottweiler considered her next move. Eventually she decided that her next move was to retreat but she promised to check with the bahaader *and* lodge a complaint with the captain.

'Stuck up cow,' Jane remarked loudly as she walked away. 'Thank you, Jack... Spider.'

'You're welcome, love,' Spider answered to Jane as he gave me a wink. Kelvin just waved over his shoulder. He was still engrossed in whatever he was doing.

'Come on, boys, make yourself comfortable,' Jane ordered. 'Nothing is spoiling our last night.'

'But tomorrow's the last night,' Johnny said.

'Well you know what I mean,' answered Jane before raising her voice so that Kelvin would hear. 'So what happens if the captain comes?'

Kelvin pointed to his left. 'He can play the tambourine.'

'OK, just checking,' she answered whilst the rest of us laughed.

We four watched as Kelvin installed and fussed and programmed and checked cables and ordered the other band members around. Spider was sent to the bar and I saw him pointing our way to a waiter and the waiter nod. I guessed what was happening. Ever attentive Kelvin might be otherwise engaged but he was arranging through Spider that our table got good, regular service.

'As Kelvin's not here then I'll say it, boys. Drinks are on us tonight.' They went to object but I stopped them. 'He will say that you are doing him a service by looking after us two, won't he Jane?'

'Without a doubt.'

'So it's settled. Order what you like when the waiter comes. Kelvin has already arranged payment by the look of it.'

Spider winked again as he passed. 'Perhaps we could dance later, little un?'

'Not a chance,' I answered. 'I'll be dancing with Tomas.'

'Well deflected,' said Jane. 'Dancing is just vertical expression of a horizontal desire.'

Tomas turned bug eyed.

'In that case, Mummy Bear, would you like to dance?' I asked all demure and fluttering my eyelashes sweetly.

And now Johnny joined him.

'They won't let you,' Tomas said. 'We tried. Dancing is strictly boy/girl.'

'Well there are four of us,' I declared. 'So if the four of us get up then how will they know who is dancing with who?'

'So I guess I'll be dancing with Johnny,' Jane played. She waited for his eyes to open wide before she spat out a laugh. 'Don't worry, I don't dance,' she finally said, putting him at his ease.

'Aww, but that spoils the plan,' I said. 'None of us can, then.'

Jane looked down her nose at me. 'Well we'll see, then.'

If I could get Jane up to dance it would be a minor victory and I'd be well in Daddy-o's good books.

The waiter arrived soon afterward and we ordered more champagne and an order of brandy all round. As he returned with our drinks the lights lowered, and an air of expectancy swiftly arose, you could almost feel it.

On the stage Kelvin had the band around him as he explained and pointed out certain things. I could see that there were questions and they looked unhappy if their body language was any judge. They moved to their places with sloping shoulders and dragging their feet like Death Row inmates. Kelvin was his normal confidant self.

'His way or the highway,' Jane said beside me. She must have noticed their attitude too.

'What do you mean?' I asked.

She turned to face me. 'I imagine he's just told them that they're doing it his way, like it or not, and to trust him and everything will be fine.'

'Well they don't look happy, that's for sure.'

'They'll learn,' she answered, crossing her fingers. 'I hope!'

'Well they'll just have to learn to trust him like we do.'

Kelvin cleared his throat and adjusted his microphone one last time. 'Good evening, ladies and gentlemen,' he started. 'This is a special night tonight and to celebrate we're going to do things a little differently. Firstly we're going to show off a bit and, hopefully, get your attention and then we're going to try and convince you to get up and dance. Also we're open to requests – polite ones.' He earned a murmur of laughter. 'So if you have any just write them on a slip of paper and hand them to the beautiful people sat at the table here to my left.' He pointed to our table and we looked to the floor, proud and embarrassed, but smiling nonetheless. 'We'll try the songs with the most requests if it's at all possible, won't we lads?' He looked behind him but the band weren't too forthcoming with enthusiasm. 'I said "won't we lads"?'

'Yeeees,' they groaned.

That brought more of a laugh from the crowd.

So that was it, I thought. Was Kelvin tempting them out of their comfort zone and off their playlist? I hoped that his faith in his box of tricks was well founded. I'd hate for it all to come crashing down around his feet. 'Jane, can he do this?' I asked in concern.

She shrugged. 'Well he thinks he can.'

'But he said his software has never dealt with a whole band before.'

She held her crossed fingers up for me to see.

'So without any more ado,' Kelvin continued as he turned and pointed to the drummer, 'let's be afraid. Hit it!'

The drummer started with a slow beat all by himself for a short while until the others joined in, Kelvin included. Then after another short while Kelvin started singing.

'Oh, this one,' Jane said.

'What is it?' I asked.

'I don't remember,' she answered. 'But he absolutely worships the guy who normally sings it. Guy with a girl's name?'

It meant nothing to me but the music sounded great.

She snapped her fingers. 'Lyndsey Buckingham!'

Who, I thought?

'Yeah, he's Kelvin's god!'

Kelvin had a god? Wow, he must be good.

'He's with Fleetwood Mac, isn't he?' Johnny offered.

'Yeah,' said Tomas.

'Shhh, let's listen!'

By now Kelvin had stopped singing and was playing his guitar and, to my ears, making it scream almost sexually. Then he was singing again. I looked at the gathered masses and saw that at least some were nodding in time to the music. A good start. I couldn't help but smile.

I must admit I already liked this song although I had personally never heard it before. It had a slow, plodding but heavy beat like somebody exhausted was walking slowly in big heavy boots, and Kelvin's voice was doing it justice not, I admitted, that I had any reference to compare. It sounded great and there were plenty of little guitar solos which suited Kelvin down to the ground.

By now Kelvin had stopped singing and was involved in a long guitar solo which I thought must mean that the song was close to the end but it just carried on and on and every time he squeezed a higher screaming note out of his guitar I thought that it just couldn't get any higher but then he would shock me by making it scream even louder. His eyes were closed and he just seemed to be as one with the guitar as he rocked back and forth and his fingers seemed to have a life of their own, feeling his way through like the instrument was an extension of his very self.

He treated women the same way in bed, I couldn't help myself from thinking.

If I didn't fancy the arse off him already then I would have by now. It was quite a performance by any standards and I was totally amazed at his skill level and the sounds his fingers produced from the strings. Part of me wondered if any of the pool bitches were present. Would their chests be heaving as they sighed in wantonness and certain parts of them oiled up?

But I shouldn't have been amazed at his performance. I'd seen and heard him play and sing quite a bit in the two weeks – I still couldn't believe it was only two weeks – since I'd met him. But tonight he was pulling all the stops out and was in his element. Part of me wondered how he was going to beat this. Had he peaked too early?

Yeah, like you know anything!

I looked at the rest of the scurvy crew. The drummer seemed to be enjoying himself the most and seemed to be beating the life out of his kit, even behind his beard I could see his toothy grin. The beat might be relatively slow but it certainly gave the drummer plenty of scope to flourish. I could see that he was almost in as much rapture as Kelvin.

When the song ended everybody cheered and there was a standing ovation. *From the very first song!* Not only that but after the last notes had been played the band themselves quit their instruments and surrounded Kelvin and shook his hand and congratulated him by thumping him on his back. Spider actually kissed him on his cheek.

I looked at Jane and she reflected the pride I felt. I saw the pride in her eyes that I felt and saw the tears she was just holding back as I felt myself doing the same.

'That was fucking awesome,' said Johnny. 'Oh shit, excuse my French,' he said when he realised his choice of words in front of ladies.

'Totally,' added Tomas. 'How's he going to top that!' he added, reflecting my earlier thoughts.

Kelvin was trying to talk but the applause was drowning him out. Eventually we began to hear him over the crowd. 'Well I think we got your interest, yeah? What do you say?'

He already had the crowd in the palm of his hand. In response they clapped and whistled and roared even louder in response to his question.

'That was 'So Afraid', an old Fleetwood Mac song,' he continued.

'But now let's try something a little softer for the ladies. Phew it's crowded in here.' He nodded to Spider and the whole band started playing.

Even I knew this, a Crowded House classic, 'Only Natural'. I found myself impressed with Spider's harmonising along to Kelvin's leading voice. Everybody at our table was dancing as we sat, rhythmically swaying back and forth from the waist up, anyway.

As that song finished they launched straight into another Crowded House number, 'Fall At Your Feet', without waiting for appreciation from the crowd and I wondered at how they did it. This was the first time they'd ever played together.

Then I noticed what Kelvin had done with the equipment that Jane and I had brought from the cabin. His laptop was on a table next to him and between songs he would reach down and carry out some task on it, but attached to the laptop using the cables we'd brought were phones. I noticed that every band member had a phone positioned close to him and, in some cases, they never took their eyes off the screens. Were they linked somehow? That must be the answer. What had Kelvin done? Whatever it was it was working brilliantly.

'I think it's time you danced,' he said as the appreciation from his Crowded House medley died down. He, they, launched immediately into a song that I recognised from some film or other. I seemed to recall it was an Australian group from possibly one of the *Crocodile Dundee* films. It was easy to dance along to and even our table got up and moved easily along to the beat.

Yes! I shouted to myself, even Jane was up. I caught Kelvin's eye and he managed to wink at me and I saw him smile. As if he wasn't busy enough!

The four of us danced along in a group, to all intents and purposes as boy/girl boy/girl, but we knew better. I looked around and was pleased to see that we weren't the only ones dancing. Far from it.

The songs kept coming. Some we knew and some we didn't but they all sounded great to me. And Jane? Getting her on her feet was one thing. Stopping her dancing was another. It was as if she was making up for all the lost time when, for reasons I'd not yet found out, she'd stopped herself from dancing or singing or doing anything in public view.

Unbelievingly and all too soon, Kelvin pronounced that it was time for the break. Had forty minutes really gone so quickly?

The crowd booed.

'We promise we'll be back in fifteen minutes,' Kelvin said in an attempt to pacify them.

They booed even louder. 'Gee you're a tough crowd,' Kelvin played as the band exited the stage and headed for their beer or whatever it was they craved.

Weed!

'Go to the toilet, get a drink. Anything! You've got just fifteen minutes to do it.'

The crowd weren't having it. They were banging tables and calling for more.

'Well, perhaps there is something we could do?' Kelvin capitulated.

A round of applause sprang from the crowd. I wondered what Kelvin had promised them.

'Whilst the band uh… wash their hands, perhaps there is something we could do.' He leaned down to his laptop and tapped away with his left hand. Eventually, satisfied, he stood back up to his full height. 'Among us tonight,' he started. 'There is an up and coming young talent that some of you may have heard of. She's been bubbling under for some time now,' he lied, 'and has just finished a small tour of New York and Miami.'

The crowd whistled in appreciation even though they had no idea what or who they were going to get. I clapped too though I didn't know either.

'So if we could convince her, perhaps she would take some time to join me on the stage and we could continue to entertain you whilst the band catch their breath. What do you say?'

He could have told them that cat food was healthy for humans to eat and they'd have agreed with him. They clapped and cheered.

'Who's he spotted?' I asked Jane as I craned my neck around to peer into the masses in an attempt to find out who he'd seen.

'So please, ladies and gentlemen, please join me in a round of applause for… Aneese Crosby!'

'Yeah, whoo whooo,' I said even as the name registered. My name. Realisation hit like a sledge hammer. 'Me?' I said as I pointed to myself.

When members of the crowd noticed it was me they started to clap as they looked my way in an attempt to cajole me into getting up.

'Me?' I said again. 'There must be some mistake?'

Jane leaned towards me and whispered, 'What was that about learning to trust him like we do?'

I could have killed her right then. I was terrified. The last thing I needed was to have my own words used against me. 'Jane tell him. I can't do this.'

'You tell him,' she answered sweetly.

'But what if he'd called your name?' I pleaded.

'He has more sense,' she answered back.

I felt my heartbeat increase. How was I going to get out of this? I met Kelvin's gaze and projected hate his way. How dare he do this to me. I was enjoying myself and now he'd spoiled it. He nodded at me, making me more angry. I projected hatred his way. He nodded at me and again and if his eyes could have glowed white they would. He was positively, silently, shouting *get your little arse up here* to me.

'Guess you'd better get up there, Aneese, before they hang you,' prompted Tomas.

I found myself standing and I heard the applause increase. It spurred me on even more and before I knew it I was on the stage. 'I will kill you!' I hissed, and I meant it.

'No, you'll thank me,' he said, his eyes boring into mine, staring me out. 'Most people dream of this moment and you're actually getting it, so you can hate me later.'

I turned around to face the audience and tried to project a smile even though it was far from what I actually felt. I felt fear, this was a terrible nightmare. I'd be such a let-down and then I'd run off and cry and I just knew that I would never forgive him for shaming me. How dare he do this to me!

Funny, it was fine when he did it to the band!

'Aneese,' he whispered to me. 'You know I would never harm you. If you don't trust me then return to the table and I'll apologise to the audience.'

I looked at him. He so needed bringing down a peg or three but he knew what buttons to push where I was concerned. 'You're using my love for you as a weapon,' I hissed. 'And it's not right.'

'Weapons hurt and kill and I'd do neither of those things to you, you know that. Now do you trust me?'

Damn him. 'You know I do!' I almost snarled.

'Then trust me now and I will make you a singer. No more mouthing silently in front of the mirror. I'm trying to give you something, here, not taking anything away.'

I recalled Jane saying something similar to me recently but about a completely different subject, not to mention Tomas. I'd forgotten who actually said it first.

'Now take a deep breath,' he said and he watched me until I did so. 'And another, then hold it and let it out.'

I did as he'd instructed.

'We're going to do that Ricky Martin duet that you didn't think I knew you've been practicing.'

My mouth dropped open. That was meant to be a surprise for him when we got home. How did he know?

'My iPod tells me you've repeat played it at least fifty times,' he said, as if reading my mind. 'And I know it's within your vocal range.'

I nodded, dumbly.

'So are you ready?'

I considered saying no. Where would he be then? 'I'm ready.'

'Ladies and gentlemen,' he started straight away. 'We've decided to do a duet, so if I just plug in the tape we'll be ready in a jiffy.' He took the guitar strap from around his shoulders and placed the instrument down. Then he moved to his laptop case and started to poke and prod inside it.

What was he doing? There was no tape. I didn't understand. After he'd made it look like he was doing something with his empty laptop case he deftly ran his fingers over his laptop keyboard and I felt and heard the microphones spring to life. As the introduction started, he indicated his laptop to me and I saw the lyrics written on the screen.

Was this an aid in case I didn't know them? I knew them. He told me himself, fifty plus times on repeat play. All the music was coming from his laptop, too. I guessed he had his box of tricks set to karaoke mode and the mention of his tape was just a ruse. Then he started to sing.

I loved this song. I'd found it on his iPod when it was set to random and I'd imagined Kelvin and I singing it together and so rehearsed it again and again in my mind. I knew every word but I appreciated the helping hand that he'd provided on the screen. My nerves might mean I needed the help.

On his laptop screen his lyrics were coloured yellow and mine blue and they coloured over into white just before we were expected to sing them. I doubt he needed to look at the screen and I looked at him and, indeed, he didn't.

I knew so much about this song and had actually started to deconstruct it. Kelvin had told me during our three days in our cave that deconstructing could be fun and that you came to really appreciate what the writer was trying to accomplish and how the song writing process developed.

This song was designed in such a way that the male lead, him (Ricky Martin), sang first and that the female, me (somebody called Meja – never heard of her), joined at a backing vocal level, initially. As the song developed, the female part gained prominence until they are singing a true duet. I'd worked this all out by myself and was very proud of my efforts.

Kelvin's voice was perfect and sounded just like I was listening to his iPod. How did he do that? Was his software compensating? I'd heard him sing and knew he could so I quickly discounted that last thought.

Then my lyrics started to turn white on the screen and I panicked. I'd been so caught up in thought that I'd totally forgotten that I was meant to be singing as well. I didn't even have a microphone. My eyes met his, his cool and rational as always and mine wide and white in terror. I was right, I was going to screw this up. As if in slow motion his arm reached around me and drew me closer to him. I wondered whether he was trying to kiss me but then I realised that he'd casually brought his microphone so that it was positioned between us.

I nervously sang my first three words, missing my introduction by a heartbeat, I thought, and feeling like I had cobwebs in my mouth, but before I repeated my words again I'd silently cleared my throat and recovered. There was then a small gap before we started singing again and by then Kelvin had found another microphone from somewhere and we moved apart and sang looking into each other's eyes.

I felt wooden and heavy at first but then I started to relax into it as I saw Kelvin had already done. By the time my voice was due to rise and overtake the lead, my confidence had grown, all in the space of a few moments. I no longer felt wooden, I felt like I could fly!

The song was over all too soon and I found tears in my eyes as I listened to the energetic applause. I sought out Jane and saw that she was standing and clapping and biting her lip as her eyes sparkled as she looked proudly up at me. Tomas and Johnny were standing too. I swallowed and looked to my left to find Kelvin. Our eyes met and he nodded twice by just moving his head a fraction of a millimetre both times. That was all I needed.

I launched myself at him and in no time at all my arms were around him and I clung on for dear life as the audience wolf whistled and I ignored them, uncaring what they thought. 'Thank you, thank you, thank you,' I gushed.

'You're welcome. You did great!'

My smile widened and I thought my chest would burst with pride. 'I want more,' I found myself saying. 'And you can have me in any way whenever you want. I love you so much.'

'But I thought you hated me?' he asked, knowingly. I just knew he'd want his chunk of flesh.

I ignored his remark, pushed away from him and stared deeply into his eyes, willing him to understand *exactly* what I'd just said. I was telling him that he could have my bum cherry anytime he wanted, could spank me over his knee any time he felt like it. Tie me up, whip me, whatever. Hell, if nostrils and ears turned him on then he could stick it there as well!

He smiled. 'What, here on the stage?'

'If that's what you want,' I almost panted. 'I know now that you *will* be giving me something and not taking.'

He moved towards me and placed his hands on my waist. 'It's called sharing,' he said, and I nodded.

'No, it's called giving,' I answered, sounding more wise than I felt. 'You're such a giving person, you know that?'

'In that case I'll *give* you a chance to *share* another song?'

I nodded quickly. 'Yes, please.'

'Well then, Miss Harry, let's get to it.'

He disentangled himself from me and went to work on his laptop. I looked down and saw him scrolling through songs and then reverse the scroll until he'd highlighted the one he wanted. The song was called 'Just Go Away' and I'd sang only half of it, once, in the cabin.

This was asking too much, I thought, and I nearly said as much but as usual it was as if he were reading my mind.

'I know you've only sang this song once but it's an easy song to sing and the words will be on the screen. What's more important in this song is attitude. Relax into it, enjoy yourself and give it some flare once you've settled.'

I nodded though my mind was actually thinking *easy for you to say!*

'I'll be accompanying you on drums.'

I have to sing alone? I felt the familiar terror arising within me. *Hang on, he plays drums too?*

'Remember, Debbie Harry wasn't big on overt shows of emotion. Sing it like you're bored and would rather be peeling potatoes in a Soho kitchen or something.'

I numbly nodded again. Not too far off the truth.

'Ready?'

I nodded.

'*ARE YOU READY?*' he said again, as if talking to a slow child.

'Yes, I'm ready,' I voiced.

As I answered him he pressed a button on his keyboard and ran to the back of the stage towards the drum kit. My gaze followed briefly but then I saw the laptop screen spring to life and my lyrics appear and my heart leapt into my mouth. The words *Introduction in 3, 2, 1* were displayed above them in green and as the numbers turned white in succession I readied myself. As the *1* turned white I almost started to sing but I realised in time that this was an instrumental introduction.

I wondered if anybody had seen my – almost – mistake. Then again, had anybody realised I'd almost fluffed the first word of my duet? The fact that they seemed not to have gave me confidence.

Bored. Pretend you're bored!

I put my left hand on my hip and bent my right leg at the knee as if

I'd been waiting too long in the Post Office queue and wanted to show my displeasure. Then I disdainfully scanned the audience, though I winked when my gaze fell on our table. Jane smiled back at me and I almost broke into a grin but caught it just in time.

Lyrics in 3, 2, 1. They started to colour and I started to sing.

I realised as I sang that the song was about a woman suggesting to her former lover ways in which he could leave, something along the lines of "I don't care how you leave JUST GO AWAY!" It was actually quite amusing.

Don't go away sad, don't go away mad. JUST GO AWAY!

And every time I said JUST GO WAY Kelvin would echo the words in a sneery, nasal voice and it was difficult for me not to smile. I tried to concentrate on appearing bored but the song had a good beat and I found my right foot balancing on its heel and tapping. I stopped it once or twice but then I thought *what the hell* and gave it free rein. Trying to control it was distracting me, anyway.

The drumming was perfect and I had to look behind me just to reassure myself that it was actually him playing. It was him, though, and he was really enjoying himself. I tried to recall whether I'd seen a drum kit back at the house. Wouldn't mind a play on that, either.

Like you'd have the time with all the things you've promised to do!

Halfway through the song the lyrics referred to a fool and the way I flicked my head left the audience in no doubt that I was referring to Kelvin. By the time the song finished the audience were smiling and laughing and some were even trying to join in with the sneery remarks. I guessed we were a hit, I WAS A HIT, and I was right. And I felt wonderful. This was almost like a double yolker... well almost. No wonder people like the Rolling Stones kept going, they just couldn't get enough of this drug.

And neither could I.

Kelvin left his drums and joined me at the front of the stage and I pounced on him.

'Samantha Fox.'

He looked at me, confused and surprised. 'She does?'

I shook my head and rolled my eyes. 'No!'

'She doesn't? Make up your mind!'

At the time I wasn't sure whether he was playing or not. I spoke slowly, enunciating each word. 'I WANT TO SING 'TOUCH ME' BY SAMANTHA FOX.'

'Are you sure? I've never heard you sing that.'

'Just because you've never heard me, doesn't mean I can't!'

He looked doubtful.

'Kelvin,' I said exasperated. 'I trust you but you have to learn to trust me... to trust you...' OK, so it sounded better in my head. 'Now do you have it in your box of tricks or not?'

'Sure.'

'Then can you set it up... please, Daddy-o?'

He stared at me as he contemplated. 'This will be the last song. The boys will be back then.'

I nodded my understanding.

'Have you ever sung this song before, I mean really sung?'

'A hundred times.' *In my head when I've been drunk.*

'You'll be by yourself?'

I suspected he was trying to dissuade me but I nodded anyway.

'Apart from me on lead guitar and backing vocals.'

So he was testing my commitment. I smiled and nodded.

'Then I guess we'll give it a go.'

I smiled victoriously.

'But you can introduce it.'

Another test? I nodded.

'OK, let's go.'

As the audience returned to their seats and quietened down, he did whatever he did on his laptop. I guessed it would be something along the lines of selecting the song and switching off drums and switching on lead guitar and backing vocals. I stole a glance at Jane and raised my eyebrows in her direction. One of hers raised questioningly in reply.

For you I mouthed in her direction, pointing as I did so. I think she got the gist. Yeah, *touch me, I want to feel your body close to mine.* This was definitely for Jane: beautiful, fragile, alluring and sexy and more. I imagined me unzipping her dress later and letting it slide off her perfect body as my mouth sought her nipples. Yeah, good music was like sex, all right. I could so be a pop star. I think I finally understood groupies, too.

The thought shocked me.

'Ready?' Kelvin asked as he picked up a guitar and went to put the strap around his shoulders.

'Yes,' I answered. 'But you aren't.'

'What do you mean?'

'You don't look like a rock star,' I finished. 'Lose this.' I pulled at his bow tie until it undid. 'And the jacket.'

I started pulling at the tuxedo and he put the guitar down and let me remove it. He was left in his gleamingly white, long sleeved shirt complete with cuff links. Members of the audience started to whistle and bang the table.

'Still not right,' I said as I bit my lip. 'The shirt's not right.'

'Well I can't lose the shirt or we'll be walking the plank.'

'Quite,' I answered, unintentionally imitating Jane but still deep in thought. Then an arm reached out and tore at Kelvin's right shirt sleeve at the shoulder until it half came apart at the seams. Another tug and it was off. My mouth dropped open and I followed the arm up until I met its owner. Spider.

'You're right, little un, he just don't look the part. I've been wanting to do this all night.' He turned to Kelvin. 'You look like a saxophone player with the Glenn Miller Band.'

Who?

The other sleeve was soon off and I took in the view. Kelvin was now bare armed, his muscles and tattoos there for all to see. As I've said before he wasn't overly muscled like some of those freaks, but his arms looked great. The audience were whistling appreciatively, males and females. I considered ripping the buttons off his shirt to get a waistcoat effect, but the shirt was too long and would just look silly. Then Spider turned his attention on me.

'And as for you,' he said as he knelt down in front of me. 'Below the knee might be fine for *some* Blondie songs, but for Samantha Fox…' I guessed he'd seen the selected song on the laptop screen. 'You need to go a bit slutty.'

I heard a tear and felt a pull on my clothing.

'My dress!' I couldn't help calling out. My killer dress, my two thousand pounds of overpriced, golden material. It was well above the knee now and, what's more, it was ragged. I looked to Kelvin for support but he was smirking. I knew what he was thinking: *If it's good enough for me, it's good enough for you.*

The wolf whistles increased in number and intensity.

'I'll buy you a new one,' he offered as he smirked.

'But it's my dress,' was all I could say.

He laughed and I looked in Jane's direction. She was theatrically shaking her head with her head buried in her hands.

'And the heels have to go,' Spider continued.

'I can't sing in bare feet.'

'Good enough for Sandie Shaw.'

Who?

'Lose 'em,' he ordered.

I paused but then surrendered and kicked my shoes in the direction of our table. Tomas and Johnny recovered them as Jane went into fits of giggles.

I felt another pull at what was left of my dress. 'Another inch or two should do it.'

'Forget it, buster!' I said, and as he tried to rip more of the material I raised my foot, put my sole flat on his chest and pushed him away. I saw him smile as he fell back onto his rump and knew that he'd got a good eyeful of my underwear. The audience thought it was hilarious.

'Now can we sing?' I pleaded to Kelvin.

He laughed. 'Well you started it!'

I had, I knew, but that wasn't the point. 'Be gone,' I said to a prostrate Spider and I indicated with my hand the direction in which he could do it, too.

He raised his hands in surrender and slithered away like the snake-spider he was.

'Shall we do it?' I asked.

'If you're sure, but the bible bashers ain't going to like it.'

'Well there's no going back now,' I answered, pulling what was left of my dress into what I hoped was some form of respectability. 'And fuck 'em, anyway!'

He stifled a laugh as I hoped the microphone hadn't picked up that last statement. 'Ready when you are.'

'Well press the button, dammit!'

I readied myself for the beginning and watched the screen as I waited it to count me in or whatever it would do on this occasion. I watched and watched and watched for, oh, five seconds, perhaps. When nothing happened I turned my head to the left to face him and shrugged. Maybe the box wasn't working now? He just looked at me and I looked at him for another few moments and then he rolled his eyes, shook his head and leaned forward into his microphone.

'I guess I'll do the introductions, then' he said drily to the audience.

Oh crap. I'd forgotten I was meant to introduce us.

'Seems she wants Samantha Fox to touch her. Or perhaps somebody in the audience will volunteer. Applications on a postcard, please…'

I saw arms shoot up on more tables than one and most of those arms received a thump or slap for their efforts from partners and wives, playfully in most cases but in some cases not. Jane's arm stayed up the longest and I beamed at her. In my peripheral vision I could see Kelvin lower his head into his hands and shake his head, just like Jane had played at earlier on.

What? I mouthed to him.

He just shook his head and pressed the button.

And just as I started my *Full moon in the city* I saw the uniformed bitch who'd tried to stop our fun and beside her was a man in a naval uniform with lots of decoration on his cuffs. He held his hat under his arm, just like I had seen actors do in the old war films that Richard liked to watch. He was watching us, stern faced, and the harridan beside him was smirking. It seems she'd called Kelvin's bluff, the cow.

My heart dropped and my singing faltered slightly. I had wanted to sing this song since I was a little girl and here I was screwing it up because of some po-faced, egotistical, rule follower. I felt a presence beside me just as I started singing *touch me, I want to feel your body* and he waited until there was a singing break and he was filling the gap with his screaming guitar before he hissed in my ear.

'The song, nothing matters but the song,' he hissed. How he could hiss at me and play the guitar at the same time I didn't know. 'Ignore them. Enjoy yourself. Everything after the song doesn't matter. The song is here and now. Nothing else!'

My concentration was wavering even more. I was on the verge of losing the beat, even forgetting words. Then I felt an electric shock as somebody touched me right where they shouldn't; they were actually touching my underwear just where that damn dog did all those years before but from behind me. I jumped and turned my head to face Kelvin and as I did I saw his hand returning to his guitar just in time to start playing again. Part of me was shocked and part of me was relieved. For a second, there, I thought it was Spider who had molested me into action.

'Now sing, damn you!'

I only missed my next line by a tiny amount but sing I did. I momentarily caught Jane's eye and guessed by her open mouth that she'd seen what he'd done. Had the audience seen too? Whether they had or hadn't didn't matter, the song was called 'Touch Me' so what did they expect. What mattered was that I was singing again. Kelvin had got my mind back on track in his own unique way.

So I ignored the skinny mean bitch and I sang. In fact I more than sang. Kelvin was right, I realised, the song, the performance, was here and now. Nothing else mattered. I felt myself relaxing and my singing feel more natural. I started to feel the music and felt my body sway as I skipped around like a wannabe pop princess. In my mind I was watching Samantha Fox singing her song on *Top of The Pops*. In my mind's eye I saw her with her fashionable ripped jeans, skipping and gyrating, and I felt myself imitating her, unashamedly.

OK, I didn't have the fashionably ripped jeans and the faded denim jacket, nor her single fingerless glove on her left hand or her big hair. I certainly didn't have her bust though, I told myself, I wasn't too far off. And I wasn't wearing black high heeled boots either, but for this briefest of moments I was Samantha Fox. Whatever she did all those years ago – I think I was eight when I saw her on Top of The Pops – I did now.

And it felt great, better than great, wonderful. I put my all into my performance. If it wasn't appreciated by the audience then it wouldn't be because I hadn't tried. What could you do but do your best.

All too soon the song was over and I almost cried as the audience, well most of them – Kelvin had been right about the religious crowd, showed their appreciation for our, my, performance. I smiled my thanks back at them, tight lipped and on the verge of tears. In apparent slow motion I turned my head and sought out Jane. She was standing and clapping and her face reflected joy and love. Tomas and Johnny stood with her and they were clapping too. I saw Tomas place two fingers in his mouth and let forth a shrill whistle. Then I turned my head to face Kelvin and saw him nod twice, as was his way of showing satisfaction at my performance.

From somewhere inside me the words *That'll do, pig* jumped to the fore as his manner of appreciating my performance was recognised by my subconscious as being just like the farmer in the film *Babe*. Funny what your mind does at certain times, isn't it?

Then I saw the uniformed pair arrive at Jane's shoulder and she jumped when they touched her arm because she hadn't seen them. I saw her face instantly cloud over as the man talked to her and the grassing bitch tried unsuccessfully to hide her smirk. I watched as Jane frowned and answered them back angrily. I knew that Kelvin would be entering the fray soon. In fact I was surprised he wasn't there already so I turned to my left just as I felt him take my microphone off me.

'Ladies and gentlemen I apologise for this,' he shouted over the still applauding audience. 'Seems I committed a capital crime earlier on this evening when I…' He theatrically paused and looked left and right as if he was going to let forth a great secret. 'Moved a table. And now the jackbooted brigade have come to take us away for execution, so there'll be no more show tonight.'

As the audience started to quieten down, no doubt in disbelief, he shrugged off his guitar strap and held out his hand to me. I looked at him, confused, but didn't move. Surely he wasn't giving in just like that? Then he winked at me and I went to smile but he stopped me with a quick shake of his head. I took his hand and we both stepped off the stage together. Just as the audience started to boo.

The booing got louder as we walked towards Jane and when we were halfway there Kelvin stopped and shrugged. This wasn't like the playful booing from earlier, this was the real stuff.

'Rules is rules,' he said as he shrugged. Only the nearest tables would have heard him but his gesture was obvious.

The boos and jeering got louder still.

'Go give Jane some support,' he whispered to me, and he patted my behind to send me on my way.

As I walked I looked over my shoulder and saw that he was heading back towards the stage.

'Sorry, I forgot my stuff,' he said as he passed a mic. He made a show of dismantling his equipment and Spider joined him on the stage. I watched as they exchanged words and saw Kelvin shake his head. Then Spider grabbed Kelvin's arm and I feared the worst. Surely they weren't going to get into it on the stage?

'Well Spider, here, wants us to continue,' I heard Kelvin say. I hadn't realised he'd switched the mic on. 'What do you guys say?' he asked the audience. 'Do you want the show to go on?'

There was a faint response.

'Sorry, I can't hear you?' Kelvin played, hand to his ear in the traditional way.

This time the response was louder.

'Sorry, say again,' Kelvin asked. 'Did you say you wanted the show?'

Some answered verbally but some just nodded.

'What?' asked Kelvin as he leaned towards the audience. 'Can't hear you. Did you say you wanted the show?'

It started as a murmur but then it changed to a mumble. Before long it was a throbbing roar as the crowd got his gist and did his bidding.

I realised that this was what he'd been working on all the while. His retreat had been a show, nothing more.

WE WANT THE SHOW! WE WANT THE SHOW! WE WANT THE SHOW!

Soon the rhythm was augmented by stamping feet and banged tables. Kelvin was helping by seemingly conducting the crowd like they were one big orchestra. His orchestra. Eventually he shushed them and when he had silence he turned towards our table and spoke into the mic. 'So what's it going to be Adolf... Eva... does the show go on or do you have a riot and five hundred complaints in the morning?'

The uniformed man swallowed and went to speak but the chant started again. I watched as the face of the bitch beside him turned purple with rage as she, at least, realised that she had lost. The man at least had the good grace to smile at the mutinous crowd as he led the bitch away.

A huge roar of victory and applause followed them out of the room.

'I think we just... what's the term? Stuck it to the man?' Kelvin said into the mic and he gained a healthy dose of laughter from the crowd. Seemed they liked sticking it to the man. 'So let's dance, yeah, what do you say?'

It was obvious from the response that they wanted to.

'Set 'em up, guys,' Kelvin said to the band members as he jumped down from the stage and joined us at the table.

'We won!' I said excitedly.

'We sure did,' he answered. 'You OK?' he asked of Jane.

She paused. 'Well I wasn't but I am now. How dare they...'

'Yeah, some inadequates! All they can do is follow pathetic rules because they haven't got the brains to think for themselves. They think they have power if they get people to do their bidding.'

He took her in his arms and kissed her. 'Wasn't she great?' he said as they moved apart.

He meant me, which was just as well, as I was starting to get a little jealous.

'She was fantastic!' Jane replied. 'Come here, you,' she ordered and she drew me into her arms and we hugged. As we parted we kissed but to anybody looking on it would look like a peck on the lips (because that's just what it was). Then Kelvin did the same to me, but lingered more than she, and my minor jealousy evaporated in an instant.

This wasn't the first time we three had openly showed affection in public, but it felt like it. I felt very wicked. And so very, very alive!

'You looking after them, boys?' Kelvin said to Tomas and Johnny.

'Doing our best,' answered Johnny.

'Well I appreciate it. Drinks are on us.'

'We've been informed,' answered Tomas, this time. 'And again we're trying our best,' he quipped, raising a full glass to show what he meant.

'Good for you. Anyway,' Kelvin said as he turned back to face us girls. 'Gotta go.'

He kissed us both quickly again and then he was gone. As he joined the guys on stage I sat beside Jane and found her hand. She squeezed back and I felt happy and content, deliriously happy, actually.

'Did you see what that horrible man did to my lovely dress?'

'Yes,' she answered. 'How dare he.' Then she looked slyly my way and lowered her voice. 'But you got to show off those great legs of yours. You're so hot!'

'Ditto!' I moved to kiss her but we both stopped just in time. Somehow we both knew that without Kelvin here it would be crossing some kind of line. I settled for, 'I want to dance with you.'

She raised an eyebrow and looked at me questioningly. 'Vertical expression of horizontal desire?'

'Oh yeah.'

'Then you're on!'

Chapter Fourteen

I wondered if the room was still spinning. It was last night. Not only was it spinning but it was buzzing too. A loud almost mechanical sound from an overly loud radio which interfered with my hearing and made understanding conversation difficult, if not impossible. I remembered having to shout a lot and people shouting back at me: Kelvin, Jane, Tomas, Spider, everybody. But I couldn't remember why or where, or what they were saying.

We'd danced, I recalled. Me with Tomas and Johnny and Jane and then me with Jane by ourselves. Nobody said a word. Don't think they'd have dared and, anyway, if they were as drunk as me they wouldn't have cared. Then we'd danced back in the cabin? That's right. I remembered now. We had an after show party in the cabin and on the balcony. Spider and the band were there and some women appeared from somewhere. Who they were I had no idea but they gave the band members something to hold onto. I had a vague memory of seeing some bare breasted woman in the bathroom with the band's drummer, and Spider with his tongue in some woman's mouth. Surely I must have imagined both those events? I mean, Spider's married.

Oh you naive child!

I tentatively opened an eye. It took great effort to force it open. It was daylight, I saw, but the throbbing in my head forced me to close my eye quickly. I convinced myself that the throbbing decreased when my eyes were closed. It had, hadn't it? I was thirsty but the thought of actually moving to do anything about it was just that, a thought. This would take some effort. Perhaps Kelvin would get me something to drink, he was the ever attentive hound, wasn't he? Isn't that what Jane had called him? Something like that, anyway. Come on, Daddy-o. Your 'ickle girl is dying of thirst, here!

It was lighter now. Had I fallen back to sleep? How long for? I could hear the distant sound of the sea now. I hadn't heard that before. I realised that the balcony door was open. Had it been open before and I just hadn't noticed? This time I opened both my eyes and forced my head up from the pillow. I was shocked to find that my pillow was actually Jane's thigh and that her feet were where her head should have been. She was naked, face down on the bed and I, myself, was laying almost perpendicular across the bed and the ache in my neck told me that I had been in this position far too long. I too was naked, we all were, and I was laying on my back with my legs draped across Kelvin's. He was almost bent double with his arm on my waist. What a sight we must look.

There was a stale, musty aroma, I realised. I recognised the smell. Surely we hadn't screwed last night? And if so, who'd done what to whom? Surely I'd know if I had. Wouldn't I? I hoped to God that I hadn't. I mean, what's the point of doing it and not remembering the next morning. I was still thirsty and my headache was worse. I needed fluids badly but I still couldn't bring myself to move. It just took too much effort. Perhaps I'll just go back to sleep.

'Oh, my head,' Kelvin murmured.

Oh good, he's awake. 'Mine, too. Need a drink,' I whispered hoarsely. There was no response for a while so I prodded him on the shoulder. 'Get me a drink.'

'You get *me* a drink,' he countered.

I gathered the strength to answer him. 'You're... meant to... look after... us,' was the best I could do. I was exhausted afterwards. Still no answer. 'Daddy-o, please?' I whined.

'OK, OK,' he answered, but still he didn't move. I was just about to speak again when I felt him move beside me. Then he paused for a little while and moved again. A few more movements like that and he was unsteadily on his feet. I watched through half-closed eyes as he swayed before lunging towards the wall and leaning on it. I listened as he slid along the wall and then I heard the water run as he filled a glass. He walked back to the bed without the support of the wall and handed me the glass.

The water was warmish, even though I'd heard him run the tap, but it tasted like heaven. 'More, please,' I said as I finished.

'Me, too,' Jane croaked, obviously awake now. By the sound of her she felt as we did.

Kelvin did three more trips to the tap before we women were sated. He'd stand before us, swaying with his eyes closed until we pressed the glass back into his hand. When we were finished he addressed his own thirst.

'We need pills,' Jane said.

'Where are they?' Kelvin asked.

'My bag. Don't know where.' She was using as few words as possible. We all were.

I heard him fumbling around the cabin for a while.

'Can't find it,' he finally said. 'Close your eyes. Turn light on.'

I screwed my eyes tight shut and heard the light switch operate. Then I heard him shuffle about and the light switch was finally flicked off.

'Found it,' he said. 'More water.'

We all took four pills, two whities and two pinkies, and washed them down with water. Kelvin found another glass and left two full glasses of water on the bedside stand. When he was halfway back into bed Jane stopped him.

'Cold. Balcony door.'

Kelvin exhaled loudly and forced himself back up and I heard him slide the door closed. When he got back into the bed we all moved until we were wrapped around each other like a litter of puppies in a box. I felt a light sheet placed over us and, despite my head, I smiled. I was warm and comfortable. Now all I had to do was wait for the pills to take effect. What was it Jane had said so long ago in New York? An hour for them to kick in, was it? There was beer, too. My stomach gurgled as I gagged at the thought of beer. Not this time.

We snoozed and sipped from the glasses occasionally and Kelvin dutifully kept the glasses filled. After what seemed like much more than an hour I started to feel more human.

'Are we ready for some breakfast yet?' Kelvin asked as if reading my mind. He sounded a lot better, certainly better than I yet felt, though I was getting there.

'I think so,' Jane answered for us both.

She was laying spooned around me with her arm around my waist. I, in turn, had my head on Kelvin's chest and his left arm was around both of us females. I felt him stretch out his right arm, slowly so as not to disturb us, as he reached for the phone.

'Room eight-four-five-five,' he said into the phone. 'Three full English breakfasts with coffee and tea and various juices, please?'

I heard a tinny gurgle as the person on the other end of the phone talked.

'Then you'll have your work cut out, then, won't you,' he said before putting the phone down.

'What was that all about?' Jane asked, saving me the trouble.

'She said they've just stopped serving lunch.'

'Lunch! What the hell time is it?' I exclaimed.

Kelvin squinted at his ever present watch. I don't think I'd ever seen it off his wrist. 'Fourteen o'clock, just gone,' he answered.

'A little after two,' Jane translated. She didn't seem shocked at all.

'Two, what time did we go to bed?'

'Haven't got a scooby. Think we finally turfed everybody out by four, including the guy sleeping in the bath. Who was he, anyway?'

Guy sleeping in the bath? First I'd heard of that.

We lay silently for a small while but it was me who broke the silence. 'Did we, uh, do anything last night?'

'You mean sex?' he asked. 'Well I know I did, but don't ask me who with.'

'Well that's just charming!' Jane played. Then she turned to me. 'Don't you know if you did?' she asked.

'Um... no.'

'Must have been the guy in the bath, then.'

'Ha ha, very funny,' he answered. Then I jumped as his fingers probed me in a most personal place. 'Well you've had some attention,' he exclaimed before moving on to Jane.

'Get away from me!' she squealed.

'As have you, looks like a full house!'

'And did I orgasm?' I asked.

'How the hell would I know,' he answered, and Jane laughed.

'Well it's your duty to ensure I do!' I exclaimed.

'Oh, is it now?'

'Yeah, it's the rules.'

'Which rules?'

'Those invisible ones which we live by.'

'Oh, those ones. Well how do you know I didn't?'

'Didn't what?'

'Make you orgasm.'

'I don't, but you have every time before that.'

'So there's the answer, then.'

'But I don't remember.'

'Not my problem. The rules say, apparently, that I have to bring you to orgasm. Nothing in the rules about me having to remember for you.'

'He has a point,' Jane ventured.

'Whose side are you on, anyway?' I asked.

'The side of peace and quiet,' she replied. 'My head is still banging.'

We lay in silence for a while more. 'I could remind you,' Kelvin finally said.

'Remind me of what?' I answered and asked.

'What an orgasm feels like? Perhaps it will jog your memory?'

Jane leaned forward and looked down at his penis. 'Oh god, it's awake.'

'Not a chance, buster!' I said a bit too loudly. My head wasn't quite there either. 'I'm a bit tender, this morning,' I said more softly.

'So I couldn't convince you?' he asked.

I felt his hand cup my left breast.

'No, I don't think so,' I answered, but as soon as I said it I felt my body responding to his touch, headache or not. Then Jane shimmied closer and started to nuzzle my ear and I knew I was lost. Kelvin pulled me closer and kissed me and I felt his hand run down my back towards my backside. Then he stopped and I felt him tense.

'What on earth is this?' he asked, pulling at something under the sheet. Every time he pulled I felt my thigh going tighter until I felt my circulation almost stop. He pushed back the sheet until we could see and then he burst out laughing. What "this" was, was half a pair of briefs. God knows where the other half was.

'Not a good day for your clothes, was it,' he said.

'What do you mean?' I asked.

'Your dress?'

'My dress?' I'd forgotten about my dress but now it all came flooding back. 'My dress,' I groaned. 'My lovely dress! That bastard Spider destroyed it!'

'Maybe he destroyed your knickers, too?'

'Oh, don't, I'll be sick!'

Jane laughed. 'We'll get you a new dress.'

'But it was special,' I whined. 'My first lovely dress and it was wrecked by that... that... man!'

'There, there now, little angel-girl,' Jane soothed. 'You just lay back now and Mummy Bear and Daddy-o will make everything better.'

I did as I was told and they both started on me, their hands all over me caressing and stroking me. 'Huh, make everything better,' I played. 'You just want to fuck me!'

'True,' they said in unison.

'Well you can't,' I finished.

'Oh? Why ever not?' asked Kelvin as he slipped a finger into my moistness, making me gasp.

'Because,' I sighed. 'Breakfast has just arrived!'

And it had.

Two hours later we were back beside the pool feeling slightly better. We'd eaten and showered and in between I'd ended up covered in the smell of bacon, sausage and egg, the full English, actually. Oh, yes, they certainly made a meal out of me and they'd both reminded me what an orgasm felt like. Jane and I were getting better at pleasing each other. Yeah, life was hell!

It seemed that everybody was wearing dark glasses that day and I don't think all of it was due to the sun. Roy Orbison, a favourite of my father's, would be smiling from heaven. I'd actually ducked into a shop and bought three matching pairs of Orbisons and we wore them as we searched for some loungers around the pool. It felt very warm but it could have been the alcohol, the breakfast, or the exercise or perhaps all three. Either way, I was looking forward to getting into the pool to cool off and Jane had prepared by bringing another set of pills for each of us just in case we weren't totally out of the woods yet.

I saw a man laying with his wife raise his hand to us and beckon us over. There were two empty loungers beside them and when he whispered to his son, he left and there were three. 'Fine show last night,

Kelvin,' the stranger said.

'Sorry, have we met?' Kelvin asked as we took the offered loungers.

'Not really. I'm Lenny and this is my wife, Carol. Our boy, Ken, just left to go find his friends.'

'Well thanks for the seats, Lenny,' Kelvin said as he shook hands with him. 'The ladies here, Jane and Aneese.'

'Pleasure to meet you. Carol and I really enjoyed the show last night.'

As they mentioned the show there was a ripple of movement all around us like a mini Mexican wave. First the dark glasses were lifted and then there was a spattering of applause. Kelvin responded to the activity with a wave as he plonked himself down on his lounger.

'Yeah, we never danced so much in years. I'm in kitchen design, by the way. Coventry Kitchen Masters. This is our twenty-fifth wedding anniversary cruise.'

'Congratulations,' Kelvin said.

I got the impression that this guy could talk for England. Hardly the peace and quiet I craved. 'I need to swim,' I said. 'Jane?'

'Yes I could do with cooling down. Nice to meet you,' she said to the couple as we slipped away.

'I'll get us some drinks,' Kelvin volunteered.

'Nothing alcoholic, please?'

'Yeah we heard about your party,' Lenny continued. 'Talk of the ship at breakfast. Not surprised you're a little worse for wear.'

He was still talking when we slipped into the pool. Jane surprised me by putting her head under the water and coming back up with her hair plastered to her face and dripping water. 'Ah, that was just what I needed.'

'You put your head under!'

'Extreme times means extreme measures must be taken... or something like that. Feel like I'm boiling away under my skin.'

'Guess it's the alcohol and the pills and stuff.'

'Probably right. I don't ever remember ever having a hangover like this.'

'You OK to swim? Come on, I'll teach you to swim underwater. It's easy and it will cool you down quicker.'

'OK, but don't let me bang into the wall. I can't open my eyes under the water.'

'I'll teach you to do that, too.'

'No you won't. Trust me on that one.'

Part of me realised that the under the water thing was one of her hang ups, like her not dancing or singing. Well I'd got her dancing so I decided to push this one. 'I'll be back in a jiffy,' I said and by the time I'd returned I'd begged the lend of two pairs of swimming goggles.

'Anything for you, singing lady,' the teenager I borrowed them off had said.

I'd graced him with the full million candles and guessed he'd be fantasising for years over my put on wiggle as I walked away. The eyes attached to his hormones were watching my bikini clad body the whole time. Lucky him.

'Here you go, put these on,' I said as I handed her a pair.

I saw her face cloud over slightly. 'I told you I wasn't opening my eyes underwater,' she said.

'They're not for that,' I lied. 'They're for stopping the chemicals in the pool hurting your eyes. Nobody says you have to open them.'

She thought a while and her eyes narrowed. 'Will you be opening your eyes?'

'Yeah, of course, but I do anyway. And anyway you asked me to stop you banging into the side of the pool, so I'll be your underwater guide dog.'

She paused some more. 'Well OK, then.'

Yes!

I was getting good at this reverse psychology lark. Thank you, Daddy-o! I'd already formulated a plan – it just came from nowhere like a lightning bolt. I'd bet my forthcoming new dress that I could get her to open her eyes within half an hour. Kelvin would be so pleased with me. And it wasn't as if I was just doing it to please Kelvin either, I was doing it for Jane, too. I got such enjoyment from swimming underwater – it was more relaxing than surface swimming – and being able to see and in turn see what others were doing was part of the appeal.

So firstly I told her that swimming underwater was just like the breast stroke she habitually did on the surface, but without the need to raise your head and give yourself that crick in the neck feeling. After a couple of below the waterline strokes, I started to teach her about holding her breath which, to all you doubters, isn't just about holding your breath, it's about and comfort and control. I taught her to take a breath and swim for a while, but to breathe out halfway when she got close to her lungs bursting. She could then stay under, comfortably, for a little while longer until she needed to breathe out again to release the pressure on her lungs. It was only when there was nothing left to breathe out that you came to the surface for another lungful.

'Come on,' I said when she had the hang of that. 'Just go under and really let go, spread your wings and enjoy yourself. I'll be right beside you and when I tap you it means to stop because we'll be close to the side.'

She looked at our route from one end of the pool to the other. 'Like that's going to be a problem. We won't be getting anywhere near the end of the pool before I run out of air.'

So she swam and I watched her. She was hesitant at first but soon she was really reaching out and using the full length of her body and arms. I smiled as I saw the glimpse of a smile on her face as she experienced the freedom and relaxation that I felt when I swam underwater. I also, OK I'll admit it, looked at her wonderful body. I wasn't too mesmerised to notice her exhale half a lungful, as I'd instructed her – she was really good at this – but I almost missed informing her that the end of the pool was in sight. I had to hurriedly reach out and tap her thigh twice and we only just made it before she would hit the end of the pool wall. We both stood and she loudly exhaled as the water dripped from her head and face. Then she took off her borrowed goggles and the first thing she saw was my superior smirk.

'That was so relaxing. What are you smiling at?' Then she noticed the pool wall behind me. 'What the…' She looked behind her at where we had just come from. 'No way!'

'Yep,' I answered simply. My turn for smug mode.

'No FRIGGIN way!'

I just crossed my arms over my chest and smiled at her as she looked behind her again, as if doubting what she had just done. Then she started jumping up and down and then she grabbed me and I was forced to join her in her excitement.

'And not only that but I got to look at you, too, without anybody seeing me do it. Wow, you are really beautiful and you swim gracefully. I could look at that glorious bum of yours all day as your thighs slowly kicked through the water, and when you stretch out your arms the material of your bikini top becomes taught and I don't have to imagine anything!'

'You know what I think?' she asked around her smile. 'I think you're a fucking pervert!'

I screamed in laughter, causing some pool goers to look our way. Jane hardly ever swore! 'Come on, let's do it again but this time I'll have to go slightly in front of you because I nearly forgot about the wall, engrossed as I was. I'll reach back and tap your shoulder or something when we get close, this time.'

We swam back and I swam further ahead than I said I would, a whole body length actually, and I swam like a whore. I made sure that my legs opened fully as I swam frog-like ahead of her. If her eyes were open, as I suspected and hoped they would be, then she would certainly be getting an eyeful. In the last quarter of our swim I flicked onto my back, but still beneath the surface, and was almost certain that her head turned away slightly as if she was indeed watching but that she didn't want me to know. I, myself, couldn't see whether her eyes were open or not because her goggles were misted over on the inside. When I reached the end of the pool I played dumb and tapped her twice on the shoulder.

'See, that's twice you've done it now,' I said. 'So it wasn't a fluke the first time. Again?'

She said nothing but just nodded and we turned around to start our next length. 'Same as last time, OK? I'll go a bit in front of you and tap your shoulder at the end. Seemed to work well last time.'

Again she just nodded. I waited for her to launch herself before I started. I soon overtook her and when I did I swam like a whore again. But this time when I gauged that there was nobody around us I quickly flicked onto my back and pulled my bikini top up, exposing my breasts for her to see. Her response was immediate. I saw bubbles escape from her mouth and nose and she kicked for the surface only a foot or so above her.

'You bitch!' she coughed after I'd surfaced next to her, treading water. It was deeper here.

'Just checking,' I said as I smiled victoriously. 'Knew you couldn't resist.'

'I hate you!' she said, but she was smiling when she said it.

I leant closer to her and lowered my voice. 'Seems I'm not the only fucking pervert in this pool!'

She guffawed and put her hand over her mouth.

'Again?' I asked.

'Well only if you keep your bikini on!'

'Done, but we can look at each other.'

So we swam and we looked and I did all the underwater tricks I knew. I somersaulted forward and backward and generally tried to impress whilst "innocently" giving her more and more of my body to look at, and I admired hers. When my lungs were nearly empty I headed for the surface and took in another lungful and immediately kicked back down beneath the surface. She'd seen what I had done and after only a moment's hesitation she copied me. When she was close to me I reached out to her and kissed her. She went rigid at first and then she relaxed and kissed me back. I hoped that nobody could see us, under the water as we were, because there would be hell if they could. All too soon we were forced to surface.

We trod water now as we were at the deeper part of the pool. We were silent and breathing heavily after our exertions and I felt my heartbeat mirrored in the throbbing of my head. Perhaps I was overdoing the swimming bit, it being the morning after a skin-full the night before.

'I'm exhausted,' she finally got the breath to say.

'Me too. Shall we go back?'

She nodded. 'But this time I'll go first.'

When we lifted ourselves out of the pool poor Kelvin was still being talked to by Sir Lenny the Boring. 'You two OK?'

'Excellent,' Jane answered. 'Aneese taught me to swim underwater.'

'She did?'

I could hear the incredulity in his voice.

'Yeah, she's quite the mermaid, my little angel-fish!'

'Wow, impressed!'

Kelvin was impressed. With ME! I'd never even heard him say "Wow" before, and he meant it! Normally all you got from him was his

That'll do, Pig nod!

'I got drinks,' he said, indicating them to us with his hands and looking at me with new respect.

'Not alcohol, I hope?' Jane said as she towelled herself down, looked on by an ogling Lenny.

'No clol,' he promised

Lenny's Carol, who let's face it was no oil painting, punched him on the arm. We weren't meant to see it but we did. 'Come on, it's tea time,' she hissed.

'No, it's early yet,' he appealed but she wasn't having her lump of a man letch at the two bathing beauties before him.

'Well I'm hungry,' she said, and then she was gone.

Poor Lenny didn't know what to do but in the end he quickly packed up and followed his frump. 'Um, later, Kelvin, yeah?'

'Yeah, later.' Then when Lenny was out of earshot. 'Much later. That guy can talk a glass eye to sleep.'

'Aw, poor you,' I played.

'So tell me about the swimming,' he said as he took over the letching duties.

So we did. His mouth dropped open when Jane recounted how I'd exposed myself to her underneath the water.

'So when I've recovered,' Jane finally said. 'We're going for a swim and you have her,' and she pointed her thumb at me, 'to thank!'

'We can all go for a swim,' he countered. 'But before then,' he asked. 'Somebody mentioned bringing a second set of pills?'

'Aw, did Lenny give Daddy-o a headache?' I teased.

'All right for you,' he said as Jane handed him the pills. 'Whilst you two were ogling each other I had to pay for our loungers, and over the odds too!'

'Well thank you, Jack,' Jane said. 'I appreciate it if she doesn't!'

He got a kiss from her and I got a playful raspberry.

'That's better,' said Kelvin. 'Now pucker up, creature of the deep, if you know what's good for you!'

Well I didn't need telling twice. 'There'll be complaints,' I said between kisses.

'Like I give a sh... damn,' he replied, and I kissed him harder for the sheer hell of it.

By the time the bahaader arrived we'd drank our drinks, ordered more and had a good half hour worth of swimming as a trio. By then we'd all three of us taken our second set of pills, too.

'See what did I tell you,' I said as Kelvin and Jane oiled me up for the later afternoon sun. We'd already oiled Jane up and Kelvin was next.

'Another complaint about pornography at the pool, Bahaader?' Kelvin asked. 'Take a seat, why don't you?'

As the bahaader sat, Kelvin tipped the wink to the barman and in no time at all a fiery ginger ale appeared, much appreciated by the security head.

'No pornography complaints, Kelvin. Just thought I'd drop by and pass some time with my fellow ex-soldier.'

'Cut the crap, Gurung, I wasn't born yesterday. What's on your mind?'

I actually thought that Kelvin had crossed the line but the bahaader just shook his head and laughed. 'I was off duty yesterday,' he started. 'Nepalese holiday of The Holi Festival. Festival of Colour, as you westerners would call it. So I missed your antics last night, but I did receive a bundle of complaints this morning.'

I rolled my eyes. 'That po-faced bitch had it coming,' I said. 'All we wanted to do was be able to see the band. Our night was disturbed so that the masses could be entertained so why shouldn't we have a front row seat?'

The head of security eyed me for a moment. 'This one has teeth, Kelvin. How do you control her?'

'Threats, coercion and psychology normally works. Haven't quite had to go any further yet, but I live in hope.'

The Gurkha laughed before continuing. 'Actually there were no complaints about you last night. None at all.'

What? Then why is he here, I asked myself.

'I had three sets of complaints,' he continued. 'One set against a certain...' He looked my way before continuing, 'Po-faced crew member.' I heard Jane stifle a laugh. 'And one set about drug abuse by certain members of the band.'

'Never touch the stuff,' Kelvin said as he held up his hands defensively. 'You know us squaddies are subject to random drug testing. You can take the man out of the army but you can't take the army out of the man. And anyway, Jane here is very anti-drugs. Wouldn't touch them even if I wanted to because it would mean losing her and I ain't going to do that.'

I saw Jane reach out and touch Kelvin's shoulder.

'I never once thought you would, but I do have a problem. On the one side I have been told that this band have earned... the gig, as they call it, for the rest of the season, but on the other I have multiple complaints of class C drug abuse which Carnival Cruise Line cannot tolerate. As you would say I am caught between a rock and a hard place. The captain asked me personally to check into this.

'I also have one complaint from a husband who says his wife was molested at your cabin party last night by a member of the same band. Her dress was torn.'

'What? Who?'

'The drummer, the one with the black beard. Said she was pulled into your rest room and sexually assaulted against her will.'

'Now hang on a minute, there,' Jane said. 'Those women were all over the band, I remember that much. And I remember the woman with the drummer. Green dress, wasn't it?'

'The same,' answered the bahaader.

'Women love the band,' Jane continued. 'They're called groupies and they know what they're doing.'

'Had the lady in question been drinking?' Kelvin asked.

'Everybody at your party was drinking.'

'Well my guess is that her alcohol reduced inhibitions got the better of her and she regretted it when she sobered up. And where was the husband while she was at our party?'

'It seemed that they'd had a falling out earlier in the evening.'

'Well that's the classic revenge fling,' Kelvin continued. 'Getting her own back on her husband, but she went too far and regrets it.'

'My thoughts exactly,' said the bahaader. 'But I have to prove it.'

'You really are a good egg, aren't you?' Jane said after a slight pause.

He opened his arms, almost a shrug. 'I try. Honour is all to a Gurkha warrior, a gift you give yourself. Honour is like a difficult woman, hard work but ultimately worth it.'

'Well said,' Jane complimented.

After my snapping when the bahaader first arrived I had kept my own counsel and said nothing, but now I had something to offer. 'I walked in on the drummer and the woman in the bathroom,' I said.

'You did?' Jane and Kelvin said together.

I nodded. 'They hadn't locked the door.'

'Well on that statement alone a good lawyer could get him off,' Kelvin pointed out. 'If you are planning to assault somebody you'd lock the door, I'm sure.'

'And there's more,' I continued. 'When I saw them he was pushed back like he was almost laying on the sink. Very uncomfortable position. She was on top of him, almost, doing all the pushing. Her dress was around her waist and her... chest was exposed, but her dress didn't look torn to me. Looked to me like she was doing all the running.'

'And you'd swear to this?'

'If I had to, yes, and it's not only men who have honour. I wouldn't lie to protect her, another woman or not. I told the truth as I saw it.'

'But you, too, were drinking last night?'

'We all were,' Kelvin interrupted before I let one fly. I felt my word was being doubted. 'But if you believe an accusation from an inebriated person then why can't you believe the defence statement from another inebriated person? Weigh them up against each other and what have you got on the level playing field?'

'I see your point.' The security man turned to me. 'Forgive me, miss, I was not meaning to doubt your word and I apologise if that is what you felt.'

'No harm done,' I answered, but I was only slightly mollified. Jane reached out her hand to me and I took it.

'Well I think we've put that one to bed, as they say,' said the security chief. 'Now all I've got to do is decide on the band as a whole.'

'Where are they?' asked Kelvin.

'Confined to their cabin under guard.'

'Are they allowed visitors?'

'Only if accompanied by the first officer. It was him with the po... with the crew member in the lounge last night. You haven't made any friends there, I am certain.'

'Nevertheless, I have an idea that might be open to all. Carnival wants the band but not the drugs? I think I can arrange that.'

'I will be in your debt if you do,' Gurung said. 'Shall we try?'

'I'll meet you back in the cabin,' Jane said. 'The place is a state after last night. I will find our steward, get it sorted and then wash these pool chemicals out of my hair. I do not want to be involved in drug use by anybody for any reason. I cannot condone it.'

'I'll come with you,' I offered, and I started to pack my belongings into our beach bag.

'If you don't mind, miss, I may need you to complete a statement if you are still willing? It may not be necessary after I present the evidence verbally but just in case I would like you to accompany us?'

I looked at Jane. 'Go with them,' she said, 'I'll be all right. As I said, I have to wash my hair. I'll wash yours later if you like?'

I nodded and she started to leave but Kelvin stopped her. 'Jane, you are more important to me than they. Just say the word and I'll let them stew in their own juices. As drug takers they deserve what they get. You know, I believe that.'

'You know I'm not happy with the situation, Kelvin, but after both your hard work getting them the gig, I couldn't allow that. I trust you and therefore I trust you'll make this plan work, but I don't want any of those men visiting my house and I don't want to see them before I leave this ship tomorrow afternoon.'

Kelvin nodded and kissed her on the cheek. 'We won't be long.'

Jane hugged me and was gone in a moment. I recalled that she had been involved with drugs and that was why, I suspected, she had lost Isobel. One day, I determined, I would know that story in full, but the look on her face told me it wouldn't be any time soon.

When we got to the band's cabin the bahaader nodded to his guard and the door was opened.

'Kelvin Turner! Knew you'd come through for us!'

'Shut it, Spider. I'm here to offer you a way out but it hasn't been painless or without cost. My Jane is vehemently anti-drugs and anybody who uses them. For the record, I don't think I'll be getting any succour there for a while.'

'Just as well you've got the spare, then, yeah, that little un, Aneese? I'm sure she could give a man a lot of warming, you know? Bet she's tighter than a fish's arse! But that's why you've got her, yeah? The older one a little saggy? A tad too loose for your liking?'

I didn't see it all because I was outside the cabin. All I saw was a blur of movement viewed between the two guards and the partially open door, but I heard the punch impact and I could fill in the blanks with the rest. Kelvin was no weakling. I don't think anybody wanted to be on the receiving end of a punch from him.

'Now hang on, there,' said the first officer. 'I won't have this on my ship!'

I heard what I guessed to be Spider being uprighted. 'I can take you, Turner!'

Then Kelvin spoke. 'Forget it, Lieutenant. Throw the book at them!'

'No!' I said.

'What, she's out there? I didn't know,' I heard Spider say in genuine sounding regret.

I moved forward and nobody stopped me. When Spider saw me he dropped his eyes to the ground, all thought of fighting or wisecracks gone. I might have been in a bikini and the answer to every red blooded jailbird's fantasies, but nobody was feasting their eyes.

'You arsehole,' one of the band said to Spider, digging him in the ribs as he did so.

'And I won't have that sort of language in front of a lady,' shouted the first officer.

'The young lady here has evidenced on behalf of your drummer,' said the security chief. 'So you are off the hook there.'

The drummer opened his mouth in shock and took in a sharp breath. 'Thank you, miss,' I heard him almost whimper. He was biting his lip. I could have been wrong but he seemed close to tears to me. I guess being released from a sexual assault charge was a whole weight off a man's shoulders.

I stood looking at Spider but he wouldn't meet my gaze. An awkward silence descended upon the whole scene. I resisted the urge to slap him after he'd insulted me *and* the woman I loved. Slowly I turned to Kelvin. 'I want your plan to proceed, though it's more than some of them deserve. And before you object you will be doing it for you. I don't want you feeling guilty about not helping when you could. I know you, Kelvin Turner. You may be a cold hearted killer and able to sleep nights afterwards, but you're also a good man. Don't let the others suffer because one of them's a low life back stabbing snake.'

He started to open his mouth but I stopped him by raising my hand. 'Just get it done,' I insisted. I turned on my heel and started to walk away.

'I'll pay for your dress,' I faintly heard Spider say.

I stopped in my tracks and spoke to Kelvin though I kept looking straight ahead. There's no way I was communicating with Spider. 'And if that excuse for a man comes anywhere near any of us then you are ordered to earn yourself another tattoo, and I'll do the inking myself!' Then there was complete silence as the implications of what I'd just said sank in. 'And for the record, there is nothing wrong with Jane's body,' I hissed again. 'If I look half as good as her when I get to her age I'll be happy as hell!'

There was another, longer, pause as I withdrew further from the cabin. I didn't go far, though.

'Let's hear this plan, then?' said the first officer, finally.

I stayed and listened, partly because I wanted to hear the plan, but mainly because I didn't want to leave Kelvin here alone or be alone myself.

Kelvin's plan was thus. He asked for their stash, which they provided. Then he asked for their standby stash which they denied having. On threat of strip search and body cavity search (which Kelvin insisted he would gladly do himself) a reserve stash was produced. Then Kelvin demanded his business card and told them in no uncertain terms that his prior invitation to visit our house was revoked. They were to stay in their cabin until we had disembarked tomorrow and were confined to the ship for the rest of the cruise. They were being watched. They could play their gigs and they would get paid the contract amount, but one misdemeanour, one whiff of anything on any of them, one complaining husband, and they were gone, and with no money, either. Kelvin then cemented the process by adding that, should the band feel that they could have the ship over a barrel by them not having a replacement band, should they be tempted to use that argument to get their own way, then Carnival Lines were to ring him and he would gladly come and complete their gigs after he'd thrown the band over the side.

I almost laughed at the last bit. It was a good plan with nowhere for the band to go. They either behaved, did their gigs and got paid, or they lost the lot. And Kelvin wasn't the type to make empty threats.

'And don't forget that I haven't put my evidence in writing yet, and nor will I,' I added from outside the cabin. 'I could suffer amnesia and then where would you be?' I knew this was coming down hard on the drummer but he was the one with all the muscles and bulk. If anybody was going to keep the rest of them in line it was going to be him.

The cabin door was banged shut like a prison cell and the guards remained as the rest of us walked away.

'And there's something else,' Kelvin said, turning to face the first officer as he did so. 'Five men in a tiny cabin that wouldn't fit one man comfortably? Any wonder they need drugs to survive? Two people max per cabin or I will kick up such a stink that everybody will hear about it and nobody in the music industry will ever grace a Carnival Lines ship again. That's disgraceful!'

'But that's—'

'No buts. Take it or leave it. I will find out if you don't do it.'

'I'll speak to the captain.'

'*I'll* speak to the captain if you want? He and the line will be the ones in trouble should the band's living conditions become common knowledge. I'm sure the captain doesn't even know, does he? I'm sure he leaves berthing and so on up to you, like all good skippers. So give me your word you are going to sort it and then sort it.

'I don't know whether you know but I am in the music industry. I *will* find out if you don't.'

'You drive a hard bargain,' the first officer finally said. 'You have my word I'll see to it.'

I could see and hear that he wasn't happy with either Kelvin or me but I had an idea. There wasn't time to bounce it off Kelvin so I just went ahead and waded in.

'And in return you get this,' I offered. 'What's going to happen to your girlfriend? You know, the crew member that called you to turf us out last night?'

It was just a guess but the look on his face confirmed it. Even Kelvin's mouth dropped open and I had to resist the urge to show my victory on my face.

'I fear she will be deemed unsuitable for her task and be sacked.' He cleared his throat. 'She is fairly new to this. There have been complaints on other cruises, though. She just gets nervous, that's all.'

'We put in a good word for your girlfriend with the Line. We request that she doesn't get sacked, that she gets retrained or something. We can even say that we were slightly out of line or whatever.'

'I don't think you'll get Jane to agree to that,' Kelvin offered.

'Well that's my problem, not yours, and I'll deal with it, not you. Now shake on it, you two, will you?'

I watched as Kelvin and the first officer reluctantly shook hands on the deal.

'Thank you, now can we go? I'm starving and I have to wash my hair before we eat.'

We turned to leave but the Gurkha stopped me with a light touch to my elbow.

'Miss, in my country women are classed as the property of their husband and, as such, are deemed to have no honour of their own. I just wanted to say that I do not hold with that assumption. It is indeed an honour to know you.'

With that he bowed slightly, and when he straightened he departed, leaving me and Kelvin agape.

I cleared my throat. 'What was all that about?'

'I think you surprised him and made a friend. You certainly surprised me. We made a good team back there.'

I smiled. 'Yes, we did.'

'And I want you to know that what Sp—'

'I know you don't. And I don't want to hear his name, ever! He insulted you, he insulted me and he insulted our sweet Jane who wouldn't hurt a fly.'

As we ambled along the deck I saw him watching me. 'What?' I asked.

'You really surprised me today, that's all. First you get Jane to swim underwater *and* open her eyes whilst doing it, then you stop me making a big mistake.'

I guessed he was on about when I stopped him letting the first officer throw the book at the band. 'You're welcome,' I simply said.

'And then the other things you did, cementing the deal by making the drummer be the enforcer, threatening Spider with your "cry havoc and let slip the dog of war", me, routine. Classic!'

I walked a few paces, smiling to myself. 'I think you underestimate me.'

'I do… or did,' he finished.

I leant on the rail and turned to face him. 'I just did what I felt was right. I had a good teacher. You!' I poked my finger into his chest.

'Christ, I couldn't have chosen better, Jane and I are so happy with you. We wouldn't swap you for the world.'

'Just as well,' I said, leaning towards him. 'Because I wouldn't let you!'

We closed on each other and kissed. I was conscious of being in plain view of any passers-by, but I didn't care. I didn't care what they thought of us two, smooching. I didn't care what they thought of me, and I didn't care what they thought of us. By us, I meant the three of us. It should have been obvious to anybody with eyes that the three of us were a loving… couple? No, that was the wrong word. *Ménage à trois*? No, that sounded wrong and sordid to boot. Love triangle? Again, that sounded too complicated. There was nothing complicated about our relationship, we just loved each other and there were three of us. We could be a perfect triangle? That would just have to do until I could think of something else.

Wordlessly, we stopped kissing and held hands as we ambled along the deck. I was deep in thought and slightly confused. It amazed me that, should I be with Kelvin I felt totally in love with him, but if Jane was here I would be head over heels with her. When there were all three of us it was like…. it was like… I don't know… different? I couldn't describe it. I don't think even the sage, Tomas, could answer this one.

'Why has Jane got so many hang-ups?' I found myself saying.

He paused, deep in thought it seemed, so I sharpened the question. 'I mean, you're the combat soldier—'

'I was an engineer.'

'An engineer with an armful of kill rings?'

'That was forced on me, it was either kill or be killed. Mostly.'

A silence formed again and I was reluctant to push any further.

'She went through bad times,' he started. 'She's strong but I know you can wear anybody down over time, never mind how strong they are.'

'So what happened?' I pushed.

'Can't tell you, it would be wrong, like a betrayal. I'm sure you'll find out eventually, but it has to come from her.'

I frowned, I didn't like being the outsider. Why wouldn't they trust me? It really annoyed me.

'In time I'm sure you'll know everything,' he continued. 'Look how good you are with her, how you've got her dancing and swimming underwater and humming when she does your hair?'

'She sang too,' I couldn't help saying. 'In New York. Under her breath, but she did.'

'And she did none of those things before you came along. You weren't...' He paused to find the right words. 'Brought in to do that, but look at what you've done? You're wonderful!'

I felt myself start to melt inside and I began to bite my lip. I couldn't be angry with these two for but a moment.

'Come on, we'd better get back,' he said, and I rested my head on his shoulder as he slipped his arm around my waist and guided me along.

Chapter Fifteen

'So tell me again,' Jane said as she washed my hair. This time we weren't doing the bending over the sink routine. I was sitting in the bath and she was washing me like you would a child. A large wine glass was used to pour water over my hair to rinse the shampoo out, as it had been used to wet my hair prior to adding shampoo. Kelvin was standing silently close by with a towel wrapped around him, shaving at the sink.

So I told her. How Spider had been rude about us both and how Kelvin had punched him – she'd admonished him about that when she'd noticed the graze on his knuckles – and how we'd made a deal with the first officer, took their drugs off them and threatened them with a cavity search – she'd loved that bit – and how I'd threatened Spider a grim death if he ever darkened our door again. She loved that bit, too, but said she wasn't happy about Kelvin having to kill again, even a "no good junkie like Spider".

'So you threw their stash into the sea?'

'Happy, happy fishes,' I said. I couldn't help but imagine some passing shark being beaten up by a couple of dolphins high on marijuana.

'So that bitch last night is the first officer's girlfriend? How did you know?'

'I don't know,' I said. 'I just thought it was odd the way she looked at him last night and got him to back her up. I thought nothing of it at the time, but this afternoon it was almost like a light went on in my head. Suddenly it seemed so obvious.'

She bent forward and kissed me on the cheek. 'Clever girl.'

'You should have seen her,' Kelvin started to say.

'Quiet, you, I'm still angry with you, fighting like a common brawler. Even though it was in my defence.'

'Yes, dear,' he said, carrying on shaving.

'Our defence! I put him straight on it, though,' I interrupted. 'Told him that you were the most beautiful woman I had ever seen and that if

I had a body even remotely like yours when I was old, I mean your age, then I would be over the moon.'

She kissed me again. 'Well you did the right thing. Better than fighting like some... man!'

'Well I am a man.'

'Be quiet, you!'

'Yes, dear.'

'Come on, out with you,' Jane said to me, tapping me on the arm as she did so.

By the time I'd stood she had a towel waiting for me and she wrapped it around me and started rubbing vigorously. It did more than just dry me. I tingled all over.

'And you can avert your eyes,' Jane said to Kelvin, even though her back was to him. 'She's mine, all mine. I washed her and I'm having her!'

I giggled. 'Lucky me!'

'I need a towel for her hair, though. Find one for me, will you?'

A few more rubs and she turned around to find Kelvin standing in front of her. He was looking at her sternly with his arms crossed.

'I asked for a towel?'

He said nothing, just lowered his eyes once or twice. Finally Jane got the message and looked down to find a towel being suspended on his flag pole. She hooted a laugh and took the towel.

'Thank you,' she said, but not to Kelvin. Then she bent forward and kissed his manhood.

Aww, I thought. I want some!

'Interesting towel rail,' she commented. 'Wonder if it has any other uses?'

'I can think of some.'

'Quiet, you, I was talking about the better part of you. The useful part!'

'Yes, dear.'

I sniggered and winked at Kelvin as Jane wrapped my hair. I knew they were just playing, that Jane wasn't really upset with him. I guessed she was a teensy bit upset with him, or at least pretended to be, so I asked her later just to be sure. She told me that of course she was not mad at him, but was just letting him know that she, as a woman, could not condone violence for any reason... even if it was in defence of her honour.

I, personally, thought it was hot and as Kelvin turned his towel rail away from me and revealed his tightly toned bum cheeks I found myself licking my lips and looking forward to the next time that I clung onto his muscled shoulders and wrapped my legs tightly around his back. Yeah, my hangover was gone, all right.

Jane saw me and must have read my thoughts because she tutted and shook her head in admonishment. 'You're such a whore,' she whispered.

'That's why you love me, right?' I shot back.

She shook her head but then smiled. 'Well maybe a bit.'

We were the three of us in such a good mood. I think part of it was the fact that our collective seriously heavy hangovers had finally gone. There was still so much about last night that I couldn't remember but at least I'd remembered the important bits that got the band's drummer off the hook. I couldn't remember, though, what song Kelvin and the band had ended up singing after the votes had been counted. I was hoping it would come to me and I was determined not to ask. I just knew they'd rib me mercilessly.

Huh, you don't even remember getting a good seeing to last night! Did you cling tightly to his shoulders and wrap your legs around him then?

I ignored my inner voice but hoped that I did cling on as he bucked and came inside me and I, no doubt, orgasmed loudly. I found myself licking my lips again and Jane, by now, knew the look.

'Oh, you're incorrigible!'

'Is that good?' I asked, once I had recovered from my shock at being found out. 'Hey, Daddy-o?' I called, and as he looked our way I dropped my towel. 'Oops!' I said innocently.

He smiled and walked towards us, taking in the view as he looked me up and down like a hungry wolf. I certainly recognised *that* look.

'I don't think we've the time,' Jane said.

'Oh, just a quickie?' I pleaded.

She rolled her eyes to heaven. 'I'll leave you two to it. I just have time to rinse the conditioner out of *my* hair.'

He grabbed me and lowered me down onto the towels that we'd dropped on the floor near the bath. There were lumps where the folds were, so it wasn't that comfortable, but I didn't care. I gasped loudly as he entered me with no preamble.

Well you asked for a quickie!

He was into the canter straight away – this was no slow screw.

'Well I think my hair will last another ten minutes,' I heard Jane say. She'd been in the shower and had even turned the water on before she'd changed her mind (or the sight and sound of us changed her mind for her). 'I hope you have enough for two!' she finished as she turned her lovely backside to me and bent down and started kissing him.

He grabbed her and man-handled her around until she was facing me, and then forced her down until she was almost astride me. Although I could see his hands roughly pawing her breasts and his mouth biting at her shoulders, whilst his other hand dropped between her legs, to all intents and purposes it looked to me that it was Jane who was thrusting a penis into me. That was too much for me, a dream come true, almost, and in no time at all I felt myself orgasming loudly and it was a strong one. No matter what control I tried to regain over my body, perhaps to stifle the sound or gain some control over my bucking spasm, the strength of it beat me down. I had no chance. I bucked and writhed and moaned until I was sure that the passengers in the cabin next door could hear me.

As I was coming down from my release Kelvin withdrew from me and quickly positioned Jane beside me and entered her. As soon as he did I could see she was close to coming, herself, and Kelvin's urgency betrayed his need.

'Quickly, Jane!' he almost snarled.

I guessed the poor thing was close to exploding but, being the man he was, he didn't want to run out on Jane and leave her in limbo. I couldn't take my eyes off her face. Her neck was arched back and her eyes were clasped tightly shut as she bit her lip. I was half expecting to see her draw blood.

'Jane!' Kelvin hissed through clenched teeth. It was more of an urgent appeal than a request.

She was close, if I was any judge, but not just close enough. How much control did he have left, I thought? Surely not a lot. Before I knew what I was doing my arm reached out and found one of her nipples and my thumb and forefinger closed around it. It was already hard as I found it but I felt it harden even more and then she was bucking as I had and being just as loud, if not louder.

'*OH JESUS CHRIST!*' she exclaimed as if she was surprised by what was happening to her.

I watched as she rode out her orgasm – I was only just calming down after mine. My breathing was still ragged and my heart was still pumping. I must have been only twenty seconds ahead of her.

Kelvin flopped down and relaxed on top of her as he thinly smiled at me. I could see his chest heaving too.

Wow, I thought, a quickie between three people. And all done in about a minute and a half! Beat that, the rest of you boring fuckers!

'Thanks for the assist,' Kelvin finally got out between breaths.

'Mmmmm,' Jane sighed, which I took to mean "Yes, thanks!" I saw her lift her arm and took it as an invitation so I moved closer. Her arm settled on my shoulder and we relaxed in the afterglow as our breathing slowed. I felt Kelvin's touch as he reached out for me and I reciprocated. I took a deep breath and closed my eyes, like a tired puppy would yawn before settling down to sleep.

Yes, I was one contented little puppy!

We were late arriving at our dinner table that night. We'd been told that everybody was to be seated by a set time on this, our last night at sea, and although it had been a request everybody seemed keen to adhere to it. We had, too. It was just that we'd got a little carried away, what with one thing and another, and as it was Jane's hair was still slightly damp and she fretted at it even though you couldn't see to look.

'Leave it alone, it looks fine,' I admonished playfully as we sat.

'It's wet underneath,' she objected.

'Nobody can see the underneath,' Kelvin pointed out.

'Quiet, you! If you hadn't been the horny hound I'd have had enough time to do my hair properly!'

'Well nobody said you had to join in, all running out of the shower all wet and panting for it!'

'I was not!' she said indignantly.

I laughed. 'Well I certainly was. You.' I nodded to Jane. 'Rubbing me all up and him with his towel rail!'

'See, it's her fault. I'm the innocent party in all this.'

'That'll be the day. You didn't have to accept her offer.'

'And you didn't have to come running from the shower, all wet and panting for it, unable to resist a quickie!'

'Yes I could resist,' Jane declared. 'I just chose not to, that's all. I mean, why cut off your nose to spite your face?'

'A good point,' offered Kelvin. 'Let's just put it down to the fact that the young miss, here, is irresistible.'

'That's right, because I am!'

'True enough,' Jane smiled, but she still stuck her tongue out at Kelvin. 'See, I have an excuse. You try resisting the irresistible!'

'Oh, I don't. Not when it's as willing as she is.'

'I am here, you know,' I played.

There'd been a spattering of applause and a light cheer as we arrived and sat and playfully bickered. Part of me wondered who they were clapping for but then I realised that they were looking at us as they did it. 'Why are they clapping and looking at us?'

'Relief that we're finally here, I think,' said Kelvin.

The clapping raised slightly in volume once they'd realised we'd noticed it was directed at us.

'Are you going to sing tonight, Kelvin?' asked two British sounding girls as they approached our table.

Kelvin's mouth fell open. A treat, it didn't happen often. 'Do I know you ladies?' he asked.

'Yeah, we were in the audience last night.'

'As were hundreds of others. So it's Mr Turner to you!'

'Ignore him, girls,' I said as they deflated. 'He's old fashioned. You haven't been introduced.'

'Well I'm Gemma and she's Donna,' the tallest of them quickly said as she pointed first at her friend and then to herself.

'Excuse me, sir?' an American sounding voice interrupted. 'My mom and dad were wondering if you or the lady, here, would be singing tonight? The band are sick, we've been told, and my parents hope to be able to dance on the last night of their cruise?'

Kelvin looked back at the English girls, a look of triumph on his face. 'See, that's the way to do it.'

'So are you, sir?' the lad continued.

'No, young man, we are not,' Kelvin said with a smile, and I felt for the poor fella as he deflated. 'This is our last night, too. We just aim to relax and take in the atmosphere and eat a good meal and get something light to drink.'

'And recover from our lingering hangovers,' Jane said under her breath.

'Oh,' the young man said. 'They'll be so disappointed,' he said before starting to turn away. 'My apologies for disturbing you.'

'I'm sorry,' Kelvin said, as he left.

'What, you're not singing?' Gemma asked incredulously.

'Hey, we're just paying passengers, just like you,' Kelvin explained.

'Aww, well that's not very good. Come on, Donna, let's find something to do.'

And with that they were gone.

We were silent for a little while but then it was me who spoke. 'So you still have a slight hangover?'

Jane nodded. 'It reminds me it's still there, every now and then. What the hell did we drink last night? I still don't remember most of what went on.'

I felt relieved. It wasn't just me, then. I could remember doing my Samantha Fox routine and I vaguely remembered singing later with Kelvin and the band. After that it was just snippets of memory here and there, like a badly edited video.

'It was those damn boys, Tomas and Johnny,' Kelvin explained. 'Drink what you like, I told them. They drank vodka neat, by the bottle, and we just joined in. And when we decided to carry on back at the cabin everybody was told to bring a bottle and they all brought a bottle of spirits. No wine, no beer, no mixers or soft drinks!'

So that was it. No wonder I remembered so little. 'That's the way the youth of today drink,' I explained. 'My little sister is the same.'

'Little sister?' Jane asked. 'How old is she to be drinking like that?'

'Well she's sixteen now.'

'Sixteen!'

I shrugged. 'Things are different now. She doesn't do it in front of Mum and Dad, of course, but if there's a party or something they're all doing it.'

'I was still in ankle socks when I was sixteen!'

'Hmmm, nice. Still got any?' the ever horny hound asked.

She smacked his arm playfully. 'Pervert!'

'So what were you doing when you were sixteen?' I asked as a waiter brought menus to the table.

He took his time to answer as he scanned his menu. 'Oh, I was a boy soldier. I started my army training when I was sixteen, more or less straight from school.'

'What, they had boy soldiers? I never knew that.'

'Yeah, when I joined we lived under the threat of the mushroom cloud and the possibility of seven million screaming Russians coming running over the inner German border. We had a real army then, quarter of a million guys in boots with nearly a million reservists. The navy and air force were extra and they even had ships and planes those days, too. Imagine that, not like these days!'

Jane rolled her eyes. 'Don't start him off on that one,' she warned me. 'I'm sure he wishes for a return to those frightening days.'

'Well maybe I do. Knew who the enemy was then. Believe it or not the world was a safer place.'

Wow, I thought again. I couldn't imagine living under the threat of being nuked every day. They were exaggerating, surely?

'Let's change the subject,' said Jane. 'Time to eat.'

We did as we were told and silently perused our menus, though I determined to ask questions of Kelvin later. The conversation had served to remind me how little I actually knew about these two people. On one hand I couldn't remember, stupid as it sounds, ever being without them; it was as if I'd known them all my life! On the other hand I knew virtually nothing, their political leanings, their favourite colours or even their birthdays.

Well you'll have to talk more and fuck less!

Yeah, like I wanted that to happen! I was so happy that I still didn't believe it and it wasn't just the sex, the *very* good sex! In the back of my mind were thoughts of my future life. What would it be like? Since finding out their intentions for me (only an unbelievable five days earlier) I'd had very little time to reflect and order my mind. I knew that tomorrow the party, the cruise, would be over. Then, I guessed, the real party would begin, me with my life as a kept woman, lover and friend to both. What could go wrong? There was so much to tell Sianna and my parents when I got back.

But what was I going to tell them? Sianna I knew I could tell everything – we'd shared everything at school, from every kiss to every fumbled attempt at getting a hand in our drawers. My parents? Hmmm, well that would take some handling. Damn it, where was Tomas when you wanted him?

'I think I'll have ribs, though they'll be messy as hell.'

'Excuse me, Kelvin,' a now familiar voice interrupted.

We'd been so engrossed in our conversation and in checking the menus (and me in my thoughts) that we hadn't noticed what was going on around us. I looked up to find the bahaader standing close and accompanied by a man wearing a uniform similar to that of the first officer. This man had more colour on his uniform and was more than just slightly older, though. His hair was greying but he had sharp intelligent eyes. I guessed he'd been doing the rounds, table to table, and as we were the last arrive it was now our turn.

'Kelvin Turner, ladies, this is Captain Hibbard.'

'Mon Capitan,' Kelvin said as he sprang to his feet and shook the offered hand.

'Ah, you speak French?' the captain remarked.

'Actually, you've just heard all of it.' Kelvin smiled. 'But *ich spreche ein wenig Deutsch!*'

'*Ah, Ja. Ich wurde gesagt, Sie ware nein ex soldat!*' the captain replied.

'*Darf ich ihnen meine Frau vorstellen.*'

I was impressed. Kelvin spoke German. Something else I didn't know about him.

'Stop showing off, Turner. It's rude to exclude others.'

I snorted, recalling how Jane had habitually spoken Spanish to Consuella at home.

'May I introduce Jane and Aneese?' he said, switching to English.

That's not what he'd said, I told myself. Even I knew that *Frau* meant wife.

'Your wife?' the captain asked of Jane as he shook her hand.

'Not his wife,' said Jane. 'Unfortunately.'

The captain looked slightly confused as he turned to me. 'And the young lady?' he asked as he held out his perfectly manicured paw to me.

'Not his wife, either,' I smiled. 'Again unfortunately.'

Then the thought hit me. I *could* actually be his wife. There was no buried under the floorboards ex-husband preventing me. Should I bring up the subject? The realisation hit me like a stone. My heart started to beat faster and it wasn't my hangover, much too early for that. Oh my god, Aneese Turner? I liked the sound of that. Perhaps I could marry Jane, too, civil partnership, or whatever it was called? Tomas would know, I'm sure. Speaking of that, where *was* he today? Surely this was a solution?

Why was everybody looking at me? Could they read my mind?

'I think you've awed her into silence, Captain. I'm impressed. I've had to come close to using the whip in the past.'

They laughed at Kelvin's quip.

'It must be the uniform. I was asking how long you'd been a singer?' repeated the captain.

'Ah, n... nearly twenty-four hours now,' I managed to stammer.

Jane snorted at my reply and the look on the captain's face.

'Last night was my first time in front of an audience,' I explained.

That's not true. Jane watches you and Kelvin all the time!

'Oh!' said the surprised captain. 'I didn't catch your performance myself, but I am told it was well worth watching. Well done.'

'It's all his doing,' I answered truthfully, pointing to Kelvin. 'He brings out the best in people.'

Well that's one way of putting it.

'Mr Gurung tells me you have had quite a cruise. For the first three days it was like you never boarded – we were going to send out search parties – and then after that it was like you were everywhere. I've heard so many good things about you.'

'And some not so good, to boot, I'd guess?' smiled Jane sweetly.

The captain had the good grace to smile before continuing. 'It's a pity about the band being...' His eyes scanned left and right like he was one of those action man toys on the Christmas toy adverts. 'Ill, isn't it?'

'Quite,' said Kelvin.

'Though I hear they'll recover after you have disembarked

tomorrow afternoon?'

'Yeah, we heard that, too.'

Kelvin and the captain stared at each other silently. There was so much going unspoken here. They each knew that the other person knew exactly what they *weren't* talking about!

'Which brings us to tonight?' said the captain.

'Thought you'd get around to that,' answered Kelvin. 'But I've already said that this is our last night, too. Just going to eat and relax, and maybe suck on a shandy. We drank a bit too much last night for one reason or another.'

'Oh,' said the captain, disappointed. 'Couldn't persuade you in some way, could I? Some sort of deal on your next cruise? I do have some pull with the booking offices, you know?'

'Sorry, Captain. Would like to help but, you know how it is? Helped last night and nearly got my fingers burnt.'

I wanted to speak up and say that it was all the fault of that horrible Spider and the rest of the drug takers. But Kelvin was right, this was our last night and he deserved some rest and relaxation. That was what holidays were for. In no time at all we'd be back in England and he'd be back at work – *but you wouldn't be!*

Ooh, I'd forgotten about that. No more work? Cool!

'I'll want to dance later,' Jane said quietly. 'Seem to have found the urge, lately, after a hiatus of some years.'

We all looked at her silently. Eventually the light came on, faster in some than it did in others.

'Well there is the pianist playing in the forward bar?' offered Gurung, sweetly.

I was convinced he knew where Jane was going with this.

'No, I was thinking something a little more... pop?'

Kelvin knew where she was going and turned his head slowly to meet her eyes.

'Look, you don't have to sing yourself,' she said. 'Just put a tape on or something. Then I can dance with you, too.'

'Karaoke!' I almost shouted. 'Set up your gizmo in karaoke mode and Bob's your uncle!'

'That's the answer,' said Jane. 'Everybody wins! And I know you,

Kelvin Turner. Give it an hour and you'll want to get up there and sing. I just know you will.'

Kelvin chewed his lip and I knew that Jane had won. Again! I was beginning to realise that she knew him so well and that I was getting there, too. He just wanted to be convinced, that's all. He just wanted to pretend that he was being dragged kicking and screaming onto the stage. I guessed it was his way of playing hard to get. And also I knew that he wanted Jane dancing as much as I did. I wondered if I would ever be able to wrap him around my little finger like she did. I did hope so!

'So it's settled then,' beamed the captain.

'I guess so,' said Kelvin in what I now knew to be pretend reluctance. 'But I'm having my ribs first.'

'Steward,' called the captain to a passing server. 'Make sure this table gets served their dinner first, or you'll answer to me.'

'Yes, Captain. Right away, sir!'

The stewards – what we'd been calling the waiters – always moved at a nifty rate, but this one was almost running. He settled at Kelvin's shoulder, ready to take our order.

'A pleasure doing business with you, ma'am,' the captain bowed to Jane. 'Excuse me, miss,' he said to me as he dipped his head in my direction. Kelvin play scowled at both the captain and the bahaader as they departed, the latter trying desperately to stifle a smirk.

'Goodnight ladies,' the bahaader finally managed to say as he passed us.

Kelvin play glared at us but we just smiled sweetly back at him. It was easy to be magnanimous in victory.

'So it's the ribs for me,' he finally said to a nervously waiting steward. 'And the ladies will have...'

'Oh, I haven't even looked,' I admitted, earning me a roll of the eyes from Kelvin and a snigger from Jane.

As I quickly scanned the menu I heard the PA system buzz to life and saw that the first officer was holding one of the mics from off the stage. I guessed captains didn't make their own announcements. They had crew for that sort of thing.

'Ladies and gentlemen,' he started. 'You have heard, no doubt, that the band are unable to perform this evening, but do we have a treat for you instead.'

'Are you going to dance a jig?' a voice shouted from the back, invoking instant laughter. 'Or walk the plank?'

'Um, no,' he answered, clearly nervous. 'There will be karaoke after dinner…' This started a collective moan. 'Arranged by the more than able Mr Kelvin Turner.' The moan turned into a cheer. 'And ably assisted, no doubt, by the lovely Miss Aneese Crosby!' This time the cheer included wolf whistles and my cheeks coloured visibly and Jane laughed. 'I have it on good authority,' the first officer continued, 'that, regrettably, nobody's clothes will be torn off on stage tonight but, I am sure,' he shouted over playful booing, 'that you will get a good night's entertainment nonetheless!'

He retreated as more applause started, this time directed at us. I found myself suddenly shy and looking down at my feet. I was wearing the same shoes as last night but, due to the demise of my dress, I was just wearing one of the cheap (well compared to my now destroyed dress it was) wrap around dresses that I'd bought in Miami. Jane wore the one I'd bought for her so as not to show me up. At least they were above the knee and not almost touching the floor.

'Looks like you're singing too!' remarked Jane.

Kelvin smiled evilly.

'I don't mind, I like singing.'

His smile vanished in an instant. 'Damn it,' he said under his breath.

I smiled victoriously at him and stuck my tongue out at him. Seems he was getting a lot of tongue tonight.

Makes a change. It's normally you!

The ribs were indeed messy and by the time he'd finished he looked like a young child who'd had his way with an open jam jar for the first time. The remains of the sauce were everywhere, his hands, his face, even the tablecloth and his napkin. His finger bowl turned up a little while later but it was a little too late. Jane and I ended up cleaning him down with our napkins or he'd have gotten it over his tuxedo jacket. He was wearing his black one this time.

'Oh, you're such a caveman!' Jane played.

'Yeah, you mucky pup!' I joined in.

Kelvin for his part was enjoying being pampered, I was sure. It dawned on me that he didn't get too much in the way of pampering. Perhaps I could do something about that in the future? Might be fun. Speaking of fun, he was also revelling in the jealous looks he was getting from men on surrounding tables. I bet they were wishing that they could be looked after by two gorgeous women such as us. Yeah, Kelvin was so much of a man that he needed two women to satisfy him!

'Thank you, lovely ladies,' he smiled as we finished cleaning him up. 'I'll just go and collect my – what was it you called it? – my "gizmo?", while you finish.'

He kissed us both before he left and I hung onto his neck and pulled him down to make mine a lingerer. Yes, I was enjoying the looks on the other diners' faces too, and not only the men. Part of me wondered what they thought of us, who was with who and all that, but part of me (most of me) didn't give a hoot. They'd obviously seen all of us kissing all of us by now, but nobody had had the nerve to ask. It dawned on me that I wouldn't know what to say if they did and what business was it of theirs anyway?

'Oh, we haven't ordered dessert,' I suddenly exclaimed. We'd both settled for the duck glazed in honey (which was fabulous) but there wasn't a lot of it. 'Not like him to miss out on some cheesecake?'

'I noticed. It means he is planning to sing, though. He doesn't like to sing on a full stomach.'

'Oh,' I simply said. Something else she knew about him that I didn't. 'But we can, right?'

'Damn right,' she said. 'Got my eye on some simple apple pie and cream.'

I smiled. 'We are *so* going to need the gym when we get back.'

'Yes, but now I'll have somebody to go with.'

I smiled even more. My new life was going to be unbelievable. I was such a lucky girl!

True to the captain's promise we got superior service from the servers and, even though Kelvin wasn't there, we were given prompt service with our dessert order. We were both sighing over out last mouthful (I had blueberry pie for the simple reason that I'd never had it before) when Kelvin returned with his laptop and some of his connecting leads. He didn't stay long at the table, just long enough to tut and murmur "fat girls" under his breath before he moved away. A used napkin followed his departure, thrown by Jane.

I watched as he deftly connected up his laptop to the band's speakers which were still left on the stage along with the rest of their equipment. I knew that they'd planned to remove some of it today but were prevented doing so by their incarceration. I also noticed that one of Gurung's security men had been discreetly keeping watch on the stuff whilst we ate, and presumed that a guard had been mounted all through the day.

Kelvin gestured to me and I eventually left the table and went to him after applying a napkin to my lips.

'I need you to do a mic test,' he said. 'Just stay here by the mic until I need you.'

I watched as he returned to our table. 'Say something?' he ordered.

I did.

'Into the microphone, dumbass!'

I knew that he was playing and so I played along. Jane hooted and some of the closer diners giggled and I looked at him through slitted eyes but did as I was told. 'Boy, you're going to get it later.'

'Sounds great.' He moved further back. 'Try it now.'

'Dumbass, is it? Just you wait!'

More people heard this time, as I'd spoken into the mic.

'Perfect,' he said, deadpan. 'Thanks a lot.'

'No, thank you,' I play snarled once more into the microphone. I tried to keep a straight face as I stepped down from the stage, but so many of our fellow diners were laughing that my play scowl cracked and I couldn't help but join in.

'That was funny,' Jane said as I rejoined her at the table.

'Dumbass? I'm so going to kill him for that!'

Jane had to reach for a glass of water she was laughing so much.

He returned to our table carrying an ice bucket, champagne and three glasses. So much for not drinking alcohol today. 'I'll just give them some time to finish their desserts. Champagne, ladies?'

'Yum,' I said. 'I've heard it makes you intelligent which is just as well, me being such a dumbass and all?'

'I'd better get a couple more bottles, then!'

'Oh, you're so dead, later!' I threatened.

'I can't wait. Playing dead can be fun, can't it Jane?'

'Well, not dead, but playing asleep can be.'

I watched her as her eyes glazed over as she recalled some memory. She shivered. 'Oh yes, playing sleep can be fun!'

What the hell did that mean? 'Care to explain?'

'Probably best if we didn't in public.'

I wracked my brains to try and imagine what the hell they were on about. 'Later, then?'

'Oh yes,' he said. 'It's a date.'

I wondered what I had left myself in for.

He looked about us and decided it was about time to start. With a wink at us he turned on his heel, went to the stage and hopped up to the microphone. 'Well here's the plan,' he said with no preamble. 'I'm going to sing, some of you, the brave ones, are going to sing. Hopefully all of us are going to dance. If anybody wants to sing then put it in writing and give it to the stewards. Stewards, if you would just drop them on the stage, here,' he pointed with his left hand, 'and we'll go from there.

'I've got over five thousand songs on my box of tricks, here,' he continued, pointing again. 'Oldest song is about sixty years old and the paint is still wet on the newest, so take a chance. If I have it then you can sing to it. If I haven't… well mention it anyway. Perhaps we can arrange something. If you have it on your iPod then I can add it in a jiffy, but please check first.'

'Get on with it, Turner, I want to dance!'

My head shot to my right. The heckler was my own quiet and shy Jane!

He play glared at our table whilst the laughing subsided.

'Whilst we're on the subject about dancing,' he continued. 'Dogs can dance with dogs tonight, and cats with cats. If I see one approached by some jobsworth who says otherwise then the party's over and I go back to being a paying passenger rather than unpaid singer. Sure the captain will be most displeased if that happens.' He paused, giving everybody – where was po-face tonight? – the chance to digest what he'd said. 'I'll start the ball rolling with a personal favourite of mine, and then a couple of songs that are easy to dance to. But after that I expect some of you to take the field so that I can dance with the lovely ladies.'

I blushed again as I knew that many heads were turned towards us.

'Speaking of lovely ladies,' he continued. 'This song is dedicated to the two loveliest.'

As I reddened further I saw him stroke his laptop and felt the buzz as the whole system sparked to life.

'It's called 'Angels'.'

He started singing as Jane and I looked at each other and smiled and bit our lips and held tightly to each other's hands under the table. The rest of the audience were clapping before he'd even started.

He sang and Jane and I gently swayed together as we held hands. As he sang he looked our way and smiled when the song allowed him to. I felt so proud of him and so special and I guessed that Jane must have felt the same. And as for the song? He sounded just like Robbie Williams. How did he do that?

He picked up a guitar and played the guitar solo in the middle of the song – Robbie Williams can't do that! – and when that was done he let the guitar hang on its strap, grabbed the microphone stand with both his hands and closed his eyes as he sang the high notes of the final verse. When he'd finished he got his standing ovation. Only Kelvin could get a standing ovation after his first song.

He simply smiled and nodded at the crowd's appreciation but he winked our way as his fingers dropped to his keyboard. 'Now it's time to dance,' he said, and before anybody could react he launched into a high tempo number which was vaguely familiar to me.

I felt a tug at my hand and realised that Jane was pulling me to my feet. Seems I was dancing whether I wanted to or not. Good thing I wanted to. Part of me remembered that Jane wouldn't dance, but here she was, first up on the floor with me a close second. We weren't the only ones.

'Who is this?' I asked over the music.

'Some Australian group, I think. Split… something or other,' she answered as she moved her lovely body in front of me. 'From the eighties, maybe. From some film but I can't remember which one.'

I must have seen the film, I thought, because the lyrics sounded familiar. Richard had liked to stay in and watch old films. I hadn't been too keen but it got to be a habit and a time to cuddle up on the settee. And it had been cheap, leaving our savings to mount up slowly rather than be spent on expensive and wasteful nights out on the town. Some of the films weren't bad, as I recall. Some were awful.

I looked around me as I loosened up. There were indeed dogs and cats dancing with each other and Jane and I weren't the only pair of cats. There was even one large group of cats all dancing together in a circle, but so far no dog on dog action. That changed quite quickly when I felt a tap on my shoulder and turned around to find Tomas and Johnny.

'Hey,' I said as Jane and I hugged and kissed them as we continued to move to the music. 'You can dance with each other,' I shouted into Tomas's ear as I cavorted happily in front of him. 'Kelvin said dogs with dogs and cats with cats or they can forget it. You're dogs.' I indicated with my fingers.

'Been called worse,' Johnny answered.

'And you're at our table,' said Jane said as she pulled me away. 'See you later.'

I smiled and shrugged as she pulled me away.

Jane was really letting it go and earning some looks from sitters and dancers alike. So much for the latent hangover. Catching up on lost time, indeed!

When the song finished Kelvin didn't wait for applause or appreciation, he just launched straight into another high tempo dancing song. Even I knew this one. Everybody knew Billy Idol's 'Dancing with Myself'.

Jane let out a whoop and kicked off her shoes towards our table where Tomas and Johnny did the gathering them up thing again. I giggled when I suddenly thought of them as Jane's... footmen?

She was really going for it, kicking her feet one minute then swaying her lovely hips suggestively the next with her eyes closed as if she was in a world of her own. I caught Kelvin's eye and raised an eyebrow at him as I indicated Jane with a nod. He was having as much fun performing as Jane seemed to be having dancing. He nodded approvingly. I felt so wooden compared to the two and I would have to change that. And to do that I would need some help.

Alcohol.

I skipped along to our table and grabbed a glass of champagne and quickly downed it. I hadn't realised how thirsty I was. 'Help yourself, boys,' I said to Tomas and Johnny as they settled at our table and I refilled the glass. 'Order what you like but get some more champers whilst you're at it.'

Yeah, I was very generous with somebody else's money.

I felt my refilled glass snatched from my hand and turned to see Jane draining it whilst continuing to jig and sway to the music. Then she banged it down on the table and pulled me back towards the dance floor without missing a beat. I let myself be pulled away and joined Jane in her happiness and abandoned myself to the music.

The next song was slower but easy to dance to. About a minute into it an old guy (well older than me) dancing with his girl near us leaned over to me. 'Wow, I have never ever heard anybody try this song apart from The Smiths. What a guy!'

I guessed he meant Kelvin so I nodded and smiled back. The Smiths? Heard of them but I don't think I'd heard any of their songs. I listened to the words as Jane and I danced. There weren't many, but I had to admit that the beat was excellent. Kind of slow and mournful but jaunty at the same time, easy to sway to. Then I heard some of the words, something about dancing by yourself in a nightclub and then going home and wanting to die.

'Such a happy song,' Jane shouted at me over the music. I was just thinking the same myself.

'You dance well,' I shouted back.

'Misspent youth,' was all she said in reply and then her eyes were closed again and she was swaying and snapping her fingers again.

As we danced I looked around and saw that the dance floor was much fuller now. As my eyes roamed I caught sight of Gurung and Captain Hibbard. Standing behind them and obviously escorted by two of Gurung's men was the unmistakable form of Topper, the band's drummer. I hadn't realised before how big he was, having mainly seen him sitting behind his drum kit. Even hunched over like he was he was huge.

'Hey, Jane?' I said as I touched her arm to get her attention.

She followed my gaze until she'd seen where I'd indicated. As we watched I saw Gurung gesture to somebody and saw that he was trying to get Kelvin's attention. As I looked back to Kelvin I saw him gesture them over with a flick of his head and they gently pushed their way through the dancers until they reached the stage.

'Come on, let's be nosey,' she said and we danced our way closer to Kelvin who was finishing singing a line whilst they awaited his attention.

When he'd finished, he leaned down to them, still playing his guitar and not missing a beat. Gurung shouted into his proffered ear above the din of the music but Jane and I couldn't hear a thing even though we were right next to him by now. I saw Kelvin look at Topper.

'I ain't no druggie, Kel, I swear. I get my kicks out of good bourbon and beer.'

And topless women!

'What I am, though, is...' He looked around as if he were revealing a great secret. 'I'm claustrophobic, see. I just can't stay in that cabin any longer. If you'd allow...'

He trailed off and his shoulders slumped. I guessed it took a lot for a big lump like him to admit that he was scared of anything.

'What do you say?' Kelvin said to Jane. 'He ain't no druggie.'

I watched as Jane pondered and as Kelvin went back to the mic and sang the next line. When he'd finished that he leaned back towards us.

'And I'll keep the other guys in line, too. I'll swear I will,' Topper added.

Jane pondered a moment longer. 'Well I guess there's nothing wrong with bourbon and beer.'

Topper's eyes lit up and he moved towards Jane but instantly checked himself. I guessed he was going to kiss her. 'Bless you, missus,' he said instead.

'He'll be your responsibility,' Gurung added. 'On parole so to speak?'

Kelvin just nodded at him as he concentrated on playing. Then he used his eyes and directed Topper to his drum kit where he went happily.

'Thanks, Jane,' Kelvin mouthed down to us.

Jane moved towards him and I followed. Well we were here to be nosey, weren't we?

Kelvin reached down and Jane kissed him on the cheek and still he didn't miss a beat. 'And in return you can keep the dance music coming,' she shouted.

'But I was going to make this my last song?' he protested.

'Think again,' she ordered.

He rolled his eyes but nodded. 'I'm going to need some refreshment,' he said. 'And some beer for Topper?'

'I'll arrange that,' I offered.

Kelvin nodded and we went to move away but he reached his foot out to touch me and got my attention. 'Keep her dancing,' he mouthed down at me.

'Don't think that'll be a problem,' I shouted back up at him. 'Stopping her might be!'

He smiled down at me and mouthed a kiss at me, which I returned before I happily turned away.

Jane grabbed my waist and held onto me as we neared our table and started to sway to the music. We were dancing close now, like a man and a woman would, and I wondered if anybody would object. Then I remembered what Kelvin had said and I smiled and dropped my woodenness. So we were rubbing up against each other. So what, so fucking what? This was the twenty-first century!

The dance music continued and Topper took over the drumming duties from Kelvin's electronic friend. And it was just as well because everybody seemed content to dance that night. No karaoke offers had been forwarded to the stage yet and if the music carried on being so good I doubted they would. Kelvin was a hard, perhaps impossible, act to follow.

Six or seven songs later – and they were great ones but I lost count – Jane finally needed a rest and I was glad of it. As we returned to our table I looked up at Kelvin and he made a thirsty face at me.

Oh shoot, I'd forgotten the drinks! Poor Kelvin must be parched!

Kelvin kept the songs coming for hours but at the end even he had to stop. Eventually he must have flicked a switch because he was beside us at the table but the music was continuing. By then most of the revellers had danced themselves to exhaustion and there were only a few die-hards dancing along to the canned music emanating from Kelvin's laptop. They were probably too far gone to notice. Everybody had been drinking heavily, it seemed to me. It was the final night, after all.

Kelvin received the appreciation of passing revellers as he transited the dance floor, which he accepted with smiles and thanks.

'I haven't danced so much in years,' a clearly tipsy Jane said as he joined us at the table.

'You don't say,' he answered. 'Come on, let's get you hydrated.' He turned to me. 'You too.'

'We're fine,' I exclaimed.

'Rubbish. All that dancing and alcohol to boot?'

'And what abouts you?' Jane nearly slurred.

'Me, too,' he said. 'Somebody kept forgetting me and poor Topper up there. It was like singing in a desert!'

I played at guiltily lowering my eyes to the floor. I had tried to keep the drinks coming but I'd gotten carried away sometimes.

'Where's the boys?' Kelvin asked.

'Back in their cabin, I think. Said they drank too much last night and hadn't quite recovered. They only came out to show their face tonight.'

'Huh, lightweights,' Kelvin said.

'I actually think they drank much more than us last night,' I offered in their defence.

A steward appeared at Kelvin's side. 'Three pints of pineapple juice with lemonade, please. Ice in all,' he ordered.

'Hey, I can order my own drinks,' Jane insisted. She turned to the steward. 'What he said,' she said, pointing to Kelvin.

I smiled. I don't think I'd ever seen Jane drunk before. Before me, that is. I'd normally been just as drunk as her and therefore hadn't noticed. She was funny.

'You played good music tonight, Jack,' she breathed over him. 'And now I want to kiss you.'

'Kiss awa...'

He never got to finish his sentence because he had a beautiful blonde woman on his face. Or close enough. She seemed a little off target.

'And now I want to kiss you,' she said to me. 'And if the others don't like it then...' Her eyes glazed over and she blinked. 'Something about dogs and cats,' she finished. She almost fell off the table as she leaned into my lips. It wasn't much of a kiss. She was well gone.

Our drinks arrived and it took nearly an hour to get Jane's into her. Kelvin and I had finished our second by then.

'Time for a walk, I think,' Kelvin finally said.

'I don't want to walk,' Jane said. 'I want to stay here and drink beer.'

'But you don't drink beer.'

'But Topper does, cos he's not a druggie!'

I smiled at her silliness. 'Where is he, anyway?' I asked.

'I told Gurung's boys to give him some latitude til midnight then escort him back to his cabin.'

I nodded. 'Think there'll be any problems?'

'God I hope not, have you seen the size of him? Oh look, fireworks!' he said as he winked at me.

I didn't get what he meant at first, but I certainly hadn't seen any fireworks.

'Oh good, I likes fireworks,' Jane said, and I got the gist.

Kelvin helped her up and we moved towards the door and in no time at all we were outside in the fresh air. There was a warm breeze blowing, even though it was after eleven. Kelvin had a firm grip on Jane even though she insisted she could walk very well by herself.

'Where, I can't see them?' she stated.

'Must be near the stern,' Kelvin answered and we set off in that direction. Anything to get her feet moving, I guessed.

I didn't know what his intentions were but I just played along. I didn't feel drunk at all, but all drunks said that, I knew. Compared to Jane, though, I was probity itself.

There weren't any fireworks at the stern so Kelvin said they must be at the bow. By the time we'd reached the bow Jane had forgotten about fireworks, thank God, because there weren't any. Although it hadn't seemed that long, the whole midships to bow, to stern manoeuvre took over an hour. Kelvin had planned it that way, I guessed. There was a lot to look at along the way and he'd pointed things out to slow us down, the moon, the stars, the phosphorous of the waves as the moonlight hit them and the ship sped along. There were even small islands in the distance and Kelvin suggested that they were the Florida Keys, as we were heading back to port. Eventually Jane seemed to snap out of it.

'I'm thirsty,' she said a few moments later. 'And hungry.' She sounded more like herself.

'What a good idea,' Kelvin said and we went in search of food.

'I want pizza.'

'You never eat pizza,' Kelvin exclaimed.

'Well I do tonight, I'm fancying.'

Kelvin looked at me and saw me licking my lips. I could almost taste the hot cheese and spices. 'Pizza it is, then,' he finished.

We found pizza, or should I say Kelvin found pizza. They were closing – it was after midnight by now – but Kelvin is very hard to say no to. And not just in the bedroom.

I knew I'd feel heavy in the morning but tonight I didn't care. We were seated outside on a small table that our three chairs would only just about fit around. Between us sat the largest pizza I had ever seen and it tasted fabulous and we all three of us ate like we'd been starved for a week. I had no idea what type it was but it had everything on it. We washed it down with iced lemonade and asked for, and received, refills.

'Hmmm, I needed that,' said Jane as she noisily licked her fingers.

'You certainly did,' Kelvin answered.

'Shut up, you, probably your fault I got drunk, anyway.'

'Probably,' he accepted as he winked at me.

'And don't wink at her.'

'Why, jealous?'

'Yes!'

He winked at her theatrically and she laughed.

That got me thinking. 'Do you get jealous?' I asked before I knew that I'd asked.

They both looked at me at the same time and I immediately thought I'd messed up big time.

'You mean of you? Of course not,' she answered. 'Do you?'

'A little,' I had to admit. 'But not of the physical things or anything. I'm jealous of the way you know each other's habits and ways and stuff.' I shrugged. 'That's all.'

There was a brief silence, broken by Jane. 'You know, it wasn't easy accepting another woman into our life,' she said. 'And a very beautiful YOUNGER woman at that, but Kelvin chose well. You're perfect for us.'

'I wasn't fishing for compliments,' I said.

'Well tough, cos you're going to get them!' Kelvin added and we all smiled.

'So what now?' I asked.

'What do you mean?' asked Jane.

'The party's over,' I said. 'Back to England.'

Jane looked at Kelvin but he said nothing. 'You *are* moving in with us, aren't you?' she asked. I saw the look of near terror on her face as she imagined that I wasn't.

'Well I haven't officially been asked,' was all I could say.

'Kelvin!' Jane admonished.

'Well we've been busy!' he said in his own defence. 'And I thought it was obvious, anyway.'

She thought for a small while. 'I think that you've taken a lot for granted,' she said, finally, then she turned to me. 'Aneese, we would be honoured if you would move in with us, we want to be with you. We're not talking short term here, forget your job and give up your little flat. If it all goes sour – which I know it won't,' she added quickly, 'then we'll make sure you're looked after, won't we?' she said, looking to Kelvin who nodded.

I suddenly felt tearful. 'I'm sorry,' I said. 'I just needed to hear it.'

They both reached out for me at once.

'It's a big step, you see. And I'm so happy and I've never been so happy in my life and I keep thinking that I don't deserve it and that it's all just a dream and that I will wake up and it will be morning again and my lovely dream will be over and—'

'Whoa, calm down, there,' he said, touching my arm softly as he pushed a fifty into the pocket of the crew member tidying up after us.

He was right, I'd been babbling.

They both moved closer to me and Kelvin spoke. 'You're staying with us, like it or not. If you try and run away I'll find you and drag you back to the house, tie you up in the basement and we'll use you repeatedly, as to our will. So there are your options, willingly or unwillingly, but believe me, either way you're coming home with us!'

I played at thinking about it. 'Sorry, what were the choices again?'

'Simple,' he continued. 'Our way, or our way with a smack!'

'Then I pick your way,' I said. 'And can I get back to you about the smack bit?'

Jane laughed and Kelvin nodded once, like a hatchet coming down on a chicken's neck. I hoped I wasn't the chicken.

'Glad we got that sorted,' said Jane finally. 'And now let's go to bed!'

'She's a silver tongued temptress, isn't she?' Kelvin played as we stood up and prepared to leave.

We walked back to our cabin through and around the other late revellers. We were arm in arm with me in the middle and life was good. I hoped it would never end.

The next morning I awoke and felt relaxed and well rested. I stretched and yawned and noticed that Kelvin was watching me. 'Watcha, Daddy-o?' I smiled, reflecting my happiness.

He put his finger to his lips and hushed me and I thought that he didn't want me to wake Jane. I looked to my left and sure enough she was there, asleep.

So what's your pleasure, Daddy-o, I thought, willing him to understand me. Last night we'd come to bed and I'd been expecting some serious action but all we'd done was some light petting, some kissing and some serious cuddling, and it felt good. I must have fallen asleep because now it was morning and now here was Kelvin after his fix. Must admit I was having withdrawal symptoms myself, so come on, Daddy-o, give it to me! Don't worry about Jane, she'll wake up halfway through and join in, I'm sure.

I waited patiently but all he could do was look at Jane.

OK, I remember we'd mentioned jealousy last night and I'd been truthful on my part, but there was the *pissed off* factor. I mean, I'm here, I'm panting for it and all you can do is look at Jane who is sleeping for Christ's sake!

She was laying beside me wearing a short, flimsy nightie and, for once, it had stayed on during the night. Normally our nightclothes, if we bothered to wear any – and we didn't often – were on the floor by the time we'd awoken up. As well as her nightie she was wearing panties which I'd guessed she'd forgotten to take off before bed. Normally, even if we wore nightdresses, neither of us habitually wore underclothes to bed. And as for Kelvin he always slept in the nude.

But what the hell was so all consuming about a sleeping Jane? Here I was, naked, everything on show, and all he could do was look at a clothed Jane!

I cleared my throat to get his attention but he shushed me.

What the fuck!

Then he reached over me and gently placed his hand in the band of her briefs and pulled the material down until it showed part of her bum cheek.

I say again, *What the fuck!*

He moved his hands further along the banding and repeated the same tactic. The fabric moved a little but then caught. The way she was laying, almost in a foetal position, had stopped it moving any further. Unperturbed he'd moved his hand elsewhere and now pulled on the material that had ridden up at the bottom of her bum cheeks. It moved, revealing her bum hole, the slight brownness of skin between the meeting of both her bum cheeks. My mouth fell open as he looked at me and smiled evilly.

His smile shocked me. For the first time in his presence I felt afraid. What the hell was he doing? Jane was asleep for chrissake! Thoughts cascaded through my brain. Had the man I trusted and loved fooled me? Was he really a… sick pervert of some kind? What was I to do?

He reached for my hand and I almost flinched as he touched me. He pulled my hand over to the sleeping form of Jane and forced me to touch her right at the join of her bum. She moved and made a noise, like you would if you were sleeping in the garden and a bee buzzed too close to your ear, and I pulled my hand away instantly. Her movement resulted in her laying on her back and that pleased Kelvin. I watched almost in disbelief as he gently pulled at the thin band at the top of her panties again. This time the material moved enough that the top of her pubic hair was in view. He looked my way and smiled that evil smile again.

I quickly reached forward and pulled his hand away, shocking him. *NO!* I mouthed at him.

WHY? He mouthed back. This time he moved the material from the side and revealed all her pubic mound as well as the dark line running down the middle and despite myself I carried on watching. I didn't want to, I swear, but there was something mesmerising about it. He gently started to rub her and she quietly moaned. Maybe she thought she was having a nice dream, I thought. I mean, I had horny dreams, had some since we'd left England, but mine hadn't been with Kelvin molesting me as I slept.

Or had they?

Suddenly my dreams of him doing things to me came rushing back to me. Perhaps I hadn't imagined it after all! And I'd felt so guilty thinking that I'd wronged him by accusing him wrongly whilst we were in New York!

Instantly I pulled his hand away from her and I glared angrily at him. I didn't want to be in the same bed as him but I had to stay and protect Jane. I thought about my options. Should I wake her and watch as her world collapsed around her as she thought that the man who'd rescued her, her Jack, was a molesting pervert? Or should I just stop him, perhaps saying that I'd tell her unless he stopped? Either way I saw a quick flight back to England in my future and a lesson learned, but that would mean leaving Jane at the hands of this monster in front of me. I made my decision – Jane could come with me! We'd make it alone, me and Jane. Yes, that would work. Surely once I'd told her she would leave him? We could both get jobs. She'd be safe!

He must have read my mind because he launched himself at me and for the first time I really struggled and, also for the first time, I felt the full strength of his muscular upper body. I was pinned beneath him with his hand over my mouth and, despite my struggles, he easily overpowered me. I writhed and I tensed all my inadequate female muscles but I was nowhere near a match for him. I had a fleeting thought that maybe the movement of the bed would wake her and she would see what he really was. I went to kick my leg – anything – but it was as if he'd anticipated all my moves. I was totally pinned underneath him and his hand firmly over my mouth was starting to restrict my breathing.

I wondered if he was going to rape or kill me, perhaps both. Surely, he couldn't succeed with Jane right beside us? *Kelvin could*, my inner voice shouted at me. OK, then I'd let him, but only because I was sure that his guard would be lowered sufficiently for me to cry out and wake Jane, or that perhaps Jane would wake up during the act, anyway.

I was in disbelief. Part of me thought that this just couldn't be happening to me but the other part of me was smug and telling me *told you so*. I'd been right all along, right that my happiness was too good to be true, right that it couldn't last. I gave in, my heart in turmoil and all fight gone from me. I felt myself start to cry for what I had lost.

'*She's not really asleep, you dick!*' he hissed into my ear, just in time.

Realisation hit me like a wall. Was he telling the truth? If he was, what did it mean?

Actually it means you're the biggest jackass since... well since forever!

He stared into my eyes, projecting what he'd just said into my inner soul.

That wall of reality hit me again and it hurt. Oh god, if she was really not asleep it meant she was awake and if she was awake it meant she was willing and if she was willing it meant that Kelvin was not a sick molesting pervert and if he wasn't a sick molesting pervert it meant that he hadn't molested me, causing my dreams, whilst I slept, and if all that were true it meant... that I was the biggest dick/jackass/dumbass (delete as appropriate) ever!

But only if she's awake!

'What's going on?' I heard her say, beside me.

This was it, the moment of truth!

'I think I'll get my workout at the gym,' replied Kelvin. 'Not as if I don't need it!'

With that he pushed himself off me and leaned over and kissed Jane. 'Laters, babies!'

I looked incredulously at his naked form as he got out of bed. What a turn of events! Then I looked at Jane. I went to look back at him but he was gone, just the cabin door closing behind him. Hell, he moved fast. Was he naked on the deck or something?

'Were you awake?' I gasped.

She lowered her eyes, bit her lip and nodded slowly.

'Damn it, I didn't know! I thought he was...'

She must have noticed the genuine distress on my face because she reached forward and took me in her arms and held me tight. 'Oh, you poor girl. Jack would never hurt me. Or you.'

'But I thought...' I almost sobbed.

'We thought we'd primed you last night? You know, when we mentioned it? Jack knows that me sleeping in underwear is the sign. We do it all the time.'

'You do?' I asked, unbelievingly.

'Christ, yes. It's *so* erotic!'

'Well remind me never to sleep in underwear,' I exclaimed, but as soon as I said it, I regretted it. I remembered my fascination as he'd revealed her flesh to me and suddenly part of me wanted him... or her, either of them, to be doing it to me. And I'd spoiled it. 'He hates me!' I suddenly exclaimed.

'Rubbish! He's probably laughing over it, right now.'

'That's just as bad!' I almost sobbed.

'I'm sorry, I'm sorry,' she started. '*We* are sorry, we pushed too far, too soon.'

She shushed me and stroked my hair and in time I settled down. I hadn't quite got to the tears stage, but it was close.

'So what now?' I eventually asked.

'Weelllll,' she said. 'They do say that if you fall off a horse you have to get straight back on... and we are alone... It's not quite like waking up beside you, alone, but it's close enough...'

'But Daddy-o?'

'Is at the gym and working himself hard. Couldn't we do with the exercise, too?'

Hell, I knew I did. Already I could see the difference in my body because we had eaten and drank to excess on our...honeymoon? But part of me knew she didn't mean the gym, either. 'Well, I guess we could...'

Yeah, I was such a whore. But you know what? I didn't give a damn.

She went to remove her underwear but I stopped her. 'No,' I said, and started to do it for her, for us, actually.

She understood, I think. It was almost like I was working back my forgiveness. She laid back and I slowly peeled away her underwear like I had seen Kelvin try to do. I watched intently as her sex was revealed and I drank in her womanly aroma. I suddenly realised what I would have felt if she had been asleep or pretending to be. My breathing quickened and I felt... wicked. In an instant – and surprising her, I think – my lips were on hers and I found her bum cheek grasped tightly in my hand as I ground myself into her. I felt like I was the man and she was my unwilling accomplice and she was only too willing to play at being unwilling. I clung onto her and pressed myself into her as deep as I could go and we kissed deeply as she played at moving her mouth away from mine. I found myself hurriedly raising her nightie to reveal her breasts and my mouth hungrily sought out her nipples. She moaned when I found them and that just spurred me on. Yes, I was almost a man when I was with Jane, but a squirming schoolgirl when I was with Kelvin.

Kelvin had indeed chosen well. But what the hell was I?

Eventually, one of us bucked and the other was soon to follow. We lay until our breathing settled from noisy and lustful to quieter and sated. We both sighed in contentment. 'I love you,' I sighed.

'I love you,' she returned.

'And I love Kelvin,'

'As do I,' she returned.

'What's it mean?' I asked as soon as my breathing would allow me.

She paused before she answered. I guessed she wanted to be sure what I was asking. I enjoyed her rubbing my back as she pondered. 'I think it means that we're very lucky,' she finished, and I nodded.

I don't recall whether I fell asleep with her left nipple in my mouth but it was sure there, or close enough, when I awoke. I needed no prompting. We were in the afterglow from our second coming when Kelvin returned.

I opened one eye as I heard the cabin door opening. I sat up instantly and ran naked to the door before Jane was even fully awake. As I did, I saw Kelvin's eyes take me in completely. 'I'm sorry,' I intoned. 'Please forgive me?'

'Nothing to forgive,' he said as he dropped his newly purchased, sweaty towel at his feet and put one arm around me.

'I didn't know,' I offered as mitigation.

'Our fault, not yours,' he said as I kissed the foul smelling beast.

'You stink,' I said with a smile.

'So do you,' he shot back. 'What *have* you two been up to?' he asked, pretending he didn't know.

'I could use a shower,' I said. 'True enough.'

'And I could use a sixty-eight,' he answered back immediately, with a knowing smile.

Well he might know but I didn't. I wracked my brain. 'What's a sixty-eight?' I finally asked as we closed the bathroom door behind us.

'Your maths knowledge depresses me,' he said. 'Verdict on the state of the nation's education system, perhaps?'

I was still none the wiser and it must have showed on my face.

He sighed. 'It's like a sixty-nine, but I owe you one?'

I got it. Finally! It was quite funny. What could I say? I certainly owed him one, that's for sure. But sixty-eight? I giggled as he led me into the bathroom leaving a beaming and sniggering Jane.

I so wanted my feeling of guilt to disappear. OK, so I'd normally only done this whilst PISSED with Richard and never enjoyed it. Strange as it may seem, with Kelvin I wanted it, looked forward to it with relish. I was happy to please him, *so* wanted to please him.

And I think I did.

When we left the shower Jane said that she'd already ordered breakfast.

'She's eaten,' Kelvin answered in his flippant way, and I took in a quick breath and looked to the floor as Jane looked at me.

'Have you?' she asked, half mock stern and half amused.

I nodded, guiltily. Hell, he wasn't meant to tell!

She laughed. 'Well just leave what you can't eat,' she said with a smile. 'That's if there is anything you can't swallow!'

I sniffled a giggle, bit my lip and played at looking ashamed but somehow I didn't feel it. I'd swallowed what he offered willingly. Somehow I always felt fully alive when I was with these two wonderful people. There was a cost, sure, but I was all too willing to pay it. I was such a whore! Their whore, and happy to be so!

SONGS MENTIONED IN THIS BOOK

The Kill – 30 Seconds to Mars
The Power of Love – Frankie Goes to Hollywood
So Afraid – Fleetwood Mac
Only Natural – Crowded House
Fall at Your Feet – Crowded House
Live It Up – Mental As Anything
Private Emotion – Ricky Martin (featuring Meja)
Just Go Away – Blondie
Touch Me – Samantha Fox
Angels – Robbie Williams
I Got You – Split Enz
Dancing With Myself – Billy Idol
What Time Is Now – The Smiths